Maya Blake's hopes of becoming a writer were born when she picked up her first romance at thirteen. Little did she know her dream would come true! Does she still pinch herself every now and then to make sure it's not a dream? Yes, she does! Feel free to pinch her, too, via Twitter, Facebook or Goodreads! Happy reading!

USA TODAY bestselling and RITA® Award–nominated author **Caitlin Crews** loves writing romance. She teaches her favourite romance novels in creative writing classes at places like UCLA Extension's prestigious Writers' Programme, where she finally gets to utilise the MA and PhD in English Literature she received from the University of York in England. She currently lives in the Pacific Northwest, with her very own hero and too many pets. Visit her at caitlincrews.com.

KIDNAPPED FOR HIS ROYAL HEIR

MAYA BLAKE

THE ITALIAN'S PREGNANT CINDERELLA

CAITLIN CREWS

MILLS & BOON

First Published in Great Britain 2020
by Mills & Boon, an imprint of HarperCollins*Publishers*
1 London Bridge Street, London, SE1 9GF

Kidnapped for His Royal Heir © 2020 by Maya Blake

The Italian's Pregnant Cinderella © 2020 by Caitlin Crews

ISBN: 978-0-263-27811-8

MIX
Paper from
responsible sources
FSC™ C007454

This book is produced from independently certified FSC™ paper
to ensure responsible forest management.
For more information visit www.harpercollins.co.uk/green.

Printed and bound in Spain
by CPI, Barcelona

KIDNAPPED FOR HIS ROYAL HEIR

MAYA BLAKE

CHAPTER ONE

Violet Barringhall held the thick envelope in her hand, mutiny brimming in her heart. She managed to dredge up a thin smile for the smartly dressed courier before shutting her apartment door.

She knew its sender without peeking inside. Its weighted richness shrieked wealth, and its creamy, seamless perfection stressed its importance. The gold-embossed emblem on the top right-hand corner was distinctive enough without her years-long exposure to the family that bore it with centuries-old pride and unapologetic arrogance.

But more than that she encountered an even purer strain of that pride and arrogance on a daily basis in the form of His Royal Highness Prince Zakary Philippe Montegova—the sender of the envelope in her hand.

It wasn't a highbrow invitation.

No, this was a *summons*.

She knew this because she'd been responsible for sending out *those* invitations for his latest fundraising event herself, in her role as his long-suffering dogsbody for the last twelve weeks.

Three months, and counting, of pure hell. Of relentless commands and impossible expectations of perfection from a man—no, a *prince*—who demanded the very best of himself and therefore of everyone else around him as well.

As Director of the House of Montegova Trust, a foundation that dealt with everything from managing Montegovan business interests abroad to charity and conservation work all over the world, the trust had gained international acclaim for the small but immensely wealthy Mediterranean kingdom.

Together with his brother, Crown Prince Remi Montegova, and their mother, the Queen, Zak had elevated the status of the kingdom to even greater heights since the untimely death of the King over a decade ago.

Where others would've grown content at achieving multi-billionaire status, unquestioning respect and reverence, and rested on their laurels, Zak was even more driven, his terrifying, breakneck work ethic inexhaustible. Heck, every facet of his *life* was lived in high octane.

Right down to the revolving-door speed of his personal liaisons.

Violet didn't want to think about that. Right now, she'd give anything to completely erase Zak Montegova from her memory. At least for the next twelve hours.

But she couldn't.

She'd committed to being at his beck and call. In fact, that clause was specifically stated in her contract with the trust. While she had several reservations about the man himself, she couldn't forget that her degree in community development and her personal career ambition as a conservationist would be given a huge boost with a stint at the trust on her CV. It was why her deliberations about accepting the secondment offer in New York had been woefully short but immensely painful.

Because, aside from her grimace-inducing personal history with Zak, it directly played into her mother's blatant and conniving plans.

Despite telling herself *that incident* was a thing of the past, Violet hadn't been able to consign it to history. Like a recurring nightmare, it leapt to life and replayed in vivid Technicolor every time she was in Zak's presence, which these days happened to be several hours of every day.

Three more months. A mere ninety-odd days. What could possibly go wrong?

Like an impossibly perfect spectre, his face loomed in her mind's eye.

Formidable perfection. Insufferably handsome, with a royal swagger that shouted his awareness of his charisma. The raw prowess she'd heard whispers about long before she'd first encountered him.

Every dismissive word he'd thrown at her that day in her mother's garden six years ago had been steeped in pure masculine arrogance. He'd carried that entitlement in his thick, broad shoulders and arrogant slant of his head as he'd walked away, secure in the knowledge that his manhood was assured, even worshipped by yet another woman, while he'd cruelly rebuffed the attention he'd garnered.

Violet's face heated up at the memory. Her hand curled tighter around the envelope, one heartbeat away from crumpling the expensive paper. Slowly, she unclenched her fist, breathed deeply to restore her equilibrium. She wasn't eighteen any more, hadn't been for six long, tough years.

She'd had to grow up pretty damned fast shortly after that eye-opening party, thanks to an unexpected heart attack taking her father, and the discovery that the life of luxury they'd led had been lived on the back of a ruthlessly guarded facade of falsehoods, humiliating ingratiation and a blatant and ultimately futile exercise of robbing Peter to pay Paul.

The shocking revelation that the Earl and Countess Barringhall weren't as esteemed or as wealthy as they'd led the world to believe, that they were in fact destitute to the point of bankruptcy, had become an open, humiliating secret. Even far away at university, Violet had been subjected to snide and cruel gossip, social media playing its part in serialising the true status of her family to the world.

It was why Violet had buried herself in her work at the International Conservation Trust. And when the opportunity came up to work away from Barringhall and her mother's ever-increasing efforts to marry her off to someone socially advantageous, Violet had grabbed it with both hands and taken the position in Oxford.

But with senior positions in the field going to more experienced colleagues, not conservationists with less than two years' experience, she'd known it was only prudent to redouble her efforts to accelerate her career path and put herself entirely out of her mother's orbit.

She'd taken this job despite knowing her mother's close friendship with the Queen of Montegova would be exploited to the utmost in her bid to marry her daughter off.

Violet had considered telling her mother not to bother because she wouldn't succeed. Little did her mother know that Zak Montegova couldn't have made his feelings for Violet any clearer than he had that night six years ago or during the last few weeks she'd been working alongside him.

To Zak, she barely existed.

So she didn't understand why this envelope had been delivered here, now. After ten hours' exposure to His Royal High-Handedness today, she'd hoped for a night's reprieve before being subjected to his disturbing presence again.

Lips pressed together to hold her feelings inside, she slid a finger beneath the flap.

The note was brief. Succinct. *Imperious.*

My assistant has been taken ill. You will take her place in accompanying me to the Conservation Society fundraiser, which starts in an hour. A chauffeur is at your disposal.

  Don't let me down.
HRHZ

The inherent threat in those four final words had kept her awake for more nights in the past three months than anything else had done in her whole life.

That need for her to be exemplary in all things lest the stain of gossip, that underlying suspicion that she was a freeloader, a *leech*, because of her parents' infamous misdeeds, attach itself to her. So far it'd proved an uphill battle, social media and her mother's relentless pursuit of status playing their part in keeping the gossip mill alive and robust.

But she only needed to withstand this for a while longer, to *earn* her place in life through hard work and dedication to her chosen career. Prove sceptics like Zakary Montegova wrong. If that included stepping into his assistant's shoes for one night…

She could gain invaluable experience from other conservationists attending the much-vaunted and anticipated event. So why were thoughts of Zak uppermost in her brain? Why was her heart hammering at the prospect of seeing him again?

She jumped when her phone rang from where it lay on the tiny console table next to the front door. Her Greenwich Village apartment was compact enough to cross in a handful of steps, although she suspected who it was before she reached for the phone. Sure enough, the cynical *HRH* she'd programmed into the contacts was displayed in green.

'Hello?'

'You have received my note, yes?'

She hated it that her fingers shook at the deep, faintly accented tones that blended Italian, French and Spanish in an enthralling mix that made up Montegova's language and history.

'Since you informed the courier to hand it over personally, no doubt you've been told exactly that. And good evening, to you too. Your Highness.' She couldn't stem the snippiness from her voice even as she grew irritated with herself for letting him get under her skin. For this heart-banging-against-ribs effect he so effortlessly commanded from her.

But hadn't he done that to her since she'd first set eyes on him at twelve? Hadn't she and her twin sister, Sage, watched him that first time from their bedroom window? Hadn't Violet, freshly done with reading her favourite fairy tale, instantly placed herself in the Princess's shoes, with Zakary Montegova in the leading role of Prince Charming, because in that seemingly serendipitous moment when he'd looked up and locked eyes with her, he'd been her every wish come to life? The answer to those desperate, seemingly futile prayers for deliverance from her parents' endless arguments, the whispers and conversations that suddenly stopped when she and her sisters walked into the room, and their mother's constant badgering about making strategic friendships?

She'd hated herself for that weak moment later, of course. Because books were books. Nothing in real life could mislead her into thinking she needed a boy...or man...to save her. That the answer to her self-worth lay in a prince whose gaze turned cool and dismissive as he stared at her from across the top of his perfectly polished sports car.

His Perfect Highness didn't immediately respond to her snippiness now, and that drawn-out extra second tightened Violet's already strung-out nerves. He'd always had a knack for making her feel self-conscious, even awkward once upon a time.

But only if you give him that power.

Where she would've rushed into further speech at twelve or eighteen, Violet forced herself to hold her tongue now. To wait him out. As if her heart wasn't banging harder just from the sound of his voice. As if her palms weren't growing clammy, reminding her how she'd *ruffled* him, for a very brief, blink-and-you'll-miss-it instant, six years ago.

It was infuriating that her brain refused to let go of that

moment, the scent and, sweet heaven, the *taste* of him still lingering, vivid and real and *affecting*, after all this time.

'Personal dealings with couriers are outside my remit, so you'll have to excuse my ignorance,' Prince Zakary drawled, dragging her attention back to the present. Back to his exclusive importance. To the reminder that he dealt with heads of state and *Fortune 500* CEOs, not the common working class. 'But I'm pleased to note the urgency of the situation was relayed. I trust you're ready?'

'No, I'm not. I received the note five minutes ago. I haven't even thought about what I'm going to wear yet.'

'Think fast, then, Violet. I'll be at your apartment in twenty minutes.'

'What? You said I had an hour before your chauffeur fetched me.'

'There's been a change of plan, which necessitated this call. My foreign minister wishes to meet with me before the fundraiser starts.'

'And what does that have to do with me?'

Again, he paused for an extra beat. 'Since you're acting as my assistant, your presence is also required at the meeting. Unless you feel you're not up to the task…?'

That barely veiled insinuation stung.

'Not that long ago I spent three weeks under an intense sun, with very little sleep, cleaning and tagging hundreds of birds after an oil tanker spilled its contents on the other side of the world, Your Highness. I'm sure I'm up to *taking notes* at a meeting. Unless you'll be conducting it in something other than one of the five languages I speak fluently?' That need to prove her worth to him, to ram her few but much prideful accomplishments down his throat, grated for a moment before she owned it.

She'd learned to her cost that *timid* didn't work with Zak.

Anything other than toe-to-toe combat was just asking to be eaten alive and spat aside with singeing indifference. He responded to challenges, usually attempted by misguided fools who dared to say no to him. But occasionally it didn't hurt to remind the man that simply because that word didn't exist in his vocabulary, it didn't mean she intended to gushingly enquire *how high* when he said *jump*.

'I'm well aware of the contents of your résumé, Lady Barringhall. You don't need to recite it to me, especially not when time is of the essence.'

'Of course not. Your Highness. Just as I won't remind you that you're the one who called me. That you're the one wasting time by keeping me on the phone when I could be getting dressed.'

'Ah.' His voice was a cool, deep exhalation. 'I imagined you were an expert at multi-tasking. Since I don't recall that listed as one of your accomplishments, I'll have to make my own judgement on that score. You now have fifteen minutes, Lady Barringhall.'

The line went dead, and Violet couldn't stop the uncouth word that erupted from her lips. That little catharsis freed a layer of tension and propelled her to her tiny bedroom, where she rummaged through her meagre wardrobe in search of the gown she hadn't worn since her twenty-first.

Recalling how different that birthday had been from her eighteenth, she pursed her lips. A three-hundred-plus guest list shrunk to a half-hearted twenty-five, so-called friends having fallen away like rats deserting a sinking ship, some exhibiting shocking cruelty on their way out that still hurt to this day.

Violet had endured the occasion only because her mother had insisted on marking the day, spending money they hadn't had for a birthday party no one had wanted to attend, wearing a dress she suspected had come from a charity shop, not the *haute couture* line her mother had insisted it'd come from.

Whatever the genesis of the dress, Violet couldn't fault

its simple but tasteful lines. The dove-grey pleated bodice swept from a shallow V over her cleavage to wrap around her upper arms and back, leaving her shoulders and lower back bare, before the soft chiffon gently moulded her hips and fell away to her ankles.

Since she'd already showered in anticipation of slipping into her pyjamas for an early night, her only task was to slip on the dress, brush and sweep her hair into a tidy chignon, add a simple string of pearls inherited from her grandmother, shoes and make-up, and spritz on her favourite perfume.

Her doorbell went for the second time within half an hour as she was tossing her keys into her small, matching clutch. Her heart attempted to jump into her throat, until she assured herself that royalty didn't conduct such mundane tasks as climbing four flights of dark, dank stairs to knock on the front doors of apartments in buildings within a short sprint of a housing project.

She went to the door, opened it and froze, her jaw sagging at the sight of the man framed in her doorway.

'Do you normally throw open your door with very little regard for your safety?' Prince Zakary Montegova asked coldly.

Violet stared, convinced that the combination of memories, exhaustion and his earlier phone call had colluded into make her hallucinate him. But, no, that steady breathing, those much too incisive grey eyes, that towering, mouth-watering body and especially *that* aftershave convinced her he was all too real.

'I… What are you doing here?'

One sleek, winged eyebrow rose, sarcasm dripping from that small motion.

'I meant you didn't have to come up and get me yourself. You could've called. Or sent one of your bodyguards.' She managed to drag her gaze from him long enough to confirm the security guards without whom he never travelled were indeed present, watchful and crowding her poorly lit hallway.

'And missed this scintillating peek into your life? One that makes me question why you have a peephole and an adequate-looking security chain on your door but chose to use neither?'

That tight bite of irritation had thickened, even as his gaze swept over her from hair to heels, dragging awareness over every inch of skin he scrutinised, all the parts he couldn't see.

It was that bite, that suppressed energy that intensified her awareness, dragged even more unnervingly arresting pieces of Zak Montegova into focus.

The sharp classiness of his bespoke tux highlighting his brooding sexiness.

An innate sensuality overlying a raw masculinity that'd earned him Most Eligible Royal status for more years than Violet cared to count.

'You told me you'd be here in fifteen minutes about… fourteen minutes ago. It doesn't take a wild leap to conclude who was knocking on my door. And, really, are we going to waste more time debating safety protocols? Because I assure you that would take up even more of my precious time.'

'*Your* precious time? You signed a piece of paper, I believe, stating that every moment of your secondment was mine. Have you forgotten?' he drawled, his gaze flickering past her shoulders and into the apartment. Sharp eyes lanced over cheap furniture, cheaper blinds and the stack of conservation books on her coffee table before returning to hers, a little less cynical and a lot more…turbulent. 'Did I interrupt something? Were you entertaining, perhaps?'

Violet pulled the door closer, unwilling to let him see the small sanctuary she'd created for herself. While she kept her space neat and tidy and as homely as a temporary living space could be, the truth was she had very little spare funds to make it any more than functional.

To a man whose kingdom delivered precious gems by the quarry-full, amongst other priceless resources, an apartment like hers would probably make him shudder. But more than that, Violet wanted nothing to escalate his belief that her mother's agenda to marry her off advantageously was hers as well. That she was here in New York for any reason other than to gain as much work experience as she could.

'I think you're a little misguided. You're my mentor for the hours I spend at the trust and perhaps a few extra-curricular duties, but I don't account to you for every moment of my time, and what I do with my private time is none of your business.'

'Are you sure about that?' he asked.

For some reason, her belly somersaulted, and her breath hitched. 'What's that supposed to mean?'

For the longest minute he simply stared at her, eyes slowly narrowing. Then he sharply veered from her doorway, granting her the freedom to shut it behind her.

'You're right. The matter of your security and extracurricular activities can await another time. I don't wish to keep my minister waiting.'

The fact that he'd simply evaded answering her question puzzled her before she assured herself she didn't really want to know what he'd meant. After all, it had nothing to do with her work.

She told herself that with every step down the long flights of stairs. With every arrogant step that testified that the man who walked beside her was no ordinary man. That he was high born and could trace his ancestry back almost half a millennium.

He gestured her forward at the front door. She stepped through, then startled at his sharp exhalation. A furtive glance over her shoulder showed the briefest flare in the straight blade of his nose. The tiniest hungry flicker in his eyes as they dropped down to her bare back.

A second later he was back under control, prompting her to wonder if she'd imagined that reaction.

Because Zak Montegova didn't betray superfluous emotion. In all things he held himself under supreme control. As if he were still in the military position he'd held in the Montegovan air force in his twenties.

But he had that night.

That hard-packed body had been *alive* with passion, impatiently aroused and breathlessly all-consuming with it. Even though he'd snapped into chilling rebuttal afterwards, she'd experienced that blistering moment when his guard had dropped. When he'd given her a glimpse beneath his armour-plated façade.

For years Violet hadn't quite been able to dismiss that fraction of a moment from her thoughts. Not as easily as the Prince had dismissed her, anyway. Even when she'd imagined she'd seen a residual memory lurking in his eyes the handful of times fate, or her mother, had thrown them together.

But it wasn't until her arrival in New York that she'd known she was mistaken. It'd all been in her imagination. And she needed to kill those thoughts once and for all if she hoped to get ahead in life.

And she had.

For the most part…

But that vital final step eluded her. The last memory of sizzling heat, masterful hands on her body that had ruined her for much longer than she cared to admit. It was why she'd rebuffed any advances from the opposite sex. Because after a few tentative tries she'd known she was wasting time better spent pursuing a fulfilling career. Because even if those advances hadn't eventually been ruined by her mother's meddling or male interest only piqued by the whiff of scandal that followed her name, the memory of Zakary Montegova had always been there, a formidable apparition, rendering every man who came close an unworthy imitation of the accomplished Prince.

The man lauded as a genius. While his brother had been tasked with preserving Montegovan interests, Zak had been tasked with interests abroad. Within a handful of years he'd had heads of states at his beck and call. And that acclaim had gained power and glory with each passing year.

The sights and sounds of New York blasted in the moment they stepped out of her apartment building.

And into the path of a bicycle courier. The cyclist swerved, just as Violet took a hurried step back. Into the hard, towering body of Zak Montegova.

Strong arms gripped her arms to steady her. Fierce eyes drilled into her with a mixture of concern and brusque irritation and that enigmatic gleam that immediately drove the breath from her lungs. Everything fell away.

The courier's irritated shout despite his blatant contravention of cycling laws.

The blare of taxi horns and loud hiss of bus brakes.

The scent of stale hot dogs and hot pretzels.

Only the searing awareness of skin-on-skin contact remained, taking up ever-expanding room in her consciousness until it was the only thing that mattered. Until even breathing became redundant. Secondary to the rush of having her every fear confirmed.

That, regardless of her mother's machinations and Zak's blatant reservations about her presence in New York, she harboured terrible secrets of her own. Secrets she'd taken turns scoffing at and then fearing.

On a sordid little street corner in New York City, Violet accepted the truth that the fairy tale was very much alive.

That the man who'd taken her in his arms, kissed her with soul-stirring expertise while murmuring husky Montegovan words to her, was still very much present beneath that stoic facade. That the man who'd come within a heartbeat of taking her virginity on the night of her eighteenth birthday was still the man she secretly yearned for.

That Zakary Montegova was the reason Violet was, at the ripe old age of twenty-four, still a virgin.

Hard on the heels of the bracing indictment came the realisation that he *knew.* It was there in the blaze of his grey eyes, in the awareness that rippled through his body. In the thumbs brushing her bare skin…testing her weaknesses?

A shiver ran through her body, spreading goosebumps all over her skin.

His gaze released hers for a moment to track her reaction while his hypnotic caress continued. When her nipples began to pearl, he didn't miss it. Didn't miss the acceleration of her heartbeat or the erratic cadence of her breathing.

As if from a distance, she watched his expression change, morph into calculation. It didn't take a genius to guess he was cataloguing his every effect on her for possible use against her.

He made a sound under his breath, a curious cross between a growl and a visceral sound of satisfaction. Of a hunter having stalked his prey into a tight corner.

It was enough to drag Violet out of her stupor. Enough to stress the urgent need to redouble her efforts to resist her mother's intentions.

But most of all to prevent Zak from confirming the truth.

At all costs.

CHAPTER TWO

WEAK MOMENTS HAD the power to bring down kingdoms.

Zakary Montegova knew this all too well.

So when Violet scurried away from him towards the limo idling at the kerb as if he'd suddenly contracted a flesh-eating plague, he let her go, following at a slower pace and absolutely rejecting what the sight of her smooth bare back and pert, rounded bottom did to his libido.

Dio mio, hadn't his father delivered an abject lesson in weakness from beyond the grave? The repercussions of it had been deep and traumatic, and still haunted the royal Montegovan household to this day in the form of his much more reserved and circumspect brother, Remi. In the form of his mother's quiet anguish, well hidden behind the façade of royal duty and the solemn, defiant refusal to be cowed by any circumstance. It was well documented in the antics of his illegitimate half-brother, Jules, the physical manifestation of their father's weakness.

Most of all, it was what he'd witnessed within hours of his father's death and the revelation of the late King's infidelity. How close the seat of power had come to being usurped by greedy generals and shameless opportunists, eager to capitalise on the kingdom's instability; that had shown Zak just how precarious temptation could be.

Weak moments had the power to bring *him* down.

It was why he led a life of hard work, harder diligence and zero trust in his fellow man. Why no woman had even the smallest chance of claiming him. Why he was more than content to leave the production of heirs to his brother, the Crown Prince.

So why had he allowed Violet Barringhall to burrow beneath his skin six years ago?

He'd nearly refused his mother's request to attend her birthday party. He'd had better things to do than indulge his mother's misguided friendship with the notorious Margot Barringhall, the infamous gossipmonger, opportunist and tabloid lover.

Everything he stood against. But his mother had insisted.

And from the first moment he'd seen the grown-up version of the girl he'd met very briefly only twice before, Zak had been unable to take his eyes off Violet. The hour he'd intended to spend at her party had turned to two, then four. Despite his distaste at the increasingly drunken behaviour of her so-called friends, he'd lingered. Followed her out into her mother's garden, enticed by the timid but alluring feminine wiles she'd seemed determined to flex.

At some point he'd believed he was testing himself, seeing how far her enthralment would last. A misguided attempt at immersion therapy, over-exposure to several hours' worth of temptation after which he'd walk away, triumphant over the pressure in his groin and the bewildering need to touch her. Taste her.

Find a mundane answer to why Lady Violet Barringhall intrigued him.

So he'd followed. He'd touched. He'd *tasted*. And craved more with an unending hunger that had dogged his waking hours for months. Driven him to investigate the Barringhalls. He'd felt no guilt over it, as it was in fact a practice he'd followed since his father's death. He'd thoroughly vetted every affiliation to his family, tenuous or otherwise, ensuring the events following his father's death never occurred again.

But he'd also secretly entertained the possibility of a liaison with Violet down the line.

Only he'd discovered there was nothing remotely honourable about the Barringhalls.

They were in hock up to their eyeballs, the Earl having depleted his substantial family resources through a dizzying series of bad investments and gluttony before his untimely death. After which his wife, Countess Margot Barringhall, had taken up the mantle, frantic to safeguard her way of life by indiscriminate dalliance with the press and, when they had come of age, attempting to marry off her daughters to any half-decent man with a large bank balance who was thirsty for a shoddy little title.

Zak's disappointment in the discovery had been searing and shocking, his fury at nearly falling into Margot Barringhall's well-laid trap elevating her and her daughters to the top of his to-be-watched list.

The phone call from his mother three months ago with the secondment request had fortified Zak's guard.

Since her arrival, he'd thrown every menial task at her to push her into admitting defeat and pleading for her mother to intercede on her behalf.

The crunch point had never arrived. Perversely, he'd detested being proven wrong about her, and had piled more work onto her slim shoulders. She'd raised her game higher, exhibiting a finely tuned talent for understanding the needs of his trust, especially the work he undertook for the less privileged.

But Zak was rarely impressed. Violet Barringhall was a tougher cookie than he'd given her credit for, but the reminder of her body straining against his, her shockingly sexy little whimpers and greedy hands, were testament to her hidden skills. And that sometimes shy demeanour that hid a tart tongue? *Si*, it'd come within a whisker of rousing his jaded humour.

And therein lay the pitfalls. Allowing himself to be impressed, *tempted*, by her had nearly resulted in a gross error of judgement that could've cost his family untold misery.

It was why he stayed away from tall, statuesque women with silky, chestnut hair and eyes the colour of the turquoise-blue waters that sparkled beneath the Montegovan sun.

He slid into the car, watched her cross her legs in a curiously elegant way that effectively angled her body away from his. Poise, no doubt drilled into her in that expensive finishing school her family had ill-afforded, was evident in her ramrod-straight spine, the hands folded neatly over her clutch in her lap, and perfectly angled jaw.

The only thing giving all that *decorum* away was the pulse leaping at her throat. Her very silky, very smooth and supple throat. Creamy skin he wanted to stroke. To taste.

Basta!

He stirred in his seat, registered what he was doing and froze.

Dio mio, since when did he *fidget*?

He told himself it was his annoyance that made him glance over her body, over her shadowed cleavage that gave a tantalising peek of her breasts. It was annoyance causing the fever in his veins.

'You're meant to be taking notes, yet you don't seem to have brought any note-taking equipment with you.'

Shrewd blue eyes met his and...*mocked* him? 'Perhaps because it's no longer necessary to bring a whole stationery cupboard to take notes. I have an app on my phone—approved by the trust, I believe—to take notes and transcribe digitally. Depending on how quickly you want it, I can have it ready in an hour.'

'And if I want it sooner?' he asked, simply because his mood was decidedly testy and she was the cause of it.

'Then I'd have to wonder why you're even bothering to

attend the fundraiser if you have far more pressing matters to deal with. Don't get me wrong, I know you're a master at multi-tasking but it would help to know what I'm supposed to prioritise.'

Their arrival at his embassy put paid to his errant thoughts and, thankfully, the need to dissect the real cause of his disgruntlement. 'Let's go and find out, shall we?'

He stepped out, ingrained courtesy dictating he hold out his hand to her.

She accepted his assistance, slid out gracefully but almost immediately attempted to regain her hand. Zak released her but not before he once again registered the smooth, supple warmth of her skin. The need to keep touching her.

General Pierre Alvardo, Montegova's defence minister, approached the moment they were inside the vast hallway of the Montegovan embassy.

'Your Highness, thank you for meeting me. This matter is urgent or I wouldn't have interrupted your evening.'

'I'll be the judge of that.' Zak had accepted the meeting because Alvardo tended to be a little trigger happy. His mother had her hands full with parliamentary duties and his brother, Crown Prince Remi, was on a diplomatic mission in the Middle East.

Alvardo slid a glance at Violet, then addressed his next request in Montegovan.

Zak stopped him with a halting hand. 'You may address me in English, Alvardo. Lady Barringhall has signed a confidentiality contract and knows the consequences of breaking it.'

Beside him, Violet gave a sanguine smile that somehow tunnelled straight into his bloodstream, heating it up several more degrees. 'Lady Barringhall hasn't forgotten, Your Highness. She doesn't need to be reminded.'

Alvardo's eyes widened but he hadn't risen to defence minister without learning a thing or two about diplomacy.

In the conference room, Zak waited for Violet to be seated before taking his place at the head of the table. The moment she set her phone to record, he got straight to the point.

'Is this about the group of dissidents you alerted us to two months ago?'

Alvardo nodded. 'Intelligence reports they've doubled in number and may be planning an insurgency in Playagova in the near future.'

Zak tensed. 'May be? You're not completely certain of their plans?'

Alvardo's gaze grew cagey. 'We haven't been able to infiltrate the group as easily as we'd hoped.'

Zak's eyes narrowed. 'You're here to seek leave to openly pursue them?' he surmised.

His minister nodded. 'As the Queen's appointed head of the Montegovan military, you will have to give express instructions for an active investigation into the group.'

'Even though such an act could fuel anxiety, cause undue panic?' he countered.

'I believe it's a small price to pay for absolute certainty.'

'I don't.'

Zak felt Violet's gaze on him. He glanced at her, registered the relief in her eyes before she broke eye contact to fiddle needlessly with her phone.

'But… Your Highness.' Alvardo paused, and Zak got the notion he was measuring his words. 'I'm of the opinion that this could get out of hand very quickly if not immediately dealt with.'

'Then redouble your efforts to turn *may be* into concrete evidence. The Montegovan people have been through enough without causing ripples with unfounded rumours. Maintain surveillance without engaging and report back to me when something changes.' Until then he'd make his own investigations, double check the general's report.

With his mother's recent but as yet unannounced intention to step down from the throne in favour of Remi, the situation would need extremely careful monitoring. The last thing Montegova needed with its recent history was another shaky period. 'That will be all.'

The general rose, gave a grave bow and left the room.

Zak noted Violet's heavy silence as he escorted her back out to the car.

It wasn't until they cleared Midtown traffic and were heading towards the Upper East Side, where the fundraiser was being held, that he turned to her.

'Ask your questions. I can see you're about to burst from the effort of maintaining your silence.'

She pressed plump lips together for a short moment. 'Is there really a threat to your country?'

He shrugged. 'There's always a threat. The trick is to separate the salient from the white noise, as it were.'

'But what the general said…it all sounded urgent.'

'Alvardo is a defence minister. He believes he wouldn't be doing his job if he didn't advocate fire and brimstone at every turn.'

She frowned. 'Are you sure? It seems a little more than that.'

'Probably because it is,' Zak confirmed, then wondered why he was giving her this leeway, letting her into secrets that might come back to bite him.

'And you're happy to go along with such dire predictions? Are you really okay with such blatant…warmongering?'

'I've learned to look beneath the surface, always. He makes his reports. I investigate further where I need to. The truth of the situation always comes out in the end.' He couldn't stem bitterness that stemmed directly from the secret his father had kept for over twenty years, only to have it explode in their faces even before the dirt had settled over his final resting place. But his statement was also aimed at Violet, more specifically at the plans she'd concocted with her mother.

He glanced at her, noted how her lashes swept down and away, pretending interest in the passing scenery outside the window. *Si*, Lady Violet Barringhall, like her mother, clearly thought they were pulling the wool over his eyes with this stint at his trust.

'And do you think this situation requires serious investigation? Are people really plotting to bring the kingdom down?' she asked after a moment with wide-eyed interest that appeared genuine. But then her interest would be genuine, wouldn't it, if she had aspirations of elevating herself from Lady to Princess?

Zak shrugged with an ease he didn't feel deep down. 'There are those who believe the era of the monarchy is long past. That the people should dispense with the royal house altogether.' He gauged her reaction. While her expression looked a little troubled, there wasn't the cutting desperation he'd expected at the possibility of her coveted position evaporating before her eyes.

Perhaps she was a better actress than he'd initially credited her with being.

'And what do you say to that?'

Centuries-old pride and the warrior's clamour of his forebears drew only one answer from him. 'My ancestors didn't carve out a kingdom through blood and battle only to hand it over to a disgruntled few who believe they know what's right for my people. Montegova isn't ruled by a power-hungry figurehead who merely sits on the throne and collects taxes at the end of a fiscal year. My mother and brother are both active members of parliament. Their votes are just two among many that operate under a system of check and balances agreed by law. As the current head of the monarchy, the Queen has certain rights, granted, but she's not above the law. Whatever injustices are felt should be addressed through the legal system, not through uprisings.'

'That's easy to say, though, some would say. Didn't your ancestors stamp out dissension when there were bloody revolutions?'

He allowed himself a smile that didn't quite unfreeze the chill in his chest, not when the memory of how close to chaos Montegova had come a mere decade ago echoed through him. 'Precisely. So why follow the same tired route when we can forge new ones? Innovate, don't imitate, isn't that the saying?'

'Why are you pretending to be flippant about this?' she asked.

Zak tensed, despising the extra layer of disgruntlement her incisive observation triggered. 'Perhaps I'm wondering what your motives are. Your task was simply to take notes. Why the sudden interest in Montegova?' he tossed back at her.

She floundered momentarily before her composure snapped back into place. 'I work for you, for the time being. Is it really so strange for me to take an interest, considering I have an affiliation with Montegova? Or have you forgotten that my mother is half-Montegovan?'

He hadn't forgotten, neither had he missed how effectively the Barringhalls used that fact when it suited them financially. 'And how many times have you visited the homeland you have a *quarter* claim to?'

She flushed, even though her gaze stayed defiantly on his. 'Not as often as I would've liked—'

'By that you mean never, am I right?'

'We both know I've never visited Montegova.'

Perhaps it was time to root her out, turn the tables on this scheme by the Barringhalls and be done with this woman who tempted him like no other.

'According to your résumé, you've been to the other side of the world. The life you choose to live on social media is fond of screaming that fact but you've never bothered to visit the homeland of your non-British ancestors on the other side of Europe? I'm sure you'll excuse me if I find your concern for the state of affairs in my kingdom some-what…lacking.'

'My travels were funded by charitable donations pains-takingly gathered over four years because I was determined to make a difference. And if by life on social media, you mean my *job*, then yes. It's called raising awareness.'

His lips twisted. 'There is a fine line between raising awareness and raising one's own profile.'

'Is there? How would you know? Isn't your royal web-page managed by a team of social media experts? Or are you one of those royals who can't resist having a secret profile so you can play the voyeur on other people's lives?'

He allowed himself a riling smile. 'If I do possess such a page, rest assured, I won't divulge it to you.'

Hot emotion flashed through her eyes. But again it was swiftly swept under the cloak of utter composure. And why did that normally laudable ability suddenly grate on his nerves?

'Because you, like everyone else, believe every single thing you hear about my family?' she demanded, her tone holding a chilled note of censure. As if she was the one dis-appointed in him, not the other way around.

'The evidence is hard to refute but I invite you to try.'

Her lips pursed again and, like a fool, he latched onto the motion, recalling far too vividly the taste and supple-ness of her lower lip. The eagerness of her response. Did she still make those insane little sounds when aroused?

'No, thank you. Far be it from me to waste my time on

a futile task. Besides, we've arrived,' she announced with more than a little relief in her voice.

Zak flicked a glance out his window, his ire increasing. He'd been so absorbed in her he'd lost all sense of time and place. He ignored his driver's presence beside the back door and concentrated on Violet. On the answer she'd given him. Had she truly just refused a silver-plated invitation to interact with him?

Zak could honestly say he didn't recall the last time the words *no, thanks* had fallen from a woman's lips in his company.

And again he was…intrigued. He stared into the blue eyes regarding him with a touch of wariness and…reproof.

'Your Highness—'

'Zak.'

Her eyes widened. 'What?'

'You may call me Zak when we're not in a formal or professional setting. I'll leave it to your discretion,' he said, reeling a little from the words falling from his own mouth.

She didn't speak the words but the refrain of *no, thanks*, blazed in her eyes.

Another first.

'We're going to be late, Your Highness.' She aimed a pointed gaze at the door. 'And I don't wish be blamed for your tardiness.'

A peculiar little blaze fired through him, fanning higher the longer he looked into her eyes. He was a prince. Second in line to the throne of a small but infinitely mighty kingdom. Not very many people dared to defy him.

Violet Barringhall was exhibiting definite signs of defiance.

The urge to put her in her place resurged. But it had a different slant to it this time. There were so many ways to deliver one's point. To those who sought to seed mistrust and dissent in his kingdom. To those who sought to gain financially on the back of his family name.

Why not try a different solution to this problem? Take that immersive therapy he'd mocked to another level. Send the Barringhalls a message once and for all.

She blinked, drawing his attention to her wide, alluring eyes. The flawless skin of her throat and neck. Lust kicked hard in his groin, reminding him that he hadn't indulged himself in a while.

She'd flashed those eyes at him just like that on her birthday. Well, two could play at this game the Barringhalls had started.

Si, it really was the perfect solution.

Decided, he flicked his wrist and his driver eased the door open.

Zak stepped out to a frenzy of paparazzi flashbulbs. Ignoring them, he offered his hand to Violet, this time holding onto her as she stepped out onto the red carpet.

In her heels, she came up to his shoulder, the perfect angle for him to gaze down at for a beat before the inevitable personal questions were shouted at him.

He didn't answer, of course. Pandering to the media was beneath him, and he'd learned long ago that the tabloid press printed what they wanted regardless of his answers or, indeed, the truth.

But when they caught sight of Violet and tripled their questions, he allowed an enigmatic smile to play on his lips as he tucked her arm into his and escorted her inside.

The paradigm had shifted.

Violet couldn't pinpoint exactly what had happened or when. But as she walked beside Zak though the throng of designer-clad guests, she sensed an edgier purpose from him. Instinctively, she knew it wasn't the challenge of attempting to meet his impossibly high standards.

Whatever Zak had up his sleeve was *personal*. Aimed at her.

It lurked in the shrewd, too-long gazes that repeatedly slanted her way as he guided her around the opulent ballroom. Halfway through the first circuit, she knew she needed to extricate herself from him.

His tight schedule, even at social functions, provided the perfect excuse. 'You have three pre-dinner drinks. The first is with the Bolivian attaché. Here he comes now,' she said briskly, hoping that flinging them both into business mode would throw him off whatever scent he seemed determined to hunt down.

Zak nodded without taking his eyes off the person he was saying goodbye to, then skilfully intercepted her with a hand on her elbow before she could walk away. 'Stay. Your presence will curtail his tendency to drone on ad nauseam. You might also pick up a tip or two to take back to your institution when you leave in a few months.'

The reminder that this position was temporary shouldn't have annoyed her, considering she'd been praying for it to end a short while ago. Perhaps it abraded her nerves because he stated it with that narrow-eyed, watchful suspicion? 'I'll stay if you think I'll be useful. My role is to assist, after all.'

'Do I detect a little displeasure in your tone, Lady Barringhall?'

Violet.

She barely stopped herself from issuing the invitation. She wouldn't. He could use that mocking tone all he liked. Right up until she extricated herself permanently from him.

'Of course not,' she said with a smile manufactured straight from the depths of the decorum rulebook.

She ignored his droll expression as he greeted the attaché, sending him on his way the moment the man's conversation grew circuitous. But after he'd introduced her to the next person with that faintly mocking tone once more, she'd had enough. 'Why do you keep throwing my title in people's faces?'

'I don't know what you mean.'

Ignoring the blatantly false claim of obliviousness, she pressed on. 'You've been in a…mood since we arrived. Is this some sort of test?'

'Everything is a test, Lady Barringhall. If you don't know that by now, then I've been wasting my time.'

'I don't mean professionally and you know it. This feels personal. Did I do something to offend you?'

The only hint that she may have strayed near a bullseye with her question was in the brief flaring of his nostrils. Then he was back under supreme control. 'I merely introduced you with your correct title. I fail to see why you would feel attacked by it.'

To push the issue felt like overkill. And yet… 'Perhaps we should clear the air. Lay things out in the open?'

His eyes gleamed. 'Ah, now we get to the heart of the matter. Is this where you confess?'

She frowned. 'Excuse me? Confess what?'

'That this so-called role of yours is just hiding your true purpose here,' he said, an edge in his tone.

'And what's my true purpose, pray tell? No, wait, let me guess. You think it's some sort of ploy to land myself somewhere in your private life? Or, goodness, perhaps even in your bed?'

That earned her more emotion. His eyes blazed wildly and ferociously, just like they had that night, before he ruthlessly smothered it. But it didn't die completely. She felt its latent heat as his gaze drilled into her. 'Is your ultimate goal to land in my *bed*? You should've said this straight out, Violet. Then we could've dispensed with all this…pretence.'

Fire intensified, flaring out from her pelvis to engulf her whole body. 'You're deliberately twisting my words. I don't want to end up in your bed. Hell, I don't want to go anywhere near your bedroom!'

A few heads turned, and she flushed as eyebrows went up at her hot, charged denial.

Just then a discreet little chime announced the end of the champagne reception. Violet breathed in relief.

'Saved by the bell but definitely to be continued, I think,' he rasped as they drifted towards an even more opulently decorated ballroom where the main event was being held.

'No, it won't,' she whispered fiercely. 'I hate to disappoint you but I've said all I'm going to say on the matter. I don't care what you think my motives are, but I'd thank you to—'

'You don't care? Have you forgotten that one major reason you're here is to get your hands on my invaluable letter of recommendation?'

'Are you threatening to withhold it unless I indulge you in your silly little game? Is that what this is about?'

His mouth twisted. 'Let's not throw around accusations on who is playing games with whom, Lady Barringhall.' His voice was silky, like a stiletto knife sliding through butter. All without losing an ounce of his arrogant composure. Hell, he even nodded greetings to a few guests in the process of cutting her down.

She refused to be cowed. 'You didn't answer my question. I've done everything you've asked of me since I arrived in New York. But if I'm wasting my time, at least have the balls to tell me so we can be rid of each other sooner rather than later,' she dared, her heart banging hard against her ribcage. She didn't want to risk irritating him more than she already seemed to be doing, but she didn't want to throw away all her efforts either.

They reached their designated high table and he slid back her chair, his strong, elegant hands braced on the sides as he waited for her to be seated.

Violet moved, incredibly aware of his proximity, of his scent and the powerful body barely leashed beneath the trappings of civilised clothing. Aware of his complete focus on her. She called on every crumb of composure she possessed, thankful when she took her seat without stumbling.

But then he lowered his head to align with hers, drawing a wild shiver as he murmured for her ears alone, 'A few weeks of running around in my office, dispensing effortless English charm, isn't going to quite cut it. If you want to earn my regard, you'll need to do a lot more than lackey work. And as for my balls, Lady Barringhall, I'd caution you not to involve them in our conversations. At least, not in this setting. Later, though…who knows? I just might accommodate you.'

Heat flared into her cheeks, whipping up a wild tornado that centred between her thighs. She refused to be thrown by the images he evoked. Nevertheless, it took considerable scrambling to get her brain to formulate an answer. 'What do I need to do to prove my worth?' she demanded once he was seated, frustration building in her chest.

'You want to prove your worth? The trust is in the process of building eco-lodges in Tanzania. It's a tourism initiative in partnership with the government to provide long-term income to the area. Tell me what you would bring to the table in this project.'

Violet ruthlessly curbed her excitement. With a few words, he'd described everything she hoped to aspire to in her career. But she didn't put it past him to dangle an offer in her face only to snatch it up the moment she expressed an interest. That gleam in his eyes had only intensified in the last few minutes, his focus on her almost rabid in its fervour.

'How many lodges?'

'Thirty to start off with catering to the discerning and

environmentally-conscious tourist in mind. Twice that in phases two and three.'

'When are you looking to vet volunteers? I could help you with that. Weed out those wanting a free ride against those committed to truly making a difference.'

'There are a few on the ground already but the majority are lined up to be vetted in the next week or two.'

She shook her head. 'The rainy season starts in less than three months. If you don't want the project severely disrupted, you need to move quicker than that.'

A smile ghosted over his lips and Violet suspected he'd been testing her.

Her shoulders went back. She lifted her chin and stared him straight in the eyes. 'You want to test my true commitment? Include me in the project. My secondment is up in about the time it'll take for this first phase to be done. Let me prove to you that this isn't just some flight of fancy.'

He wasn't impressed by her declaration. If anything, his scepticism increased. 'You wouldn't be the first royal seeking to elevate their status by affiliating themselves with a project like this. Just so we're clear, that's not going to happen here.'

'All I'm asking is that you suspend your suspicion of my motives for a few weeks and let me do what I came here to do. Or are you so cynical that you won't even give me that chance?'

His smile turned hard, edgy. 'You seem in a mood to throw around taunts.'

'I'm defending my character. I'm a hard worker. Take my word for it or let my actions speak for themselves.'

Stormcloud eyes pinned her to her seat. But before he could respond, a hush descended, drawing their attention to the podium as the patron of the fundraising charity rose to make her welcoming speech. The world-renowned socialite, known for her skills in raising millions for charitable causes, repeatedly glanced over at Zak as she spoke.

Despite being over a decade older than him, her interest was blatant, a fact, Violet suspected, that had contributed to her hosting this event.

For a cynical moment Violet wondered if Zak had taken advantage of it. Whether he'd had even a moment's pause before aligning himself with a woman whose gaze caressed his face even as she delivered a charming, quick-witted speech.

She only registered that she'd been staring at him for an indecent amount of time when his gaze swung sharply to her, one eyebrow cocked at whatever he read in her expression.

She resisted the urge to drop her gaze, allowed hers to linger before, feigning boredom, she turned towards the podium as the socialite ended her speech to applause.

Violet couldn't fault her. As her own mother had repeatedly striven to maximise every opportunity by hosting such events, people were more prone to opening their wallets when in a good mood.

And the sight of Prince Zak Montegova, rising with masterful grace and long-limbed elegance to step up to the podium, made them feel extra-special.

His speech was a sublime combination of wit, gravitas and arrogant challenge, rousing consciences and stirring sluggish apathy. Heads nodded and any remaining sceptics couldn't help but be moved by the video presentation of the trust's needs, especially in deprived communities.

'And just so you'll appreciate the urgency of my latest project, I've been informed by Lady Violet Barringhall, my newly appointed special advisor on our latest project in Tanzania, that time is even more of the essence if we're to meet our goals. Which means you'll also need to move fast or this particular train will leave without you. And if you miss this one, you won't be guaranteed a seat on the next one.'

And, simply because everyone in the room wanted a connection with the Royal House of Montegova and its representative Prince, they laughed a little more eagerly, their glances sharper as they turned to her, prying and assessing whether *she* was the conduit to their ultimate prize—access to Zak Montegova.

But Violet wasn't interested in them. She was wholly consumed by Zak's revelation. Her heart banged anew when he stared at her in blatant challenge for a sizzling few seconds, absorbed the applause at the end of his speech, before stepping off the podium.

He neither paused nor smiled in acknowledgement of the accolades dropped in his wake as he returned to the table.

Soft music struck up from a string quartet as he resumed his seat.

'You couldn't have told me before you made the announcement?' she asked, wondering why her excitement, while effervescent—because this was what she'd dreamed of for as long as she could recall—was tinged with an even sharper thrill she suspected had nothing to do with her new role and everything to do with the man who'd granted it.

'I believe this is the moment in the process where you thank me for giving you this opportunity?' he drawled silkily, dark grey eyes fixed on her face.

Violet swallowed her sharp reply. Regardless of how the package had been delivered it was the content, the chance to start to make a difference, that mattered. 'Thank you for the opportunity. And before you taunt me by asking me if I'm up to the task, I assure you I am.'

'You urged me to test your mettle. Consider this the first lesson. But I'll be watching you every step of the way. One misstep and you're done.'

'There won't be any,' she stressed, for him and especially

for herself. She couldn't afford any, not if she wanted to drag herself out of the shadow of her parents' misdeeds.

'Good. We leave in seven days. You can have tomorrow morning off to pack.'

Something wild and urgent fluttered in her belly. *We?*

'Did I not mention it? I'll be in on the ground in Tanzania too. Which means you'll be working directly under me,' he said, his voice deep, weighted with evocative meaning that sent blood surging through her body to concentrate traitorously between her thighs.

He stared at her long enough to register the effect of his words on her. Then he turned away and addressed the other guests at the table.

Violet sat back, attempted to absorb the swift turn of events, and the image she couldn't erase from her mind— of her trapped beneath the sensual power and might of Zak Montegova—quickly enough.

The gauntlet had been thrown down, and her with it, right into the spotlight. Perhaps in more ways than one.

Either way, it was up to her to show him, to show everyone, that she wasn't just a tainted title, biding her time until a rich, preferably titled man swept her off her feet and answered all her mother's prayers.

CHAPTER THREE

TANZANIA WAS HOT, humid and stunningly beautiful. Even the humid bustle of Dar es Salaam held a unique vibe that escalated Violet's excitement as they disembarked from Zak's private jet and headed out of Tanzania's largest city.

Air-conditioned SUVs allayed a little of the discomfort travelling into the heart of the country caused with pot-holed roads, but Violet absorbed every second of it, still pinching herself that she'd managed to get herself into the field so quickly.

Their final destination, Lake Ngoro, was still a good two hours away, according to the satnav, when they stopped for lunch.

Despite the stunning and picturesque vista, the restaurant was little more than a few thatched huts with tables and chairs grouped under shaded umbrellas. When the procession of four SUVs stopped, Violet hid a grimace as the suited bodyguards alighted stiffly and formed a loose semicircle around their Prince.

'Something annoying you already?' Zak enquired, his laconic drawl suggesting he wasn't surprised. 'The heat perhaps? Or the sparse surroundings? Five-star establishments a little thin on the ground for you?'

Violet ground her teeth and breathed through her irritation as a waiter hurried towards them. 'None of the above. If you must know, I was thinking that six bodyguards seem a little…excessive, don't you think?'

'Protocol dictates it needs to be this way. And I'd rather

not incur my mother's wrath by going against her wishes,' he added with a wry twist of his lips.

Queen Isadora was a formidable woman. Even though she and her mother were friends, Violet had met the Queen only twice in her life. Both times she'd been awed by the woman's utter poise and the shrewd intelligence that shone from grey eyes she'd passed to her sons, along with her strength and resilience.

'Does their presence ever get overwhelming?'

He cracked open a bottle of iced water and poured her a glass before filling his own. 'That's like asking if breathing is tedious. It is what it is.'

Her fingers curled around the chilled glass. 'Would you change it if you could?'

Despite the shades concealing his eyes, she felt his probing gaze. 'Why would I want to change a status only a fraction of people ever get to experience? I'm deemed one of the luckiest men in the world to be surrounded by yes men and women all too eager to obey my every command,' he stated with a thick layer of cynicism.

'And yet your tone suggests otherwise,' she replied.

For a fraction of a moment he seemed startled by the observation. As if he'd let something slip he hadn't intended to. Then his face resumed its stoic mask. 'I was taught not only to appreciate the advantages of my status but also to help preserve it. And to deal effectively with those parasites who would attempt to leech their way into riches on my family's coattails.'

It didn't take a genius to know she'd been lumped in with that deplorable crowd. 'But you don't mind using those yes men and women to accomplish your goals?'

His eyes narrowed. 'Are we being specific here, Violet? Are you asking me if I take advantage of my status?'

The man-eating eyes of that fundraising socialite flashed

to mind and she tried to curb the curious sting in her chest.
'Do you?'

'I earn my dues in business. And in pleasure. No one
has left my presence dissatisfied. Unless they absolutely
deserved it, of course.'

The urge to pluck the sunglasses off his face so she could
read his expression warred with the very real need to deny
that they were speaking about the same thing—the night
of her eighteenth birthday. Had she deserved to be left dissatisfied like that?

And why was he referring to it now?

The waiter's arrival with platters of food put paid to the
dangerous train of thought she seemed to stray into with
maddening frequency.

'Are you done?' He nodded at her plate twenty minutes
later, a frown in his voice.

She looked down at her plate. The food had been tasty so
she attributed her elusive appetite to Zak's presence more
than anything else. 'Turns out I'm not very hungry.'

His lips firmed but he rose without saying a word.

Back in the SUV, Zak Montegova handled the vehicle
with effortless grace, his body packed with latent power that
repeatedly drove the very air from her lungs each time she
glanced his way. Bouncing over potholes and being jostled
about, it was difficult not to be aware of her own body and
its close proximity to Zak's.

So she was relieved to arrive two long hours later, to
breathe the fresh, clean air of Lake Ngoro, the mostly
flat green landscape where Zak had sited the Trust's eco-
lodges.

Events had proceeded at breakneck pace after the fundraiser. As she'd predicted, donations had flooded in from
the great and good, easily ensuring that they could fund
another five projects within the year.

And Zak's confirmation on Monday that the rains were

indeed expected in a few weeks sparked an urgency for the trip. Violet had read through hundreds of résumés, sat in on in-person and video conference interviews, and grilled each volunteer until she was certain the sixty-five they'd chosen would be up to the daunting task of constructing the eco-lodges in time.

As she looked around now, she was gratified to see that the local construction crew who'd already been on site for two weeks were already at the final stages of laying the foundations.

A man broke away from a group of workers hammering a sign board into the ground and hurried towards them. His dark bronze skin, curly mahogany hair and light eyes indicated a mixed heritage. Despite the sweat pouring down his face and sticking to his tie-dyed T-shirt, his grin was infectious and as open as his outstretched hand.

'Hey, there. I'm Peter Awadhi, foreman slash friendly face slash official representative of the Tourist Board. We've spoken a few times on the phone but let me formally welcome you to Tanzania…um… Prince…er… Your Highness.'

Violet hid a smile as he stumbled over Zak's title.

Zak shook his hand. 'Zak is fine,' he offered, although he didn't return the man's smile.

Peter nodded, then glanced at her.

She held out her hand. 'I'm Violet Barringhall. Special advisor, volunteer co-ordinator and general dogsbody.'

'Ah, you're the new one in charge of the volunteers? Sweet. I have a few requests to swing by you later when you've had a chance to settle in.'

'Of course. That's what I'm here for.'

His grin widened and Zak's face soured further. 'Are our tents ready?' Zak asked.

Peter released her hand, looked over towards the SUVs and shouted instructions in Kiswahili at the group erecting the sign. 'They are. I'll have your luggage taken to your assigned tents when you're ready.'

'We will. The sample lodge is ready to view?' Zak asked.

Peter nodded. 'In the west compound, as you instructed.'

'Take me there, I'd like to inspect it.'

'Sure thing,' Peter replied, in no way daunted by Zak's hit-the-ground-running attitude.

'When we're done, I'd like a tour of the rest of the site, if that's not too much trouble?' Violet asked.

Zak frowned. 'We just arrived. You should rest.'

She shook her head. 'I'm not tired and I've been cooped up in the car for hours. I'd like to stretch my legs and familiarise myself with the landscape in preparation for when the volunteers arrive tomorrow.'

His lips firmed and he clicked his fingers. One of his bodyguards rushed forward and a low exchange took place in Montegovan. Before Violet could blink, a wide-brimmed straw hat magically appeared. Zak held it out to her. 'Heatstroke is a serious issue here. I'd hate to have to use the chopper on our very first day.'

She'd packed a hat for herself but with her luggage still stowed in the SUV, she had no choice but to accept Zak's offering.

'Thanks.' She pulled on the hat, glad for the shade it offered.

They made their way from the parking area to the heart of the site, where the large building that would house the reception, restaurant and spa were located.

The construction crew were in the final stages of pouring concrete for the foundations. The handful of volunteers who'd been on site from the beginning would leave as soon as the new volunteers Violet had helped select arrived to start their work erecting the lodges.

They bypassed the central building and she spotted a sleek helicopter, the one Zak had referred to, on the far north side of the flat landscape. Its discreet little red and white cross caught her attention.

'Why the medical chopper? I didn't think it'd be needed at a project like this,' she said to Peter.

He glanced briefly at Zak before he answered. 'This isn't strictly a medical helicopter but it's useful since the nearest medical facility is thirty miles away. It's purely a worst-case scenario option.'

Of course, with the VIP royal who happened to be second in line to the Montegovan throne on site, safeguarding him was paramount. Looking closer, Violet spotted the monogram of the Montegovan royal house on the tail fin of the aircraft, confirming her theory.

Zak sent her a sidelong glance. 'Before you think the pampered Prince has a chopper on tap to deal with his splinters, you should know that the chef in charge of feeding the whole camp happens to be eight months pregnant. She refuses to leave before her rotation is up in two weeks. The helicopter is primarily for her in case she goes into early labour.'

Shame lanced her and she was glad for the wide brim of the hat hiding her chagrin. Zak's mocking gaze returned to the path as they left the first row of lodges and headed west.

The eco-lodge came into view as they rounded an acacia tree.

The single storey building was functional, compact but beautiful, designed for a small family. It blended into the landscape and had a simple wraparound veranda at the front to make the most of west-facing sunlight.

Zak stepped onto the veranda and opened the front door.

The functional theme was echoed inside with an openplan living room and kitchen, and two small bedrooms tucked into the back of the house. But it was the hidden extras that Violet was interested in.

'Bath water is recycled into sanitary plumbing?' she asked.

Zak nodded. 'And solar panels on the roof at the back provide energy. A central borehole has been dug ready to harvest natural artesian water and rain. There's a large borehole for the whole village.'

According to the report she'd read back in New York, the eco-lodges had been a joint-design between Zak and Tanzanian architects to exact specifications, with as much locally sourced materials as possible, after which they were constructed and flat-packed in Montegova and shipped three weeks ago. It was clear this project was close to his heart as he inspected every corner of the dwelling, pointing out areas he wanted rechecked and improved in the yet-to-be-built units.

Peter answered every query, providing intelligent solutions when Zak demanded them. Before they left the sample house, it was clear why he'd been chosen as foreman.

Thinking she would be left alone with Peter to conduct her tour, she inhaled sharply when Zak fell into step beside her. Violet refused to glance his way, a little resentful that he brimmed with vitality after endless hours in the vehicle, whereas she felt hot and sticky and wilted.

They were circling back to the heart of the site when a volunteer arrived with a query for Peter. He made his excuses and left, leaving her alone with Zak.

'First impressions?' Zak asked.

She was impressed. She couldn't deny it, so she didn't. 'It's exceptional.'

Zak nodded. 'There will also be a Montegovan specialist on site for the first three months to train homeowners on how to fix basic things should they go wrong.'

There was a pulse of pride in his voice that threatened to destabilise the picture she'd drawn of him. Threatened to soften a place inside her she needed to keep under tight guard. Lofty thoughts of the charming Prince saving the less privileged belonged in fairy tales.

'Should I take that frown to mean you don't approve?'

She shook her head. 'I approve of all this. But I'm wondering about you,' she blurted. 'You have thousands at your command to do all of this. Why are you here?'

He'd taken off his shades when they'd entered the lodge and now speared her with the full force of his grey eyes. 'You want to know why I'm supervising a project that bears my name?' he asked, his tone bone-dry.

'Don't you worry that people will wonder what a Harvard-educated Mediterranean prince needs to prove by digging around in the dirt? That this is really some PR stunt? Like you said, it wouldn't be the first time a privileged royal did this sort of thing in the hope of gaining points with the media.'

His shrug was chock-full of dismissive arrogance. 'I'm in the unique position of not having to impress anyone or caring what anyone thinks.'

Because he had the advantage of status, wealth and drop-dead gorgeous good looks?

'Not even that you want to make a difference?' she pressed, a little unsure why she wanted to probe so deeply.

'The results of my work speak for themselves.'

She couldn't deny that. Beyond his military and academic accolades, Zak Montegova had made a name for himself with his family trust. Had rivalled and in some ways elevated his family name more than his semi-reclusive brother had.

But then Remi Montegova's loss of his fiancée had resulted in his withdrawal from the social scene and the world in general, leaving his mother and brother to become the face of the royal house.

Had that put extra pressure on Zak? Was that why he held himself so stoically? Or was that ingrained in him for another reason? Realising she was back to dwelling much too long on the enigmatic man and not enough on her professional role, Violet turned away.

Only to have her elbow snagged in a firm hold. 'The bush might look harmless but be careful about wandering too close to it. Stick to the designated paths. You don't know what's lurking in there.'

Right at that moment she was more worried about the heat singeing her whole being from his touch than bugs or snakes. 'If I spend all my time worrying about what will jump out at me from the bushes, I'll never enjoy my surroundings.'

Peter heard her response as he re-joined them and nodded his approval. 'That's the spirit.'

Zak sent him a chilled glance that had the man's smile evaporating. Muttering an excuse about checking on their luggage, Peter left again.

'You're not here to enjoy yourself. You're here to work. Taking unnecessary precautions could end up inconveniencing others,' Zak declared.

He was right. And yet his retort stung deep. 'That's the difference between us, Your Highness. I give myself permission to enjoy my work. And by the way, I hadn't forgotten why I was here but, thanks, I'll bear your concern in mind.'

'You'll do more than that. I can't afford to have my schedule disrupted because of carelessness.'

She fought the urge to roll her eyes. 'I've just got here. I haven't had time to be careless!'

His gaze flicked pointedly to the hat on her head. 'Haven't you?'

She snatched it off and held it out to him. 'I'm not as fragile as you'd like to think I am. Besides, the worst of the heat is over.'

He didn't reclaim the hat. Instead, he conducted a slow scrutiny of her body.

By the time his gaze returned to her face, she was hot and tingly all over, and it had nothing to do with the blaze of the late afternoon sun or the trail of sticky sweat meandering its way down her spine.

'When was the last time you applied sunscreen?' he rasped, his voice a shade deeper.

She couldn't remember. 'I'm not doing this with you. I'm a grown woman capable of taking care of myself. Find someone else to snarl at.'

They'd circled back to where they'd left the vehicles and Violet saw with relief that their luggage was being unloaded. She seized the opportunity to wrest herself away from Zak's all-encompassing, disturbing presence. 'I'm going to unpack. If we don't have anything else to discuss, I'll see you in the morning.'

'You'll see me in an hour and a half, when we meet for dinner to go over the schedule for tomorrow,' he said silkily, but with that stamp of authority that said he expected his command to be obeyed.

Unable to resist, she glanced over her shoulder at him. Dark grey eyes regarded her steadily with a hint of challenge.

Violet resisted the urge to grind her teeth, reminding herself for the umpteenth time that he was her boss. He was calling the shots. For the next few months he virtually held her professional life in his hands.

Despite repeating all of that to herself, her temper still simmered by the time she reached the area where the tents had been erected on the east side of the site. She spotted Zak's immediately since it was quite impossible to miss. It was the largest structure, set away from the rest of the tents on its own little hill. Plus the presence of two bodyguards guarding the entrance gave it away.

'Miss?' The volunteer who'd been escorting her had stopped several feet from her, drawing her attention from Zak's imposing tent. 'Your tent is this way.' He indicated the path that went past the row of empty tents set a short distance away.

Frowning, she followed, her breath growing shorter the closer they got to Zak's tent. Surely he wasn't expecting her to share a tent with him?

'I thought I'd be using one of these smaller tents,' she said, aware her voice had grown husky and uneven. Hell, even a touch agitated. All at the thought of sharing a tent with Zak?

Yes.

No matter how much she tried to dice it, she recognised that exposure to him would fray what composure she'd managed to secure around him.

'You are,' the volunteer said, pointing to a medium sized tent tucked behind Zak's and away from the smaller ones down the hill. 'Well, it's kind of small,' he amended at her frown. 'But you're sharing Prince Zak's shower, not sharing with everyone else down the hill, so that's a bonus, right?'

Violet refused to examine the twinge that lanced her midriff at the realisation that she wasn't sharing a tent with Zak. Part disappointment, part relief? She pushed the emotion aside and thanked the man, who propped her large backpack in front of the tent and left.

She dragged her luggage inside and looked around. A small desk and chair had been set up on one side, with a carafe of water and glasses on a tray. The single bed on the other side held a surprisingly comfortable mattress and beside it was a nightstand on which sat a small but powerful lamp. At the foot of the bed was a shelved cabinet and a wash basin.

Simple. Rustic. A world removed from the opulent Park Avenue offices of the Royal House of Montegova Trust and the glitz and glamour of the fundraising ballroom in New York. And even the country manor house her mother had moved heaven and earth to cling to despite their questionable financial circumstances.

Yet Violet felt a sense of rightness and homecoming as she set her case down to unpack. Done minutes later, she set up her laptop on the desk, checked her emails—thanks to the newly installed Wi-Fi system—and ensured there were no last-minute emergencies to deal with before re-checking the volunteer roster.

Then, because her roiling emotions needed sorting through, she lay down on the bed, her gaze fixed on the apex of the tent.

Zak Montegova was here and was staying for the duration of the project. She needed to get used to seeing him every day. As long as she maintained professional distance, she had nothing to worry about.

A few short weeks. That was all she needed to endure Zak's presence…

Violet jerked awake, the realisation that she'd fallen asleep filling her with mild horror. A quick check on her phone showed she was ten minutes from being late to dinner. So much for her lofty assertion that she wasn't tired.

She flew to the cabinet holding her clothes, selected a white T-shirt, khaki shorts and brown espadrilles. Washing as best she could in the basin, she changed her clothes, brushed and tied back her hair.

She stepped out of her tent and stumbled to a halt. 'Oh, my God,' she murmured, awed by the sight before her. The cloud was awash with bursts of orange, greys and indigos. The hues were so powerful and spectacular she lost the ability to breathe as she stared at the stunning sunset. Thoughts of being late melted away, the sheer beauty of her surroundings holding her firmly in place.

'Is this your first?' a deep voice asked.

She hadn't heard Zak approach. Her stomach dipped alarmingly at the hushed gruffness in his tone. It was almost as if he didn't want to ruin the moment with their earlier animosity. She didn't want to look at him, fearing he would only add to the dramatic enchantment around her. But the sheer magnetism of the man drew her attention from the magnificent sky and sunset blazing over the lake, and she glanced at him to find his stormy gaze wholly fixed on her.

Heart thumping, she tried to recall what he'd asked her. 'My first?'

He turned away, presenting her with his haughty and perfect profile. 'African sunset.'

'I… Yes,' she whispered, a little afraid that speaking too loudly would make the glorious vision disappear.

The smallest hint of a smile tilted his lips, but it disappeared far too soon. 'It has the ability to evoke weak-kneed reactions.'

She stemmed the wild urge to ask him about *his* first. Had he been alone? If not, with whom? It was none of her business. So why the next words tripped from her lips, she would never know. 'I find it hard to believe you're capable of getting weak-kneed about anything.'

Did he tense just then? Thinking it wasn't wise to investigate too closely, and dying for another hit of magnificence, she turned back to the view.

But then he replied, 'If I didn't know better, I'd think you were feeling me out, Violet. Are you?'

She opened her mouth to deny it, but the words stuck in her throat. Did she want a demonstration of Zak's passion? Did she want to hear that deep voice murmur her name in that lightly accented timbre that slipped into his speech every now and then? Heat rushed through her, concentrating in her breasts and between her thighs as the power of his scrutiny singed her. Layer upon layer of sensation swelled, attempting to bury every precaution she'd recited to herself in the tent before sleep had overtaken her.

'Because if you truly are, you only need to say the word,' he added silkily.

Then she knew he was toying with her. Again.

It was there in the smoky mockery lurking in his eyes. There in the enthralling loose-limbed stance with in he held himself. But there was something else. Something ferocious that made her heart pound. That same intensity she'd spotted right before the ball, had sworn to stay away from because it was too dangerous but was now tempting her to peer into, brush her fingers against to test its true risk.

He shifted, turned to fully face her, as if offering her the very thing she needed to resist.

Her throat dried as the power of his masculinity threatened to knock her over. 'I don't need a demonstration, thanks,' she blurted, almost too afraid of the tingling in her body as his gaze lanced over her. 'I'll let you practise your dubious skills on some other unsuspecting female.'

She stepped away from him but not before she heard his low laughter.

Far from thinking he'd received the message, Zak fell into step beside her, his long-limbed stride shortening to match hers. Violet clenched her fists, freshly helpless against what the scent of rugged man and aftershave did to her insides.

'I don't dally with unsuspecting females, *cara*. Every woman who's graced my bed knows exactly what they're getting.'

She stopped abruptly, the images he once again evoked wreaking havoc of the jealous, unpleasant kind with her equilibrium. 'You shouldn't take everything I say as a challenge.'

'Ah, but then you have a unique way of saying things that makes me believe there's more, always more you're actually not quite saying,' he murmured, his gaze conducting that skin-tingling scrutiny of her face that left her feeling exposed.

Sensually vulnerable.

'How am I doing that, exactly?'

He stepped closer, filling every corner of her vision with his presence. 'It's your eyes, *dolcella*. You have the most expressive eyes I've ever seen. And unfortunately for you, they're in constant conflict with the words coming out of your mouth.'

His gaze dropped to her mouth and the rush intensified until her whole body was on fire. 'You either have an overactive imagination or you insist on seeing things that are simply not there.'

'Do I? I guess we'll make the discovery as to whether I'm right or wrong together.'

'We'll do nothing of the sort. They only thing we'll do together is—'

'Go to dinner?' he supplied, more with amusement than with his customary mockery.

Violet wasn't sure why his humour, even at her expense, eased and lightened something inside her. Made her almost…pleased to have been the source of his mirth.

This was totally insane.

'There you go again, *cara*,' he murmured. 'Your innermost thoughts blaze almost as fierce as this sunset.'

She forced a shrug. 'You believe you know what makes me tick. Perhaps I'm wondering the same about you. It's natural curiosity that I'm unsure it's worth fully indulging. That's all this is.'

An edgy little smile twitched at his lips, but he waved her forward with a smooth elegance that proclaimed his royal status. 'Then let's go and eat. Perhaps by the time we're done, you'll have decided one way or the other.'

She wanted to ask him why he was taking an interest. But then that would be prolonging this...*exploration*. So, while she would've enjoyed lingering for a little while longer to watch fiery day blend into star-filled night, she headed for the large tent designated for meals and gatherings.

The scent of sausages, grilled meats and fish assailed her nose as she entered, sparking a growling in her stomach that reminded her that she'd barely touched her lunch.

She was aware of heads turning their way as she and Zak headed for the food table, just as she was aware that the interest was all for him. Helping herself to small portions of local dishes, fried plantains, *ugali*, a thick maize porridge, and sauce, and a sausage on a stick while Zak chatted with Peter, she chose a seat at the end of the long banquet-style table. This was supposed to be a working dinner, and she didn't want things to veer off course again, so she activated her small tablet as soon as Zak joined her.

An email alert brought her up short. She clicked it, her heart sinking when she read the message.

'Problem?' Zak's deep voice rolled over her.

She bit her lip, loath to start their meeting by confessing a setback. But there was no avoiding it. 'Two of the volunteers have pulled out. One has an urgent family matter she needs to deal with, and the other's changed his mind. I won't be able to get replacements for a few days.'

'How are you going to fix that?' There was no challenge in his tone, only simple expectation.

'I'm going to move a few people around, ensure there's an even spread of skillsets to cover until the new volunteers arrive. And I guess this is where my general dogsbody role comes in handy. I'll lend a hand where needed until the replacements get here.'

He nodded. 'I'll do the same. You and I can make up the shortfall.'

Something snagged in her midriff, robbing her of breath

for a moment. 'You'll be helping to build lodges?' she asked, frowning. 'You… I wasn't made aware of that.'

'Would it have changed any part of your role?'

Yes, she would've been better prepared.

Before she could answer, he continued, 'I designed the lodges and worked closely with the company that developed them in Montegova. I'm best suited to step in more than anyone else at short notice. Even you, Violet.'

When it came right down to it, she couldn't object. This was his project, his name on the letterhead. It would've been easy to dismiss him if he'd been a spoilt, pampered prince, obsessed with his looks and getting his picture in the tabloids at every opportunity. But he was offering a sound solution to what could be an irritating setback.

'If you're sure…'

'I'm sure, Violet.' At her continued hesitancy, that edgy gleam returned to his eyes. One brow slowly rose. 'Unless there's another reason for your objection?' he drawled.

Aware that the table had grown quiet, she firmed her resolve and shook her head. 'Absolutely not.'

'Good. Welcome to my team.'

The emphasis on *my* ignited that blaze between them again. She held his gaze for as long as she could withstand the flame, then focused on her tablet, aware that once again she'd been outplayed, had slid that much closer to the edge of an abyss whose depths she couldn't quite fathom.

CHAPTER FOUR

VIOLET GAVE UP tossing and turning at five a.m.

She yearned to blame her restlessness on the different time zone and environment. But she knew the prospect of not only being in Zak's presence but the steel trap of working closely with him for however long he intended to remain here was the reason she'd lain wide awake for long stretches of the night.

Showered and dressed within half an hour, she headed to the food tent, where the local construction crew and skeleton volunteer staff were gathered. She spotted Peter the moment she entered and joined him after getting her breakfast.

'Good morning,' he greeted with a wide smile, pulling out a chair for her. His scrutiny was quick but appreciative, exhibiting harmless male interest a polar opposite from the kind she was used to. The kind her mother keenly invited constantly in a bid to find her and her sisters the 'right' husband. Refusal to accommodate their mother was the reason her twin sister, Sage, had taken a job on the other side of the world in New Zealand and rarely visited Barringhall these days.

She glanced up as Zak stepped into the tent, immediately sucking up all the oxygen from the space and directing more female gazes to him.

For the first time since she'd known him, Zak was dressed at his most casual. Yet even the expensive light-coloured cargo pants and white T-shirt shrieked their exclusivity. Although she suspected that dressed in rags, he'd somehow find a way to exude effortless sophistication and suave elegance. With his broad shoulders, potent good looks and dark hair that gleamed damply from his recent shower, it was near impossible to look away from him as he sauntered over to where she sat.

His grey gaze went from her almost empty plate to her half-finished coffee. Unlike Peter's, his scrutiny triggered fireworks in her body before it met her eyes. *'Buon giorno,'* he said, his deep, raspy voice making her skin tingle even more. 'I didn't expect you to be up this early.'

She shrugged, aware of Peter's interest in the exchange. 'I couldn't sleep so I thought I'd make an early start. The quicker I acclimatise to the routine, the quicker I'll shake off the jet-lag. Besides, the volunteers and trucks should be arriving soon.' And as soon as she rid herself of this disturbing reaction to Zak's presence, she could focus her excitement elsewhere.

'That's the best part—when the long wait is over and we get to see the structures actually going up,' Peter enthused.

Violet smiled at him, his effervescence infecting her.

'Let's hope all that enthusiasm doesn't suffer in the face of hard work,' Zak drawled, folding powerful arms across a wide chest.

She swallowed against the electrifying effect of his muscled biceps and glanced away.

Peter frowned, then shrugged. 'Everyone flags a little when faced with the scale of the work to be done but the ultimate goal is what pushes us all on. It's why I love what I do.'

Violet couldn't help but respond to his infectious attitude. She was still smiling when a female volunteer hurried over with a fresh pot of coffee and offered Zak a cup. For an infinitesimal moment, he didn't respond. His gaze remained locked on Violet a touch longer before he gave an abrupt nod.

Perhaps it was a good thing he was in a disgruntled

mood. It kept her mind from wandering into dangerous territory. Allowed her to steer her attention back to Peter.

'How long have you been in the tourism industry?' she asked him.

'I've never really done anything else. I started off as a tour guide and volunteer, then joined the tourism board to find ways to help the rural areas like these find ways to sustain themselves. It's in my blood,' he said with a grin. 'My Norwegian mother met my Tanzanian father on her gap year volunteering at an animal sanctuary in Dodoma. I was born a year after she finished her veterinary studies. When the opportunity came up to join forces with Zak's and tourist board's vision, I couldn't jump on board fast enough.'

The sound of large engines ended the conversation. The arrival of the volunteers was followed an hour later by excited shouts announcing the arrival of the eco lodges.

Excitement and a keen desire to please the Royal Prince kept everyone on their toes all though the first day. Violet allocated tents and assisted where she could, all the while ensuring she kept a safe distance from Zak.

That plan shattered when he approached where she was filling water bottles to distribute to volunteers. 'You were supposed to join me at lodge two after lunch,' he said, his shoulder brushing hers as he joined her to watch the last of the lodges being laid out in front of their designated sites.

She shifted away from him, her insides a little too jumpy and tingly at even that tiny contact. 'I'd planned to, right after I did this.' She started to lift the tray of bottles but he beat her to it, brushing her aside to balance the tray on one hand as he stared down at her with a fierce smoulder.

'Avoiding me isn't going to work with this thing you're fighting. You know that, don't you?' he rasped.

Despite her stomach hollowing out, she lifted her chin, daringly met his gaze and attempted to bluff her way through it. 'Since I don't know what you're talking about, I'm not equipped to give you an accurate answer.'

He stepped closer to make his point because surely a man like him didn't give a little damn about being over-heard? 'I'm talking about the fact that you're attracted to me, Violet. Have been for quite a while. The fact that you've been attempting to deny it. And the fact that your every action simply emphasises your naughty little dilemma.'

Should she bother denying it? Or should she confront it head on? Would the former merely attract further mock-ery because the evidence of it had lain like an unexploded firework between them since she'd made the mistake of throwing herself at him six years ago?

With a deep breath that failed to steady her, she chose the second option. 'So what if I am? You're decent enough to look at, and since you seem intent on alluding to my lapse in judgement six years ago, yes, we kissed, and, yes, that was halfway decent enough too. But let's not make a moun-tain out a molehill, shall we?' She wanted to fist pump for sounding convincingly nonchalant.

'Decent enough?' he echoed, something close to aston-ishment blazing in his eyes.

'Did you expect a higher rating? My memory isn't that great about the whole thing so you'll have to accept my generous verdict,' she said.

A circumspect gaze raked over her face. 'You have more fire than I remember. Fire I can't help but be tempted to stoke, to test the veracity of your claim. Perhaps even re-fresh your flawed memory.'

That sizzling need to throw herself into his particular fire blazed higher. She fought it with every shred of com-posure she could find. 'You're not going to get the chance. I don't particularly care to repeat the performance. Now, are we going to deliver this water or waste time recount-ing insignificant incidents?'

A long pause followed by an enigmatic smile was all she received in answer before he pivoted and walked away with her tray. With no choice but to follow, Violet gritted her teeth and did just that. Of course, with his help, the job took half the time, meaning that within minutes he was striding purposefully towards their designated lodge, where the team was waiting for Zak's signal to start.

His switch from sensually mocking into efficient commander was stunning and a little intimidating to witness. God, he would've been even more formidable in his military days.

Even more?

She shivered, drawing back from imagining Zak Montegova's jaw-dropping body in uniform, those lips issuing commands and talented hands manning the controls of the fighter jets he used to fly—

'Are you planning on joining in?' he drawled.

She focused to find the small group looking her way, one gaze in particular transmitting his knowledge of exactly what she'd been thinking about.

Aware of the faint blush staining her cheeks, Violet pursed her lips and strode over, avoiding Zak's gaze as she tore into the first pack. Luckily, he didn't comment further on her lapse of concentration and fell back into instructor mode.

Once she and the volunteers understood the basic instructions on how to construct an eco-lodge, the time flew by. Violet grimaced at the ruthless efficiency with which Zak worked, the fact that he worked harder than most on even the most mundane task in a fraction of the time it took for the rest of the volunteers to achieve the same result.

She wanted to resent him for yet another skill, but the sensation that burned within her every time she allowed her gaze to stray towards him was...admiration.

He wasn't afraid to put his mouth where his money was

and relished leading by example. Of course, when sweat and the heat of the day resulted in Zak pulling off his T-shirt and tossing it aside to reveal a hard-packed, flawless and gleaming torso that rippled and enticed with every moment, she especially despised the fact that she couldn't keep her gaze on her work, that her mouth watered and flames blazed deeper in that aching place between her thighs.

While his complete focus was on his task, unaware of or ignoring her stolen glances, which disgruntled her even more.

By sundown, the outer shell of their lodge had been erected and the primary emotion as she and the team felt as they took in the fruits of their labour beneath another spectacular sky awash with streaks of purple, red and orange was immense pride.

She joined the exodus towards the food tent, conscious that a shirtless Zak walked a few paces behind. Knowing the battle to keep her gaze off him would be harder, she lingered after she dished out her food until he was seated. Then she took the seat farthest away from him.

Peter joined her minutes later. But even as she kept a fairly easy conversation flowing, she was aware of Zak's growing scowl from the end of the long table. Aware that the presence of the other man next to her irritated the enigmatic Prince.

Too bad.

Perhaps it might do his ego some good to know that she wasn't one of the many females falling over themselves to hang onto his every word! With that wicked thought in mind, she laughed a little more enthusiastically at Peter's jokes, met his gaze a little longer and didn't object when he offered to walk her back to her tent, via the long way by the lake.

And when he bade her a perfectly gentlemanly good-night, she retreated inside with a smile, ignoring the little dissatisfied hollow in her stomach as she gathered her toiletries and headed back out to take a shower.

While she was all for the luxury of a proper bathroom and conveniences, Violet couldn't fault the special and simple delight of showering under the Tanzanian sky after sunset. The simple pump system delivered fresh water via a shower head and she sighed with pleasure as the cool water washed away the day's grime.

Of course all that delight turned to chagrin when she realised she'd forgotten her towel. With no choice but to stuff her underwear into her wash bag and don her shorts and T-shirt, she re-dressed as quickly as her damp skin would allow and stepped out.

Directly into the path of Zak Montegova, leaning against a slim acacia tree, clad in only a towel.

He straightened at the sight of her, sauntering over with a mouth-drying swagger that made her every nerve ending jump to attention. Dear God, how was it fair for one man to be this attractive?

'For a minute there I wondered whether I'd need to take a dip in the lake, in case you decided to use up all the water,' he said.

She made a vague gesture towards the half-full pump to the side of the shower stall. 'As you can see, I didn't. There's more than enough for you.'

He kept his gaze trained on her, not deigning to glance at the pump. And with each second she grew even more aware of her dripping hair, of the T-shirt sticking to her stomach and breasts, outlining her stiffening nipples. Of the heat gathering between her thighs when his gaze dropped down her body.

Had his breathing altered? Did that naked chest expand as he sucked in a long breath?

Get yourself together!

She started to turn away, keen to heed her screeching senses.

'A word of advice, Violet. Whatever it is you're up to with Awadhi, be sure it's a choice you won't eventually regret.'

Was he cautioning her as her boss? Or was this... personal? 'You have a say in the work that I do. I don't believe you have a say in how I spend my free time.'

'Are you attracted to him?' he pressed, a definite bite to his voice. 'Can't get enough of all that wholesome, salt-of-the-earth, tie-dyed goodness? Is that it?' he mocked.

'Why? Are you jealous?' she taunted, exhaustion, a sense of injustice from being the butt of his cynicism and, yes, that constant, overwhelming need to give into the sizzling temptation he evoked just by *breathing* finally cracking her composure.

His nostrils flared. 'That would imply he has something that I do not.'

That stung deep, made her even more rash. 'If you're not interested then why are we having this conversation?'

He stepped closer, bringing his tower of virile masculinity and solid potency far too close. Her mouth dried and her fist clenched with the need to touch. To explore. To taste.

'You misunderstand me. The issue isn't what I want. It's what he doesn't have. Which is you. Because I won't allow it.'

Shocked, hollow laughter ripped from her throat, thankfully eroding a layer of need. *'Won't allow?* You have a nerve! Who do you think you are, telling me what you will or won't—?'

The rest of her inflamed accusation evaporated as he speared his fingers into her wet hair and drew her abruptly against his body. Hot, demanding lips slanted over hers, his arm banding her waist. He picked her up as if she weighed nothing, took three long strides and before she could take a breath she was plastered against the side of the shower stall, out of view of passers-by.

Zak held her immobile, angling her head as his tongue delved between her lips to begin a torrid little dance that instantly beaded her nipples, driving sharp, sweet pain between her thighs.

Violet had far too often relived their encounter six years ago, wondered if her recollections had been exaggerated because of the occasion, wondered if her childish crush on him was what had heightened her emotions.

This re-introduction was so much more than she remembered, her senses stunned anew as he expertly nipped her lower lip with his teeth and fresh, explosive sensation spiralled through her.

Perhaps she was older, hungry enough to appreciate him better, to savour this raw, intoxicating contact that had her questioning her sanity in allowing it one minute, then straining onto tiptoe, her arms trailing delightedly up those muscled biceps she'd admired to lock around his neck.

Whatever.

Caution evaporated away as she threw herself into kiss, tentatively nipping in return.

Zak made a hungry, greedy sound under his breath, muttered words in Montegovan she only half understood. Words that would've made her blush had she not craved it, yearned for satiation of the hunger growing inside her, demanding gratification.

She strained against him as Zak freed her mouth to explore the newly discovered erogenous zone beneath one ear. She shivered and gasped, clung tighter as he trailed his lips down her throat to her collarbone, then lower to one hard nipple.

His mouth surrounded the peak, taking flesh and cotton in one powerful pull. One hand slipped beneath the hem of her shorts to boldly cup her naked bottom.

Flames lit up her veins, pooling in a torrent between her legs. She gasped as, keeping their gazes locked, he moved his hand purposefully between her thighs, his fingers intent on one destination.

He absorbed her reaction, hungrily devoured her every shiver. With it came a speculative gleam in his eyes as he traced the heat suffusing her face.

'No bra, and no panties. I'm not sure whether to spank your naughty little bottom for exhibiting yourself like this or accept this gift you seem intent on giving me,' he growled against her lips.

Violet cried out as his fingers caressed her damp heat, breached her outer lips to rest against the soaked entrance of her womanhood. The hot brand of his own arousal jerked against her stomach as he absorbed her reaction, hungrily devoured her every shiver.

'Is it my touch that excites you like this, Violet, or the thought of being spanked, I wonder?' he rasped in a low, deep voice that strummed and deepened her need.

Frankly, Violet suspected it was both. And the more the thought seeped into her consciousness, the shorter her already compromised breathing grew.

Dear God, was she kinky on top of all her unwelcome woes?

Zak laughed beneath his breath, clearly witnessing her freaked-out expression. But slowly his laughter died, leaving a deeper carnal intent on his face. 'Is there something you wish to tell me, Violet?'

'I don't know what you're talking about,' she gasped.

'Don't you? You react too strongly to such an ordinary pleasure.' He squeezed her bottom again, kneading her flesh while boldly holding her gaze. 'You're all but hovering on the brink of orgasm from just this simple touch alone.'

He slanted his lips over hers once more, his tongue brazen, positively possessive as it slid against hers, determined to draw an even more potent reaction from her. Reaction she was helpless to deny as hunger clawed through her, wrenching her onto tiptoe again so she could taste more, drown more, *feel* more.

But that dim light of warning at the back of her head brightened, steadily but surely, slowing her reaction enough for her to pull back. A little too late she recalled what had happened the last time she'd allowed herself to give in to this sensation. He'd rejected her.

Nothing had changed.

Except this time she would reject him first. The last thing she wanted was to spend the next few weeks drowning in humiliation if he repeated the experience.

So, gathering the dregs of her composure, she bunched her fists against his shoulders. And pushed.

He growled beneath his breath for a second before he allowed her to break the kiss. 'Violet—'

'I don't care what you think. I don't want this.'

'Define *this*,' he insisted, narrowed gaze fixed on her wet lips for a tight moment before it rose to spear hers.

'Any…all of it. I'm not interested in scratching whatever itch you may have. Now or ever.'

'Such dire, sweeping pronouncements. Are you certain it won't come back to bite you?'

She took a step back, then another since one wasn't enough. His gaze dropped to her chest, landed precisely on one beaded nipple before switching to the other. And stayed.

Violet wished she could halt her agitated breathing. Wished she could stop her flesh from reacting to the ravenous hunger in his eyes. But he'd rejected her once and become entrenched in whatever dire opinions he had of her and her family ever since.

Falling into his bed would be as good as confirming

everything he'd accused her of. And she wouldn't be jeopardising just her body but the career she'd set her heart on.

'Yes. I'm one hundred per cent certain I don't want you to touch me.'

Dark rebellion glinted in his eyes but his words were smooth and immediate. 'Very well. You have my word I will not touch you until you ask...*no*, until you beg me to.'

Alarm strangled her lungs.

Why did that feel very much like a challenge?

And as she watched him walk into the shower without a backward glance, why did she feel like he was simply biding his time until he *won*?

What the hell had he been thinking, making that prediction?

Five days had passed since their torrid little encounter by his shower. Five days of hell when either she plotted to drive him out of his mind or the little witch cast a spell on him.

Zak swiped an arm across his sweaty forehead and stepped back to survey another excellent day's result. They'd shaved a whole day off their target, building two eco lodges in five days instead of six.

He didn't apologise for being a harsh taskmaster when the occasion demanded, and the high fives happening behind him suggested the team didn't mind, either.

Violet's husky laugh made his stomach clench tight.

He didn't want to turn around. Didn't want to be drawn to her attention-absorbing face, her supple, curvy body or those control-wrecking legs she insisted on displaying in the bottom-moulding shorts she favoured.

As for her work ethic...

Contrary to his dim prognosis, she'd delved into every task with wholehearted enthusiasm, more often than not going over and above expectations. Not once had she protested.

Of course, he still had his reservations that she could sustain it in the long run—

A choking cough shattered his thoughts and intentions. He turned and found Violet doubled over, the subject of the team's humour as she spluttered.

'A little warning next time, please?' She laughed through the coughing.

Zak's gaze narrowed at the volunteer holding the suspicious-looking bottle as he approached, unable to take his eyes off Violet's legs and plump, shapely behind as she bent over to cough again. The reason for her state became apparent when he caught the scent.

Pombe, the local alcoholic brew, was lethal to the unschooled. 'What do you think you're doing?' he demanded.

Everyone froze, their gazes avoiding his.

'We're celebrating. What does it look like?' Violet responded, the humour dying from her eyes.

'Perhaps you should consider celebrating with something a little less…potent?' he suggested.

While the rest of the team sent him wary glances, Violet shot him a challenge-filled glare. All week she'd treated him to those defiant little looks. Having grown up in a Royal household where most people fell over themselves in deference and yearned to please, Zak found her attitude… uniquely interesting. Perhaps a little too much? Was that why he couldn't resist needling her whenever the opportunity arose?

He shoved the suggestion away when her chin lifted.

'Where's the fun in that?' she taunted, her eyes still shiny from her coughing episode.

Perhaps it was frustration. Perhaps it was disgruntlement that she wouldn't fit into the mould he'd cast for her. Before he could stop himself, his fingers were wrapping around her forearm. 'For those of you who prefer it, I've had champagne delivered to the tent to celebrate finishing early. Feel free to go and help yourselves,' he said to the group.

Predictably, his announcement was met with a chorus of cheers and the team dispersed quickly.

'Would you please stop manhandling me?' she sniped as soon as they were alone.

He released her but planted himself in front of her. 'How much of that did you drink?'

'Policing my activities yet again?'

'Only in the sense that you're inviting a hell of a hang-over by indulging in that stuff.'

She swiped the back of her hand across her lips, drag-ging his attention back to the full, luscious mouth he'd tasted. The mouth he couldn't get out of his head. 'Thanks for your concern but that's my problem, surely? Have I done anything so far to compromise my work?'

He pursed his lips. 'Not yet, but there's always a first time.'

A flash of emotion, possibly hurt, darted across her face. 'And you're, what, positioning yourself as my champion? To save me from myself? Why?'

'Because we're leaving tomorrow. And I'd prefer you to be at your best, not hung over and jet-lagged when we return to New York.'

Her alluring eyes widened, right before she frowned. 'We're leaving? But we've only been here a week.'

Considering the words spilling from his lips were a sur-prise to him as well, he absorbed the astonishment well, he thought. Congratulated himself on the inspired thinking, even. 'Do you think there's something more you can learn by remaining here?' he countered.

She bit her lip. 'No, I'm sure I can put together an eco-lodge in my sleep now. But I thought we...that *I* was stay-ing to see this project through.'

'I've changed my mind. Why waste more time here when you can gain more experience on the next project?'

He could tell she was torn between the need to argue and the need to accept the carrot he was dangling. 'Where are we going next?'

Zak shrugged. 'I have to return to Montegova at the end of the month. Until then, my itinerary is fluid but it doesn't lack requests for my presence at various projects. Who knows, perhaps I'll let you pick the next destination.'

She turned away, casting a longing look over the site and the surrounding landscape. 'This is a beautiful place. I was looking forward to my half-day off tomorrow to explore.'

Another spur-of-the-moment thought hit him. 'You'll have to make do with a visit to the phase two site, provided you can be ready to go immediately?'

She faced him again, surprise reflected in her eyes. 'I... Of course.' She looked down at her stained and work-worn clothes. 'Give me a few minutes to change and clean up and I'll join you.'

He shook his head, a stab of impatience driving him harder. 'You're not attending a red carpet event, Violet. You're fine as you are. You can shower when we get back. Or, if you insist, there's a lake you can use to wash up when we get to the site.'

Mutiny rose in her eyes and Zak's muscles tightened, anticipation flowing through him at the thought of tussling further with her. But she tossed her head and with a shrug waved a hand at him. 'Fine. Let's go.'

She headed towards the area where the vehicles were parked. Zak let her go while he issued quick instructions to his bodyguard. The guard nodded and sprinted into action.

'How long is the drive?' she asked when he reached her.

'Normally an hour, but we're not driving. We're taking the chopper. Come.'

The pregnant chef had been evacuated two days previously at the first signs of her labour, reducing the likelihood that the aircraft would be needed in the next few hours.

When they reached it, he held the door open for her, unable to resist glancing at her smooth bare legs as she slid into the seat. Her eyes widened when he took the pilot's seat, leaving three of his bodyguards in the main cabin.

'You're flying this thing?' she asked, tentatively taking the headset from him.

He didn't miss her scepticism. 'Courtesy of a full licence from the air force, I'm quite capable of it, Violet. No need to be afraid.'

He was gratified to see the scepticism melt from her eyes, although he wasn't quite sure how long his groin would sustain the pressure at the sight of her breasts outlined by the dissection of the seat belt.

He was still debating the wisdom of this tour when he lifted off and headed east.

Through the mic attached to the headset, Zak heard her soft gasp as he set down ten minutes later on the flat landscape near the edge of Lake Lengai. Once again Tanzania was showing off its jaw-dropping beauty with another stunning sunset but this time against the backdrop of a cascading waterfall thundering into a shallow pool that fed into the lake below.

He'd chosen this spot for phase two primarily for the ready fresh-water source, but watching Violet dart from the chopper, unabashed joy on her face as she raced towards the waterfall, Zak took a reluctant beat to see the land through her eyes, to appreciate the beauty of his surroundings.

When he joined her, she was straightening from leaning down to run her fingers through the clear water. 'It's…beyond spectacular,' she said a touch reverently, a lot mournfully.

'Your tone suggests differently.'

'Because the pool is shallow and wildlife-free. I would've brought a swimsuit with me if I'd known.'

Immediately, his brain supplied him with a vivid picture of her clad in a bikini. He shifted, almost growling at his body's eager response.

His shrug was a masterclass in fabricated calm. 'We're both adults, Violet. Unless you're once again naked beneath those shorts and T-shirt, you can improvise.'

In the fading light, colour washed her cheeks, strumming an elusive thought that faded before he could grasp it. 'That's none of your business. Shall we get on with the tour?'

The tour took fifteen minutes, and again she asked pertinent questions, her thoughtful observations backing her conduct on the project so far.

It didn't prove anything, he told himself.

Her mother was equally as passionate about landing a fat cat for her daughter, preferably one with a title and bottomless wallet. All this…passion could be a carefully orchestrated plan.

Just like the general's nearly successful strategy in those crucial and terrifying days after his father's death. Just like the restless factions whose motives and whereabouts were still proving elusive to pinpoint in his homeland.

The reminder restored a little more calm, reasserting his sense and control. Enabled him to summon up appropriate dispassion when they returned to the edge of the lake, where his bodyguards, following his instructions, had set up their evening meal.

He walked past a frozen Violet to their picnic blanket. 'Are you going to just stand there all night or join me?'

Suspicion filled her eyes as she ventured closer. 'I… You set this up?'

'I thought we could kill two birds with one stone. The

likelihood that there'll be anything left to eat when we return is slim. Sit down, Violet.'

Four solar lamps were positioned on each corner of the picnic blanket, providing ambient light as darkness fell.

He watched her sink down, fold her long, shapely legs beneath her before plucking a grape from a bowl. 'You're a prince. Isn't it the done thing to summon a chef to prepare a meal from scratch if the fancy takes you?'

'Of course, just as it's this easy to arrange a picnic by a lake because I wish it.'

She'd fully expected him to deny her veiled insult, and he watched, amused, as she blushed again. He reached for the champagne bottle set in the ice bucket and worked the cork free, aware her gaze lingered on him.

'Something on your mind, Violet?'

'You mentioned your pilot's licence from the air force. Why did you leave the service?'

Because the man he'd been dying to impress, the man he'd looked up to and called Father, had died unexpectedly, shattering a secret dream and leaving a nightmare in his wake. Not only had his father not been the man he'd thought him to be, his weaknesses had left the kingdom he should've been safeguarding in jeopardy. Only by strengthening their foundations in the eyes of the world had they kept from toppling over into the abyss the King had left by his death.

Not a subject he was in the mood to revisit right now. 'I served my time until I realised I could better serve my kingdom in another role.'

'But, from that meeting with the minister, it looks like you're still in charge?'

'Some matters of national security will always fall within my remit, yes,' he said, aware his voice was clipped. He ended her questioning by popping the cork. She flinched but accepted the glass he passed her.

'You were in a celebratory mood earlier. No reason why you can't raise a toast to your achievements this week.'

'You say that with a straight face, yet your dry tone mocks the very thing I'm supposed to be celebrating.'

'Let's leave the analysis for now, Violet.'

'Because you don't like hearing the truth?'

'Because I'm famished and don't wish to invite indigestion.'

For the rest of the meal they ate in silence that drew far too much of his attention to her face, her body, the movement of her throat when she swallowed.

The moment they were done, she rose.

'Where are you going?'

She threw him another defiant glare as she walked away. 'To take a better look at the lake, after all. At the moment it's a little more appealing than the company.'

CHAPTER FIVE

HE GAVE HER five minutes while the remains of their picnic were tidied away. Then Zak approached the water.

Flames leapt in his bloodstream when he saw that she'd more than just taken a look. Her T-shirt and shorts were neatly folded on the grass near the water's edge and Violet was submerged up to her neck, her body turned from him as she performed unhurried breaststroke.

Without stopping to debate the wisdom of it, Zak tugged off his clothes and slipped into the water. The fresh water did nothing to cool the pounding in his groin as she sent him another glare over her shoulder, then purposefully increased the distance between them.

He wanted to breach it, wanted to truly explore why this woman got beneath his skin so effortlessly when every woman before her had failed to even crack his veneer.

He managed to resist the urge for as long as it took her to swim within metres of the waterfall.

'Are you going to avoid me all night?'

She gave a rich chuckle. 'Now, there's a thought worth serious consideration.'

Laughter spilled from his throat, surprising them both, if the slight widening of her eyes was an indication. 'Have I really been so fearsome?'

'Don't flatter yourself. You've been disagreeable, discourteous and downright rude, but you'll have to go a long way to be fearsome. To me at least. Can't speak for the masses.'

He raised his eyebrow at her list. 'I've been all of those things? How very trying for you.'

'Like I said, don't flatter yourself. I can more than handle you.'

The flames leapt higher. 'Can you really?'

She hesitated, her gaze meeting his for one bold moment before sliding away.

'How about we make a deal? For tonight only, you have my word that I'll be more…accommodating.'

That regained her attention. 'And what does that entail, pray tell, seeing as it'll be a complete novelty to me?'

He shrugged. 'I'll leave the testing of it up to you. But if you intend to interrogate me, I suggest you come closer. I don't wish to compete with the mighty waterfall for conversation.'

She glanced from him to the thundering waterfall, then swam in lazy, graceful strokes towards him until she was just beyond arm's length.

His fingers vibrated with the strongest urge to snatch her, plaster the body that had shattered every night's sleep since their arrival against his.

It took a monumental effort to resist the urge, to stay put as she eyed him with thinly veiled suspicion. His poker face must have passed muster because she ventured a shade closer. Until he could count every moonlit pearl-shaped drop on her flawless skin. Trace the fullness of her lower lip and watch the sensual sweep of her tongue lick away the droplets that clung to her soft flesh.

His fist bunched as need climbed higher. She saw his reaction and for a moment triumph flashed through her eyes. The foolish little witch… 'Has no one taught you it's unwise to play with fire?'

One shapely eyebrow lifted. 'All I'm doing is swimming, Zak. You're the one who seems to be…disturbed.'

Even as she said the word her nostrils fluttered, and he

was willing to bet the moonlight hid her blush. That innocent reaction triggered an even more urgent question.

'Do you have a boyfriend, Violet?' He suspected not, considering her mother's end goal, and the certainty that if mother and daughter's goals were aligned, they would be circumspect about publicising such a relationship. But that wasn't to say Violet, like any other matrimonially ambitious socialite, wouldn't seek to amuse herself along the way to landing herself a rich husband. The sudden need for confirmation intensified the longer she hesitated. She opened her mouth and he interrupted the heated rebuttal. 'Or a conveniently clandestine lover, willing to keep your bed warm until he's no longer of use to you?'

Expecting anger or even a heated denial, all he received was a withering look. 'This is you on your *accommodating* behaviour? What is it about me that chafes at you so badly you feel the need to keep picking at my character?'

For the first time in his life, Zak suffered the sting of... shame. He refused to give it another name, refused to consider that this form of attack spoke to a vulnerability in his own character.

'Or is it because you're unwilling to admit you're stumped when it comes to me?'

'Hardly.' He infused his tone with as much boredom as he could muster.

Head tilted, she regarded him with something close to... enlightenment. 'That's it, isn't it? All these weeks you've been expecting me to behave a certain way, confirm all your suspicions. And I'm not, am I?'

Those last words were uttered so softly the thunder of the waterfall almost snatched them away. But he heard them. Heard and refused to acknowledge even a fraction of them held any truth. He wasn't stumped. He simply needed more proof.

The last time he'd accepted anyone or anything at face

value, he and his family had paid a steep price. Shattered trust was a difficult thing to regain.

While Violet Barringhall may not represent a toppling of his family's throne or epitomise his personal anguish, Zak had learned not to give any quarter.

'Your mother has been hounding me with emails, demanding to know how her precious daughter is doing.'

She stiffened, her hands momentarily stilling in the water. 'What did you tell her?'

'Nothing, so far. She doesn't quite rate in my list of priorities. Not yet anyway.'

She tried to hide her relief by glancing away. Zak allowed her a moment's reprieve before he continued, 'That's not to say I won't send her the response she seems to crave. I was curious about one thing, though…'

Her gaze snapped back to his, apprehension flashing in her eyes. 'What?'

'Her continued insinuation that this project, you being out here, is all some sort of perfunctory exercise for you. A stepping stone to what you're really after.'

Again, emotion flashed in her eyes, frustration and perhaps even hurt. But she mastered her expression, a little too admirably. A different need hammered at him, one that wanted to see her…undone. Unfettered.

'If you think I'm going to dishonour my mother by maligning her just to prove a point, you'll be waiting a long time,' she snapped.

Loyalty. A quality he would've admired if not for the disturbing reactions teeming inside him. 'You want me to make up my mind one way or the other about you, then prove it.'

'I thought I already had this past week.'

'Work is work, and I've yet to make up my mind on that score. Like you said, this is personal. Prove that all this isn't some sort of tedious playing-hard-to-get game.'

Her beautiful eyes narrowed and she expelled a stunned breath. 'Reverse psychology? Really? What do you want? For me to prove I can indulge myself with you for a few minutes, then walk away instead of begging for a ring on my finger the way you believe I yearn to?'

The curiously husky note in her voice intensified the pressure in his groin. The scenario wasn't as deplorable to her as she pretended.

He smiled, the voice whispering at the back of his mind that he was enjoying this far too much ignored as he replied, 'It doesn't necessarily have to be a few minutes. A fraction of time to show me you can operate with no strings attached. An hour or two will suffice.'

She gasped, and this time he swore he saw the colour suffusing her face. Either the challenging Lady Barringhall was prone to blushing or her innocence was more than surface deep.

The hot coil of possessiveness and need was totally misplaced and deeply unwelcome. And yet there it was, sinking twin talons into him as he watched her alluring face.

'You want to kiss me as much I desire you to, Violet. There's no shame in admitting it,' he stated boldly. 'Or perhaps it's the begging part that worries you? Would it please you if I took that off the table too?'

She inhaled sharply. But despite her desire to cling to outrage, Zak read her interest loud and clear. Saw the way her gaze dropped to linger on his mouth before darting away. 'You can have any woman you want, according to the giddy tabloid headlines. Why are you here, needling me, *Your Highness*?'

Never had his title sounded so sultry, so insistently *arousing*, falling from a woman's lips. He wanted to hear her breathe it all over his skin, wanted her gasping it when he buried himself deep inside her.

His fists bunched beneath the water as the powerful

surge of need momentarily stunned him. 'I could never resist a challenge. Perhaps I wish to see how long you can truly hold out.'

Her eyes glinted and for a moment Zak feared he'd finally pushed her too far.

In the next moment, however, Violet tripped him up completely by slicing through the water. She came straight at him, one hand sliding up his nape to fist his wet hair while the other curled around his shoulder.

And because he absolutely didn't want to spook her into changing her mind, Zak held stone-still, watching a touch of confusion then resolution settle on her face. Held his breath as she levered herself closer, plastered her chest against his.

And slid her lips over his.

One moment. Two. Five excruciating seconds he managed to hold out.

Then he sealed her in his arms, glorying in the smooth, supple feel of her skin as he locked her to him and took over her far too tentative exploration.

She tasted even headier than before, the sensual slide of her tongue when he breached her sweet lips a lightning bolt to his system.

Dio, how was she doing this to him? Even as he tasted and savoured, his hunger built, threatening to shatter his control. A soft, throaty moan left her mouth. The sound curled around him, hardening his already rock-hard shaft.

She registered her effect on him, gasped against his lips as he groaned, and deepened the kiss until he was unsure where her body ended and his started.

Until only his lazy kicks kept them afloat.

Until Zak suspected nothing would douse the flames leaping within him save for the ultimate act. The thought staggered him, made him wonder if he was willing to take things that far.

Si, his charged libido insisted. She'd accepted his challenge.

Perhaps he needed to prove his own point, deliver a message to the Barringhalls and every grasping leech out there that the Montegovas weren't to be trifled with.

They were both consenting adults. Even if one of them exuded innocence that hinted she might be unschooled in some aspects of sex.

Again the thought sent a pulse of primitive possession smashing through him, even though he refused to believe it. Made his caresses bolder, hungrier as he cupped her breast and toyed mercilessly with the stiff peak. Her unfettered shiver and sharp cry drove him even further into insanity. Drowned him in the urge to devour her.

He growled in protest when her fingers slid out of his hair. About to command her to return them, to pull tighter… harder, he stopped when she dropped her hands to his shoulders. Anticipating more, Zak trailed his lips down her throat, tongued that leaping pulse he'd been thirsting for all evening. Gratified when she gave another delicious shudder.

Right before she altered her touch. The hands on his shoulders weren't caressing. They were insistently pushing him away. A little stunned, he watched her kick away from him. 'Is that enough for you? Are you convinced now?' she asked, her voice passion-husky but determined.

'No, I'm not. Because that wasn't enough, *mia bella*,' he growled, lunging forward to recapture her. Drag her close once more. 'Not nearly enough.'

Electrifying sensation threatened to douse the warning signs flashing through Violet's brain as Zak lowered his head. The thought of experiencing his explosive kiss once more, of feeling his tongue and teeth and lips saturate her senses made her whole body grow weak, wantonly needy.

It was a good thing he still held onto her or Violet was sure she'd be a useless lump at the bottom of the pool right now.

He drew closer still, his sensual lips a tempting whisper away.

Dear God, what was she doing?

Proving a point. But one that she'd already proven, surely?

Not nearly enough.

His words echoed in her head, louder, more insistent, eroding her common sense. Because he was right. That taste hadn't been nearly enough. All it'd done was rake over every dampener she'd put over her emotions and re-awakened them so rudely, so effortlessly it'd set her whole body on fire.

Now the very thought of walking, or swimming away, felt like an insurmountable task. One that would be made easier by giving in one more time?

She ignored the voice mocking her logic, made a noise that sounded suspiciously like a whimper when he held himself that last scant inch away. Ruthlessly teasing? Or perhaps as unsure as she was?

She ventured a glance into his eyes. And was met with blazing arousal that left her in no doubt that Zak was as into this as she was. Still, his lips brushed furtively over hers. Sizzling but way too brief.

With a helpless groan she sealed her lips to his once more, ignoring his grunt of pure male satisfaction.

Just once more. One more minute and she'd end this insanity.

They strained against one another, determined to best each other in this battle of wills and kisses that required a victor. When the hot steel rod of his arousal imprinted itself against her belly, she whimpered some more, a driven urge to touch him, stroke him driving her hand beneath the water.

At her first touch, he tore his lips from hers. Eyes dark and mysterious in the failing light raked over her face. At first, Violet thought the thundering in her ears would surely deafen her. Until she realised they'd swum right up to the waterfall.

She blinked against the drops pelting her face, gasped softly when Zak's large hand framed her jaw, tilted her head upward to meet her gaze. Without releasing her, the arm banding her waist lifted her onto one flat boulder.

He moved between her legs, ferocious intent in his eyes.

She wanted to compare this moment to those in her mother's garden six years ago, but Violet knew she couldn't.

For one thing, the cool reserve lurking in his eyes then was nowhere in sight now. The hands trailing up her knees to frame her hips were possessive, purposeful enough to convince her that he wasn't about to stop any time soon. That unless she stopped it this time, Zak was fully intent on accepting whatever she gave.

His gaze dropped from hers to trail a fiery path down her throat to the agitated rise and fall of her breasts. One hand moved from her hip, up her ribcage to rest beneath one breast. Momentarily freed from his gaze, she glanced around her.

He'd set her down on a flat boulder large enough to recline on, solid enough to take both their weight. And with the thundering waterfall now shielding them from the outside world, it seemed like the perfect place for a seduction.

Was this what he'd intended all along?

Her heartbeat tripled as she stared at him. Whatever words she was cobbling together to ask him, they dried in her throat as his thumb grazed one tight nipple, his gaze riveted on her face, absorbing her every reaction.

Another pass and she shuddered, biting back a moan.

'You like that?' he rasped.

Violet caught her lower lip between her teeth, absurdly

reluctant to admit she did despite the blatant evidence he couldn't miss. A twist of his lips told her he had his answer and was perhaps content to let her off the hook.

In the next instant his other hand joined in the torture, moulding the twin globe until she couldn't help the tight cry that fell from her lips.

After an electrifying minute, he started to draw back the wet fabric of her bra. And at last she found a shred of common sense. 'Your guards—'

He shook his head. 'They won't disturb us. Their job is less about watching me and more about watching out for potential threats.'

Her privacy protest battered away, she was confronted with another question that loomed large in her mind.

Was this really happening?

'Should I be pleased or insulted to be excluded from that scenario?' The question was a throwaway one, meant to buy her time to regroup and rebalance, but she was nowhere near sane, shuddering as he caught her flesh between his thumb and forefinger and squeezed.

Expecting a rapier-sharp comeback, perhaps even desperate for one to restore her sanity, Violet was mildly stunned when his face grew dark and dangerous. 'Any misjudgement will be down to me. Not them.'

She couldn't help but wonder if there was a hidden meaning behind his words. A meaning she herself needed to heed before it was too late. 'Zak—'

'I believe that's the first time you've used my name. Say it again, Violet.'

'Why?'

Expert fingers caught her chin, angling her face so he could better scour her expression with his electric gaze. 'Because I find my name on your lips…pleasurable.'

'Zak.'

Ferocious eyes spiked into hers. 'I want to taste you,' he

announced, his voice hot, raspy, setting fire to her pelvis. 'Stop me now if you don't wish this to continue, Violet.'

She opened her mouth intending to do exactly that or at the very least slow down this relentless freight train of passion threatening to run away with her. At the last moment her throat closed up. Was this a turning point? Or was this her opportunity to draw a line under what had started six years ago?

She'd spent long endless nights craving more of that brief taste of desire. Now he was offering her a feast on a platter. Wasn't he? She searched his gaze, eager to discover whether this was another prelude to a rejection. She found only a fierce hunger that matched her own.

But hadn't he looked the same that night too?

Sensing her reticence, Zak dropped his hands from her body and rested them on the rock beside her hips, holding her in place just with the look in his eyes. 'Don't overthink this. What happens here stays here, Violet.'

'You mean in the light of day we forget that this ever happened?' Why did that press on a tender spot in her chest?

He shrugged. 'If that is what you wish. What it will not be is a pretence that what happens between us here will lead to something more. That is not on the table.'

Why not? she wanted to ask, but she already knew the answer deep in her bones. Something more would never include the likes of her. She only needed to glance at his family history to see the sort of pedigree the Montegovas chose to have lengthy relationships with.

Remi had been engaged to a woman with a flawless background, despite her commoner status, and their mother was a renowned ex-beauty queen, coming from a prestigious family and an heiress before she'd married the King.

Even now, the Crown Prince was said to be hunting for a woman of impeccable pedigree to replace his dead fiancée. Violet was sure nowhere on that list was a minor aristocrat with a background soiled with near bankruptcy, disgrace and a tabloid-hungry mother who sold gossip on a regular basis.

'This isn't a world-altering decision,' he insisted.

But in a way it was to her. A few mind-blowing kisses were one thing but giving herself to Zak Montegova completely was quite another.

And just like that the issue of her virginity loomed large before her eyes. She bit her lip, nerves eating fresh at her as she contemplated how to break the news to him. Perhaps he would be turned off, just as he had been by her awkward crush on him six years ago. Was she better off keeping it to herself?

'You want me,' he insisted, his tone deep and fierce, angling his mouthwatering body closer.

'I'm not denying that.'

'Then what is this about?'

His eyes gradually grew icy as he stared at her. 'You didn't answer me before. Is there someone else? Is that why you hesitate?'

A wave of anger swept over her. 'You really think I would be here doing this with you if I was in another relationship? What sort of women do you date?'

He barely flinched at her accusation. 'While I'm inclined to think that heated response answers my question, I don't wish to assume. Is there someone else, Violet?' he demanded again, his voice terse.

'No, there isn't. I haven't had the time or the inclination to do…this or have a relationship. Of any kind,' she added, just so he would understand she was including whatever schemes he believed she was hatching with her mother.

'I have an understanding with my liaisons and I've set out what my expectations are.' He stopped, his eyes heatedly scouring her body before returning to hers. 'I despise deceit. So this is your chance to end this or give me your answer.' He brought his body another tempting inch closer. 'If you want me, touch me.'

The invitation was too much to resist.

In that moment, Violet knew she'd passed the point of no return. As for her virginity, one way or the other he would find out that she was truly innocent soon enough.

Even if he didn't realise it, after this she only needed to proceed as normal for a few more months. Then she would be out of this life. Why that thought sent a lance of pain through her chest, she refused to examine.

She would take this moment out of time, slay the dragon of need that'd consumed her for so long and then put it all behind her. Then she could go on with her life.

'*Dio mio*, do I really need to beg?' he demanded roughly.

'Perhaps you do. Perhaps I want to see that unique event,' she teased.

A smile twisted his lips, but it was the raw need in his eyes that threatened to stop her breath. A feeling of urgency rose inside her, and without waiting to see whether he would actually resort to begging, she hooked her fingers behind his neck.

The blaze of triumph in his eyes should have made her hesitate, but all Violet could think of was that her fierce hunger was about to be sated.

He delivered a hard, consuming kiss to her lips, and every thought melted from her brain. The tasting was over in an instant and then his lips were trailing down her neck again. This time his destination was purposeful as he caressed the skin with one hand while his other eased in a downward trajectory to one breast.

He lightly bit the plump slope, causing her to cry out again. Before the sound died, he was wrapping his lips around one tight peak. He licked, tortured and delivered heady sensation the likes of which Violet had never expe-

rienced. Flames flared from the point of contact throughout her body, coalescing in that tight space between her
legs and making her hips jerk and strain with the need for
satisfaction.

Because this was Zak, because he was effortlessly at-
tuned to her needs, he didn't leave her waiting for long.
Taut fingers trailed over the sensitive skin of her belly before stopping at the boundary of her panties.

Bold and brazen, his fingers delved beneath the wet
fabric. Her breath strangled in her throat. She hung on the
edge, every molecule in her body strained at the twin points
of contact.

And then his finger slipped between her folds, igniting
raw, acute pleasure through her veins. Her head dropped
back on her shoulders, the effort to keep herself upright
weakening as Zak spread her knees wider, sought better
access.

Access she couldn't deny him as her craving escalated.

He caressed her swollen flesh, growling in satisfaction
as he encountered the slick evidence of her need. In raspy
Montegovan, he muttered against her nipple, the sound lost
in the thundering waterfall but no less arousing. For endless
minutes he toyed with her while swirling his tongue around
one nipple until need gathered unbearably in her pelvis.

'Zak…'

He laid her back against the rock, dragged down the
straps of her bra and bared her breasts to his eyes. Then he
drew back, taking his time to conduct a sizzling scrutiny of
her body. '*Madonna mia*, you are exquisite,' he breathed.

Flames of lust lit through her at his words, her reaction
pleasing him, if the turbulence in his eyes was any indication. He returned to his attention to her breast, catching
the sensitive flesh between his teeth as his fingers delved
deeper between her thighs. He breached her core, growling

a torrent of Montegovan when he encountered even more evidence of her need.

Slippery, hot, ready, he caressed her expertly before pressing one finger to her core. Violet tensed momentarily. It wasn't enough to change her mind but the knowledge that this was actually happening was enough to attract fresh nervousness.

'So tight. So snug. It's almost enough to make me wonder if you're untouched,' he said.

Here's your chance. Tell him.

She didn't know why she held back or why she dropped her gaze instead to watch the magic he was evoking between her legs. The sight of the carnal, erotic caress made her whimper.

His head surged up. 'Violet? Is there something you wish to tell me?'

She swallowed, then dredged up the keenest poker face she could muster. 'Is this a Q&A or are we going to get on with it?' she asked boldly.

His gaze raked her face, narrow eyes probing hers. Violet undulated her body, straining closer to his touch. She wasn't aware her nails dug into his shoulder until he relaxed and gave a low laugh.

'Is my little hellcat impatient?'

'You're the one who seems to have all the answers. What do you think?'

Without answering, he sucked one nipple into his mouth, and then the other, groaning at her fresh shudder before licking the space between the globes.

She lost the ability to string thoughts together, falling backwards on one elbow as he charted a path down her midriff to her navel and then lower.

Aware of what he intended to do, Violet was torn between stopping him and going with the flow. 'Please…'

He lifted his head, speared her with those intense grey eyes. 'Will you give me what I want, Violet?' he rasped.

'And what's that?' she whispered.

'To taste you. Here,' he said, running his knuckles over her heated core.

She cried out. He gave a harsh exhalation, dispensed with the teasing and tormenting, lifted her hips off the rock and sealed his mouth to her aching body.

Sensation like she'd never known rushed through her. Her body twisted and jerked as Zach boldly explored her. Her clitoris became his plaything, her centre his playground as he took his time to deliver pleasure heaped upon pleasure.

Eyes squeezed shut, Violet could only ride the wave as paradise beckoned. She was vaguely aware of tiny screams ejecting from her throat, of cool water lapping against her shoulders and the hot solid column of Zak's body positioned between her legs. Everything else ceased to matter as her climax gathered with fierce concentration between her legs. And when that moment came, when with a bold caress he shoved her off that peak, she screamed, certain she would never be the same again as every cell exploded in ecstasy.

For endless minutes she floated, almost afraid to open her eyes, afraid to discover if this had just been another lurid dream. Even though none of her dreams had ever felt this earth-shattering.

Violet opened her eyes, her heart lurching when she was confronted with the solid reality of Zak in his full magnificence, totally focused on her.

She understood at that moment why women went crazy for this man. If what he'd done to her moments ago was even a fraction of the pleasure he could deliver, then every flick of his arrogant eyebrow and every word that fell from his lips in utter self-confidence was justified.

Not that she was about to tell him any of that. His ego didn't need the boost from her.

Certainly not in the manhood stakes, she thought in stunned wonder at her first glimpse of his arousal. At some point between laying her down on the rock and gifting her that mind-blowing orgasm, Zak had removed his boxers. Unashamedly naked and magnificently virile, he held himself over her, making room for himself between her thighs.

The faintest flicker of uncertainty slid through her mind. Could she accommodate him? Perhaps he spotted it. One corner of his mouth lifted in a tense little smile. He lowered his head and brought his lips to hers, his tongue easily breaching her lips to commence a slow gliding dance that evoked what he intended to do to her.

Apprehension melted away but a warning tweaked the back of her mind. It evaporated when he settled his mouthwatering body against hers, leaving her gasping as every erogenous zone in her body roared to life.

'Look at me, Violet,' he urged, his gaze fusing with hers when she raised her eyes to his. 'Touch me,' he commanded.

All along she'd fooled herself into thinking that this was simply an experience to indulge in and move on. But even before he had settled his hard length against her core, Violet suspected that this was so much more.

'I want to see your eyes as I take you,' he said, his voice deep, profound, soul-stirring enough to make her tremble with something more than pleasure.

Too much. It was too much.

Thoughts loomed large and impossibly momentous in her mind as Zak surged inside her, filling her up, breaking through that final barrier of her innocence.

He froze, shock filming his eyes and slackening his jaw as he stared down at her with something close to icy condemnation and searing regret.

CHAPTER SIX

'MOTHER OF GOD. You're untouched?'

Violet struggled to breathe, struggled to drag her mind from the sensations ricocheting through her body. The initial sting of his penetration had receded fast to leave behind a wild hunger that demanded fulfilment. Hunger she was immediately terrified he wouldn't sate as he started to withdraw.

'Please.'

Zak shook his head once, a tight, shaken expression still on his face as he glanced down at where they were still joined and then up to meet her gaze once more. 'Why didn't you tell me?'

'Does it matter?'

A rough sound barked from his throat. 'You think it didn't?'

'Perhaps I didn't want to make a big deal out of it.'

He started to pull back even further. She clamped her legs around his waist, somehow believing that would stop him. Miraculously it did, fresh tension shadowing his face as he paused. 'It is a big deal, Violet.'

'Why?' she asked, then winced inwardly. Dear God, was she really having this discussion with him? Right now?

Shock and a touch of bewilderment washed over his face. 'You really think me so callous that I wouldn't have minded whether you were innocent or not?'

She clamped her legs tighter. He shuddered, his body falling forward as he groaned. 'It's already done, Zak. Let's not overthink it.'

For the first time in her life she spotted indecision on his face. It made her bolder, the thought that here, now, her femininity was more powerful than his resistance, sending a wave of triumph through her. 'You wanted to take me. Well, here I am,' she dared.

With a torn grunt, he surged forward, driving the last dregs of apprehension away and filling her with searing pleasure. One stroke. Two. On the third stroke, Violet was introduced to a new platform of sensation that made her jaw drop. Whatever came next, she was sure that this sublime feeling would never be surpassed.

'Why, even now when I know I should be stopping this, can't I end this thing?' he groaned almost under his breath, his bewildered gaze dancing over her face. The gleam morphed, turning deeper. Possessive.

Why that infused her with even more pleasure, Violet didn't want to pause to examine. Emboldened, she spiked her fingers through his hair, raking her nails over his scalp the way she'd tested at some point and discovered he liked. He shuddered, his eyes glinting in the dark as he stared at her.

'You're determined to bewitch me, aren't you?'

'Am I? Then why am I being denied?'

He sucked in a harsh breath, his chest expanding, dragging it against her nipples. They both shuddered. She undulated, that peculiar need surging high as her body demanded more. Zak thrust inside her one more time.

From then on no words were necessary. The slide of hands, the stroking of tongues, the slippery penetration transmitted need and propelled her towards another earth-shattering climax.

Violet was almost afraid that she would be wholly consumed by the depth of her pleasure, so much so she tightened her grip on him, attaching every part of her body to his solid frame, revelling in the deep shudders that racked his frame as he found his own climax. Eventually the tide receded, hearts slowed, reality intruded, leaving behind a slow-cooling lava of alarm that hollowed her stomach.

Because while throwing caution to the wind had been freeing and eye-opening in the pleasure stakes, she was terrified that she may have given a whole lot more than she had intended to.

Even now as Zak withdrew from her and turned to swim a few feet away, she wanted to grab him and pull him back, beg him for more of what he'd just given her. Like her distress as he'd taken up her thoughts and invaded her dreams for the last six years, with this experience she was suddenly terrified there would be none other like the man who had just taken her virginity.

There was no such profundity on his face when he tugged on his boxers and faced her, however. Just grim-faced shock.

'Violet,' he rasped, his voice ashen with something close to horror. 'I didn't use any protection.' Regret and fierce condemnation drove away pleasure as reality smashed into her brain.

Oh, my God.

How could she have been so reckless?

He needed a moment to think. Scratch that. He needed several moments.

A week. A *month*.

Perhaps a stint in an asylum because only that would explain what he'd just done. His error of judgement came rushing back in a torrent wilder than the waterfall thundering behind him.

He'd taken her innocence.

Even while that admission sent another spike of primitive possessiveness through him, Zach was reeling from how he'd spectacularly compounded the severity of the situation.

He'd not only taken her, he'd taken her innocence without protection.

Dio mio.

He'd handed her everything she needed to destroy him. He wasn't a wet-behind-the-ears schoolboy, so how could he have been so monumentally stupid? Acrid bitterness wove through him, enough to make him bunch his fists as he sorted through his shaken thoughts. Was this what had driven his father, too? Desire so strong common sense had ceased to exist?

Unwilling to dwell on his father right now, he returned to Violet.

The women he usually slept with had two modes of post-coital interactions—sultry invitations for a repeat performance or, more usually, a gentle probing as to how soon they could once again grace his presence.

One look at her showed Violet was far from exhibiting either of those cloying signs. If anything, she was in a tearing hurry to dress, her movements clumsy as she secured her bra and panties.

Momentarily arrested by her beauty and disarmed by the thought of never experiencing sex with her again, it took a moment to realise she was glaring at him.

'If you're worried this is some scheme to trap you, don't. I'm on the Pill.'

The relief he should've felt was…minimal, stunning him anew at his actions tonight. He shuddered to think what else would surprise him.

He'd never dared a woman into sleeping with him, for starters.

When several indicators had pointed to her innocence, he'd still forged ahead. He gritted his teeth at the unfortunate pun, instantly reminded of her snug, mind-melting heat.

'Why am I surprised that you're freezing me out?' she accused. 'Everything you said was a lie, wasn't it?' she threw at him, refocused, affront coating every word.

'I don't believe I've even uttered a word,' he returned, attempting to gather the control that'd shattered into a million pieces.

'Believe me, your body language speaks volumes.'

'And what is it saying exactly that has you so riled up?'

Dark blue eyes sparked flames at him. 'Don't patronise me. What happened to "what happens between us stays between us"?'

He shrugged. 'Have I done anything to indicate otherwise?'

'You're not already wondering if this wasn't some sort of trick that I performed on you?'

Since he'd thought exactly that, and he wasn't about to admit it, he merely shrugged.

'You're unbelievable.'

'You said you're on the Pill. I'll return the favour by saying you have nothing to risk healthwise from being with me. But your overly emotional reaction is…concerning.'

His icy delivery stopped her cold. Her eyes widened with apprehension as she stared at him.

'Whatever happens after this please promise me that this isn't when you decide to pay me back for what we both indulged in by ruining my life. My work is the most important thing in my life.'

Fresh shock unravelled through him. Did she really think him that callous? 'I gave you my word and I intend to keep it.'

For a moment after she'd slid off the rock and stepped into the water, she searched his features.

Zak wanted to lower his gaze, evade whatever it was that she was looking for. Because he wasn't thinking straight. Probably hadn't since he'd got into the helicopter to come here.

Slowly, he let the ruthlessness his ancestors were renowned for, the ruthlessness some had accused him of, fill his veins.

What was done was done.

He'd slept with Violet Barringhall, despite his intention to stay away from temptation. He still craved her, if truth be told. Even now as she determinedly swam away from him and surged out of the lake towards where she had left the rest of her clothes, he couldn't drag his eyes away from her curvaceous body.

But that didn't matter.

There was no point wishing she was anyone but who she was, a risky venture he should never have tangled with. As he followed, his mind raced through every pitfall that could arise from this. By the time he boarded his helicopter again, he knew only one option was open to him and that was to ensure this never happened again.

Because contrary to what he had so loftily attempted to deny, Violet had almost come within a whisker of sliding beneath his guard, creating havoc.

He didn't intend for it to happen again.

Two months later

Violet stood up shakily along with the cathedral full of the *crème de la crème* of European royalty, a Russian oligarch or six, and wall-to-wall dignitaries and celebrities. In unison, they watched the wide doors of the Duomo di Montegova, the sixteenth-century cathedral located on its own picturesque hill in Montegova's capital, Playagova, to catch a first glimpse of the bride as she slowly made her way down the aisle.

While she made a pretence of being agog, her mind was

far away, spinning wildly enough to give a whirling dervish a run for its money.

She wished she could stop thinking about everything that'd happened since that night in Tanzania. At least then her head wouldn't spin so hard she feared she would pass out.

Fists discreetly clenched, she fought through the sensation. Under no circumstances could she break down here, now. Her mother's eagle eyes would zero in on her and Margot would demand an explanation of what she'd termed 'Violet's odd behaviour' in the past few days. Violet could only thank goodness her twin sister Sage had flatly refused to attend, and her older sister Charlotte, who'd held a secret flame for the Crown Prince, had been too morose at the announcement of Remi's marriage to notice Violet's less than radiant appearance.

No, she couldn't give in to the hysteria bubbling beneath her skin.

She definitely couldn't give in to tears. She'd succumbed to them a few times already, and these days it seemed as if tears waited around the corner, ready to exploit any unsuspecting emotion she succumbed to.

So she plastered a smile on her face, turned towards the advancing bride, hoping that her make-up would cover the worst of the shadows that had gleefully mocked her when she'd looked in the mirror that morning.

Thank God she'd declined her mother's invitation to share a suite at the five-star hotel they'd been booked into for their stay in Montegova.

And thank God her mother was too busy lamenting the fact that Crown Prince Remi had slipped through her clutches, eliminating himself as suitor for her older daughter, to pay closer attention to Violet.

As she'd been doing for the last few weeks, her mother would spend most of her time gossiping and giving her opinion about the longevity of the upcoming nuptials, freeing Violet to wallow in her misery.

Violet didn't have an opinion one way or the other. She'd only seen the bride, Maddie Myers, very briefly at the pre-wedding party thrown by the Queen two nights before, and Violet would be the first to admit that she hadn't been at her best that evening either.

But then who could blame her?

You only have yourself to blame, the voice that had been haranguing her endlessly insisted. Recalling her behaviour that night at the waterfall, she felt the blood drain from her face. Weeks later, she could barely believe that had been her.

How she'd wrapped her thighs around him and urged him on. How she'd flaunted her rock-solid contraception in his face afterwards and promised he had nothing to worry about.

How very wrong she'd been.

Wrong and completely compromised.

She'd stopped bothering to decipher the ins and outs of how the contraception that was meant to be reliable had failed her. All she knew was that it had, and the promise she'd given now needed to be taken back. Because the very thing he'd feared had happened.

She was pregnant with Zak Montegova's child.

An incontrovertible fact that had the power to render her speechless every time she thought of it. And she'd had a lot of time to think about it ever since her period had failed to make an appearance.

'Ah, here's Zak now,' her mother said, anticipation throbbing in her voice. Completely unaware of the fresh barrage of shock she'd just delivered to her daughter.

Heart banging against her ribs, she followed her mother's gaze.

Zak was escorting the bride, the confident half-smile

aimed at Maddie sending discreet sighs throughout the cathedral.

Violet wasn't one of swooning crowd. Been there, done that. The consequence of it was growing inside her this very minute. Nevertheless, she couldn't help but gaze at the stunning image he made in his impeccable best man's suit.

In the weeks since she'd last seen him, he'd stayed true to his word and given her nothing to worry about in the work stakes. What he'd failed to mention the morning after their night by the waterfall when they'd boarded his private jet back to New York was that his way of ensuring nothing would adversely affect their working relationship was to remove himself completely from any interaction with her.

Because no sooner had they arrived back in New York than he'd absented himself from the House of Montegova Trust, and departed for parts unknown.

She'd been left with more than enough to occupy her, had even gained much-needed experience on other projects, sent detailed reports to Zak after every completed task. But he'd neither acknowledged them nor made a reappearance in the New York office, leaving her with nothing but time to absorb the earth-shattering confirmation that she was pregnant.

With Zak's baby.

Steeling herself against a fresh barrage of bewilderment, she attempted to drag her gaze from him as he neared, to hide herself behind elaborate fascinators and wedding hats.

But, with the accuracy of a guided missile, his head swivelled towards her, dark and stormy grey eyes singling her out of the crowd. The smile he'd been sharing with his soon-to-be sister-in-law evaporated. And perhaps she was deluding herself, seeing what she wanted to see, but Violet could have sworn he stumbled as he saw her.

Of course, that wasn't true.

Her mother was godmother to his older brother. Her name was on the guest list.

And if neither of those facts had registered and suggested the possibility of her attendance, Violet had sent him emails, requesting a meeting with him, none of which he'd unanswered.

Leaving her with no choice but to succumb to her mother's pressure to attend this wedding. She may not have been ready in any way for the news she now bore, but neither did she want to keep it from him.

It didn't matter that she suspected he would treat it with even more of that icy disdain he was showing her now. It couldn't be helped.

He was the father of her child and he deserved to know. Once she'd delivered the news, she could get down to the reality of how she would work her life around a child.

Her child.

Her hand crept towards her flat belly, as it'd been wont to do with terrifying frequency and a stunned joy these past few days. Sucking in a breath, she hastily dropped her hand. She needed to remain on her guard before her mother spotted the tell-tale sign.

The last thing she needed was her mother's opportunistic interest ratcheting up the pressure that was inevitably heading her way now that Remi was off the market.

As if intuiting her thoughts, her mother turned towards her. 'Be sure to find Zak and have him confirm that he'll be writing you that letter of recommendation. I don't really see the point of why you would go to such lengths to do the work and not capitalise on it.'

Violet bit the inside of her cheek to stop herself from responding. She would be hunting Zak down but not to pursue the letter of recommendation. At least, not immediately.

While she needed the letter, it wasn't her priority at the moment.

Besides, she had no right to the letter, not when she still had weeks left on her secondment contract.

She composed her expression when her mother sent her a sidelong look, turned to face forward and silently prayed for the time to whizz by so she could leave Montegova.

Her mother believed she was staying on for the post-wedding festivities planned by the Queen but Violet had changed her ticket for an earlier flight out of Montegova to-morrow. In all the scenarios she'd cast through her mind of how Zak would react to the news, she didn't believe it would include an invitation to celebrate at the Royal Palace. Hell, he would probably throw her out of his kingdom himself.

'Violet?' her mother demanded under her breath, her eyes narrowing.

God, she really needed to get herself under control.

'The bride looks stunning, doesn't she?' she said hur-riedly, momentarily distracting her mother.

The ceremony began in earnest then, thankfully excus-ing her from conversation. Drowning in her own thoughts, Violet barely registered the ceremony. She offered congrat-ulations when she needed to, smiled during the photographs afterwards and before she knew it she was being whisked into the jaw-dropping ballroom in the equally magnificent Montegovan Royal Palace.

Throughout the long speeches and the long line to offer congratulations to the Crown Prince and his new Princess, Violet was aware of Zak's overshadowing presence. Just as she was aware that he was ignoring her.

More, she was painfully aware of the single socialites gravitating towards him with a sickening covetousness that set her teeth on edge.

She told herself she was irritated simply because his en-gagement with other guests was eating into the time she needed to tell him her news and make her exit. But the ex-cuse rang hollow inside her.

Because, as she'd predicted that night after they've made love, he'd invaded her thoughts even more insidiously than he had six years ago. It was as if now she'd experienced true passion, it...*he'd* imprinted himself indelibly on her psyche. His absence from New York had sharpened her hunger, intensified it exponentially. So much so that even when she promised she wouldn't glance his way now, her gaze defied her will, seeking him out as he danced with one stunning woman after another, exchanged laughs with his brother and courteously escorted his mother around the ballroom.

Knowing she needed to get herself under control if she was to remain level-headed for their upcoming meeting, Violet excused herself and made a beeline for the cloakroom. Retouching her make-up and taking several deep breaths lowered her heart rate by a laughable fraction, but beggars couldn't be choosers.

Neither could they afford to linger interminably in the cloakroom.

Passing shaky hands over her dark peach floor-length gown, she headed for the door, a half-smile plastered on her face. The smile dissolved to nothing when she opened the door to find her elusive Prince framed in the doorway.

No.

He wasn't *her* elusive Prince. He was simply the elusive man who'd treated her like a pariah since taking her virginity. No, that wasn't wholly accurate either, her inner voice mocked. She'd been a willing participant in the act, urging him on when he'd attempted to put the brakes on their passion.

While she wasn't one to dwell on might-have-beens, Violet needed to face reality. And she needed to face it head on. With that in mind she angled her head to meet his gaze, even summoning that elusive smile to counter his mocking one.

'Hello, Zak.'

'For someone who's been feverishly chasing me, you don't seem particularly happy to see me,' he drawled, his lazy tone belying the fiery intensity in the gaze that raked her from head to toe and back again.

Her heart dropped. 'So you knew I was looking for you? And you didn't bother to return my emails or get in touch?'

His arrogant, dismissive shrug sent an arrow of hurt deep into her chest.

'The reports you sent regarding your projects were adequate enough not to require further discussion. Beyond that, I fail to see what you'd have to discuss with me. But seeing as you're making personal demands, I thought I should double check.'

She barely managed to stop her fist from clenching. 'I've been in Montegova for two days and at this wedding going on four hours,' she said, not bothering to hide her caustic tone. 'Are you making some sort of point by avoiding me?'

His gaze blatantly raked her again, lingering at the pulse racing at her throat before rising to meet hers once more. That intensity had risen, giving him an almost dangerous look. 'You look stunning, Violet.'

Flames lit through her blood. She attempted to ignore it. 'Don't change the subject.'

His jaw tightened. 'As I've said, your reports came in regularly and since nothing demanded my immediate attention, I drew my own conclusions as to why you were clamouring to see me.'

She refused to acknowledge the wild lurching of her heart. 'Which were?'

'That this demand is extremely personal. And since we discussed in detail how we wouldn't make personal demands of each other in the aftermath of our…coming together, I thought it wise to give you a chance to rethink this meeting. Obviously, you have no intention of doing so, so let's get this over with, shall we?' he drawled, his tone extremely bored.

'Wait, you think I'm gagging for more of the same?'

His eyes narrowed at her caustic tone. Then he caught her by the elbow.

Anyone who saw them would've believed he was escorting her but his firm hold told her otherwise. 'Where are you taking me?'

'Where the scene you seem to be intent on having will have minimal impact.'

Violet couldn't help herself, she laughed. 'You really are full of yourself, aren't you?'

He didn't respond, simply led her towards a set of double doors flanked by two uniformed sentries. With smooth precision, they opened the doors as Zak walked her through, and then closed them.

Despite having primed herself for this meeting, Violet was unprepared for the full impact of finding herself alone with Zak in a room that look like a smaller version of the one holding the wedding reception.

He hadn't changed much. There was a tautness about his jaw and his hair seemed a little bit longer, lending him an edgier aura of danger.

'I love a good appreciative scrutiny, but your timing leaves a lot to be desired,' he drawled.

'What are you talking about?'

'Maman has admonished me not to attract attention or gossip at my brother's wedding. Being locked in a room with an attractive woman isn't the best way to avoid it.'

Violet felt heat wash up her cheeks and devour her face. He wanted nothing to do with her. Wished no hint of their association to be broadcast. For a moment, she contemplated just turning around and walking out. Let him discover the news that his indiscretion had borne fruit in a little over seven months.

But even as she contemplated doing so, she remained rooted to the spot. She'd barely been able to sleep in the last few weeks. There was no way she could do this to herself any longer.

'Violet?' Her name was a terse command from his lips.

'Don't worry, Zak, I don't want to be here any more than you want me to be. But while I came to Montegova out of courtesy to your brother, I also did want to speak to you. And it has nothing to do with work.'

His eyes narrowed, suspicion growing with each second that passed between them. The blood rushed in her ears, the knowledge that once she released the words there would be no taking them back strangling her vocal cords.

'You wish me to fetch the string quartet, perhaps? Add a little suspenseful music to this dramatic performance?' he mocked.

'You may find all this amusing or boring or whatever emotion you're trying to project but, believe me, this is the last place I want to be.'

He tensed, his body solidifying to stone as he continued to watch her with an intensity that sent skitters of apprehension over her. 'Then make it fast.'

Simply because her heart was threatening to hammer itself out of existence, her head spinning with the effort of keeping herself under control, Violet exhaled and let the words fall from her lips. 'I'm pregnant.'

For the longest stretch of time he simply stared at her. Then his breath hissed in a sizzling exhalation. 'Repeat that,' he ordered.

'There's nothing wrong with your hearing, Zak. You heard me right the first time.'

Several emotions chased across his face, none of them calming her roiling senses. The ones she managed to decipher only accelerated her heartbeat, the shock at his discovery of her virginity in no way competing with the icy shock and anger that finally remained once he'd composed himself.

'You are not reckless enough to attempt to trick me so I'm going to take you at your word,' he rasped through flattened lips.

How she managed to locate her vocal cords to respond would remain a mystery to her. 'I won't thank you for that because I'm sure there's an insult in there somewhere. Facts are facts, though.'

His nostrils flared as his gaze dropped down to her belly, drawing her attention to that telling gesture that had once again taken her by surprise. This time her hand stayed, splayed over her stomach in a protective gesture. When his eyes rose to hers, Violet could tell he'd fully acknowledged it.

A moment later he pivoted away, reached into his pocket and extracted his phone.

He spoke too fast in Montegovan for her to decipher even the word or two she understood of the language she should've mastered a long time ago if only her mother hadn't pandered more to her English side. 'What are you doing?' she asked when he hung up.

'You know my family's history so you know I have a half-brother who was sprung on us the day of my father's funeral.'

She frowned. 'Yes. That isn't news, is it?' she replied, wondering where he was going with this. 'What does that have to do with—?'

'Very few people will ever know the depth of the chaos Jules's unexpected arrival caused in our lives. Like you, her mother chose a significant occasion to deliver her news.'

She gasped. 'Surely you don't think—'

He cut across her once more, his tone icier than ever. 'Believe me when I say that I'm not going to sit back and watch it all happen all over again.'

Her heart lurched at the intensity and determination in his voice. 'I don't understand.'

'You will,' he replied.

Heading for the door, he summoned one of the guards and returned to where she stood. 'You will watch her. Make sure she doesn't leave this room. Is that understood?'

The guard snapped to attention. 'Yes, of course, Your Highness.'

Violet rushed forward. 'Wait, what do you think you're—?'

He turned towards her, his face a mask of determination as his eyes speared into hers. 'Who else knows?' he demanded.

'I… No one.'

'For your sake I hope that's the truth.'

'I'm not a liar, Zak!'

Without acknowledging her response, he turned and started walking towards the door.

'Zak, if you think I'm going to be left here cooling my heels whilst you waltz off and do…whatever, know that it's not going to happen.'

He stopped, pivoted towards her without approaching. 'Tell me, Violet, was your intention in coming here to have a discussion with me?'

She slanted a glance at the guard, who stared into the middle distance, effectively mimicking a seen-but-not-heard stance most likely drummed into him as part of royal protocol training. Her gaze returned to Zak's. 'Yes.'

'My duties are mostly finished but I cannot carve out the time for this without first going back to make my excuses. You will wait here for me to return.'

'But—'

'Unless you've changed your mind about the supposed urgency of this situation?'

For the life of her, Violet couldn't see the web he was spinning even though silky threads whispered over her skin. She would've loved to flounce off after delivering the news, but she couldn't sustain any more shocks. Couldn't live in limbo as she tried to decrypt his full and eventual reaction to her pregnancy. She had to stay, see this through in order to better inform her next steps.

'But we don't have to do this right this minute, do we?'

'And when do you propose we do it? That we get together at another state occasion, perhaps?'

'That wasn't my fault. If you had bothered to answer my emails—'

He waved that away with a flick of his wrist. 'The past is past. I know what you have come to tell me now. And I am going to do something about it.'

She opened her mouth, but again he halted her speech with a slash of his hand. 'I'm willing to bet my mother has noticed my absence and is already sending someone to look for me as we speak. Do you wish me to handle this and come back to you or not?'

What could she say to that except, 'Yes. Okay.'

With an abrupt nod he walked out the door, leaving her with an icy dread she couldn't quite explain. A wave of dizziness rushed over her, and Violet stumbled over to the nearest set of sumptuous matching sofas and sank into the nearest seat. Scenarios raced through her mind as an hour ticked by without Zak returning. She had the absurd thought that he'd abandoned her, was circulating the ballroom, secretly laughing at the absurd news she'd delivered.

The doors opened and a second guard entered. Violet watched, a little bemused, as the two guards exchange a low-voiced conversation before advancing towards her.

'Would you come with me please, miss?' one said.

'Where are we going?' she demanded suspiciously.

'His Highness has requested that you meet him at a different location.'

Frowning, she glanced towards the double doors that led back to the wedding reception. 'But…my mother…'

Her words were met with a blank stare.

Aware that returning to the ballroom now would attract questions, Violet concluded it was wisest to get this meeting with Zak out of the way. Rising, she smoothed at her hand down her thighs and nodded at the guards. 'Lead the way.'

They led her away from where the reception was still in full swing, traversing a series of hallways until they emerged into an enclosed courtyard where a gleaming black unoccupied limousine stood idling. The back door was open with the driver poised at attention beside it.

She resisted the urge to ask the guards where the driver was taking her, suspecting that she'd be stonewalled. Sucking in a breath that did nothing to sustain or restore her equilibrium, Violet slid into the car and fought back a shiver as it was shut softly but precisely behind her.

The car rolled forward. Through tinted windows, she saw the palace grounds whizz past. Mourned the beautiful architecture and stunning city of Playagova she'd been too preoccupied to fully appreciate.

Within minutes they were pulling up to a building that looked suspiciously like an aircraft hangar. Her suspicions were confirmed when the car glided to a smooth stop next to a gleaming jet a size smaller than the one in which they'd flown to Tanzania.

Its tail fin bore the same royal logo. The driver opened the door, courteously holding out his hand. For a moment, Violet hesitated. Sensing she would get no answers from the driver either, she alighted, then watched in surprise as he rounded the bonnet, slid behind the wheel and drove off.

'Hey, where are you—?' Realising she was alone in the cavernous space, and that she was speaking to thin air, she turned and eyed the steps that led into the plane.

Apprehension eating at her, she climbed the stairs and

entered another sumptuous, custom-designed interior. Aged cherry wood complemented gold-veined marble in a masterful display of opulence that would have completely bowled her over had the sight of Zak, lounging in a large club chair at the far end of the plane, not absorbed every ounce of her attention. She approached him only because she didn't want to conduct this meeting by shouting the length of the plane, her feet moving soundlessly over the thick carpet. She stopped within ten feet, close enough to talk but not enough to be overwhelmed by his presence. *Much.*

'What is this, Zak? What am I doing here?'

He didn't immediately reply, instead looked past her and nodded.

Glancing sharply over a shoulder, Violet saw the pilot acknowledge Zak's silent command and retreat into the cockpit.

Only then did Zak address her. 'Sit down, Violet.'

She eyed the doorway, swallowing with relief to see it was still open. 'No. Not until you tell me what's going on.'

'I thought we could speak privately about your...news.'

'You can't say the words, can you?'

His gaze dropped again to her belly, a look slashing across his face but disappearing far too quickly for her to decipher. 'That you're pregnant? That you claim to be carrying my child?'

'Claim? I thought you said I'd be too reckless to pull the wool over your eyes with such a claim?'

'We'll get to the details of that in a moment. First, I really wish you would sit down.'

Two things pierced her consciousness simultaneously.

The first was that the engines of the plane had started up, the stairs electronically retracting until the door shut with a soft whoosh.

The second, as icy foreboding raced down her spine,

was the sight of the weekend bag that should've been in her hotel room sitting against an interior door of the plane.

The enormity of what was happening weakened her knees. Before she could collapse and disgrace herself, she sank into the nearest chair, which happened to be the one directly opposite him. He rose with lithe, efficient movements, secured her seat belt, then stayed put, crouched before her as if he expected her to jerk upright and sprint for the door. As she wildly wanted to do.

But already the jet was rolling forward, slowly gathering speed once it had left the hangar.

'What the hell do you think you're doing?' Her voice was nowhere as firm as she wanted it to be. Because she suspected she knew what was happening. Knew but refused to acknowledge it.

'You've been demanding my attention, *mia bella*. So I'm giving you what you want.'

CHAPTER SEVEN

ZAK STARED DOWN at the sleeping form of the woman who claimed to be carrying his child. He wanted to be amused at the hours of silent treatment she'd punished him with following his announcement, right before she'd just as silently taken him up on his offer of the master suite to rest.

He couldn't dredge up an ounce of humour.

He'd instructed his personal security chief to dig into every second of Violet's movements since their night in Tanzania. Preliminary reports indicated that besides work and being in her apartment in New York, she'd done little else.

No secret lover hovered in the wings, aiding her plot to deliver this bombshell into his life. Even communication with her own mother had been kept to a minimum, fuelling his impression from what he'd spotted of the strain between the two women during Remi's wedding reception that Violet was avoiding her own mother.

That notion had been confirmed when Margot Barringhall had, under the guise of congratulating the new royal couple, cornered Zak to demand if he knew what was up with her daughter.

If even her own mother didn't know…

He shook his head, knowing he was avoiding the main subject that need to be addressed. His feelings towards her news.

He was going to be a father.

Simultaneous waves of ice-cold shock and a red-hot need to claim thundered through him, as had been happening ever since Violet had made the life-changing announcement.

A child.

His heir.

He didn't regret the steps he was taking to ensure that no whiff of scandal accompanied this news. His mother's announcement that she was stepping down from the throne with immediate effect, together with his brother's imminent coronation, would be fodder for those who sought to take advantage of the changes going through the kingdom to further their own nefarious ends.

But kidnap? Really?

Si, he affirmed to himself. His actions were justified. As he had learned to his cost when his father had died, delaying in taking action could prove detrimental.

While she may have lapsed into mutinous silence following his announcement that he was in effect kidnapping her, he wasn't in any doubt that this was merely the calm before the storm.

Zak shoved his hands into pockets, refusing to acknowledge the act was to stop him from tracing his fingers down her smooth cheek, then running them through silky hair loosened by sleep. Long eyelashes curled against her paler than normal cheeks, her make-up having failed at its job of disguising the shadows under her eyes or the weariness turning down her sensual lips.

He'd spotted the signs of strain long before he'd approached her at the reception. Had spent far too long wondering if he'd overworked her.

He frowned, belatedly realising he hadn't asked after her health. How was she coping with the baby? Was his child the reason she looked so pale?

His child...

He exhaled long and hard, registering that with the passage of time the icy dread was receding, and in its place was an even greater clamour. One that demanded immediate and definitive resolution to her claim with a claiming of his own.

As if she could intuit his thoughts, she shifted in her sleep, angling her body away from him and cradling her belly with her right hand.

Another hard smile curled his lips.

Whether she knew and expected it or not, she'd sealed her fate by informing him that she carried his child. No Montegovan child born of the royal family had ever gone unclaimed. When his father's indiscretions had come home to roost, they'd been forced to accept his half-brother, despite Jules's existence creating chaos within the royal household.

Even the very thought of a small part of history repeating itself made him grit his teeth. He turned and strode to the nearest window. They were still hours away from landing at their final destination. He needed to return to his seat, ensure his plan was firmly in place.

But even as the thought rippled through his mind, he was looking over his shoulder at Violet as she tossed again in bed. For a moment he entertained the notion of joining her there.

Almost immediately he rejected the idea.

Temptation was what had led them here in the first place. Temptation was what had driven him to Australia for the last two months, pursuing his trust's interests on the other side of the world secure in the knowledge that she was on her way out of his life.

Except she hadn't been. And she couldn't have found a more permanent solution if she'd tried.

Bitterness twisted inside him. She'd well and truly pulled the wool over his eyes.

But no more.

If the child she carried was his—and he was still of the

opinion that she wouldn't dare to attempt to foist another man's baby on him—Violet would be left in no doubt that he fully intended to claim what was his.

That thought settled deep within him, finally erasing any doubt or apprehension about the course of action he was taking.

Slowly retracing his steps back to her, he paused long enough to pull the light coverlet over her body before he exited the master suite. Passing the sitting area, he made his way to the conference table on the lower deck of the plane. Within the hour, he had temporarily relocated the hub of his trust, prioritised the most urgent matters, and effectively rearranged his immediate future in anticipation of what was to come.

By the time the plane touched down on his private runway, Zak was ready and armed with every weapon he needed to ensure the outcome he wanted.

The thought that ripped through him, the one that boldly hinted that claiming his child was no guarantee that he would be a better father than his own had been, he pushed away, and rose when the plane slowed to a stop.

First he would claim his child. Then he would attempt to do what his father hadn't been able to do. Not irreparably shatter his child's life with lies and callous betrayal.

Even more determined, he headed for the master suite to wake Violet.

It was time to face this thing head on.

'Where are we?' Violet asked, blinking at the blinding sunshine pouring through the aircraft windows.

She hadn't expected to sleep for this long. Was sure she looked a sight.

The strain of delivering the news of her pregnancy and what had come afterwards had been too much to withstand. And once she'd realised there had been no way to escape

Zak, she'd barely been able to contain her composure, seeking solace in silence as a way to counteract the wild hysteria simmering just beneath the surface.

When Zak had offered the master suite, it'd been all she could do not to race from his presence and lock herself in the room as quickly as possible. Expecting to stay awake from her churning thoughts, she'd fallen into a deep sleep, the most restful she'd had since discovering she was pregnant.

Now she was awake, the enormity of the situation was even more overwhelming, not less. Aware he hadn't answered, she sucked in a breath and glanced his way.

He was waiting for her, incisive gaze devouring her as he answered, 'We're at my private island in the Caribbean.'

Of course they were.

He would hardly kidnap her and take her to a bustling metropolis where she could scream her head off and attract attention at the first opportunity, now, would he?

She shook her head. She was getting ahead of herself, fearing the worst. But how else could she explain what he done? 'You kidnapped me,' she accused, while hoping he would deny it.

He merely shrugged. 'Let's not place labels on actions just yet, shall we?'

'Of course not. Because what could be more damning than a royal prince intent on protecting his pristine image?'

His eyes narrowed on her face. 'You look better rested,' he said, smoothly changing the subject.

'In time for the interrogation you have in store for me, I'm sure.'

His sensual lips pursed and he advanced towards her, holding out his hand. 'It doesn't have to be an interrogation.'

'Oh? What do you call this, then, spiriting me thousands of miles away just to have a *discussion* with me? Did you even think to ask me or are my wishes completely irrelevant to you?'

His hand dropped like a stone, his face hardening even further. 'I told you why I was taking steps to safeguard my family's privacy. My brother just got married. My mother is weeks away from stepping down from the throne. Have you forgotten that there are those who will take advantage of another hint of scandal to further their own agendas?'

Her heart lurched, a reminder of that meeting with his defence minister rising to the fore. 'You really think they would use news of a child as a tool?' she muttered.

His hand rose again, this time more commanding. 'It's not a scenario I'm willing to wait around for or risk discovering first-hand. You will stay here until we settle things between us.'

He wasn't going to take no for an answer.

That much was evident in the watchful intensity in his eyes. But the suspicion that he wasn't giving her the full picture and that she really couldn't very well stay on the plane for ever forced her to toss aside covers she couldn't remember pulling over herself and, ignoring his outstretched hand simply because she didn't think she could withstand his touch on top of everything else, rose to her feet.

Her shoes were nowhere in sight, neither was her weekend bag.

Before she could demand their whereabouts, he reached for her, sweeping her smoothly into his arms.

She suppressed a gasp as he pressed her against his hard-muscled body, reminding her with sizzling efficiency of everything she'd tried to forget about his physical perfection. And failed. 'Put me down. I'm quite capable of walking.'

'Your things have been packed in the car, including your shoes. Unless you wish to burn your feet on the baking asphalt outside, I'm your ride.'

There was no use arguing because he was already striding out of the plane.

If it hadn't been the height of absurd childishness, she would have squeezed her eyes shut and pretended he didn't exist.

But he did exist.

He was a solid unshakeable presence in her life, intent on...

What were Zak's true intentions besides the excuses he'd tossed at her? And why couldn't she stop the rush of awareness at being pressed so tightly against him?

Violet took a keener interest in her surroundings, eagerly wishing for anything to dissipate his effect on her. But even her surroundings were intent on assaulting her senses with an overload of beauty.

Tall palm trees swayed in the distance, a carpet of lush greenery extending left and right of the long runway as far as the eye could see. What she knew of private Caribbean islands was that they were compact, easily traversable from one end to the other.

Not this one, of course.

Several minutes after Zak had placed her in the front seat of a gleaming SUV and slid behind the wheel, they were still nowhere near their destination. Sunglasses shielded his expression from her and, apparently deciding to take a leaf from her book, he'd lapsed into silence once they were in the car.

Behind them, two more SUVs followed, one containing his bodyguards and the other with a boot full of luggage, triggering the suspicion that Zak intended to remain here for a while. It was that thought that triggered her speech.

'How long do you expect this theatre to play out?'

He slanted a glance at her. 'Theatre?'

She waved her hand at the scenery. 'You say you're trying to protect your family from the scandal you think my announcement will bring. But we could've had this con-versation anywhere. Instead, you've brought me here to yet another symbol of your status. To what? Drive home the fact that I'm a mere commoner? You want to put me in my place, is that it?'

'Yes. All of the above,' he replied drily.

So drily, she couldn't decipher whether he was serious or joking. Then she called herself ten kinds of fool for think-ing he would deny the accusation.

'I also intend to limit your access to the outside world, at least until we have a few things straightened out be-tween us.'

'There's nothing to straighten out. I'm pregnant. I'm having a baby. End of.'

She wasn't aware of the full extent of his tension until his grip visibly relaxed on the steering wheel. 'I believe we've just settled the first thing to my satisfaction.'

About to frown, her jaw dropped as she stared at him. 'You brought me here suspecting that I wasn't going to go through with this pregnancy?'

One shoulder lifted in an eloquent shrug.

'Establishing there's a pregnancy and telling a father of his child's existence doesn't automatically mean the state is willingly accepted. Not yet, anyway.'

'What other reason could I…?' She froze, then gasped again, growing a little light-headed as his meaning sank in. 'You believe I told you about the pregnancy to lever-age it? For what?'

'Off the top of my head? Everything you've ever desired since you were old enough to desire it. But your outrage is duly noted. As is your protectiveness.'

The last bit was uttered in a gruff voice, his gaze drop-ping to where her hand had somehow found itself over her belly again.

This time she didn't drop it or attempt to disguise the

action. They were alone, and really she was done being the soul of discretion about the child she carried. Zak had brought her here just so she'd be out of the public eye. She wasn't about to deny her child's existence.

She was still absorbing the twisted cynicism that informed his every action when they crested a low hill.

The white, sprawling plantation style house sat on top of another hill, surrounded on either side by tall swaying palm trees. And sloping away on either side, lush grass rolled away several hundred feet before turning into the white sand of a pristine beach.

All that perfection was set against a backdrop of a sparkling sea that couldn't have more stunning if it had been drawn by the world's most talented artist.

As prisons went, it was magnificent enough to snatch her breath from her lungs. On any other occasion, Violet wouldn't have stopped herself from vocalising her appreciation.

But this wasn't any other occasion. She'd been brought here for the sole purpose of being kept away from the world, a problematic stain that Prince Zakary Montegova had yet to decide what to do with.

The stony ache in her chest bruised her but she managed, barely, to hang onto her composure. She'd displayed far too many weaknesses in his presence already. The even bigger battle was ahead of her, so she had to keep her wits about her. Remain calm in the face of his highhandedness.

And find a way off this gilded paradise as soon as possible.

The moment the car drew to a stop, she reached for the door handle.

'Violet, wait—'

She ignored his growled instruction. And stepped out onto baking paving stones.

With a yelp, she sprinted towards the front door of the

mansion, fleeing the suppressed curse that sounded behind her and Zak's quick strides as he chased her down.

So much for maintaining her composure.

The doors opened smoothly and Violet skidded to a halt, her face flaming as she caught the stares of a dozen uniformed men and women who comprised the household staff.

A few glances at her attire reminded her that she was still in the gown she'd worn to Remi's wedding. Despite the air-conditioned interior, the heavy silk stuck to her skin, the short train dragging and out of place in this place where shorts and bikinis were the norm.

With her feet bare and her hair in disarray, she knew she looked a sight. Nevertheless, she plastered on a tentative smile as Zak sauntered to a stop beside her.

In deep languid tones, he made introductions, the amusement in his voice as he introduced her as Lady Violet Barringhall setting her teeth on edge.

There was nothing ladylike about her appearance. And it was all his fault. Once the majority of the staff had dispersed, they were left with the head butler.

'We'll take refreshments in the living room, Patrick,' Zak said, and then he caught hold of her wrist.

Violet went along with him simply because she didn't want to give an even worse impression of herself in front of his staff. The moment they were alone, she wrenched herself from his grasp.

'We can finish this thing now. I'm sure it'll only take a few minutes. Then you can get me off this island.'

He waved a hand at one exquisite striped sofa. 'Sit down, Violet.'

'I'm getting tired of you ordering me about, Zak.'

'You're a guest in my house and I'm offering you due courtesy.'

'I'm not a guest. I'm your prisoner. Let's get at least one thing straight.'

His face tightened. 'Very well. If you think yourself a prisoner then you should be aware of a few things. There is no way off the island except by boat or air, both of which are under my strict command. Attempt to solicit help from the staff and you will merely be embarrassing yourself. Is that clear?'

She swallowed a knot of disappointment.

He raised an eyebrow. 'Did I just shatter your dreams?'

She forced a laugh. 'Don't flatter yourself.'

For a second, a bewildered look chased across his face but it was extinguished just as quickly. 'Would you like a tour of the property? Most people are content with being in the lap of luxury. Perhaps you'll change your mind after you've seen the place properly?'

'If you wanted me to view this place as anything but a prison, you should've tried inviting me instead of kidnapping me.'

'Would you have come?'

The question was so unexpected it left her speechless for a moment. Would she have dropped everything to spend time with Zak on his island paradise? When self-preservation alone dictated that she stay as far away from him as possible? 'No.'

His nostrils flared briefly. 'Then I have my answer.'

'For someone so hell-bent on safeguarding your family's reputation, don't you think this is merely compounding it? What's to stop me from going straight to the tabloids and reporting you to the authorities once you set me free? Or do you intend to keep me here for ever?'

'Now, there's a thought,' he drawled.

The notion that he would even consider such a thing had her stalking over to where he lounged in the chair, master and commander of all he surveyed. 'This isn't funny, Zak.'

'I'm most definitely not laughing. Sit down, Violet,' he invited silkily, but with an edge to his voice that sent a shiver over her skin.

Because close proximity to Zak was a bad idea, and because she needed to gain some much-needed solid ground, she retreated to the farthest seat from him and sat down just as the butler entered, bearing a tray of drinks.

She accepted a glass of fruit punch, only realising how thirsty she was after the first sip. She set the glass down with a resolute click. 'How long do you intend to keep me here?'

'That depends.'

'On what?'

'On how agreeable you are to my terms.'

'What terms?'

Dark grey eyes locked on hers.

'No child, besides Jules, has been born out of wedlock in Montegovan royal history. And I'm sure you know the circumstances surrounding how my half-brother arrived in my family.'

'I only know what I read in the tabloids. So unless you're claiming those allegations weren't true?'

'For the most part, *si*, they were true,' he stated tightly, his voice discouraging further interest.

It was clear this was a subject Zak didn't like discussing. 'Okay, but what does that have to do with the child I'm carrying?'

He regarded her with unwavering intent. 'What do you think, Violet?'

Suspecting what was coming, she reeled in disbelief and shock. 'Whatever it is, the answer is no.'

One eyebrow lifted. 'I haven't even asked you yet.'

'No,' she repeated.

'Yes, Violet. I bear responsibility for the lack of protection when we had sex, but you also assured me that there was no risk of pregnancy. But what's done is done. While I'm curious to know why your contraception failed, it's immaterial at this point. You're carrying my child and I intend to claim it.'

A handful of words with consequences that stretched far into her future. She folded her hands tightly in her lap to disguise their trembling. 'What exactly does that mean?'

'It means my child will bear my name, be brought up in Montegova under my care, take pride in his or her heritage, be afforded every privilege and welcome the responsibilities every royal Montegovan is due. And all of that will come about if his birth comes with the benefit of true legitimacy. Which is why the only sensible recourse is for you to marry me.'

Contrary to the near hysteria that had threatened to overwhelm her mere moments ago, an eerie sense of calm settled over Violet once he'd said the actual words.

'No,' she stated once again, thrilled when her voice emerged firm and solid.

Shock flashed crossed his face. Then his eyes narrowed. 'No? That's all you have to say? No?'

'Pardon me, where are my manners? No, *thank you*,' she amended, secretly thrilled when he immediately looked... perturbed again.

'Perhaps you didn't hear me properly. I want you to marry me, Violet. You will have the title of Princess, wealth beyond your wildest imagination, and, if you wish it a place in my trust to continue your career.'

Marry me.

Her heart lurched as those two words, contrary to everything she'd believed of herself and her future path, making her waver for a moment as she was inundated with might-have-beens. Her fingers bunched tighter. 'I heard you, loud and clear. And you heard my answer.'

For a full minute Zak stared at her, his gaze unashamedly probing, seeming to delve beneath her skin. Then he eased back in his seat, his face turning alarmingly neutral.

She wasn't fooled for a second by the arm he raised to rest on the back of his sofa, or the legs he casually crossed.

'It's been an...unsettling twenty-four hours. Perhaps you would like some time to consider all this?' he suggested.

She summoned a small, hopefully dismissive smile. 'What, the fragile little lady needs some time to wrap her head around everything that's happening to her? Isn't that just typical of your sort?'

One eyebrow elevated. And was that a tic going in his jaw? 'My sort?'

'Half-decent-looking men of means who believe all they need to do is crook their finger at a woman to have her swooning at their feet.'

'Since I have first-hand evidence that you've never been intimately acquainted with any other man, even my sort, I'll assume this is a sweeping generalisation?'

Her pretended calm threatened to evaporate as a warm flush consumed her face. Still, she managed a shrug. 'Are you sure you can trust this evidence? For all you know, I could've been living it up in New York while you were... wherever you decided to swan off to.'

The tic intensified and the look he sent her was anything but neutral. It thrummed with volcanic fury. 'I was in Australia. And for your sake, I hope you're merely attempting to get a rise out of me.'

'What if I am? Will that earn me a quick exit off this island?' she countered.

His face tightened and she could've sworn his stomach muscles clenched hard. 'It won't, but confirmation of a dalliance with another man while you carry my child will definitely not sit well. Did you?' he enquired with smooth, silky lethality.

Violet held his gaze in bold silence for a handful of seconds before the denial erupted from her throat. 'No, I didn't. But I assure you, I won't be a well-behaved little prisoner if you insist on keeping me here. In fact, I'm certain you will regret it if you don't put me back on that plane immediately.'

A layer of that ferocious tension eased from his frame as he took a slow, controlled breath, that regal head cocked mockingly. 'We have time. Please, enlighten me as to how you plan to make my life difficult.'

And allow him to use that shrewd steel trap of a mind to counter her strategy? Not likely. 'Don't worry, you'll find out soon enough if you insist on pursuing this absurd caper. And it's not just me you'll have to contend with, you know. Did you stop to think about how my mother would take my disappearance at all? Do you think she's going to just sit by and allow you to kidnap her daughter?'

Without the slightest hint of unease, he shrugged. 'I'm confident I can handle your mother. Next.'

Unfortunately, Violet believed him. She suspected he could have her mother eating out of his hand with minimum effort.

Her heart clenched with that shame she'd never managed to shrug off when it came to her mother's blatantly grasping antics. Heck, she was fairly certain Zak would receive a resounding endorsement of this kidnapping from her mother if it meant she could brag about it ad nauseam at future dinner parties.

As for the discovery that Violet was pregnant, it was why she'd guarded her new state with feverish zeal. Why she intended to keep it under wraps for as long as possible. Her mother's discovery that she carried the next Montegovan royal would see her thrust into the sort of limelight her mother adored but Violet desperately abhorred.

Nevertheless, she couldn't keep this a secret for ever. Neither could she avoid her mother for ever.

And it certainly didn't mean she wanted to be kept here against her will, regardless of how stunning this prison was. She pursed her lips. 'How about your staff? You employ the type of people who condone kidnapping, do you?' she taunted.

'Their loyalty is absolute and faultless or they wouldn't be here,' he stated, his voice deep, firm and completely unfazed by her cold accusations.

About to challenge him some more, she froze for a moment, unsure why until the distant rumble of aircraft engines had her surging to her feet. She rushed to the French doors in time to see the jet rising gracefully into the sky, its wings glinting in the dappling sunlight.

'No!' She whirled towards him, fury and an emotion she refused to name flaming through her veins at the realisation that she was alone, secluded and stranded, on an island with Zak Montegova.

'Yes,' he countered smoothly. 'Calm down, Violet.'

'No, I won't calm down. You want another reason? How about the simple fact that I don't want this? That what you're doing is plain wrong?'

He simply shrugged, unfazed by her outburst. 'As you can see, it's going to take more than the seductive promise of a temper tantrum to change my mind about this.' His voice was low, deep, sexy in an authoritative way that highlighted his innate masculinity.

A shiver danced through her.

Seductive? Did Zak actually want her to throw a tantrum? Recalling that their last two arguments had ended up with varying degrees of intimacy, the second achieving the ultimate, she fought a blush and decided then and there to do the exact opposite.

She was paying the ultimate price for her folly in Tanzania. There was no need to throw more fuel on a fire that had almost consumed her once already.

And how could she have forgotten that mere hours after the fact he'd done a disappearing act on her? That he wouldn't be taking this course of action if he didn't have a selfish reason in mind.

By flailing and protesting at every turn, was she playing right into his hands? Several scenarios tumbled through her mind, each one as disturbing as the last. She slowly sucked in a calm breath, ignoring her thundering heart.

After one last longing look at the aircraft, which was now a tiny speck in the sky, she turned back to him. 'Very well. You want to play this game? Don't say I didn't warn you.'

The raw glint that lit his eyes for a few stomach-hollowing seconds sent a wave of panic through her. It reeked of relished anticipation. Of the kind of marauding conquests his ancestors were renowned for and Montegovans were intensely proud of. He didn't exactly say the words, *bring it on*, but they flamed in his eyes for those seconds before Zak rose, all litheness, power and blood-quickening animalistic grace, to stride assuredly to where she stood. And up close, she saw something else.

Sexual attraction.

He may have avoided her for weeks after Tanzania, may have pretended she didn't exist at his brother's wedding. But Zak still desired her.

And, damn her, her body's wild and fierce surging to life announced that the feeling was intensely mutual. But feeling was one thing. Acting on those feelings quite another. She intended to deny every ounce of this fevered attraction if it was the last thing she did. She'd already spent far too many nights dwelling on why she couldn't get this man out of her damned head.

'Now that we've established you're staying for the foreseeable future, would you like to familiarise yourself with the property?' he asked, all arrogant charm and effortless masculinity.

About to snap that she wasn't in the mood to tour her prison, she swallowed the heated words.

Self-containment.

Aloofness.

Grace.

She would epitomise the very word if it killed her. 'Maybe later. I'm rather tired. Just point me in the direction of where I'm to sleep and I'll get out of your hair.'

Wary suspicion narrowed his eyes. She would've laughed if she wasn't terrified he would see through her intentions, somehow find a way to dismantle them. Hadn't he done that very thing by that waterfall in Tanzania?

After an interminable minute, he gave a curt nod. He curled his fingers around her wrist and Violet fought a wild, frenzied battle not to pull away. That would be admitting his touch seared her deep, awakening sensations she was absolutely loath to admit she'd missed—even craved—in the weeks of his absence.

Nevertheless, she didn't intend to allow him such careless courtesies. So, under the pretext of returning to her seat to retrieve her clutch, she smoothly eased her hand from his.

The merest flaring of his nostrils was the only indication that he'd noticed. Making sure to keep a few necessary feet between them, she walked with him to the door.

Together they climbed a wide, sweeping staircase, at the top of which were hallways that branched out in two directions. Zak took the east hallway, leading her to the farthest set of doors.

He threw them open and Violet barely suppressed a gasp. The suite was tasteful magnificence personified. A different level of luxury from the rooms at the Montegovan palace but jaw-dropping nonetheless. Eggshell-blue walls and white muslin curtains gave the room a light and airy feel.

Cleverly accented with pale gold fixtures and furnishings, she felt as if she was floating in the sunlit sky.

The grounding force in the form of the solid, powerful man who was watching her with a steady gaze brought her back down to earth.

'A tray of refreshments will be brought up to you. We will have dinner at seven. If you need me before then, the staff will tell you where to find me.'

'Why on earth would I need you?'

A mocking smile twitched the corner of his sensual lips. 'To give me your answer, of course.'

In all the furore surrounding her kidnap, she'd momentarily forgotten that he'd asked her, *no, decreed* that she marry him.

A pulse of shock ricocheted through her. She curbed a hysterical snort. If anyone had told her just yesterday that Zak would demand that she wed him, and that she would actually *forget* that demand, she'd have crowed with laughter.

She raised a hand to her head as it threatened to spin. Instantly, he was before her, cupping her shoulders in a firm hold and frowning down at her. 'What's wrong?' he asked tersely.

'I'm just…a little dizzy.' And the warm, seductive fire of his touch wasn't helping.

His lips flattened. 'You've worn yourself out.'

'No, *you've* worn me out. Leave, please. I really want to be alone.'

He didn't release her. As he'd done when they'd left the plane, he swung her up into his arms, strode a few steps to where the huge, queen-size bed, festooned with pillows, waited. With a gentleness belying the bristling purpose stamped on his face, he set her down in the middle of it, slid the cover from beneath her and, with one sizzling scrutiny from head to toe, settled it back over her.

'I'd offer to help remove that dress, but I'm guessing you're going to oppose me on principle,' he drawled.

'Give the Prince a prize,' she responded drily.

For a moment he froze, his eyes narrowing ominously. She held her breath, a curiously hot and heavy anticipation oozing through her belly.

Then, instead of the sharp retort she'd expected, he extended his hand, trailed his forefinger down one cheek in a silent, electrifying caress.

Violet was glad the covers hid her body's reaction. And while she was battling the pearling of her nipples and the damp neediness between her thighs, he stepped back.

'Rest now. We will pick this up again later.'

She chose silence. Because all of a sudden she wasn't sure she wanted him to leave. Actually felt curiously bereft in the pit of her stomach as his broad-shouldered frame headed for the door.

And when she winced at the gentle but definitive snick of the door shutting, she feared how deflated she felt, as if he'd taken her very vitality with him. As if he'd dimmed the sun with his absence.

More than anything that'd happened since she'd stepped onto the plane what felt like a lifetime ago, it was what terrified her the most.

CHAPTER EIGHT

SHE WAS STILL choosing silence two weeks later.

A fact, she was very pleased to note, that had increasingly aggravated the hitherto unflappable Prince Zak Montegova. He didn't overtly display his displeasure at her attitude, but it was there in the flattening of his sensual lips when she left the table immediately after a civil but silent meal.

In the brisk stride of his departure when her monosyllabic answers stifled his attempt at conversation.

In her ability to project an outwardly cool and dismissive demeanour when she caught him staring at her with blatant heat in his eyes, while every cell in her body thrilled to that electric look.

In the flaring of his nostrils when he asked, 'Are you ready to give me your answer?'

And was met with an even-toned, 'Yes. It's still no.'

For the most part Violet congratulated herself on maintaining a decent enough composure. The only moments of vulnerability happened six days into her enforced stay, when she woke to hear the sound of a different sort of engine. The sleek speedboat had delivered a distinguished-looking Montegovan doctor and his two assistants, and myriad quantity of medical equipment, including a state-of-the-art portable ultrasound machine.

She hid her joy, unwilling to show Zak how much she'd been yearning to hear her baby's heartbeat for the first time.

He threatened to ruin the moment when, watching the equipment being set up, he leaned low to rasp in her ear,

'If you're thinking of spilling your guts to the doctor or his team, don't bother. He's been my personal physician since birth. I trust him implicitly. But should he even consider being disloyal, trust that I have far more extensive resources to secure his discretion than you could ever dream up.'

She hated herself for her sharp, vulnerable intake of breath. For the arrow of hurt that lodged in her midriff. More than anything, she hated herself for having considered doing exactly that, then instantly dismissing it with no clear reason why she'd abandon such an expedient route off the island. 'You're a bastard, do you know that?' she hissed.

His face hardened as he stared down at her. 'I'm a lot of things, *mia carina*, but that label isn't one of them. It's also a label I wish to prevent my child from wearing, if only you'd see sense,' he sliced at her, the edge in his voice momentarily setting hers aflame.

That she was absurdly glad for that glimpse of a deeper reaction from him only intensified when, stretched out in her bed minutes later, she watched the monitor in awe as she looked at the grainy picture of her child, and then redirected her gaze to Zak at his unfettered intake of breath.

His raw, naked expression, his inability to look away from the monitor or his complete unawareness that he'd grasped her hand, wrapped dangerously tender strings around her chest. She clung to him, aware that her guard had disintegrated, that she yearned to ask him how he truly felt about the baby she was carrying.

'Everything is precisely as it should be,' the doctor announced then, shattering the moment. 'Congratulations, Your Highness.' He turned to her, his professionalism not quite hiding the speculation in his eyes. 'And to you, Lady Barringhall.'

Zak started, his stormy gaze dropping down to hers. The next instant, he'd reclaimed his composure, directing a dark frown at their entwined hands before calmly disengaging his. Then, arms stiffly folded, he proceeded to direct questions at his doctor.

Despite his withdrawal, Violet hadn't been able to quite catch her breath, the notion that Zak might feel something deeper for his child other than as his heir threatening her composure.

Made her pause for a millisecond to consider...possibilities. Rationally, she knew his imperiously worded proposal was because of the child she carried. That he intended to wrap the tight cloak of royalty and privilege and years of history around his child.

But was there something more?

And what about her?

If she'd learned anything from her mother's feverish ambitions to marry her daughters off to rich, titled husbands for her own selfish ends, it was that those kinds of marriages were shockingly common. And, more often than not, it left one or both participants jaded and miserable within a few years, resulting in infidelity or the kind of open marriages whispered about at dinner parties.

The very thing she'd striven for years to get away from.

But had this gone beyond *her*?

Was she holding out for what she wanted in complete disregard for the needs of her child? Would her baby despise her one day for the choices she'd made? For choosing her own path instead of bowing down to the decree of its father?

Was she allowing her own childhood experiences to cloud her judgement to the detriment of her unborn child? But wasn't that what parents were supposed to do? Carefully weigh options and decide what was best for their child?

Was that what Zak had been doing? It occurred to her then that everything she knew about Zak had been mostly second-hand.

Except for that kiss.

Except for that unforgettable episode in Tanzania.

But that was just sex. She didn't actually know the man. And…some of that blame lay with her. Didn't it?

Do you even know anything about his childhood?

She pushed the thought away, the notion that she was beginning to make excuses for her chilly silence these past two weeks eating at her.

He'd kidnapped her.

Yes, but it hadn't turned out to be the nightmare she'd envisaged, had it? While she'd refused to explore the island on principle, she'd availed herself of the extensive library adjoining Zak's study, been secretly thrilled to discover a wealth of conservation books she'd been dying to read.

Not to mention the personal treats he'd showered on her.

For the first week, a new delivery had arrived by boat every day, starting with two dozen boxes stuffed with designer wear perfect for idling about on a tropical island. Light, airy sundresses, tasteful bikinis and sandals, sunglasses and wide-brimmed hats in every shade. No detail had been left unsatisfied.

Then came the daily delivery of flowers, each time with a different gift.

A diamond tennis bracelet. A large basket of cashmere knitting yarn following her brief conversation with the housekeeper about wanting to pick up the hobby. Expensive exquisitely scented candles specially crafted for expectant mothers. A pen drive containing a drone's-eye view of the completed project in Tanzania.

But best of the lot had been the small, framed photo of the ultrasound image of her baby. A photo she kept propped up on her bedside and the first thing she saw each morning.

It was that gesture that had triggered her questioning the unshakeable *no* she'd delivered every time Zak had asked her to marry him. Or perhaps it was more the fact that he hadn't asked in the last three days?

She massaged mildly throbbing temples. Was she suffering some weird form of Stockholm syndrome? Softening just when she needed to harden her heart against her captor?

She looked around her now, at the sparkling pool and the pristine beach beyond. At the stunning beauty all around her. It didn't look or feel like a prison. The staff were friendly and courteous with her, treated Zak with a respect and reverence that went beyond employee/prince boundaries.

Impatient with her thoughts and unable to concentrate on the book she was reading, she rose from the sun lounger that had become her outdoor refuge. She would've stayed in her room the whole time had it not signalled weakness. Instead, she'd flaunted her calm indifference in his face, let him taste her triumph, the way she had when he'd walked in on her opening the clothing boxes after their arrival.

He'd studied her with those piercing eyes, probably expecting her to gush her gratitude or throw a tantrum at her incarceration. Instead she'd calmly thanked him, instructed the staff to deposit the clothes in her dressing room, then, after sliding into the most provocative bikini she could find, she'd returned downstairs.

She knew she'd succeeded in scoring a point when he'd inhaled sharply at her appearance in the library with a shockingly large surface area of her body on display. Ignoring him, she'd sashayed to the extensive bookcase, taken her time to select a psychological thriller, then made her exit, head held high.

So why was she faltering now?

Because this stand-off couldn't continue for ever.

Her mother's emails were getting more frequent and strident and she wasn't being mollified by Violet's evasive replies. It was only a matter of time before Margot connected the dots and did something foolish. Like pick up the phone to her favourite tabloid magazine to voice her concern for her daughter's whereabouts.

With a sigh, she turned away from the breathtaking view, her mind whirling as she entered the living room.

And came face to face with Zak.

They stared at each other. No, it was more than that. They *absorbed* each other. The air thickened with a heavy, crackling awareness, churning displeasure and...*sex* in a volatile mix that quickened her heartbeat.

Or was it the vitality and pure, raw masculinity that brimmed from him, the mouth she couldn't stop thinking about kissing even as she remained steeped in her role of indifference, and the blinding white linen lounge clothes he'd taken to wearing on the island that was severely wrecking her equilibrium?

Whatever it was, it locked her in place. Until her lungs burned, and her senses screamed for self-preservation.

They snapped into motion at the same time, Zak heading for her with ferocious determination etched into his face. She attempted to bypass him by skirting the sofa. And failed when he cornered her a few feet from the door, his towering body barring her way.

'Excuse me,' she said, cringing when her customary coolness emerged hot and husky.

'No, *cara*, you're not excused.'

He blocked her escape by the simple act of placing his hands on the exquisite Venetian-papered wall on either side of her, caging her in, making her shockingly aware of how much of her skin was exposed in the orange bikini and the matching sarong that only covered her hips and upper thighs.

'What are you—?'

'Enough of this, Violet,' he breathed, his voice a dangerous volcanic rumble that merely heightened her sensual awareness of him. 'It's been two weeks.'

In a wild bid to reverse the frantic beat of her heart at his proximity, she took her time to slot her bookmark between the pages of her novel before tossing it on a console table nearby. Only then did she gather every shred of composure to meet his eyes. 'If it's too much for you, you know what you need to do to end it.'

For a long stretch he didn't answer, the only sound in the room the lazy whirling of the ceiling fan. And her agitated breathing.

His gaze raked her body before returning to rest on her face. 'You intend to go on letting us both suffer in silence?'

'Which one bothers you more, the suffering or the silence?' she asked, noting again how her voice missed the flippancy she'd aimed for.

An arrogant, sexy smile draped his lips, even while his eyes remained shrewd, watchful. Calculating. 'You wish me to bare myself so you can subject me to even more of the same treatment?'

Her smile was saccharine sweet. 'If you would be so kind.'

The smile evaporated. Her skin tingled and her senses jumped as rigid purpose tightened his features. He leaned forward until his lips were a scant inch from her ear. 'Did you not learn your lesson about crossing swords with me in Tanzania, Violet?' he murmured softly, dangerously in her ear.

She couldn't stop the shiver that racked her frame. She angled herself away from him, aware she was in danger of disgracing herself by toppling over but not caring in that moment. 'Are you threatening me?' Why did the very thought make her senses shiver in anticipation, make the flesh between her legs swell with need?

'I'm threatening you with the exact reaction you've been hoping for since embarking on this...escapade.'

* * *

Just like in Tanzania, just like in every interaction he'd ever had with this breathtaking creature, Zak felt unnerved, unbalanced. For as long as he could remember, every moment of his life had been shaped in strict conformity, that secret yearning to be an exemplary son to a seemingly exemplary father directing him to life in the military. While he'd had his share of liaisons, they'd been discreet, with no incidence of drama that might bring embarrassment to him or his family.

His father had not only betrayed *him* and everything Zak had believed was an honourable legacy, he'd plunged his entire family into scandal and endangered Montegova. That time was seared onto his psyche, had driven him to be extremely circumspect in his own relationships. He staunchly believed his immunity to soft words and lofty promises granted him a gratifying insight into people's true characters. He'd learned never to accept anyone at face value. Never to fall into seductive traps.

So far, his only stumbling blocks had been an unforgettable kiss six years ago, a moment of insanity at a stunning waterfall, and a ruthless decision to kidnap.

All incidents that involved Violet.

The unsettling part of it all was…he wouldn't change a single thing.

With each passing day, he wanted the child in her womb with a deeper fervour. Blood of his blood. Flesh of his flesh. Under his care.

A chance to rewrite history?

Perhaps it was a little selfish, but what if he achieved the impossible and got right what his father had got so wrong? What if he engendered loyalty, trust, integrity…even affection in his child, traits he'd believed were a cornerstone of his own life until he'd discovered otherwise. What if he could help his heir…thrive?

Wasn't that worth pursuing this course of action with Violet? Wasn't it worth living temporarily with this hollow pit in his stomach that whispered that he could fail?

He wouldn't, of course. He *couldn't*. This was too... vital. But he did admit things hadn't turned out the way he'd envisaged.

For starters, he'd expected her to throw a tantrum. Perhaps even pout and plead while she pretended to play hard to get over his proposal. Right before she fell into line with his wishes.

Instead she'd treated him with cool, sustained, never-ending *indifference*.

It *grated*. He was used to women falling over themselves to gain his attention. Had experienced it at a near nauseating level at Remi's wedding when, with his brother newly off the market, even more avid eyes had turned his way.

On that occasion, he'd withstood their interest simply to avoid the temptation to stare at and fill his senses again with Violet at every opportunity.

Now he wanted an *engagement* of a specific sort. The kind that gave him free rein to touch her glowing skin, to attract a smile that didn't start and end with mild disdain.

To have her not deliver that vacant smile when their paths crossed, then look through him as if he wasn't there. The first few days he'd been amused. Then he'd been irritated.

Then a dismaying feeling had overwhelmed him that she was getting steeped in this role she'd determinedly taken to freeze him out. It was that feeling ballooning out of proportion that'd ejected him from his study in the middle of a workday, his concentration a shambles of shattered focus and intense vexation. The sensation of losing time and ground with Violet had demanded he seek her out, finally end this nonsense.

Of course, the impact of her smooth golden skin, long-legged grace and those blue eyes had seemed more vivid each time he looked into them had all played a part, too, wreaking carnage with his body.

So…one way or the other, the cold, silent treatment was ending now. Before he lost his mind.

One side effect of pregnancy she'd dreaded was morning sickness. Another one Violet hadn't quite anticipated was a heightened sense of smell.

The moment she inhaled Zak's unique masculine scent, her senses went into overdrive. Heat fired up in her pelvis, the blood rushed into her breasts, hardening her nipples as fine tremors invaded her body.

In desperation, she licked her lips. His eyes darkened as he followed the swipe of her tongue, his chest expanding on a deep breath.

'We'll need to discuss this rationally sooner or later—'

'Why do you want to saddle yourself with me, Zak?' she blurted, her earlier misgivings furiously resurfacing. 'You don't even know me. Not really. And I don't know you, save for what's bandied about on the internet. I could be your worst nightmare. Let me go and in a few months' time we can discuss shared custody—'

'No.' A blaze of possessiveness in his eyes accompanied the hard refusal.

'You won't even—'

'Let's change things a little,' he said smoothly, intent eyes riveted on the pulse leaping at her throat.

'What?'

'Let's call a temporary truce to all this nonsense. You say I don't know you. So show me the real Violet Barringhall underneath all this stiff upper lip thing that I assure you has got quite tedious.'

The offer tantalised and tempted. But it felt one-sided,

especially in the light of her own thoughts about him only minutes ago. 'What do I get in return?'

'Reciprocity.' Before her senses could jump in wild giddiness at the offer, he added, 'Up to a point.'

Disappointment bit deep. 'You're already ring-fencing your offer?'

An inscrutable veil descended over his face. 'I'm not in the habit of offering myself up *carte blanche* to anyone. I'm not going to start now.'

Disappointment turned to hurt. Why was she surprised? She was just another being beneath his regard, one who just happened to be carrying his child.

But since it was clear Zak intended to claim this child in one way or another, wasn't she better off knowing the man better? Knowledge was power, wasn't it?

About to grudgingly accept his offer of a truce, she snatched in a breath as another scent pervaded her nostrils. Geraldine, the housekeeper, was probably preparing another delectable snack. But not one Violet's senses appreciated. She felt her stomach fold in on itself as nausea rose, harsh and fast.

The frantic need to make it to the bathroom, to not disgrace herself, had her ducking beneath his arm.

'Violet?' Zak reached for her, concern etched into his face.

She shook her head, fleeing towards one of the endless bathrooms in the villa. She barely made it before emptying the contents of her stomach into the bowl.

Over and over her insides surged as the mild morning sickness she'd experienced only once three days ago and had foolishly believed had permanently disappeared returned with a vengeance.

She'd dislodged her hat during her mad dash, and now she felt strong, gentle hands gather her hair in a loose hold, away from the trajectory of her humiliation. Squeezing her eyes shut, she willed the nausea down, grasping for a modicum of self-respect. Just as another bout hit her hard.

'Easy, *carina*,' Zak crooned in a deep, low voice, one hand sweeping down her back in a gentle caress.

Spent and breathless, she laughed. Or at least attempted to. 'There's nothing easy about morning sickness. It's horrible and humiliating and…' She stopped, closed her eyes as tears threatened to compound her misery.

'*Si*, I get the picture.'

Opening her eyes, she glared at him. 'And you standing there, looking like the spokesperson for health and vitality isn't helping, trust me.'

'I shall locate my sackcloth forthwith,' he said with deep solemnity.

Against all sense of self-preservation, her lips curved in a small smile. 'This isn't funny.'

'No,' he agreed.

'Stop trying to humour me.'

Again he nodded. 'How can I help, Violet?'

Utterly disarmed by the offer, she stared nonplussed for several seconds before reason kicked in. All this was for his child's benefit. Nothing more. 'You can go away.'

'No. I believe you were about to accept my offer of a truce before this unfortunate incident. Let's not ruin the progress we were making.' The words slid smoothly from his lips, one hand held out to her while the other flushed the toilet.

Perhaps she was weak. Perhaps she was tired of this chilly standoff that had achieved nothing but a stalemate and fleeting satisfaction at childish needling.

Before she could stop herself, Violet slid her hand into his. He helped her up and led her to the marble-topped sink. From the discreet little vanity, he took out a bottle of mouth-wash, poured a measure in a glass and handed it to her.

'Thank you.'

While she rinsed her mouth, and welcomed the minty taste that replaced the vileness, he ran a towel under cool water and dabbed it against her temples.

It felt heavenly, so soothing she couldn't hold back a moan.

Zak froze, his eyes dark and ravenous as he stared down at her. Her breath caught, her temperature ramping up at the blatantly carnal gaze he didn't bother to disguise. His hand continued its gentle ministrations, over her cheeks, her jaw, down to the wild tattoo beating at her throat.

He noted the helpless little shiver that went through her, tossed the towel into the sink, then moved purposefully between her knees. Still pinning her with his potent gaze, he slid his fingers into her hair, angled her face up to his.

'Wh-what are you doing?'

'We're having a moment, Violet. Just let it be,' he rasped.

A deep yearning to do exactly as he wished saturated her veins. But all he did was run his thumb over her lower lip, seemingly content to just caress her, while she craved more. So much more than was wise.

Sharp disappointment lanced her when he stepped back and released her.

His gaze remained latched on her mouth for another spell before his eyes rose to hers. 'The truce, Violet. Will you accept it?' he pressed.

The thought of returning to cold detachment didn't appeal. She didn't intend to turn warm and fuzzy, she remained his captive after all. But… 'Yes. But with a stipulation of my own.'

He tensed. *'Si?'*

'Three days. That's all I'll give you.'

Determination blazed in his eyes. 'One week.'

She rolled hers. 'Fine. One week. After that I'm getting off this island, even if I have to swim.'

One brow mockingly cocked. 'Is that so?'

'*Si,*' she mimicked him. 'That, or I go back to driving you crazy.'

His nostrils flared and something curiously close to relish lit his eyes before he veiled his expression. 'Agreed.'

It felt far too easy but with his iron-willed control back in place, she couldn't read him. Especially not when he held out his hand again.

'Despite your stubborn refusal to stray beyond the swimming pool, you must be dying to see the rest of the island.'

She was. Especially the green hills teeming with vegetation that bordered the north side of the island. She looked down at herself. 'Do I need to change?'

His hot gaze raked her, leaving every exposed inch of her skin hyperaware and sensitive. 'You're fine as you are. Come.'

Not even the imperious command eroded her excitement as they left the villa and headed for the fleet of sleek custom-made golf buggies she'd seen the staff use. Zak chose the most pristine one, a six-seater complete with air-conditioning and drinks cabinet.

After seeing her seated, he slid behind the wheel. Violet averted her gaze from his strong, muscled thighs and the brawny forearms. She knew the chaos that body could wreak on hers.

Despite having her world reduced to several thousand square feet for the last two weeks, albeit in unspeakable luxury, she experienced a trace of apprehension as they left the villa behind.

Realising she was in danger of growing attached to her prison or, even worse, falling in love with Zak's villa, she stopped herself from looking back, concentrating on the swaying palm trees that gradually gave way to denser vegetation and steeper hills.

'How big is this place?' she asked, desperate to dilute

the sensually charged atmosphere and Zak's unapologetic gaze that raked over her every few minutes.

If she'd devised a way to drive him to the edge by her indifference, he'd found a much more effective way of returning the favour with his blatant scrutiny.

'Altogether, it's over three thousand square acres. There are three separate beaches and a natural diving platform, among several interesting things.'

Those interesting things left her awed and dumbstruck.

The island was ninety per cent self-sufficient. A small desalination and water purification plant recycled sea-and rainwater for the island, solar panels provided electricity and an unobtrusive water irrigation system served a farm that reared a handful of Wagyu beef cattle, free-range chickens and provided an extensive selection of vegetables.

Despite the size of the island, it turned out that less than a quarter of the acreage had been developed, leaving the rest as a nature preserve with a dozen tastefully blended eco-lodges for the super-wealthy who wished to enhance their awareness of conservation.

Violet didn't want to be impressed but she couldn't quite hide her stunned awe. Neither could she dismiss the troubling revelation that under normal circumstances she would've enjoyed spending time exploring the island. Even…stayed of her own free will.

The wide-scale alarm she'd expected at the thought never arrived.

God, what was wrong with her? Was she softening? Falling in love with her prison? Pardoning Zak when she should be fighting him every step of the way?

'What were you doing in Australia?' she asked, desperate to dredge up her outrage, remind herself that he couldn't get away from her fast enough after Tanzania.

Zak turned away from the bluff at the highest point of the island where they'd stopped to enjoy the breathtaking view. His shrug bore no hint of regret. 'That part of the world suffers the same humanitarian challenges.'

'Did you leave to avoid me?' she pressed. The question was infinitely presumptuous but she didn't take it back. She needed to know. Despite her thumping heart. Despite the hurt that would accompany his confirmation.

He stiffened, his eyes narrowing on her face. 'Are we dropping our civility already, Violet?'

'You think it's uncivil to ask for the truth?'

'Not at all. But are you prepared for the answer?'

She bit the inside of her cheek, suddenly afraid of his answer. But wasn't this a laying-yourself-bare exercise, at least on her part, so she would truly know the type of man she was dealing with?

She swallowed, boldly met his gaze. 'Yes.'

His jaw tensed. Silence stretched, the wind ruffling his thick hair drawing her gaze to the perfection of his face. When he stepped closer, she gasped at the raw, carnal look in his eyes. 'You're not unaware of your beauty, Violet. I left because I didn't trust my ability to stick to what we'd agreed.'

'Wh-what are you saying?'

He reached for a strand of hair, tossed against her cheek by the breeze. For another short stretch he caressed the silky tendril. Then he pierced her with his gaze. 'That I would've wanted you in my bed, repeatedly, if I'd stayed in New York,' he stated baldly.

Her breath strangled to nothing, her body screaming awake at the imagery his words evoked. 'Zak…'

'I had to go to the other side of the world to get this… need under control.'

'Was that all?' The idea that there could be another reason, perhaps the same one that'd made him walk away from her that night six years ago, burned deep and painful. 'I'm only asking because, despite this little confession, you barely acknowledged me at your brother's wedding,' she said, hating herself for the lash of jealousy and irritation the reminder brought.

Or was she fooling herself? Was it just bruised pride? Or something more precious?

She pushed the thought away as he laughed. 'You believe you're that easily forgettable?' With the growled words, he reached for her, driving his fingers into her hair.

Unlike the charged coming together that had fuelled their past intimate encounters, this was a slow burn of a kiss. But it was no less earth-shattering or all-consuming. Perhaps even more so because the sensations coursing through her body were even more frightening, a clamour that scared her with its sheer depth.

The sweep of his tongue over her lips, the tightening of his hold, and the scent of him all converged to fire up a need so strong she didn't question the wisdom of sliding her hands around his trim waist, digging her fingers into the small of his back and, with another deep moan, straining upward to deepen the kiss.

One hand left her hair to glide down her back, his touch more urgent, more insistent as he dragged her closer. Her sensitive breasts flattened against his chest, his hard body a hot, living column branding her.

She opened for him, their tongues dancing an erotic tango, driving every thought from her head save the need to perpetuate this heady encounter.

'*Dio mio*, but you intoxicate me,' he muttered against her lips.

And he more than intoxicated her. He made her *need*. Made her crave the impossible.

Their breaths mingled, sharing the same air as he deepened the kiss.

When the need for more oxygen drove them apart, hot slashes of colour heating his chiselled cheekbones. Against her belly, he was as hard as steel and it fired up that hot and needy space between her legs.

'Does this feel under control to you, Violet?' he breathed. 'I've watched you parade around with your haughty little nose in the air and your sinful body on display, and I can barely think straight for wanting you beneath me.'

There was nowhere to hide. Her nipples puckered, her lips parting on a desperate intake of breath as she struggled to contain the fire raging through her.

He tucked her hair over one ear. 'You need to do better at hiding your reaction, *cara mia*. A less scrupulous man would take advantage of it,' he murmured.

With more strength than she'd thought herself capable of, Violet drew away from him, her hands dropping to clench at her sides. The observation stung far deeper than it should've. Made her lash out. 'You think yourself scrupulous? Enlighten me again as to who kidnapped whom?'

The briefest glimpse of regret flashed in his eyes, then he was back to being the imperious Prince who expected everyone to fall in with his wishes, whether they wanted to or not.

'That was different. And necessary.'

'Why?'

Thunder gathered on his brow. 'Besides taking steps to safeguard my child?'

What had happened to him to fuel this raging mistrust? Was it even worth her attempting to find out the reason?

'We agreed on reciprocity, Zak. Are you going back on your word already?'

The gleam in his eyes was almost...approving. Saluting her for turning his words back on him. 'Very well. Ask your questions.'

Given the freedom, she almost feared his answers. Not because they would turn her off him...but because they might *not*. Nevertheless, she couldn't resist. 'When I told you I was pregnant, you reminded me of your half-brother

and what his arrival did to your family. But Europe is lit-
tered with royal scandals and no one even blinks at them
any more. So what am I missing, Zak?'

Dio mio, but she fired with both guns and aimed for the
heart, didn't she?

He tensed, anticipating that bolt of anguish. On cue it
arrived, accompanied by a heavy dose of bitterness. He
considered deflecting her question, but how could he? This
truce had been his idea, a way to end the deadlock between
them. He couldn't backtrack now.

Hell, perhaps baring himself a little might work to his
advantage, just as he'd hoped for and witnessed her genuine appreciation for the better qualities of his island during their tour.

Still, the exercise was...hard.

'Is it really that bad?' she enquired, her voice soft, oozing sympathy he perhaps didn't deserve but couldn't help
absorbing regardless. Because he realised that when it came
to her, he was extremely selfish. Wanted more and more
and *more*.

Everything?

He clenched his gut, denying that horrifyingly damning
word that required far too much self-examination. 'Your
family isn't without its own...challenges, no?' he stalled,
brazenly buying himself time before reopening old wounds
of disgrace and betrayal.

Pained shadows flitted across her breathtaking face and
fleetingly he regretted his parry.

She stared down at her knotted fingers, then met his
gaze. 'No, it isn't, but mine is an open, ugly secret. And
before you dig deeper, I'll confess that I've hated every
single moment of it. Finding out my parents would do just
about anything, even risk bankruptcy, for the sake of social ladder-climbing was...horrifying. Being whispered

about, mocked and sometimes openly taunted about a fall from grace and being regarded as scum isn't fun. Neither is being paraded about like a prized heifer at a meat market.'

'No. I don't believe it is,' he found himself answering, for the first time catching a glimpse of what her mother's actions had done to her. He recognised the torment. But he also saw the fight in her. The ferocity it took to stand her ground. Against him. Against the world. Zak couldn't deny that the flame this added to her allure continually drew him.

Her chin lifted, eyes swimming with anguish striking him deeper than he wanted to admit. 'I can't escape my past neither can I disown my parents, but, regardless of what anyone believes, I've no wish to follow in their footsteps. If nothing else, please believe that.'

He believed her. If the past two weeks had achieved anything it was the revelation that she wasn't holding out for more. That, should he feel inclined to grant her passage off this island, Violet would walk away from him without a backward glance, his proposal and enticements and his increasing need to bestow the title of Princess on her be damned.

Again that hollow feeling of dismay threatened to consume him. He ruthlessly stemmed it. Aware that the spotlight was firmly back on him, he gritted his jaw. And bared himself. 'I looked up to him. Perhaps that was my first mistake.' He couldn't contain the deep bitterness that spilled out.

She frowned. 'Your father?'

He nodded. 'He was flawless in my eyes. The embodiment of my every aspiration. I wanted to be just like him. I wasn't going to inherit the throne, but I could walk in his footsteps.' He stopped, the words sounding foolish in his ears.

'No one is flawless, Zak,' she replied gently. 'He may have been larger than life itself to you but he was still human. Nothing more.'

Zak swallowed hard, heat and ice cascading through him at her hushed words. Hadn't he fallen for temptation himself after swearing he never would?

Had he held his father up to stricter standards than were warranted? Idolised him when he should've remembered he was mere flesh and blood? No.

'He was a *king*. He was supposed to have been above reproach. Beyond base flaws—especially flaws that caused harm to his family,' he gritted out.

'You've accepted Jules into your family. Can't you find a way to get past what your father did?'

'No! His affair with Jules's mother wasn't a fleeting thing. It went on for *years*. And while he was busy letting his family down, others were plotting behind his back. He put his kingdom in peril, gave a platform to those who would destabilise the government,' he seethed.

Violet's eyes widened in surprise. 'I...didn't know that.'

His lips twisted. 'Very few people do.'

Silence stretched tight between them. Then she laid a hand on his forearm. He looked into her brilliant blue eyes. Yearned to lose herself in them.

'Do you hate him for that or hate that he died before he could give you the answers you seek? I know I felt...robbed of the need to understand why my father would risk everything just for money.'

Damn this woman! From the very first she'd seen too much, burrowed far deeper than he'd allowed anyone else to go, save perhaps the father he now condemned.

'What does it matter?' he rasped bitterly.

'Because if it's the latter, you'll have to learn to let it go some time, Zak. To forgive and move on before it consumes you. Be the better version of the man your father couldn't be.'

The urge to rail, issue commands, assert his royal will rose fast and furious. But he knew he would be wasting his breath. Violet had no fear of him or his station. If any-thing, she would laugh in his face. So he pursed his lips, even as her words seeped deep into his soul, the truth of it ringing in his ears.

For the first time Zak knew real fear. Because what if he couldn't be a better man? What if Violet and his child found him…lacking?

With a ferocity that would've done his ancestors proud, he cut off the weakening train of thought. He was a *prince*. The blood of warriors ran through his veins. He'd never cowered before anyone. He wasn't about to start now.

'Are we done with this sharing or do you have more questions?'

Violet barely managed to stop herself from gasping at the transformation from vulnerable man to imperious prince. The loss, even more than baring her soul about her past, caught her on the raw. Because she'd glimpsed beneath the power and majesty, seen the real man who, like her, had been let down by his parent. One he'd put on a pedestal.

This was what she'd feared.

That his revelations would end up costing her even more emotionally.

Because even now, watching his stony face, she wanted to wrap her arms around him, lay her head on his chest and just…*be with him*. Be the cushion his hard edges landed on. But he was distancing himself even as she watched, his gaze growing impenetrable as he stared down at her.

Wasn't it wise to do the same?

'You said there hadn't been illegitimacy in your family besides Jules. But what about divorces?'

Grey eyes bored into hers, his attempt to read between the lines clear in his incisive gaze. 'A few, yes.'

Why did that not bring the relief she'd hoped for?

Slowly his face hardened. 'If you're already contemplating the end of a union before it's even begun—'

She forced a laugh. 'Please don't pretend what you proposed is some sort of love match. We both know it was only because I'm pregnant.'

'It's a very powerful reason. One not to be dismissed, as you seem so hell-bent on doing.'

'On our first day here you took pains to spell out what you wanted. Let me tell you what I want. I want the freedom to choose who I spend the rest of my life with. I won't settle for you simply because you happen to be the father of the child I'm carrying.'

A storm brewed in his eyes. '*Settle?* Perhaps you've been blind to the fact that all of Europe and large swathes of the Western world consider me a very big catch indeed.'

'Then they're more than welcome to you!' she responded heatedly, hurt and jealousy and the yearning for the man who'd bared himself to her minutes ago creating a wild, volatile tornado in her heart.

His eyes gleamed and Violet knew something had changed. For one thing, this was the most animated she'd allowed herself to be in his presence for quite some time. And he was savouring his triumph. 'Are you awakened at last, my sweet?'

'Don't call me that, I'm not your anything.'

Keen speculation brimmed in his eyes. 'But you could be, if only—'

'I see sense?' she finished for him. 'Your new offer is to marry you and gain the side benefit of hot sex?'

One sleek thumb brushed over her full bottom lip, a gesture that reeked too boldly of *ownership*. The kind that triggered a shivery response within her. 'I'm glad you acknowledge it will be hot. And, yes, it could be an infinitely pleasurable benefit of our marriage. Think about it.'

'You're forgetting something, Your Highness.'

'What's that?'

She took a decided step back away from temptation. 'Chemistry doesn't last for ever. Or even long enough for the ink to dry on a marriage certificate,' she pointed out. 'Thanks but, no, thanks, I won't base my future on that.'

Seconds ticked by, then Zak dragged his hands through his hair, a tense, self-mocking smile curving his lips. 'A hell of a way to start a truce, hmm?'

She shrugged. 'We seem to bring out the worst in each other, it seems.'

'I wouldn't quite call it that,' he murmured, his voice low and thick.

Alarmed she was about to drown in another torrent of emotional vulnerability, she averted her gaze from the rakish tousle of his hair and the strong bronzed throat that made her fingers itch to caress him.

He glanced at his sleek wristwatch. 'We've done enough for one day, I think. Let's get back to the villa. Dinner will be served in an hour.'

And just like that, the thought that she would be spending some more time with him sent twin pulses of pleasure and fear through her.

Because, more than anything, she wanted another glimpse at the man beneath the stiff royal exterior. Wanted to soothe his fears, share his dreams. Wanted to take her place next to him. Because *that man* was the one she hadn't quite allowed herself to dream about.

But she'd seen him, witnessed a crack in his façade. And as Zak held out his hand to her once more, Violet couldn't help the sensation growing in her heart. Or quieten the voice that whispered that the crack might fracture...perhaps even break apart to reveal his true self...with time and patience.

With love?

CHAPTER NINE

VIOLET REFUSED TO admit that the truce was the reason she took her time with dressing that evening. She was simply sharing an animosity-free meal with Zak.

He was waiting for her in the elegant dining room that opened up into a wide terrace. A sea breeze wafted in, the reminder that she was on a true tropical paradise lingering in the air.

A paradise she hadn't chosen to be on, true, but with their truce in place, she chose to suspend her outrage. Perhaps it was a foolish and slippery slope, but as she watched Zak, clad in dark tailored trousers and white, open-necked shirt, confidently stroll over to her, his gaze taking in her sea-green chiffon dress and returning to her face with latent fire in his eyes, Violet decided to just…go with the flow.

'You look exquisite,' he breathed, his low voice low pulsing with a cadence that trebled her heartbeat.

'I… Thank you.'

His lips curved in a smile as he picked up a frosted glass from the table and held it out to her. 'Here, try this.'

She accepted the offering. 'What is it?'

'A special fruit punch prepared by Geraldine. She swears it works wonders with morning sickness.'

About to ask what conversation had gone on between Zak and his housekeeper regarding her pregnancy, she decided to let it go. He'd lauded their loyalty and discretion on the day of their arrival. It stood to reason that they'd already know that she was pregnant.

She lifted the glass, the umbrella perched on it tickling

her nose as she took a sip. Delicious bursts of coconut underlain with ginger delighted her taste buds. She groaned and took the second sip.

'I take it you like it,' he said, amused.

'Oh, my God, yes, it's amazing.'

His smile widened and that treacherous, giddy sensation inside her expanded. At that exact moment she recalled her throwaway comment earlier this afternoon about the women of Europe being welcome to him.

Violet wanted to blurt out that she hadn't meant it. They weren't welcome to him. Because *she* wanted him. She bit her tongue in time, redirecting her attention to the dining table. Complete with exquisite twin candelabra, fine crystal and sterling silver cutlery, it was the most elaborate setting she'd seen since her arrival.

It was almost as if this evening was different. *Special.*

Furiously wrestling her leaping senses under control, she allowed Zak to guide her to the table.

He refilled her punch glass, poured a white Chablis for himself and sat back as the first course of poached fish and flavoured rice was served.

Registering that Zak was more interested in staring at her than in his own meal, Violet scrambled for a neutral topic. 'What's on the other side of the island?'

Again he smiled, and again her heart tripped with alarming giddiness and the mouth-watering sight of it. God, she really needed to get herself together. She couldn't swoon each time he smiled.

'It's a surprise,' he replied.

'You know all it'll take is a conversation with the staff to have my answer, don't you?'

He sat back and shrugged, unaffected by her harmless threat. 'If you wish to deny yourself the pleasure of an unbiased experience, go ahead.'

Intrigued, she stared at him, his eyes gleaming challengingly at her.

Violet was enjoying this. Far too much. While he wasn't allowing her another glimpse of the man she'd seen this afternoon, she appreciated this more casual side of Zak. Enough to explore it, see where it went?

Temptation swelling inside her, she lifted her glass and, keeping eye contact with him, took a long, deep pull of the tangy drink.

His gaze dropped to her mouth, his eyes darkening dramatically. Tiny flames leapt in her belly and her fingers trembled when she set the glass down. That set the tone for their meal, a pulse-elevating mix of heavy-lidded looks, light conversation and good food.

It took a moment for her to admit the emotion she experienced when their plates were cleared away was regret. It was barely eight, and the thought of spending the rest of the evening alone in her room dimmed her spirits.

'A non-alcoholic nightcap on the beach? Or would you like coffee here?'

He'd barely issued the invitation when she caught a whiff of coffee and her stomach lurched alarmingly. She swallowed hard, fervently praying she wouldn't disgrace herself. 'Definite *no* to the coffee. For the next few weeks at least.'

Zak stared at her with a small frown. With a flick of his hand he summoned the butler. 'Cancel the coffee and inform Geraldine she's not to serve coffee at any meal until further notice.'

'Of course, Your Highness,' Patrick responded, then swiftly exited.

'You didn't need to do that.'

Again he gestured, and the action she used to find so irritating was suddenly the sexiest thing she'd seen.

'Of course I do. Your comfort is of paramount importance.'

Violet scrambled for her good sense before it fled. 'You mean the baby's, of course.'

A weighted emotion crossed his face but was gone the next second. 'You're carrying my child but that doesn't mean your personal well-being isn't also essential.' His gaze dropped to her stomach, stayed for a pulse-racing few seconds. 'I intend to be careful with you both.'

The words burrowed deep, infusing her with warmth and eroding her attempts to guard her vulnerable emotions. She was still struggling when he rose from the table and held out his hand to her.

'A little fresh air will do you good. Hopefully by the time we return the offensive smell will be gone.'

Unable to argue with that, she placed her hand in his. He laced his fingers with hers, immediately setting off tiny fireworks beneath her skin.

Again, Violet decided to let it be.

Beyond the terrace and pristine gardens they went down shallow steps that led to the beach bathed in moonlight. When he tossed his shoes away and urged her to do the same, she didn't object. She was sticking to the spirit of their truce, she told herself.

But gradually it became much more than that.

Heavy, sensual tension lingered in the air, the kind that made her aware of every cell in her body.

When it grew too thick to bear, she frantically cast around for something to dissipate it. 'How long have you owned this place?'

His gaze slanted to her, stayed and lingered over her hair, her jaw, the swell of her bust before he answered. 'Five years. I'd been looking a long time for a place like this and made the owner an offer he didn't refuse.'

'It seems like an it's-been-in-my-family-since-the-dawn-of-time kind of place.'

One corner of his mouth lifted. 'Why would you think that?'

She shrugged. 'Isn't that the way it goes with royalty?'

He gave a low, husky laugh. The sound settled low in her pelvis, heating her up from the inside out. 'Am I being pigeonholed again, Violet?'

'Merely returning the favour,' she parried.

His smile disappeared, and he tugged on her hand to still her. 'Explain.' His voice was terse.

'Isn't that how you see me? In a specific way you won't be swayed from?' She couldn't quite keep the hurt from her voice.

'Several weeks ago, perhaps.'

The unexpected response drew a soft gasp. 'Are you saying that you no longer think I'm scheming to get my hands on your royal billions?' she tossed at him.

He studied her as a scientist would a rare and exotic specimen. 'You may be exceptional in many ways, but I don't think hiding your true character is sustainable in the long run.' He stepped closer, saturating her with his power and might and utter gorgeousness. 'I heard what you said this afternoon, Violet,' he rasped low and deep.

Heard was one thing. But did he believe her?

She wanted to ask. Wanted to lay bare every fear and secret yearning, every hope and fantasy in a way that scared her enough to pull away, attempt to disentangle her fingers from his.

He held her tight as his hand slowly rose, splayed with reverent gentleness on her stomach. Grey eyes gleaming with an emotion she couldn't name, he tugged her close once more. 'We're going to be indefinitely connected by this unique and sacred experience. Let's not default to animosity.'

'I never wanted animosity in the first place.'

His hand shifted, his palm caressing her stomach almost

possessively. 'Good, then let's address something else. This thing between us,' he drawled.

Her mouth dried, her senses jumping as she fought her own yearnings. 'What are you talking about?'

His free hand slid beneath her thick braid to grip her tighter. He pulled her closer, rested his forehead against hers. 'You're like a fever in my blood, Violet. I crave you beneath me, satisfying your every need, your beautiful body bare to my every whim.'

A deeper shiver attacked her, unravelling her from head to toe. Zak didn't miss her reaction, and smiled in pure, arrogant male satisfaction at her response to his words.

'I… I don't…'

He grazed his thumb over her lips, dredging another tremble from her soul. 'Before you deny us, think for a moment, my sweet, of how much better this truce could be if you can have me, without guilt or hesitation, anytime and anywhere you want,' he urged thickly. His voice oozed pure temptation, so much carnal promise Violet could barely keep her body upright.

Seven days of untold pleasure.

The thought that with one move he'd imprisoned her and with the other he was granting her sexual freedom was almost too much to wrap her head around.

His fierce intelligence had always astounded her, but Zak was demonstrating how he held the world effortlessly in the palm of his hand.

Even the acknowledgement that he'd guided her into the middle of this maelstrom, that she would most likely be annihilated before the tempest was over, wasn't enough to compel her back from the dizzying edge his words had propelled her to.

Seven days of indulging her every fantasy.

And then what?

She couldn't lose sight of his ultimate purpose. Everything he was doing was for his child. Well, except maybe the urge to scratch this particular itch.

But…it was the same craving she was experiencing. And wasn't this the perfect opportunity to crack that hardened emotional shell? Heal him even as she attempted to heal herself?

Her insides shook at the gleaming possibility of what could be.

His fingers drifted from her nape to her jaw, caressed her cheek as he tilted her head to meet his. 'Everything you desire will be yours,' he vowed thickly.

Did that include his heart?

She shook her head to dissipate the sudden, explosive yearning but it piled higher, dug deeper, frightening her with the strength of it. But even as she fought, she knew she was going to accept Zak's proposition.

The chance for something *more* was too tempting.

Lifting a trembling hand, she glided it over his wrist, laid over her cheek, and pressed his touch deeper into her skin.

Flames leapt in his eyes but he remained a solid, desperate foot away from her. 'Do you agree, Violet?'

'What do you think?'

'I think I want the pleasure of hearing you say yes,' he answered, a sensual edge rimming his voice.

Her heart banged against her ribs. 'Yes, I agree.'

With a thick groan, he freed their connecting fingers, placed his palm in the small of her back, and tugged her into his body.

Violet experienced a stunning new level of sensuality as his tongue probed raw and deep, with an edge of possessiveness that snatched the breath from her lungs. With effortless ease, he lifted her, plastered her body against his in a shameless demonstration of his physical prowess that had her groaning and clinging to him.

When he urged her legs around his waist, Violet gladly

complied, her sense swimming when the action imprinted his thick potent manhood against her heated core.

They both groaned, their breaths growing ragged as they strained together, right there on his perfect beach.

'I want to lay you here on the sand, share you with the moonlight as I bury myself deep inside you. But not tonight. Tonight I will take you in my bed.'

Zak was already moving, only one destination in mind as he strode with gritted-jaw purpose back to the villa.

Violet didn't take a breath until the doors of his master suite slammed behind them. Then the reality of what she'd agreed threatened to overwhelm her. As if he knew her depths of her emotion, Zak placed a gentle kiss on her lips.

Eyes locked on hers, he walked over to the wide, inviting bed and eased her to her feet. 'Turn around,' he instructed gruffly.

Glad for the brief reprieve of not staring at his overwhelming perfection, she obliged him. But the brush of his hand at her nape, the sound of him lowering her zipper created a whole new set of sizzling anticipation.

The dress pooled at her feet, and he inhaled sharply. 'Once again I find you without a bra. Is it your intention to torture me at every turn?'

She cast a glance over her shoulder. 'How is this torture?'

'Because now I'll spend far too much time obsessing over your state of undress beneath your clothes,' he griped.

Female satisfaction curled through her. 'Oh.'

His teeth bared in a smile that was near feral enough to make her toes curl into the carpet, Zak stepped forward, curling one large hand over her bottom. Her breath hitched in her throat as he squeezed her bottom and one breast at the same time.

'It's going to drive me insane, you know that, don't you?'

Violet groaned, the idea of Zak thinking about her in

that way not an unpleasant one. In fact, it was so pleasing she smiled.

'Ah, there it is again, that sassy little acknowledgement of your power. Are you ready to experience mine now, my sweet?'

He plucked one nipple, squeezed and tormented that tight little bud until her body was a column of fire racked with deep, carnal shivers.

Her gasps only spurred him on, his body bowing over hers as he stoked her pleasure with his other hand.

She moaned his name again as he lightly bit the sensitive skin beneath her ear. Expertly manipulating those three little points of sensation was all it took for Violet to tumble over the edge, free-falling into bliss so acute, a wild scream erupted from her throat.

When she came to, her upper body was draped over the side of the bed, Zak's arm around her waist holding up as he dragged her panties down her legs.

'I've dreamt of taking you like this,' he rasped, his voice barely discernible through the miasma of lust. 'Do you want this, Principessa?'

'Please,' she begged.

He gave a gruff exhalation, then came the sound of him impatiently disrobing.

One hand caressed her from nape to spine, then with a firm grip on her waist Zak thrust deep into her liquid core.

Pleasure lit up her spine, making Violet toss her head as he stroked inside her.

'*Dio mio*, you're so beautiful. Exceptional.' Words tumbled from his lips, alternately in English and Montegovan, every time driving her closer to another peak of wonder that robbed her of the ability to breathe.

All she could do was grip the sheets, her cries urging him on until with a soul-deep scream she gave herself over to deeper, more intense bliss.

Zak followed close behind, wrapping his body around hers and holding her tight as his guttural shouts echoed alongside hers, filling the room with the ferocity of their pleasure.

He held on tight to her as she floated, weightless, through her climax. When they were both spent, he eased her back onto the bed before joining her and draping her over his body.

Violet's heart dipped alarmingly when he drifted soft kisses over her face and tucked her head beneath his chin. It was a world removed from the aftermath of their coming together in Tanzania. So...special that Violet didn't even want to breathe, lest the moment be ruined.

'You're deafening me with how hard you're thinking, *carissima*.' He caught his finger beneath her chin and lifted her gaze to his. 'Don't tie yourself in knots over this.'

'Fine, then distract me,' she said.

It was like offering the Big Bad Wolf a feast. Pure male anticipation dripped from his blinding smile. 'Oh, the things I have in mind for you...' He kissed her deep and long, and then reluctantly pulled back. 'But for now it would please me if you rested.'

Almost as if her body was designed to obey his every command, a pleasant sort of weariness swept over her. And with her arm wrapped tight over his waist she slept.

While she hadn't quite doubted his words, Violet had no frame of reference for what Zak meant. She could only bear slack-jawed witness to both his sexual prowess and the sheer depth of his intelligence over the next seven days.

By specific instruction, or simply because they were trained that well, the staff kept a discreet distance as Zak introduced her to sensual pleasure all over his villa.

And they talked. Politics, diplomacy and her favourite

subject—conservation. Deep, illuminating conversation that challenged and enlightened.

While he was reluctant to revisit the subject of his father, she gleaned that he adored his mother, perhaps even appreciated her more for her strength in the face of scandal and betrayal.

It was in the aftermath of one such exchange that a kernel of apprehension sprouted. Because it was basking in the spotlight of his full attention, revelling in another heated debate while he caressed her body, and his growing reluctance to leave her side for any length of time that made Violet start to fear for her heart.

In those moments her yearning for him bloomed, threatened to scatter wild and free. To open her most secret emotions to this god of a man with almost overbearing intelligence and faultless pedigree.

The man who leaned attentively closer when she made a point, who challenged her opinion and nodded with appreciation when she succinctly delivered it. Who held her in his arms while she pretended to sleep, the fear that she was losing herself in him leaving her wide awake and terrified. Because she was right, after all. The man beneath the princely surface was the man she wanted for herself. The father she craved for her child.

So it was with mingled relief and trepidation that she opened her eyes on the seventh day since their little tryst and truce began. She struggled not to read anything into the fact that it was the only day she'd woken alone in all that time.

Their lovemaking had been even more intense the night before, the unspoken knowledge that this was their last night together driving the need to extract the most from their last encounter. She'd lost count of how many times she'd shattered with ultimate bliss, had been boneless when Zak had lowered them both into a soothing bath, had washed and dried her body before placing her back in his bed.

The conflicting thoughts stayed with her as she readied herself for breakfast. Dressed in a knee-length yellow wraparound dress, she sat at her dressing table, her fingers tight around her hairbrush.

Zak hadn't asked her to marry him at any point in the last seven days and, perversely, the absence of it had only made her obsess over it.

Would marriage to him be so bad?

He was a royal with billions at his disposal, but he was as committed to conservation and preservation as she was. Could they make a marriage work based on common interests and amazing sex alone or was she deluding herself?

What about her mother?

Margot had gone suspiciously silent in the last few days. The tabloids had been equally silent on her mother's activities, an unusual occurrence since Margot lived for the society pages. Unease slid down Violet's spine as she set the brush down and left the room.

She'd have to face her mother sooner or later. Deliver news of the pregnancy. And then what? Tell her that she'd turned down Zak's proposal or that she'd agreed?

Her heart flipped over. Was she really considering saying yes? To seeing him every day, to sharing his bed, connecting with someone who shared her professional passion?

What about love? The suspicion that ultimately this was only about the child she carried?

She froze as she neared the terrace. Could she marry Zak knowing she was second best behind his need to claim his child? Could she live with that?

Yes, her inner voice urged, even while her spirits dipped.

Could they build on that too, find their way to emotional fulfilment the way they already enjoyed sex and conversation?

She ignored the widening dismay that mocked her scrambled, pathetic excuses. Either she was going into this with her eyes wide open to the fact that Zak didn't see her as anything other than the womb carrying his child and the woman warming his bed, or this threatening heartache would flatten her harder the—

'Do you intend to linger in the doorway all day, *cara*?'

She jumped at the sound of his deep voice and despite the misgivings eating her alive stepped outside, her gaze magnetically drawn to where he sat, resplendent in the sunlight. She went hot all over again not at all surprised when her heart slammed against her ribs at the sight of him.

The thought of losing him sent an acute chill through her, and Violet knew she couldn't turn her back on whatever Zak's proposal entailed.

'What's wrong?'

The sharp enquiry was edged with the fierce determination in his eyes. Her breath stalled, her tongue clinging to the words she wanted to utter. Registering that his edginess had been present when he'd swept her off to bed last night, that she'd been too caught up to heed the look, never mind uncover what it meant, sent another wave of anxiety over her.

Dragging in a steadying breath, she approached and sat down. 'Zak, we need to talk.'

Shadows sharpened his features as he raised a laconic eyebrow at her. 'Do we?'

She slicked her tongue over her lower lip, the enormity of the step she was about to take consuming her whole. 'You know we do.'

Stormy eyes held hers for another ferocious second before he waved at the table. 'Geraldine has prepared everything you like. Don't let it go to waste.'

Suspicion that he was avoiding the subject jangled her nerves even more. She should be grateful for the brief reprieve to consider her decision. But with each morsel she swallowed, the giddiness grew, the urge to blurt that *Yes, I'll marry you*, even entertain that very male satisfaction at finally extracting the answer he wanted, suffusing her.

She thought of what would come after, the many nights and days she would spend with Zak, welcoming their child into the world, nurturing him or her...

Her hand shook with sheer elation, a world removed from the initial dismay she'd felt minutes ago. Setting her teacup down before it spilled, she laced her fingers in her lap and cleared her throat. 'It's been seven days, Zak—'

'Technically, it hasn't. Label me pedantic but we have until mid-afternoon before our time is truly up.'

She couldn't wait that long. She couldn't wait another *minute*. 'Fine, but I think you should know I'm...considering—'

The butler's diplomatic throat-clearing interrupted her.

'What it is?' Zak asked, his eyes narrowed on her face, cataloguing the nerves eating her alive.

'My apologies for the interruption, Your Highness, but His Majesty, your brother, is on the phone for you.'

He rose. 'I have to take it. Excuse me, Violet.'

'But—'

'I don't think it's a good idea to keep the King waiting, do you?' he said drily.

And yet as he walked away, she suspected he would've done exactly that if it'd suited him.

The real possibility that he'd changed his mind siphoned every scrap of joy she'd managed to fool herself into believing she would enjoy by agreeing to marry him.

She finished breakfast, eating more for sustenance than enjoyment. As if to match her mood, stormclouds rolled fast and frantic over the horizon, throwing dark shadows over the villa within minutes.

Torn between awaiting Zak's return and retreating, she

lingered until heavy raindrops began to hammer the pave-stones. Then, restless, anxious and more than a little hor-rified at the sheer depths of a loss she hadn't even suffered yet, she went up to her suite and opened her laptop.

There was still no word from her mother but her boss back in the UK had emailed, asking for a tentative date for her return.

The need to inform Zak of her decision resurged, pro-pelling her from the room. As she'd done so many times since her arrival, she entered his domain via the library, a habit that drew a small smile.

The sound of Zak's deep voice stopped her short. She didn't want to interrupt his conversation with his brother. Deciding to wait rather than return to her suite, Violet froze as a painfully familiar voice answered Zak's crisp query via speakerphone.

Zak was talking to her mother?

She barely registered moving closer to the study door, pressing her ear against the cool wood. The dulcet tones that announced her mother's excitement contained another much-too-familiar pitch, one that spelled absolute triumph, a coup she couldn't wait to crow about. A chill swept over her skin, seeping ice into Violet's soul. Decades of shame lashed her as her mother continued, 'You have my word, Zak. The interview will be tasteful and any that follow will be arranged in consultation with your people.'

'And the nondisclosure agreement?'

Violet pressed her fist to her mouth to prevent an an-guished gasp from escaping.

'My lawyer looked it over yesterday and all is well. Your lawyers should have the signed copies by now. But it really wasn't necessary. You're going to be family soon enough,' her mother gushed, 'and you've already been so generous, paying off my debts and gifting me a house in Montegova for when my grandchild arrives. I should be offended that you'd even feel the need for a non-disclosure agreement.' She laughed off the insult.

Violet couldn't see it but well imagined Zak's arrogant shrug. 'I'm sure your sensibilities will recover from my need to ensure no loopholes are left in securing what's mine.'

Violet's soul shrivelled to dust.

'Of course,' Margot gushed even more. 'The crew is arriving shortly. May I be excused?'

'You may,' Zach answered, his voice containing that edge Violet had heard at the breakfast table. 'I look forward to seeing the outcome.'

'You won't be disappointed, Your Highness.'

Her mother's voice was cut off abruptly, leaving only the sound of the blood rushing through Violet's ears as the ominous death knell of the foolish dreams she'd harboured.

She stumbled back from the door, glad for the Aubusson rug that hid her footfalls, even while she prayed she wouldn't be discovered, granting Zak the excuse to keep her here, devise another cold, calculated strategy to claim his child.

She didn't take a breath until she reached the kitchen.

Geraldine took one look at her and went into mother hen mode, the exact reaction she wanted.

'I'm not feeling great. I think the storm disturbed me more than I thought,' Violet said.

'Oh, don't worry, miss. They tend to pass quickly here.'

Violet nodded abstractly. 'I'm going to lie down. Can you make sure I'm not disturbed by anyone, including Zak?'

The housekeeper frowned but nodded. 'Of course, miss.'

She fled, feeling a twinge of guilt at using her pregnancy as an excuse. A sob clogged her throat as she hurried up the steps. She held it in until she reached her suite.

Then the torrent came.

He'd used the truce to pull the wool over her eyes, while

orchestrating her mother's co-operation with financial incentives and the limelight Margot adored so much. He'd made Violet believe they had a foundation to build a relationship on. And she'd fallen wholesale for the illusion. Given her body, soul, mind and one vital part she desperately feared would never be reclaimed.

She'd given Zak Montegova her heart.

And he'd shattered it.

CHAPTER TEN

Violet feared she would never be whole again.

But gluing her shattered pieces together would have to come later. Right now, she was still trapped on this island, her every vulnerability exposed.

She pulled herself up in bed, her jaw clenching tight. He may have imprisoned her, but hadn't she turned the tables on him for two weeks? She scrubbed at her eyes, blinking when further tears threatened. All she needed was to stage the performance of a lifetime once again, and finally convince him that she would co-operate.

Her heart screamed with agony, strenuously fighting the thought of being separated from the owner, who had no regard for it. Fists clenched tight, she rehearsed her role, acted out every imaginable outcome in her head.

Rising, she entered the bathroom, washed away all traces of tears and touched up the blotchiness with make-up.

The sooner she confronted Zak, the sooner she would gain her freedom.

The gown she wore to Remi's wedding had been dry-cleaned. Matching shoes located, she hurriedly dressed and retrieved her weekend bag. She exited, denying herself one last look at the room. The staccato echo of her heels fell in tandem with her racing heart as she approached the hallway leading to Zak's study.

Her heart lurched when the door was wrenched open.

Zak stood framed in the doorway. '*Cara*, I was told you weren't feeling—' He stopped, his expression morphing from false concern to shock to fury when he took in her attire and the case in her hand. 'What the hell do you think you're doing?' he demanded.

'What does it look like? I'm leaving.'

For a fraction of time she fooled herself into thinking she glimpsed utter bleakness in his eyes. Then his arrogant head reared up, his gaze icing over. 'What happened to talking?'

'I think we've said everything that needs saying.'

He jerked away from the doorway, bringing that deceptive, irresistible magnificence one step closer. 'Violet—'

She stopped him with a dismissive flick of her hand, silently congratulating herself for emulating his imperious gesture. 'There's no point rehashing this all over again, Zak. As you said last week, it's grown boring and tedious.'

Aquiline nostrils flared. 'This has gone infinite ways beyond that and you know it.'

'All I know is that you're holding me here against my will. Your time's up, Zak. Let's end this now before any of this comes back to bite you.' He opened his mouth but again she stopped him. 'Think of the scandal that you're courting by perpetuating this farce, and let's be sensible about it.'

Eyes narrowed, his strong jaw worked as he stared at her with a ferocity that nearly unseated her performance. 'You wanted to talk to me at breakfast. Was this what you intended to say?' he asked, his voice a blade of ice.

She pretended to frown. 'Possibly. I forget now. Blame my hormones.' Again she sent a tiny plea for forgiveness to her baby. 'It's inconsequential now.'

Laser beam eyes probed her. 'What the hell is going on here, Violet? What exactly are you trying to achieve with this performance?'

Terror struck at the threat of discovery. Somehow, she dredged up a scornful laugh. 'You keep saying it's a performance. Is it really so hard to accept that I've had enough of this place? Enough of you?'

His face grew tight, the skin surrounding his lips whitening. Still he came at her, as if he wanted to test her determination up close.

Violet stood her ground, barely holding it together when every cell in her body wanted to retreat from the overwhelming potency of him. She didn't even dare breathe for fear that his addictive scent would demolish her. She raised her chin a fraction higher and met his gaze. 'You have no choice, Zak. You gave me your word. Now let me go.'

For the longest time he didn't respond. His gaze blazed with fury, but Violet caught another emotion in the grey depths. Uncertainty. A hint of vulnerability.

But soon they evaporated as his gaze dropped with sizzling intent to her belly. To the hint of a curve where their child grew. 'You won't get very far with what's mine, Violet,' he vowed.

Her heart lurched at the throb of deep possession in his voice, but it was nothing compared to the leap of her senses at the thought that leaving here today wouldn't quite be the last time she encountered Zak. They would be tied together for ever by their child.

But at what cost? Her sanity? This deep craving she knew in her bones was more than lust? More than simple enthralment with every single thing about him?

It would shatter her completely. She knew that too in her bones. 'I had a feeling you would say that. Expect a letter from my solicitors in the next week or so.'

He inhaled sharply. 'Are you sure you wish to engage in legal battles with me?' he enquired, his tone deadly.

'Of course not. I expect a *civil* discourse between us concerning this baby. It's up to you if you wish to turn it into a battle.'

He shook his head, as if he couldn't quite grasp her response.

Violet wanted to laugh but she daren't, fearing she'd

most likely dissolve into more sobs. She'd cried enough already.

His face turned into a cold mask. 'You should really reconsider. You don't know what you're inviting on yourself with this course of action.'

'I have. You may have wealth, but I have the power and I suspect you won't want to drag your brother and his sparkling new reign through the dirt, all in the name of taking my child away from me. Try it and I'll tell the world everything you've done to me in the last three weeks.'

Stark shock mingled with the fury. 'How did I fool myself into thinking you were different?' he rasped.

Violet allowed herself a small, stiff smile and no more. 'Go easy on yourself, Zak. After all, I fooled myself into thinking the very same of you.'

He stiffened with rigid affront, thunderclouds rolling over his face as he stared at her.

Unable to stand it any longer, she pivoted away from him.

'I'm happy to leave by speedboat if that gets me off this island quicker. I'll be in the living room when it's ready to leave. Goodbye, Zak.'

He didn't respond. And with every step she took away from him, Violet felt his ferocious gaze boring into her skin. She prayed that he wouldn't follow even as her shockingly traitorous heart prayed he would.

When he didn't…when all she received was a message from the butler to say his plane would arrive in three hours to take her off the island, she cursed the silent, defiant tears that poured out of her broken heart.

Zak stood at his study window, eyes fixed on the plane poised at the start of the runway. The intermittent thunderstorms that had pummelled the villa throughout the day had finally receded and his pilot had been cleared for take-off.

His fingers clenched hard, shooting pain up his arms. He ignored it, the strain of remaining in control demanding every ounce of his willpower.

He couldn't believe he'd spent the past week with an illusion. That Violet had taken exactly she'd wanted and then left him.

What he had offered her, the inner voice insisted.

He snarled under his breath, wishing with every bone in his body that he could move from the window, wrench his gaze from the plane taking her away from him.

She never belonged to you.

He'd taken steps to protect his family, his child, and it'd backfired. That was all.

No, that wasn't all. At this exact moment she was taking his heart away from him and he didn't mean the child she carried.

Her beautiful smile.

Her laughter.

Her intelligence, vitality and passion.

Everything he hadn't known was essential to him until the moment he'd seen her in that blasted gown, clutching that godforsaken weekend bag. She'd walked away with everything he feared he would need to be able to breathe again.

Because somewhere between New York and Tanzania and the Caribbean, he'd fallen in love with Violet Barringhall. And once again he'd experienced the true depths of betrayal and shattered dreams.

But…had she really betrayed him?

She'd promised him nothing save the pleasure of the body she'd given selflessly.

In his supreme arrogance he'd believed he could sway her with his royal pedigree and the title of Princess, when the only thing that brought her truly alive was her work.

The irony of it, he reflected bitterly, that he'd thrown a

proposal at the feet of the only woman who would reject him so resoundingly. What did Violet want that he lacked? The question echoed in his mind as he watched the plane gather speed.

Fingers unclenched, he braced them against the cool glass window, a deep rumble erupting from his chest, gaining momentum as the plane's engines grew louder, forcefully announcing that he'd failed, that he'd gambled and lost, his very heart torn from his chest.

The pain grew. Unable to contain it, Zak released it in a loud bellow, both hands clenching in his hair as the aircraft lifted into the air and banked steeply. Its sleek wings caught the sunlight, delivering a mocking wink before righting itself again.

He barely registered stumbling to his desk, blinded by the overwhelming sense of loss hollowing his insides. Every sinew strained for action, specifically one that involved calling his pilot, ordering the plane back to the island. But what Violet didn't know was that all his excuses for his actions were no longer valid.

His general had finally located the rebels.

And with Remi's own news this morning that his new wife was pregnant, and a public announcement was imminent, any immediate threat to Montegova and his family were effectively neutralised.

By ordering Violet back, wasn't he compounding his sins by acting as his bloodthirsty ancestors had in centuries past? The simple truth was that she didn't want him. Had no interest in his royal pedigree, his wealth...*nothing*.

Accepting the stark truth took several swigs from his favourite vintage cognac. But an hour later Zak was still clear-eyed, his pain just as all-consuming. With a grimace, he tossed the mostly full bottle aside. He'd suffered through his father's betrayal, through the scandal of Jules's arrival in their lives, had put out several different fires in the name of family since then.

He would handle this too.

First thing tomorrow he'd instruct his lawyers to begin the process of claiming his child.

And you're happy with her hating you even more than she does now?

He growled at the inner voice. It persisted, his conscience…an almost evangelic need to make Violet happy despite her rejection of him forcing him to reconsider that action.

Desperate, he mentally replayed their last conversation at the breakfast table.

'Zach, I think you should know I'm considering…'

His heart leapt, defying his usual circumspection and cynicism. Considering what? Accepting his proposal?

Had he shut her off too soon, fearing the very rejection she'd delivered such a short time later? He dragged frantic fingers through his hair. Had he destroyed any chance of making her his? *Dio mio…* Or becoming hers?

He reached for the phone, this time to summon his pilot to turn the plane around for a completely different reason. To plead for the woman he loved.

Instead, the phone rang.

Wild hope flaring in his heart, he picked it up.

Margot Barringhall's panicked voice cut through his greeting. 'Zak… Your Highness, we have a problem.'

Ice doused his veins. 'What is it?'

'I don't know how it happened but… Violet just called me. I… She knows about you paying off my debts, about the house in Montegova… She knows everything—'

His vision blurred for a moment, that wild hope dying a swift, merciless death. 'How?' Even as the hoarse demand erupted from his throat, he knew.

She'd overheard him.

Heard and had rightly condemned him for his actions. Dread spiralled through him. 'Did you explain things to her?'

'No… I couldn't, could I? I signed the NDA—'

Zak bit back a snarl, the thought that she would leave her daughter to suffer just so she wouldn't lose out financially making him want to lash out.

But he couldn't. The blame was his alone. He'd acted without consulting her, taken steps to mitigate circumstances that might never have arisen. For all he knew, Margot Barringhall could've surprised him the way her daughter had already stunned him.

But hard lessons that'd shaped his life had urged him to react in the only way he knew how. He refocused as Margot's undisguised panic drilled into his skull.

'She's threatening to disown me, Zak. She wants nothing to do with me. I might never meet my grandchild. I… You need to do something. *Please*. I can't lose her.'

Zak hung up, his skin ashen, his mouth a thin white line. Margot Barringhall may have discovered her humanity too late to salvage her relationship with her daughter. And if Violet was threatening to disown her own mother, what chance did he have with her?

He'd faced down tyrants and dictators in his time in the military, thwarted threats against his family. Why did the thought of dealing with one woman terrify him?

Because she wasn't just any woman.

She was the woman he loved.

Violet focused the fragments of attention she could summon on the wide screen that tracked the plane's flight path to London. As if keeping it in sight would dull the pain rippling through her veins. She'd prayed she'd got it wrong, that she'd misinterpreted Zak's conversation. But her mother's caginess and eventual confession that her NDA forbade her from discussing her agreement with Zak had killed any last dregs of hope.

Seven short hours.

Then she could find a quiet hotel to hide away in. Having given up the flat she'd shared with Sage after her twin's departure and her own temporary relocation to New York, Violet had nowhere to go save the house she'd grown up in, and she had no intention of returning to Barringhall. It hadn't felt like home in a long time anyway. Knowing the very roof over her head was paid for with greed and shameless money-grabbing antics had soured it for her a long time ago.

She would give herself a few days, then start flat-and job-hunting. She had a baby coming. As much as she wanted to wallow in misery she—

She sucked in a breath as the plane banked sharply to the left. That in itself wasn't unusual, but the onscreen map flickering off for a moment before returning with a different destination was what stopped her breath completely.

He wouldn't dare!

Please, God, let him not do this. Violet didn't think she could stand it. The moment the plane righted itself, she grabbed the phone that handily announced its connection with the pilot.

He answered on the first ring. 'My apologies, Lady Barringhall, I was about to step out and apprise you of the flight plan change.'

'Tell me we're not returning to the island?'

'Ah… I'm afraid I can't.' It didn't help that he sounded genuinely regretful.

It didn't help that her heart leapt for a wild, shameful moment before crashing harder than before. It didn't help that when they landed back on the island an hour later, Zak stood on the tarmac, uncaring that his hair was wildly tousled by the turbulent air or that the all-white linen shirt and trousers only highlighted his perfection.

But she *could* help staying in her seat long after the pilot disembarked with his crew.

And she remained seated, her heart in her throat, as Zak watched her through the window until his staff drove away. Only then did he mount the stairs into the plane.

It'd only been a few hours since she'd seen him, but it felt like a lifetime had passed. He still looked devilishly breathtaking.

Formidable. Imperious. Calculating as he paused at the front of the plane, stormcloud eyes devouring her. After an age he turned to the door and pressed a series of buttons. In under a minute they were sealed in.

Panic flared through her but she fought to keep it from showing. 'I'm starting to think you have a bondage fetish, Your Highness. Shall I add that to the list of your sins?'

He sauntered down the aisle, his watchful gaze unwavering. Expecting him to take the seat opposite, Violet let out a soft gasp when he sank to his knees in front of her. 'Tell me what you intended to say at breakfast this morning, Violet.'

'I told you, I don't remember—'

He leaned forward, his throat moving convulsively. 'Please, *carissima*. Tell me,' he implored.

'Why?' she whispered.

His hands suddenly gripped hers, their fine tremor triggering an earthquake inside her. 'Because I suspect I made a very terrible mistake in not delaying taking my brother's call.'

The air left her lungs but she fought against the tendrils of hope teasing her shattered emotions. 'Did Remi really call?'

He frowned, then nodded. 'Of course. He called to tell me I'm to become an uncle. Why would you think otherwise?'

She held his gaze without answering, her eyes widening when sharp regret darkened his eyes. 'You think I deceived you,' he declared.

'I spoke to my mother, Zak. And I heard you this morning.'

'I know you did. She called to inform me.'

She gasped, pain stabbing her heart. 'So what is this? Why bring me back here?'

'Because I'm learning that my way of doing things won't always reap the results I want.'

'You think?'

His eyes glinted, his gaze dropping to her mouth before his expression tightened. 'The moment you informed me you were carrying our child, very little else ceased to matter except ensuring your safety and welfare.'

She shook her head. 'Don't wrap it up in concern for me. You wanted me out of the way, hidden away like some dirty little secret—'

'Hidden away, yes, but not like a secret.' His jaw gritted for a moment before he continued. 'My other reasons still apply but...my father's generals, men he trusted, tried to target the throne within hours of his death. Montegova was birthed through war and bloodshed. My people can be a little...bloodthirsty. Luckily, I had a network of trusted men who don't believe in senseless violence and tyranny.'

'Is that why you've kept an eye on the current general?'

He nodded. 'I vowed that we wouldn't get caught with our guard down ever again. That included removing you from any possible line of attack.'

She gasped. 'Why didn't you tell me?'

'I was going to, eventually. But...this last week was special and I selfishly wanted to hang onto it.' She was busy catching her breath when he added, 'And then I was made aware of your mother's activities.'

Her heart dropped. 'My mother?'

His lips firmed. 'She was pitting tabloids against each other, hoping to start a bidding war on a story about you. And me.'

A hot wave of shame engulfed her. But even through it, bitterness at his actions remained. 'And so you bought her off.'

'I offered her a different...better alternative.'

'An alternative?'

'A chance to celebrate her coming grandchild, rather than capitalise financially on the occasion. An interview with a journalist of my choice, to be aired with your strict approval once the baby was born and once you'd vetted every word. In return, I offered to settle her debts.'

'What else did you do? Tell her to pressure me to marry you? To keep all of this from her own daughter under threat of persecution from your non-disclosure agreement?'

His lips firmed, but he didn't deny any of it. 'Perhaps I was delusional but I didn't want to entertain the thought that this week would end with you refusing to marry me. *Dio mio*, the possibility of you leaving me, despite everything I'd done...' He shook his head. 'I'm used to winning, Violet. To being in control.'

'Because everyone around you expects it? Don't you know that's unrealistic?'

'If I can't hold myself accountable, how can I expect others to be?'

She frowned, her heart lurching at the pain in his voice. 'Are you talking about your father again?'

Cold bleakness filled his eyes before they dropped to the hands clutching hers. 'I wasted years believing he could walk on water. I even excused him when he didn't display much affection, when he seemed especially harsh.' He shrugged. 'Trying to live with that lie has been...hard.'

She didn't realise she'd twisted her fingers to entwine

with his until he lifted hers to kiss her knuckles. 'He shattered your trust, but not everyone is like that.'

'Perhaps it was my misfortune to encounter those who reinforced that belief.'

'Am I lumped with that lot?'

Her heart leapt when he immediately shook his head. 'Not you, Violet. You turned my suspicions inside out. *Dio*, you turned me inside out,' he rasped fervently. 'Your passion. Your beauty. Your spirit, challenging me at every turn. I was addicted to you long before I had you in Tanzania.'

Her heart banged against her ribs. 'What…what are you saying, Zak?'

'That telling me about the baby was the perfect strategy I used to attempt to bind you to me. I could've picked anywhere in the world to bring you but I picked this island because I wanted to show you what we had in common. What we could achieve together.'

'I saw,' she murmured, almost too afraid to hope. 'I saw and I yearned for it. So much it frightened me.'

He froze. 'Violet?' Her name was a thick, husky imploration.

She swayed towards him. 'Yes, Zak.'

'Tell me what you meant to say this morning,' he repeated.

'Why?'

Piercing eyes probed hers, his intentions blazing ferociously. 'Because I love you. I will give my life to protect you and our child. I regret taking your choices away. Because I'm obsessed with you, with your passion. With your body. With your grace. With the humbling thought that you're the one carrying my child, giving me the opportunity to be the kind of father I wanted mine to be.'

The depth of feeling in his voice shook her to the core. 'Zak…'

'Most of all, I want to do everything in my power to

make you the happiest woman alive if it's your intention to stay or move mountains to earn your love at some point in the future.'

'So you're not going to sic your lawyers on me?' she teased.

'They're at the ready to agree to your every stipulation.'

'*Carte blanche*? Really?'

A humbled look crossed his face, but since Zak was who he was, it didn't linger for long. 'I trust you, Violet. I've seen into your heart. I know you won't keep my child from me simply to make us both suffer.'

Perhaps it was that final endorsement. Perhaps it was the pregnancy hormones. With a tearful gasp, she leaned into him until their noses brushed, until she was breathing his essence into herself, filling every cracked corner of her heart with him, letting him make her whole again.

'Zak?'

'*Si, cara?*' he replied thickly, his gaze shifting from her eyes to her mouth.

'I was going to say yes. Because I love and adore you too. Because I want to wear that ring you kept threatening me with. Because I want to be not just the Principessa on paper but the queen of your heart. Because I want half a dozen babies, and you seem enthusiastic enough to fulfil that particular fantasy.'

He caught her in his arms and laid her on the plush carpet in the aisle. 'I don't know, *amore*, it's been a whole twelve hours since I last had you. I could be rusty, you know.'

She slid her arms around his neck. 'Then we'd better find out, yes?'

'Indeed, *mi amore*,' he breathed as he divested her of her clothes. 'With my love, my soul, and my everlasting pleasure.'

* * * * *

THE ITALIAN'S
PREGNANT
CINDERELLA

CAITLIN CREWS

CHAPTER ONE

MONACO AGAIN.

It was fitting, really.

Julienne Boucher had been working toward this moment with single-minded passion and bone-deep determination for the past ten years, and it made a certain sense that when she crossed the finish line at long last, she would do it here. At the Grand Hotel in Monte Carlo where she had first come ten years ago.

To sell herself.

Julienne's perilously high heels clicked against the sumptuous marble floors of the Grand Hotel as she walked, passing the flower arrangements that had looked like colorful, exotic jungles to her unsophisticated eyes back then. The lobby had been just as smugly opulent, but the difference was that back then, she'd been terrified that everyone was looking at her. That they knew what she'd come to do. That they could *see* her shame and panic, and more, her determination to go ahead and do it anyway.

Because she had to.

She'd wondered if the horrible men in the village

she'd come from—and had escaped earlier that same day—had been right all along. That Boucher women were made for one thing only, the whores. And if that was true, could *everyone* see that truth all over her? Or was it more of a bad smell…in this place that was lightly scented with ease and wealth and refinement?

Now she knew that if anyone bothered to look at her, what they would see was the elegant, self-possessed woman she'd fought so hard to become. Day by day. Year by year. A woman who was not only sophisticated, but looked as if she belonged in hotels like this one that were more properly works of art.

Because she did. She'd made sure she did.

Julienne could almost see the ghost of her former self walking beside her, reflecting all those nerves and that bone-deep desolation back from the gilt-edged, shiny surfaces, the fragrant orchids, the giddy chandeliers.

This time around, she was healthy. Well fed and well clothed instead of balancing on the precarious edge of total destruction, homeless and penniless. Most important, she was no longer a desperate teenager. No longer a scared sixteen-year-old, bleakly determined to do what she had to do to save her younger sister. Even if that meant losing herself.

Thinking of Fleurette cut through the haunting memories of ten years back and Julienne paused, there outside the famously luxurious lounge bar that catered to the world's wealthiest. Something she had guessed at then, but knew for a fact now.

Fleurette did not believe in ghosts. She had grown these last ten years, too, and was no longer a fragile waif, sickly and scared. These days Julienne's younger sister was a force to be reckoned with in every regard. From her brash sleeves of brightly colored tattoos to her defiant piercings and multicolored hair forever cut short, Fleurette made it clear with her every word and deed that she would never be *desperate* again. For anything.

"You've finally done it," Fleurette had said with her usual brisk impatience when Julienne had called her earlier. "That last deal has to be worth billions alone. I think we can both agree that you've adequately repaid the man's kindness. In spades."

Julienne had made an assenting noise, but she wasn't as certain as her sister. About anything, if she was honest—but particularly about this.

Because Cristiano Cassara had saved them. And not in a metaphoric sense. He had literally saved their lives that evening ten years ago when he could as easily have hastened their decline or simply ignored their predicament altogether. He had kept the two of them from a dark spiral into almost certain death on the streets—if not that night, then not long after it, because that was how that particular trajectory went. Julienne knew that all too well. But she hadn't had to test herself against a downward slope into hell that ate girls just like her alive every day. Because Cristiano had whisked both Julienne and Fleurette away into a brand-new life, asked for nothing in return and had left them to it with no interference.

Which meant that repaying him for what he'd done had consumed Julienne's life ever since.

She had followed him here, to the place it was rumored he came to relax once a year—though Julienne could not imagine the stern, austere head of the Cassara Corporation allowing his spine to curve the faintest inch, much less *relaxing* in any meaningful way. Julienne had worked for the man for almost ten full years and had never seen the faintest stirrings of a smile on his forbidding face.

Not even a *hint*.

Julienne blew out a long breath and checked her appearance for the hundredth time in one of the shiny mirrors that graced nearly every wall and surface, the better to reflect back to the rich and famous their most favorite view of all—themselves.

Another thing it had taken years to learn. No one in a place like this had time to look at others. Not when they were so busy gazing at themselves.

The truth was, she already knew full well that she was groomed to perfection.

That had been part of the payment she had offered her benefactor from almost the first, though he had never asked for such a thing. Nor noticed that she'd provided it.

But then, she was the one who had been there that night ten years ago, right here in this hotel. She was the one who'd taken her sister and run from the vicious little hill town where they'd been born, abandoned and repeatedly betrayed by what little family they'd had, supposed friends, and vindictive neighbors. All of whom had known what kind of women they were going to become since birth, and had always, always treated them accordingly.

Julienne had used her last handful of euros to buy the bus tickets to get the two of them out of the dead-end place, choked on the fumes of feuds ages old. She'd brazenly stolen a dress from a rack outside a boutique in the Centre Commercial de Fontvieille.

And then, she'd snuck into a bathroom, and done herself up the best she could. The pretty dress. The cheap heels. The lipstick she'd saved from their long-dead mother, though it was crumbling and sad after so long. Enough eye makeup to disguise her shame.

And hopefully her fear, too, which she'd been afraid might have a scent all its own. Acrid. Sharp. Obvious.

She'd snuck into the Grand Hotel, leaving Fleurette hidden as best she could in an alley. Terrified that she'd be grabbed and tossed out at any moment, she'd found her way to the very bar she was approaching now. Back then she'd been astonished by the place, particularly the deep, shining wood that ached with pedigrees and fat purses. Better still, it had been filled with her quarry.

Rich men.

Who everyone knew were more than happy to purchase anything.

Including sixteen-year-old girls desperate for some cash.

Julienne had learned that lesson back in the village, where she had declined the butcher's offer to toss her a few coins if she "made him happy." It wasn't his bad teeth or that he smelled like blood, though neither had helped. It was that she'd already known what became of girls like her who listened to the promises of older men in that town. Or any men in that town. She was the result of her own mother's bad decisions years back, and she knew where they ended. Strung out and eventually dead, leaving behind two daughters to the same fate.

If it was her fate, Julienne had decided, she would face it. But not in that place of echoes, built vertically into a cold hillside and filled with all the people who had watched her mother spiral into horror without lifting a finger to help. She would take Fleurette and go south to glittering Monaco, where at least their own inevitable spiral would gleam a good deal brighter all the way down.

Tonight Julienne bore no resemblance to that gaunt, terrified child. Her hair was a fall of fine caramel, polished to shine, and she wore it twisted back into a deceptively effortless chignon. She was not wearing a stolen dress—the balance for which she'd left, years later, at that same boutique with a note of apology. Julienne had built herself into a sophisticated professional in these intervening years. She preferred sleek pencil skirts and the feeling of real silk against her skin, no less than what was expected for a woman with a big job at a multinational company. She favored statement heels and understated pearls at her ears, complete with a slim gold watch on her wrist.

Cristiano Cassara had done that, too. He'd given her the means not only to become the best version of herself possible, but to repay her debts. And to change her world.

Now it was time to change it again.

Julienne paused a few steps into the lush, dimly lit bar. She looked around, seeing what could have been the same old men, rich and jaded, lounging at the same tables. Then she looked toward the expanse of the bar itself, and it was as if he'd planned it.

As if he remembered, too.

Because Cristiano Cassara sat where she remembered him, there at a bar so glossy and luxurious that sixteen-year-old Julienne had gaped at it as if all those bottles lined up so prettily were precious jewels.

This time, her heart beat hard against her ribs again, but it wasn't fear.

It was a heady mix of victory and regret, and a strong dose of anticipation, for good measure.

She headed toward him, ready to do this at last.

Cristiano Cassara had been beautiful enough ten years ago, for all he had seemed remote. Carved from the same stone as the statues that graced the wide hall that had led her here. He'd been a relatively young man then, yet already wealthier than Julienne could have possibly imagined. The heir apparent to the Cassara chocolate fortune, he had worn his wealth and consequence in the cut of the exquisite suit he'd worn and in the very breadth of his shoulders. Not to mention the way he regarded the world around him, as if it, too, belonged to him.

Not that Julienne had known any of that, then. She'd looked at him and known that he was wealthy, that was all.

Tonight, he was all of that and more, a study in sheer masculine power.

She took a moment to really gaze at him, because this was not a Cassara Corporation boardroom where she'd always had too much to prove to waste her time making eyes at a man who she was fairly certain saw only numbers, profits and losses in return. In all the meetings she'd ever attended with him, Cristiano was steely, edging toward grim. He made no attempt to disguise his ruthlessness, and dispensed praise so sparingly that Julienne rather thought an actual murmur of vague approval might send her into a swoon.

Something that had never been put to the test.

Cristiano had been wealthy ten years ago. Today he was one of the richest men alive. She knew that if she looked around, she would likely find his security detail fanned out around the bar, unobtrusively keeping tabs on the man whose annual net worth was a number so vast that most people were unable to fully grasp it. There were too many zeroes. She would no doubt also see the hungry eyes of the women who trailed after him wherever he went, singed through but never quite burned to ash by all his steel and banked flame. She might even see the sneers of men who imagined him their rival, when it was obvious he was without peer.

As far as Julienne was concerned, he was perfect.

Sixteen-year-old Julienne had made a beeline for him because he was closest. And because, after her first, terrified look around this bar for a likely first client, he had been the only one in the place without gray hair. A fat belly. Or both.

She had told herself then that if she must do the thing, far better to do it with a man like him, who songs could have been written about. And likely had been.

She'd walked up to him, desperation making her bold

enough to put a hand on his arm. And she had waited for him to look away from the drink that sat before him on the bar, seemingly untouched.

When he'd raised his gaze to hers, it had burned.

He was too intense, they said. Too harsh. Needlessly grim and cold for a man who made sweets.

But Julienne thought he had a poet's mouth, for all that it was forever in that same flat line. His dark hair was thick and had yet to surrender to the ravages of age. It wasn't only that he kept himself in such magnificent shape, though that helped add to his mystique. It was that he seemed far larger and more threatening than he was. A vast giant lurking in the form of a man. As if the shadow he cast could engulf anyone unwary enough to venture close.

But by the time Julienne had realized that ten years ago, it had been too late.

Her hand had been on his arm.

Her heart had nearly exploded from her chest.

"Would you like to buy me a drink?" Julienne had asked the man with the eyes that burned, her voice squeaking with panic.

That was what a girl said, she'd been told by brittle, hard edged Annette, who had never been much of a mother. Every time Annette went off to what she called her *parties*, she came back with less of herself. As if someone had reached inside her, scraped out everything in there and left her to walk around an empty hollow.

She had died when Julienne was fourteen and everyone had called it a blessing.

Julienne had intended to survive, no matter how hollow she was inside. And unlike Annette, Julienne did not plan to forget her obligations to Fleurette, who had only been ten, then. She would take care of her sister if it killed her. And she would not consign Fleurette to the same fate.

At least one of them should survive without that scraped-out emptiness. Just one.

"How old are you?" he had replied, in richly compelling French blurred slightly with an Italian accent. Julienne hadn't expected the question. Who knew men were discerning—about anything? Her experience so far had not allowed for the possibility. She drew in a breath, prepared to claim she was a more palatable eighteen, despite the fact sixteen was perfectly legal. But his dark eyes flashed as if he knew what she meant to do. "Don't lie to me."

"Old enough," she replied, trying to sound husky. Throaty. Wasn't that how women sounded in situations like this? "Past the age of consent, if that is what you mean."

He had looked at her, through her. In her whole life, before and since, Julienne had never felt so *seen.* In that moment she was certain that Cristiano Cassara could see everything. *Everything.* What had happened, what she'd had planned. The one-way spiral of the life before her and the squalid bleakness she'd left behind. Fleurette out there in an alley, the emptiness in Julienne's wallet and belly alike, and what she was prepared to do to change both.

All the things she was prepared to do, starting here. With him.

More than that, she was certain he could also see the dreams and hopes she had long since jettisoned in her committed attempts to keep her sister and her warm and reasonably fed—if never safe or happy.

"I rather think not," he had said, a quiet thunder stroke of a comment.

And then Cristiano Cassara had changed her life.

With a lift of one hand.

The déjà vu was intense tonight. Cristiano again sat at the bar, another untouched drink before him. He fiddled with it, turning it this way and that, but he did not lift it to his lips. She now knew the rumors about him—every rumor, in fact. That he never drank, that his father had loved his liquor too well but his wife and child too little, and that these were the rituals Cristiano performed when he was alone. The untouched drink. The sober vigil.

He still had that poet's mouth, with its hint of sensuality she had never seen him succumb to, not once. Not even in the odd, stolen paparazzi shot of him when he couldn't have known he was being watched. His face was a terrible kind of beautiful, harsh and brutal, with cheekbones that made a woman dream of saints and martyrs. And those dark, flashing eyes that still burned when he looked at a person directly.

She remembered what his arm had felt like beneath her hand as if her palm was a scar. All that hard, hot power.

And Julienne was not a child any longer. She was not a scared teenager, prepared to sell herself to the highest bidder—or any bidder at all—because she was devoid of options and out of choices.

Still, there was a particular agony to this moment, so long in coming.

She slid her bejeweled evening purse onto the glossy bar, and angled her body toward his.

And knew, without his having glanced her way or indicated he was anything but alone, that he had been aware of her all along. Perhaps even before she'd stepped inside the dark, deliberately close space.

But she was too good at making him into a myth, as Fleurette often complained. Tonight she planned to focus on the man.

Cristiano had succeeded his grandfather to become the CEO and president of the company not long after she'd met him ten years ago. More than that, and more importantly, he was Julienne's boss. She had started at the company headquarters in Milan ten years ago, as a part-time job she fit in around the private studies Cristiano had arranged for her and Fleurette. First she'd been an intern. And then, once she'd finished her schooling at eighteen, she'd taken the lowest position offered and had worked her way steadily up.

That she was, in effect, Cristiano's ward had never signified. It was never discussed, and Julienne often wondered if anyone else even knew how generous he was, or how she had personally benefitted from it. But then, it wasn't as if she'd ever lived with him. He had put them up in one of his houses in Milan, complete with staff to tend to them, and in essence, they'd raised themselves.

We were too old already, Fleurette liked to say.

These days, Julienne lived across the sea in New York City. She'd fought hard to get to her position as the vice president of North American operations for the Cassara Corporation, reporting directly to Cristiano himself. And she'd fought even harder to close the kind of deals that would not only pay Cristiano back for his generosity all those years ago, but give back more than he'd given.

It had taken years.

He looked at her now, that dark gaze of his cool and assessing.

But no less harsh.

She would have felt let down if it had been, she understood.

"Thank you for coming," she said, as politely as if she was looking at him across a table in one of the Cassara Corporation's many offices.

"You were insistent, Ms. Boucher," he said, and there was that undercurrent of disapproval in his voice that let her know that he was astonished that she'd dared. And that she'd persisted, despite his secretary's best efforts.

Julienne smiled, still polite and calm. "You met me here once before."

And she knew as she said it that she was breaking all their rules. The unspoken boundaries all three of them had maintained for a decade. She and Fleurette never mentioned him or how they'd made it from a sad, half-abandoned French hill town to a lavishly appointed, semidetached townhouse in the center of Milan. He never indicated he knew either one of them. Sometimes

Julienne had worried that he'd forgotten what he'd done for them—that it had meant so little to him when it had altered the whole of hers and Fleurette's lives.

But no, she could see he hadn't forgotten. More, she could see his astonishment, there in his eyes like a thread of gold in the brown depths. His dark brows rose, and he looked almost…arrested.

"I did." His study of her made her want to shake. She didn't, somehow. Not outwardly. "A meeting neither one of us has referenced in a decade. To what do I owe the pleasure of this unexpected trip down memory lane, Ms. Boucher?"

His voice was crisp. A distinct and deliberate slap, though as stern and controlled as everything else he did.

He meant her to wilt and she wanted to, but then, she had built herself in his image. She was made of sterner stuff because he was, and because she'd always assumed he expected it. She kept her cool smile on her face.

"In that decade, I have kept track of what you must have spent to rescue Fleurette and me. Then care for us." She named a staggering number and saw that light in his eyes change again, to something far more sharp and assessing that she could feel like a fist in her belly. And lower, like heat. "With the latest deal we closed and the amount I have in a separate fund with your name on it, I believe I have repaid that sum. With interest."

His eyes were dark brown, like the bittersweet chocolate his family made. And yet that could hardly begin to describe their ferocity, or the intense way they narrowed on her now.

"I do not recall asking for repayment. Or even acknowledgment."

"Nonetheless." She took a deep breath. "My resignation letter waits for you in Milan."

He blinked. "I beg your pardon. You are resigning?"

"I am. I have."

She reached out and did what she'd done ten years ago. She put her hand on his arm, but this time, she meant it.

Oh, how she meant it.

"Cristiano," she said quietly. Invitingly, she hoped. "Would you like to buy me that drink?"

CHAPTER TWO

CRISTIANO CASSARA DID NOT care for surprises.

He had arranged his life with great precision, the better to avoid the unpleasant shock of events that went in directions he had not already foreseen. Cristiano had a deep and abiding dismay for chaos or mess of any kind, thanks to a childhood brimming over with nothing but, and had therefore dedicated himself to organizing as much of the world as possible to suit his requirements.

Something that was easier than perhaps it ought to have been when one was a Cassara.

He should have deeply disliked the fact that this woman had deliberately shifted the ground beneath their feet. That she had not stayed put in the compartment where he'd placed her years ago.

He told himself he did.

But it was too late. Something in him had shifted, too, without a care for how little he liked the sensation. And he suddenly found himself looking at Julienne Boucher as if he'd never seen her before.

As if she was a beautiful woman he'd happened to meet in a bar in Monte Carlo, instead of all the other things she'd been to him over time. His attempt at kindness, at a kind of redemption. The embodiment of his guilt. And possibly the best vice president the Cassara Corporation had ever had, save himself.

"What exactly are you offering me?" he asked, finding his gaze intent on hers. He did nothing to temper it. "And more important, why are you offering it?"

"You could have taken what I was offering ten years ago. You didn't."

He gazed down at the hand she'd laid on his arm as if it was a writhing, poisonous snake. When he raised his gaze to hers once more, he felt certain it was frigid.

Yet somehow, she did not retreat.

"Are you suggesting that because I did not behave like an animal then I might reverse course now?" He blinked in an astonishment that was in no way exaggerated. "I don't know what is more offensive. That you think I require pity sex or worse, that you imagine I might accept it."

He had meant to sound cold. Exacting. And yet somehow the word *sex* seemed to linger between them, making its own weather.

"That's not what I meant to suggest at all."

And through the kick of the temper he usually fought much harder to keep under wraps, he was aware that Julienne did not seem upset. She gazed back at him calmly, her face open and her eyes clear, and he was forced to think back to all the other times this woman had sat before him in her other role. As his employee.

Which was the only way he had thought about her since she'd joined the company as an intern approximately a thousand years ago. He had watched her meteoric rise from intern to vice president with a detached sort of interest, the way he would have noted any other rapid ascent, and he had sat in many meetings face-to-face with her coolness. Cristiano would not have had said he'd admired the way she handled herself, but he had appreciated it. On behalf of the Cassara Corporation, of course.

It occurred to him now that she was not afraid of him. Not intimidated in the least, which was unusual.

Remarkable, even.

"I have always been enormously grateful to you," she said, leaving her viper of a hand where it was. Cristiano had the notion he could feel the heat of it through the fine wool of the suit his tailors had crafted precisely for the late October weather, when that was unlikely. As unlikely as the wholly unexpected response his body was having to her. "How could I not be? And I always planned to repay you, because that is the decent thing to do, is it not?"

His mouth was full of ice, it seemed. "It is unnecessary."

"To you, yes. Which only makes it more necessary to me."

Again he stared down at her hand, trying to recall the last time someone had dared place a hand upon him without an invitation and his express permission. Nothing came to mind.

Not even his father had dared, after a certain point. When Cristiano had finally grown too tall.

And the longer her hand rested there on his forearm,

the less unpleasant he found it, no matter what he told himself. Quite the opposite, in fact. That heat instead seemed to wind through him, a peculiar treachery.

There were more betrayals. The longer she stood there, too close to him, he *noticed* things. He noticed *her.* Her narrow, elegant fingers. The carefully polished nails, in a quietly sophisticated shade that made him think of what her skin might look like, flushed with pleasure against smooth sheets.

Unbidden, Cristiano remembered the last time she'd put her hand on him, here in this same bar a lifetime ago. He couldn't say he'd thought about it since—and yet now he suddenly had a perfect recollection of her same hand in the same place, though she had been altogether rougher then. Her nails had been ragged and untended, or bitten down to the quick. And her eyes had been glazed with misery and fear, not...

But he did not wish to define what it was he saw in Julienne's gaze just then.

No matter his body's enthusiastic response.

"The Cassara Corporation has been mother and father to me," Julienne said, with a soft intensity that he ordered himself to ignore. But couldn't. "A family as well as a job. But you were the one who saved me. Right here. And then again and again over the years by providing me every opportunity to save myself. So I did, but all the while, I had you there as a guide. Or a goal, maybe."

"If you mean in a business sense, I must tell you, Ms. Boucher, that this is no way to go about—"

Her hand tightened on his arm. Cristiano felt the sensation race through him like an electric shock.

"It's not about business. Or why would I resign?" Julienne looked far more composed than he felt, and Cristiano hardly knew how to account for such a thing. "I wanted to repay our debt to you in ten years. I've done that now. But as those ten years passed, I found myself wishing that I could convince you to take my initial offer, after all."

When he glared at her, she only smiled. "Not for money, of course. I'm not in the same circumstances I was then. I'm not sixteen. I'm an adult woman, no longer your employee, and fully in control of her own faculties. I am not coerced. I am not desperate. When I found out you were going to be in Monaco again so soon after my last deal went through, it seemed the perfect bookend."

"A 'bookend'?" Cristiano repeated, and it was bad enough that he was looking at her now. Truly *seeing* her, after so long making it his business to act as if she wasn't quite there.

It was distinctly uncomfortable.

Because Julienne might have been a scraggly, terrified teenager ten years ago, covered in too much mascara and obvious misery. But that version of her was gone. She had grown into a beautiful woman, whether he chose to admit it or not. Her hair gleamed that burnished gold and brown that made him…hungry. Her eyes were too clever by half, fixed on him with an intensity and a sincerity that made his blood heat.

And he would have to be a dead man not to notice that her body, no longer packaged in a tacky dress that had been much too old for her, was a quiet symphony of curves and grace.

Cristiano did not indulge himself with his employees, as a matter of honor and good business sense alike. Both virtues, to his mind, and both traits his own father had distinctly lacked.

But Julienne had tendered her resignation.

And enveloped as they were in the dim embrace of a quiet bar tucked away in the midst of Monte Carlo's frenetic opulence, he could hardly remember why he should have objected to any of this in the first place.

Julienne did not know it, but she was already connected to him in ways that would have made him far more than merely *uncomfortable*, had he allowed the strict compartments he kept inside him to open wide at any point in the past ten years. He never had.

He wasn't sure he wanted to now, but her hand was on his arm and there was that *heat*—

Cristiano had not been in this specific bar by chance ten years ago. He disliked Monaco intensely, associating it as he did with the worst of his father's notorious excesses. It had been in this very bar that he had indulged in the last of those terrible scenes with Giacomo Cassara. His father had been cruel. Cristiano had returned the favor. And he had been sitting right here, staring at his father's favorite drink—the demon Giacomo had carried about on his back, night and day, for as long as Cristiano could remember, wondering at his own descent into cruelty and what it might herald—when Julienne had appeared beside him.

He had been engaged in nothing less than a battle for his own soul that night. The endless war with his father was one of attrition, and any victories Cristiano scored grew more Pyrrhic by the day. He had begun to wonder if it was worth attempting to live up to his grandfather's antiquated notions of honor when Giacomo was so busy dedicating himself to living down to every expectation.

Cristiano had been raised by two men, one a saint and one a devil, and that night he'd been wavering between them.

That was the mess that Julienne Boucher had walked in on, tottering on heels she clearly didn't yet know how to walk in.

He had glanced up to find her there beside him, as pale as she was determined. And there had never been any question that he might help himself to her, as his tastes ran to the enthusiastic, not the unwilling. Or the transactional. He'd felt for a moment as if he had his grandfather on one shoulder and his father on the other.

And in the middle stood a girl with poverty all over her like the too-tight dress she wore and a fixed smile on her too-young face, offering herself to him.

Cristiano had not been tempted to sample her wares. He wasn't remotely interested in teenagers, heaven forbid. And he certainly did not troll for sex from the streets. But it had taken him a beat too long to say so. To brush off the whispering devil spilling poison into his ear—the one telling him to ignore her, the one insisting she wasn't his problem when he had enough of his own, the one who wanted him to turn his back on her and get back to his already messy evening—and do what was right.

That he had wavered at all, that he was that selfish, disgusted him.

And perhaps that was why he had not simply given her some money from his pocket and gone on his way. It was the guilt he couldn't shake that had made him go further. It was the stain of his shame that had turned him into her benefactor.

To prove that he was nothing like his father.

Even if, later that same night, he had learned that in truth, he was worse.

But tonight, Julienne did not come to him as a desperate child determined to sell her body for survival. She came to him as a woman, and a beautiful one at that, with a body she could have shared with any man in Monaco, if she so chose.

And still she'd chosen him.

He couldn't deny he liked the symmetry of it.

Cristiano couldn't go back in time and change that brief, terrible moment when he'd very nearly turned his back on the girl she'd been. Very nearly abandoning her to her fate with whatever jackals populated places like this. Vile men like his own father, selfish and destructive and heedless of the damage he caused.

So easily could Cristiano have broken her and condemned her younger sister, too, simply by walking away from Julienne that night.

He carried the weight of that, two bright lives he could have extinguished in one fell swoop, around with him. They were an enduring reminder of how close he'd come to becoming more like his father, the cost of housing and educating and outfitting them negligible to a man of his wealth—and a small dent indeed next to the soul he'd nearly lost.

They had been an act of kindness to prove he had it in him. Then an act of penance for the other things he'd lost that night.

One way or another, Julienne and her sister had long been his personal cross to bear.

And it was tempting, oh, so tempting, to put them down once and for all.

"Are you going to answer me?" Julienne asked, and she tilted her head slightly to one side as she asked it, once again signaling how little she was intimidated by him. It was a novel experience. Cristiano should have been outraged at her temerity. Her lack of respect.

Instead, he found himself intrigued.

"How can I?" he replied after a moment. "I don't know what it is you are offering."

"Me. I'm offering me."

"I appreciate the offer. And that you are no longer making it while barely legal." He considered her, the light from behind the bar making her face seem very nearly luminous. "But you see, I have rules."

"I've worked for you for ten years, Mr. Cassara. If, all of a sudden, you did not have rules for every given situation, *that* would be concerning."

He thought of his guilt, his shame. That brief, glaring moment when he had understood himself to be no better than the father he disdained with every particle of his being. The father who had humiliated him, rampaged through his childhood and laughed in the face of his pain.

How easy would it be to wash that moment away. He had saved the girl, after all. And the result of what he'd actually done—instead of merely *thought*—was Julienne.

Julienne, the youngest vice president in the history of the Cassara Corporation—aside from Cristiano himself.

Julienne, who looked at him without the calculation he had grown to expect in the eyes of women who dared attempt to get close to him—or rather, to his plump bank accounts. Julienne, whose toffee-colored eyes were filled with heat. Longing, even.

He had come back to this terrible place at least once each year since that night to stand a vigil. To remember who he'd nearly become.

Maybe, a voice in him suggested, *it is time to let it go.*

Cristiano followed an urge he would normally have tamped down, hard, and reached across the scant inches between them. He fit his hand to the curve of her cheek, and traced his way down the delicate line of her neck to find the hollow of her throat. Then, lower, to the soft skin visible in the open neck of her silk blouse that hinted at her breasts below.

And watched in a dark delight as she flushed, bright and hot.

The precise shade of her nail polish.

"I do not do entanglements," he told her severely. Though he was questioning himself already, as the heat in her skin shot through him, pooling in his sex. His body was tight, ready. And suddenly, it was as if he'd spent years wanting nothing more than to drive himself deep and hard inside her. "I like sex, Ms. Boucher. But I do not traffic in emotional displays."

Her breath was choppy and her eyes were hot, but

her voice was cool when she spoke. "I hope I have never given you reason to imagine that I was particularly emotional."

"The boardroom is not the bedroom."

"Indeed it is not. Or you would have found me distinctly indecent, long before now."

He liked the notion of that. And suddenly there were too many images in his head of missed opportunities in the office...the kinds of images he never allowed to pollute his mind. The kinds of images he kept behind the walls of all those compartments inside him, because to lose those separations was to become too much like his father. When he wanted instead to be like his grandfather, the man who had taught him how to build partitions. And use them.

But walls were coming down all around them tonight.

"You have always struck me as a woman who likes to be in charge." He continued to trace an absent pattern this way and that, in and around her low collar, drawing in the wild heat she generated. And far too aware of each breath she took. "But I'm afraid I am far too demanding for that."

Julienne shivered, as if the prospect of his demands was too delicious to bear, and he thought he might actually eat her alive. Here and now. Hoist her up on the bar and indulge himself at last.

That would be a bookend, indeed.

"What sort of demands do you mean?" she asked, and her voice changed. Gone was all that coolness, lost in a husky sort of heat that he could feel like a caress, there where he hungered for her the most.

It made him think of dark rooms, deep sighs.

He shifted again, and looked around, trying his best not to surrender to that drumming thing inside him. His blood, his pulse.

His need and his hunger.

Not cut out of him, as he'd believed all this time. But waiting.

Only waiting for a woman who dared.

But despite the riot inside him and the delicious idea he'd had concerning the bar, this was not the place to indulge himself. There were too many unfriendly eyes that watched his every move, especially in the money-eyed halls of Monte Carlo, where too many well-fed enemies would leap at the chance to see and exploit his weaknesses.

Or his wants.

To Cristiano's mind, they were the same.

He took Julienne's hand in his and then he tugged her behind him, leading her back out of the dimly lit bar and into the hotel proper. He didn't look back at her. He didn't need to. He could see her in the mirrors they passed, looking flushed and ready.

He felt the pulse of greed deep in his sex.

Instead of leading her out into the grand lobby that was filled with guests and tourists alike, he moved deeper into the hotel. Then branched off into one of the smaller marble halls festooned with luxury shops. He kept going until he found an alcove, tucked between a shop filled with disgracefully overpriced perfume and another stocked entirely with nonsensical shoes.

And once there, away from prying eyes if not entirely private, he backed her to the wall. Then propped himself over her there, one hand on either side of her head.

Cristiano watched, rapt, as she fought for breath.

How had he failed to truly *see* her all this time?

"Any and all demands," he said, finally answering her question. What demands, indeed. He could write a book or two and it would only skim the surface of the things he wanted. Needed. And would demand of her. "I like things the way I like them. Is that a problem for you?"

"I've been taking your orders for ten years."

He liked the way her eyes flashed. He liked that simmering defiance, right there beneath her cool exterior. He wanted to lick up all that elegance and see how she burned.

"One night, Julienne."

"You say that as if you imagine I might have started making a hope chest." She tossed her head with that same defiance and a streak of temper, too. "I assure you, Mr. Cassara, this is a sexual invitation. That's all."

"One night," he said again.

"I heard you the first time."

"It bears repeating, *cara*. I would hate for there to be any…confusion."

And he watched as another streak of temper made her toffee-colored eyes darken.

"How patronizing." And she scowled at him as if he wasn't caging her against the wall. "I'm the one who propositioned you, in case you're the one who's confused. Twice, now. Perhaps that's what bears repeating."

"The only word I wish you to repeat is my name," he told her, low and dark, and leaned in then to get the scent of her in his nose. Sweet and hot at once. His pulse thickened, beating hard into his sex. "No more of this *Mr. Cassara* when we are naked. *Cristiano*, please. Shout it, sob it, scream it. All are acceptable. And all bear endless repeating, as I think you'll find soon enough."

And he was so close he could see her delicate shiver.

"How sure you seem that you won't be the one crying out my name." Julienne smirked at him. She actually dared *smirk* at him. "Particularly when we have yet to establish if there's the slightest bit of chemistry between us. Perhaps there will be nothing here but apologetic grimaces and embarrassment."

"My mistake," Cristiano said.

He didn't argue the point.

He moved closer and took her mouth with his.

No finesse. No gentility or politeness. Simple, potent greed.

He took what he wanted, a bold mating of lips and tongues. He tasted her, he took her, providing a comprehensive example of precisely the kind of demands he meant.

He didn't go easy on her at all.

And she met him, his Julienne. She pushed herself off the wall, twined herself around him, and the fire of it roared through him. The gut punch, hot and mad, slammed into him. It made him question the limits of his own control, when he prided himself on never, ever losing his grip—

When he pulled away, his own breath was hard to catch. Her eyes had gone dark and wide, and Cristiano wanted nothing on this earth but to bury himself inside her, again and again.

Assuming he lived through the single night he would allow her.

The single night he would allow *himself.*

And as he fought to find his control again, he wondered, for the first time in his life, if one night would be enough.

A sentiment that should have sent him reeling. Running for the hills, but her taste was in his mouth. Sweet and salt, all woman, and he thought it entirely possible that she might be the undoing of him, after all.

The mad part of it was, he couldn't seem to care.

"One night," he said again, rougher this time. Because he was talking to himself. "That's all I have to offer."

"All you have to offer me? Or all you have to offer, in general?"

He didn't know how she knew to ask him that.

But the grief was always in him, the shame his constant shadow, and he told himself that was what made him reach over and run his thumb over her full, tempting lower lip. He wanted to sink his teeth into her. He wanted to breathe her in, then get his mouth where she was sweetest.

"Does it matter?"

He watched her chest rise, then fall. He could see

her nipples, tight and hard beneath the silk blouse she wore. He caught the faintest hint of her arousal and his mouth watered.

"One night," she agreed. Almost solemnly. But then she smiled. "But I hope you don't have performance anxiety. It would be depressing if you failed somehow to live up to all this hype."

He smiled then, edgy and wrong, and had the distinct pleasure of watching goose bumps break out all over her body.

"Let me worry about that. All you need to worry about is how many times you scream my name." He leaned closer and sampled the goose bumps on her neck, then smiled there, against her skin. "Remember it, please. *Cristiano*. Though in desperate circumstances *Oh, God* is also acceptable."

When all she did was pant a little, her eyes glazed over with heat when he angled himself back to look at her, he laughed.

And then he took by the hand this woman who he intended to purge tonight, one way or the other. He led her out of the alcove, back to the lobby elevators, and then spirited her away to the penthouse suite he'd taken on the very top floor.

Where he intended to keep her until dawn.

Using every last scrap of the dark.

Until they were both fully sated.

And perhaps, at last, truly saved from the mistakes he'd made ten years ago.

CHAPTER THREE

THIS WAS WHAT she'd wanted.

Julienne's mouth felt beautifully tender. She pressed her fingertips against her lips as Cristiano ushered her into his hotel suite, sensation pulsing hot and raw from that point of contact all the way down to her toes.

She expected him to turn on the lights. Indulge in suitably urbane conversation, dry to match the cocktails. Or whatever it was men like him did in situations like these.

But instead, he kissed her again, barely getting the door closed before his mouth was on hers.

Dark. Hot.

So greedy it almost hurt.

And there was some part of her that couldn't quite believe that a man so controlled, so deeply ascetic, could carry all this passion within him. Could have been carrying it deep inside him somewhere, all this time.

But she couldn't care about that now. Not when his mouth was on hers and his hands roamed everywhere, finding her breasts and then taking possession of her nipples.

As if they were his.

As if *she* was his.

They were still in the entryway, though she hardly saw it. Or cared. She had the sense of more marble, more mirrors, and the pervasive sense of tremendous wealth— which was to say, nothing special in the Cassara world.

But his mouth was still on hers, beguiling her and bewildering her, and she stopped worrying about where they were. Only that he was with her.

Cristiano's hands were restless, moving where they pleased. One dove beneath the waistband of her skirt to find the curve of her bottom. The other drifted to her waist, then up, pushing her bra out of his way to hold her naked breast in his palm.

All the while he kissed her, intoxicating her. Making her press into him. Making her wish she could crawl inside him.

She had never understood the word *demanding* before. Not really.

Cristiano was overwhelming behind a desk. But here, unleashed…

He was like a hurricane.

He kissed her with a ferocity that should have terrified her. That might have, if it hadn't been for the sensation that howled and shook through her with every stroke of his hand, his tongue. She felt strung out between his taste and his touch. The insistent fingers on her breast and then, below, the way he traced his way over her bottom. And kept going until he found his way to her front, and the furrow of her molten heat.

And then he was inside her, two fingers deep into the center of her need.

A wicked twist, and then more of that unreal dark laughter against her mouth as she bucked into him. And moaned.

"My name," he murmured.

Another demand.

Then he pressed down hard, thrusting deep, and Julienne dissolved.

She heard a keening sound, but all she was conscious of were those thick, strong fingers inside of her—thrusting so wickedly, with such certainty and skill.

She sank from one peak only to find herself tossed up hard into another.

And all the while, Cristiano laughed.

Low, male, deeply satisfied.

But still, it was laughter. And Julienne wanted to hoard it. Gather it up and hold it close, for all those years she would have sworn to anyone who would listen that this man didn't know how to laugh. That he never had. That he simply wasn't made that way.

He pulled his fingers from the tight grip of her sex. Then, impossibly, he lifted them to his own mouth.

Julienne watched, torn somewhere between a sharp, hot longing and a crisp embarrassment as he licked his fingers clean.

"All this time." His voice was a wondering rasp. "All this time you sat across tables and desks from me. You've walked in and out of my offices on five continents. And all this time, you have tasted like this."

She felt as if she ought to apologize, though she couldn't quite speak. And her heart felt fragile and fierce at once, there where it swelled behind her ribs.

Cristiano peeled her away from the wall and her knees wobbled beneath her when she meant to stand.

Her reward for that was that dark laugh of his again, a rough, masculine music she thought she would hear inside her forever.

Then he picked her up, tossing her over his shoulder with an easy strength that reminded her of the ancient conquerors who surely lived in his blood.

He strode through the darkened rooms of his hotel suite and she saw glimpses of bright lights heralding the Monte Carlo nightlife through the windows, gleaming antiques strewn about the palatial living spaces, and with every step, the quiet whisper of five-star luxury.

And when he put her down, he tipped her over onto her belly. Julienne tried to orient herself in the dimness of a new room, taking longer than she should have to recognize that he'd bent her over the side of a tall bed. And she tried to take stock, she did—but her body was his now. Not hers.

Never again yours, a voice said in her so clearly she almost flinched at the sound. *His always. His forever.*

And she could no longer tell if she was shuddering because of that voice, or because of him. Or some wicked, ruthless combination of both.

She felt him behind her, crouched down with a hand on one ankle, and all she could manage to do was moan.

"These legs," he said, in that same tone, like a dark incantation. "I worked so hard to keep myself from noticing these legs, Julienne. The temptation of them. And the shoes. Always the shoes, higher and higher by the year."

And all she could think was, *You weren't invisible to him after all.*

She almost felt herself shatter into pieces at that notion alone.

And then she was shivering all over, everywhere, as he slid his palms up the back of her legs. Not quite gently. Not quite softly. And the firm pressure was all about heat and want, making her delirious. Making her ripe and half-mad with that drumming desire.

It was only when he slid his hands down the length of her legs again that she realized he'd pushed up her skirt and left it bunched up at her waist.

She felt a wallop of that bright hot pulsing thing that had nearly knocked her over in the hall. It was mixed now with the image of what she must look like, bent over his bed in such a wanton display, with only the bright red thong she wore between them.

Julienne was breathing so hard now that it was all she could hear. That gasping thing not quite a breath, high and wild.

"Feel free to bite down on the linens," Cristiano told her, dark and amused. "I won't tell."

She didn't bite down. But she did grip the soft bedclothes beneath her, twisting the outrageously soft material into fists.

His fingers moved beneath her thong, almost absently, when she could *feel* the intensity coming off of him in waves. She felt him peel it down her leg, then tug it from one ankle. But not the other, and she understood—with another wallop—that he'd left her thong there.

How must she *look*…?

She was naked from the waist down, wearing only her impractical heels with her lacy red thong at one ankle. And she was making that *sound*. And his shoulders were between her legs, tipping her forward even more and lifting her at the same time, so she was braced even more fully on the bed—

"Oh, God," she moaned, as understanding slammed into her with all the force of a train.

"There you go," he murmured.

Approvingly.

And she could hear him well enough, but worse—or better—his mouth was *right there*. Right there at her core, where she felt herself clenching, melting, shuddering—

Then Cristiano took her in his mouth from behind, like an overripe peach.

And ate her like dessert.

And this time, when she exploded, she screamed.

Sometime later, he rolled her over. Julienne lay there, splayed wide, because she couldn't seem to get her limbs to work. Nor could she manage to care about that strange paralysis the way she knew she should.

All the while her heart clattered so hard against her ribs that she was worried they might crack. Or she would.

She had the vague sense that he was moving, but then he was touching her again. Stripping her, she worked out after a moment, with a ruthless efficiency that made her shiver all over again.

"Cristiano…" she murmured.

"Good girl," he replied.

She had no idea why that made her want to sob.

Though she couldn't have said, if her life depended upon it, what sort of sob that might have been. Another explosion of sensation. Or a deep well of something that had ached inside her for much too long now, too fiercely to be sadness.

All of the above, she said to herself.

At least, she thought it was to herself. It was impossible to tell.

And then he was crawling over her, tasting her as he went.

No part of her was safe from him, and she felt blazingly hot. Gloriously alight and alive. She tasted him too, so male and hard. Until she was sure they both glowed in the dark with the force of this endless temptation, wild and needy.

She wanted it to go on and on forever.

And then she felt him, hard and huge against her hip.

She realized she must have made a noise when he laughed again, softly.

"You're going to take all of me, Julienne," he told her, with that quiet certainty that made her doubt—not for the first time—that she was really going to survive this. Not in one piece, anyway. Not intact. But she'd known that before she'd come here, hadn't she? Not the particulars of *how*, exactly, he would ruin her. Only that he would. "Do you understand?"

All Julienne could do was nod. She didn't know if she was apprehensive, or desperate—but this time, in a whole new way. She wanted to prove to him that she could do exactly that. That she could do whatever he wanted, whatever he needed.

He smiled again, and it was even more devastating than before.

And she was such a fool. Had she really worried that the sight of his smile might make her swoon?

If only.

The sad truth of her situation was like another wallop, and now it was connected to that molten fire between her legs, the pounding of her heart, and the dark, demanding man propped up over her.

She had fallen hopelessly in love with this man when she was sixteen years old. She had loved him with all the mad fervency of a teenage girl, because she'd been one. And more, with the unwavering passion a girl could only have for the hero who had saved her.

It had never wavered. Over the years, it had grown stronger. Deeper.

Until even her own sister despaired of her.

Tonight was meant to be the cure. Because no man could possibly live up to the fantasies in her head. Julienne knew that. She'd been sure of it.

And tonight was nothing like her fantasies, it was true.

Cristiano was far, far better than she ever could have imagined.

And she could see the vast gulf between the teenage crush she'd had on him all this time and the reality that was this. *Him.* His ruthless physicality. His rampant, commanding masculinity, his certainty in her responses and his dark demands.

God help her, but she was lost.

He thrust into her then, a slow and steady ruthlessness that had her coming apart at the feel of it. The thickness. That deep, aching stretch. The tug of it, there at her entrance, that he barely heeded.

Then the ruthless, peremptory way he seated himself deep inside her, looked down at her face and smiled.

Julienne shattered all around him. She loved him with every last inch of her woman's body, shattering what was left of her teenage heart and loving him all the more with the far darker, far more complicated adult heart that remained.

Fantasies were nothing next to this.

She shook and she shook, and she heard his name on her lips.

A song she'd already been singing for a decade, and would likely keep singing all the days of her life.

She told herself she accepted it. She *needed* to accept it.

Cristiano gathered him to her, laughing again. It was dark music to her ears, she buckled anew, and only then did he begin to move.

And Julienne lost track of the things she sobbed, or the times she screamed. He was insatiable, and he was thorough. He taught her things she was sure she could never put into words, so she used the only one that she could remember.

His name.

It could have been hours or whole lifetimes when he finally rolled her over for the last time, pulled her knees up high and let himself go.

And it was her name she heard then, roared out into the crook of her neck as he found his own release.

One more thing that she would hoard, later.

One more piece of treasure to tuck away.

He had said one night, and he used every last scrap of it.

Julienne woke as the first hint of dawn crept across the sky, and had no idea how she was supposed to go on. Not now she knew.

She'd come here to exorcise her own, personal demons. And instead, she had lost herself all the more. Irrevocably.

But none of that mattered, because they had agreed.

One night.

"You need your own life," Fleurette had told her, time and again. "Not *his* life, his company, his world. You're not a princess locked away in a tower, waiting for some fool to ride up on a white horse. That's what Annette dreamed of, you know. Every time she went out. And look what happened."

Julienne had always agreed, safe in the knowledge that it was easy enough to agree with whatever Fleurette said as long as she still had to pay him back. And could therefore agree and also carry on doing what she was doing.

But she'd paid him back in full before she'd met him in the bar last night, transferring the last of the money to the account she'd set up for that purpose. He had bought her, in a sense, but she had bought herself back.

She was sure that once she recovered from this night—once she walked away from him, reminded herself how to breathe, and found her way into the new life she planned to build for herself far away from the Cassara Corporation or anything that reminded her of

Monaco and the girl she'd been when she'd come here the first time—she would treasure that.

You will have to, she told herself, a new sob building inside her.

She twisted in the bed, looking over her shoulder to where Cristiano slept.

Even in sleep, he looked stern. Unyielding.

Both of which he'd proved himself to be, over and over again.

Julienne didn't let herself touch him again. Because she knew that if she did, she would never manage to tear herself away.

Instead she pressed one palm hard against her treacherous heart.

One night, he had said.

And any emotional complications she had were her own.

She made herself get up, then pull on her clothes. She picked up her shoes in one hand, then found her way out through the maze of rooms toward that entryway where he'd feasted on her like a wild thing.

Julienne shuddered all over again, instantly hot and wet and ready. She lectured herself as she looked in the mirror, dismayed to find that she did not look nearly as rumpled and used as she thought she should. Her hair was wild, but it was easily tamed. She smoothed it back, then tied it into a knot.

And then she looked the way she always did.

As if nothing had changed. As if she was somehow the same person she'd been when she'd walked in here last night.

When the truth was, she had saved herself for the only man she had ever looked at twice. The only man she had ever loved. She'd saved herself for him, and he had taken her as ruthlessly as he did everything, none the wiser.

And as she let herself out of the hotel room, closing the door quietly behind her, Julienne found herself smiling.

It was hardly on par with rescuing a sixteen-year-old girl from prostituting herself, but it was a gift in return for a gift all the same.

He had protected her innocence all those years ago. And last night she had joyfully, happily, given it to him.

"You can move on now," she told herself, ignoring the way her heart thudded so painfully in her chest. She leaned down to slip on one shoe, then the next. And she could still feel him everywhere, the rasp of his rough jaw on her inner thighs. His hard, gloriously male hands so big and bold against her skin. "It's over now, Julienne. You'll move on."

You will have to, came the voice inside, too much like her sister's.

And she made herself walk away—from Monaco, from her sordid past, from the Cassara Corporation, and from Cristiano himself—without looking back.

CHAPTER FOUR

Six months later

CRISTIANO SCOWLED DOWN at his mobile as he crossed the Piazza del Duomo, then shoved it into his pocket. It was a blustery spring evening in Milan, and he had no intention of answering the call coming in. Or any call, because he did not wish to risk getting sucked back into the latest set of fires he would be duty bound to extinguish tonight.

And tonight he had other plans. Tonight he thought he might spend some time in his home for a change. The glorious penthouse that was as sleek and modern and stark as he liked, with no hint of sweetness. No chocolate. And best of all, not in his office. He thought he might try his hand at pretending he was a real man with a real life, instead of the walking, talking embodiment of the Cassara Corporation.

He would never admit such a thing aloud, and certainly not in a place like Milan where his grandfather had worked so very hard for so long and had admirers everywhere, but sometimes he wondered if he might not take a great deal of pleasure in watching it all burn.

Another vicious little thought that should have been unworthy of him. He filed that away with the rest of them, the evidence of who he really was no matter how he tried to pretend otherwise, and shoved his hands into the pockets of his coat.

As if he needed any more proof that he was his father's son, through and through.

Still, he collected each and every damning morsel himself. And kept a very thorough dossier, right there where his heart ought to be.

And he was thinking about all the ways he'd failed himself and his grandfather's memory again when he saw her.

One more thing he was sick of, he thought with an internal snarl, when the initial kick of it passed.

Cristiano loved women. He loved sex. And he indulged himself, one night at a time. He had never wanted more than one night with anyone. Ever.

And yet he had spent six months being haunted by that single night he'd spent with Julienne Boucher in Monaco.

He'd woken up that morning after to find Julienne gone, and had hated the fact that her absence hadn't brought him the usual peace or satisfaction. Instead, he'd been forced to acknowledge the distinctly unsavory truth.

He, Cristiano Cassara, had wanted *more*.

Had he woken to find her still there in his bed, he

would have broken every last one of his rules and indulged himself further.

It was unthinkable and unprecedented—but that didn't make the unfamiliar urge any less real.

He'd assured himself that the odd need in him he'd never felt before, that ravenous hunger, would fade. Give it a week's time, he'd told himself confidently as he'd left Monaco with no plans to return, and he would forget her like all the rest.

But he didn't.

He saw Julienne's face everywhere. A gleaming bit of caramel-colored hair and he was instantly distracted. The turn of a particular cheek, soft and elegant, and he trailed off in the middle of a sentence—no matter what he happened to be doing. Negotiating deals, handling problems, whatever.

She would not leave him alone, and yet she was nowhere to be found.

It was a nuisance. It was madness.

And it didn't fade with time.

Julienne's letter of resignation had been on his desk in Milan, as promised. She had left a dutiful forwarding address—the Manhattan residence she'd used throughout her tenure at the Cassara Corporation. But when, a month or so later, Cristiano had broken and actually attempted to contact her there, it turned out she'd moved on again.

This time, with no forwarding details.

She had turned into his own, personal ghost.

When Cristiano had never believed in ghosts before.

And so he scowled at the woman there in the *piazza*,

wearing an overly bulky coat and an unnecessary scarf as if it was the dead of winter instead of April, because it wasn't her. It was never her.

Except this time, the caramel-haired woman in question held his gaze. And smiled back.

The bright red ribbon inside him that he'd been calling *self-loathing* brightened, then. And shifted into a new kind of fury.

He didn't know what else to call it.

Cristiano realized he had come to a complete stop. And was now standing perfectly still, his eyes locked to hers across the coming dusk. He was vaguely aware of the usual crowds that flocked to the *piazza*. Tourists and locals alike, gazing up at the ancient cathedral and taking photographs of its spires. But all he saw was Julienne.

That *smile*.

And, as he watched, it shifted from some kind of greeting, laced with hope if he had to characterize it, into that cool weapon he recalled from the bar in Monaco.

Either way, she made his body tighten into a hard, driving greed.

She was standing still herself, her gaze on him and that puffy down coat arranged around her like a circus tent.

It suggested to him that she'd been standing out here a long while.

Cristiano was moving then, cutting through the crowd, or perhaps it was simply that they leaped out of the way of a man with that much hunger on his face.

He kept his gaze trained on Julienne, half-convinced that if he so much as blinked she might disappear like smoke.

Then he was standing before her, astonished at the new kind of greed that swelled in him. He wanted to get his hands on her again—that hadn't changed—but it was more than that. For a moment, he was content simply to gaze at her.

Like a puppy, a cold voice inside him chimed in.

A voice he recognized, snide and sneering. Like Giacomo at his worst.

Cristiano clenched his jaw, fighting back the darker urges inside him, because that was the point, wasn't it? It wasn't the urges that mattered. It wasn't the part of him that could match his father's snideness all too easily. He knew those things existed. It was what he did with them that mattered, surely.

"Julienne," he made himself say, by way of greeting. As if this was a business meeting that required his cold ruthlessness, and had nothing to do with that *smile.* "There must be a reason you are lurking about out here in the elements. I'm astonished you felt the urge to play tourist on such a wet, cold evening."

"I'm an excellent tourist, actually," she replied, and he was sure he saw some trace of emotion in her toffee-colored eyes. Here a moment, then gone. "But that's not why I'm here."

"Dare I flatter myself that you have come back to Milan to see me?" He couldn't help the iciness in his tone. The frigid bite of it. Maybe he didn't want to help himself. "You know where the Cassara offices are located, do you not? And last I checked you knew where my residence was located as well. Surely either choice would be more appropriate than stalking me in the shadow of the Duomo."

"I've been waiting for you, Mr. Cassara. Not stalking you."

"Have we reverted, then, to Mr. Cassara? Fascinating. I had my mouth between your legs, *cara*. Surely that buys a man some measure of intimacy."

"I didn't want to presume."

She sounded prim, but there was heat on her cheeks. And the oddest notion occurred to him, then. Could it be that his favorite ice queen was less cool and unbothered than she looked? How...delightful.

He didn't really want to think too hard about *how* delightful he found it. Because that brought him right back to snide commentary from a dead man.

"I told you what name to use," he said quietly now, his gaze on hers while the night they'd shared played in his head. "You may sob it again, if you wish. If that makes you more comfortable."

"I need a moment of your time, that's all," she said. Almost formally. But then there was that heat on her cheeks again, brighter than before, and he wondered what images she played in her head. "Not your name."

Cristiano lifted his hands and spread them wide, in keeping with a casualness he in no way felt. "I have nothing but time, naturally. I am a man of leisure, capable at any moment of playing tourist in my own city."

She blinked at that, her cheeks reddened further, and

he got the distinct impression that she'd expected him to put up a fight. That she was braced for it.

"You're not the only one interested in another taste, Julienne," he said, feeling magnanimous. Because she was here, finally. Because it wasn't yet another ghost to haunt him and distract him, whether he believed in ghosts or not. It was her, this time. It was finally *her*. "I tried to find you in Manhattan, but you'd moved."

She coughed, as if to cover a sound of shock. "You came to Manhattan?"

He arched a brow. "I often have business in Manhattan. As you are well aware."

But there was a different, softer light in her gaze. "Yes, right. You didn't make a special trip. I understand." She smiled at him and he didn't know how he kept his hands off her. "It was my sister's turn, you see."

"Her turn?"

A fresh flush made her cheeks glow. "I can't imagine why you'd be interested in this story."

"Her turn to do what?" Cristiano inquired silkily. "I trust it will not involve any Monte Carlo reenactments."

"God. No." She seemed to hear her own vehemence then, and looked away, that belligerent chin of hers firming. "Ever since you rescued us that night, we followed my path through the Cassara Corporation because it was the fastest way to meet our goals. To repay you and reclaim our lives. But once I resigned, it was time to follow Fleurette's path. It's only fair."

"Why must you choose? Why can't you both do as you like instead of hiding away so theatrically?"

It was only after he asked the question, out here

as the moody spring night drew close, that Cristiano thought to question why on earth it was he was standing about having random conversations with this woman. When he'd spent six months dreaming of all the other things he could do with her. With her mouth. With every square inch of her delectable body. With that heat he could feel between them even now. Even though they weren't touching.

"That was the deal we made ten years ago," Julienne said, stoutly. "And I didn't imagine anyone would be looking for me after my resignation or I would have left my forwarding details, with no theater whatsoever. We're in Seattle now."

"Seattle." He pronounced the name of the American city as if it might bite. "That is off to the west, is it not?"

"The Pacific Northwest, actually."

"You will forgive me if I do not spend a great amount of time tramping about the primeval forests of the American northwest, Pacific or otherwise," Cristiano said, his voice going edgy despite his best efforts. "As I traffic neither in legacy technology nor flannel shirts."

"I don't recall asking you for a review of Seattle's charms," Julienne said, with a smile he realized was fixed. "I'm merely telling you that we moved. And time passed."

"That is what time does." His jaw was tight. And impatience beat in him, hard and hot. "Have you turned up in the *piazza* to tell me bedtime stories, *cara*? If I'm a good boy, will you provide me with warm milk and a pat on the head? You will understand if I decline the kind offer, I hope."

He watched her straighten her shoulders. Then that chin of hers tipped up. "My sister wants me to have nothing to do with you or Cassara chocolates ever again. She claims she is the practical one, you understand, but it's actually because she cannot bear to think about where we came from. If she could, I think she would wipe Monaco from the map entirely. To say nothing of that hill town where we were born."

"I find the emotional travails of your sister at least as interesting as the story of your domestic arrangements. In case you wondered."

"She argued strenuously against my coming here."

"Had you reached out to me, I would have offered a counterargument." Because she kept talking, and all he could concentrate on was her mouth.

"Cristiano—" she began.

"First, the counterargument, if you please."

And he indulged himself, because he no longer had the strength to hold himself back. Or the will. Or the slightest inclination.

Cristiano reached over, taking his time as he slid his palm along her jawline to cup her cheek. Because he wanted to feel her silky softness. And her heat.

Her breath fanned out, half a gasp and half something else. It was like music to him.

And her eyes were sweet like candy, if darker tonight. Dark enough to remind him of the precise shade they'd been when he'd been deep inside of her. He felt himself harden, until his need was more like an ache.

He felt those iron chains he kept locked tight around

him, to keep all his compartments in a tidy order, snap open—but not as if she'd broken them.

It was as if she was the key.

And Cristiano couldn't allow himself to think about that.

Instead, he leaned forward and nipped at that lower lip of hers, full and tempting.

And maybe she said his name. He couldn't tell because his blood was roaring in his ears, and the faintest taste of her was enough to make his whole body clench tight.

He bent again, and covered her mouth with his.

And on some level he expected it to be a disappointment. Because no kiss could possibly live up to his memories. He had exaggerated her taste. Her fit. He expected to find that he'd sold himself a fantasy no reality could ever match.

But instead, Julienne took the top of his head off.

He forgot where they were. He forgot the crowd, the weather. The ancient cathedral that blocked out the better part of the sky.

All of that was so much dust in the wind to him, because Julienne was kissing him again, and it was better than anything Cristiano could possibly have remembered.

It was better.

It was her.

He swept her into his arms like the romantic he had never been, tilting her back so he could take more, taste more, lose himself more—

And it was only when he heard the high-pitched tittering sound of a set of teenage girls nearby that reality reasserted itself.

"Dio santo!" he growled furiously, there against her mouth. "What have you done to me, woman?"

But Julienne pulled back, stepping out of his embrace. And the expression he saw on her face made no sense at all, because she looked…stricken. More, she'd gone pale, leaving only two bright splotches on those cheekbones of hers, like flags.

"I'm afraid my sister was right." Her voice was husky. Distressed. "I shouldn't have come here."

"Indeed not," he agreed. "You should have found me somewhere private, so I could greet you properly. And without risk of arrest."

And he watched her change again, a sweep of pink taking over her face as if she'd leaped from an ice bath into a furnace. She even laughed a little, fanning at her face while she did.

"You're overheating, Julienne," he said shortly. "It is obviously that ridiculous coat."

Cristiano reached over, grasped the zipper that she'd tugged up to just beneath her chin, and pulled it loose.

And later, he would remember that she'd made a noise. That her arms came up as if to ward him off.

Here, now, he watched her mouth drop open. He watched her eyes darken, just the way he liked them. And then his gaze dropped down to trace the curves of that body he'd learned in such exquisite detail that their single night together was branded forever into his mind.

His first thought was that she must have augmented

her breasts, however little that made sense with what he knew of her, because they were bigger. Rounder and plumper, which made his mouth water. His palms itch.

And his gaze moved lower still, to take her all in—

But he stopped.

Because his mind simply refused to make sense of what he saw.

Worse, what it meant.

The bells of the city began to ring out the hour. Eight strikes, and each one like a poisoned spear thrust deep into his chest.

Her hands crept up and covered her belly, but it was too late. And her hands were too small.

Because Julienne Boucher had a giant belly. It was big, round and unmistakably pregnant.

Six months, something in him intoned. *Six. Months.*

Cristiano could not comprehend it.

He could not do more than stare.

"I didn't know for a long time," Julienne told him, hurriedly, though he wasn't sure he could make sense of her words. Or anything outside of that lurching in him. That great, deep howl. "I wasn't ill, you see. I was fairly fatigued, that's all. But a bit of fatigue seemed like a reasonable response to working as hard as I've done for the past ten years. Or to what happened in Monte Carlo, even. And then there was the move out west and all the details of setting up a new life. All of those things are fatiguing, are they not?"

She was talking too fast. And he kept staring at that belly of hers, that enormous belly.

Where she carried a child.

Where she carried *his*—

But he couldn't go there. His entire body and mind rejected it.

Julienne was still talking, her words tripping over each other. "When my clothes stopped fitting, I assumed it was because I was finally relaxing. Enjoying my food and no longer desperate to keep up appearances, always pretending I had nothing in common with that trashy little wannabe tramp who found you in Monte Carlo all those years ago. I congratulated myself on letting go, at last."

Was that what she expected? His congratulations?

Cristiano's throat worked, but he could not seem to produce a sound.

"So I didn't understand until quite late," she told him, her gaze wide and solemn. "A month ago, maybe six weeks, I happened to get out of the bath and look at myself in a mirror sideways. And then I began to count back."

"Six months," Cristiano said, as if from a great distance, and across the great desert of that howling thing in him.

"Six months," Julienne agreed. She cleared her throat. "And I want to make something perfectly clear, Cristiano. This was not my intention. This was never my intention. I wanted the bookends we spoke of that night, nothing more. You owe me nothing."

All he could do was stare at her. Not a ghost tonight. Not a common haunt, a memory he couldn't shake.

But his own, personal demon, come to destroy him.

"I'm here because I thought it was the right thing to

do. To tell you, I mean, but you should feel no sense of obligation. I truly mean that. Fleurette doesn't think I need to tell you at all, but I know you are an honorable man. You have always been an honorable man. And I felt certain that you would wish to know, even if you don't—"

The howling thing inside him stopped. But behind it was something far blacker. His rage.

He lifted his gaze to meet hers, his eyes like fire, and Julienne stopped talking.

Abruptly.

As if he'd slapped her.

Cristiano had never slapped a woman in his life, but in that moment, the chaos in him had control. And he could not have said what he might do next. He was a man allergic to uncertainty, and yet he had *no idea*.

"Cristiano," she began, carefully.

"You have said enough, I think."

He hardly recognized his own voice. It was stark. Harsh. As gray and cold as the city all around them. And inside him, the guilt and the shame that had always lurked there, waiting, rose up like the tide. Sweeping him under at last, then dragging him out to sea.

And that was the trouble with shame. With guilt. It only felt like drowning when the harder truth was he lived on. Despite everything, he lived on.

"Cristiano. Please." Julienne's eyes took on a particular sheen that some part of him recognized as tears. An emotion he did not wish to name.

He was far past that.

Out in that cold sea, going under, far away from any land.

"I will never forgive you for this," he told her, whole winters on his face. In his soul. And that terrible sea that choked him in his voice. "Mark my words, Julienne. I will never forgive you."

CHAPTER FIVE

THERE WAS SOMETHING raw and frozen in his gaze, and Julienne's chest hurt as if she'd breathed in too deep on a frigid morning, but Cristiano did not say anything further. Not to her.

He made two terse phone calls in a clipped, dark tone, then ushered her back across the *piazza*, his long, athletic stride giving her no quarter.

But it didn't occur to her not to go with him.

She didn't know what she'd been expecting, if she was honest with herself. Him to cry out in joy? Gather her into an embrace and dance around the *piazza*, like one of those strange American commercials for prescription medication?

"He will hate you," Fleurette had said, a judge handing down a verdict. "He will hate you, he will hate the baby, and I cannot see why it's the moral thing to do to subject either one of you to him. You repaid him already, Julienne. You do not owe him anything else. Ever."

She had not wanted to believe her sister.

More than that, she could admit—with a creeping sense of shame that bloomed all the brighter as he marched her to a waiting car, then bundled her into the back—she had wanted…

This, she supposed. Whatever *this* looked like.

Maybe all she'd wanted was to see him again. And this particular excuse to see him again was unassailable, whether he forgave her or not. She wasn't seeking his forgiveness. She was having his child.

And she would have to live with the part of her that exulted in that, and not because there was a life inside her that she was already desperately, hopelessly in love with. Or not *only* that. There was also the part of her that took far too much pleasure in the notion that their lives would forevermore be tangled together now, hers and Cristiano's, no matter what reaction he had to her pregnancy.

Julienne was certain that a better person would not feel such things. A good mother would be focused on the baby and not on her own treacherous heart. But as hard as she tried to expunge herself of such self-interested, foolish emotion, it remained.

Taunting her.

Making her wonder if he knew—and if that was why he couldn't forgive her. God knew she wasn't sure she could forgive herself, either.

Julienne did not ask where they were headed. He did not offer the information. They sat in the backseat of the car, separated by a few tense inches and a vast, unconquerable gulf of the fury that came off him in thick waves.

But she recognized the building they arrived at, sometime later. It was the house where she and Fleurette had lived in those first years after Monte Carlo, only leaving when Julienne had gotten her first real job at in the Cassara Corporation's UK office.

She shot him a sharp look as he ushered her out of the car and into the old house, but his face was closed down tight. Unreadable, save for that black, cold thing.

And Julienne understood that this was not a trip down memory lane when she saw the men waiting for them in the kitchen.

"I am a doctor," the oldest of the men said, smiling slightly while his white hair gleamed. "I believe I once treated you for bronchitis."

"Of course," Julienne murmured politely, feeling faintly ridiculous. She had no memory of having bronchitis or meeting any doctors, but then, that first six months or so after Cristiano had rescued them from Monte Carlo remained a blessed blur, even now.

The old man nodded. "If you'll come with me...?"

And it was not until the examination was done—until the necessary samples were taken and Julienne was dressed and sitting in the old living room that she had once believed was the very pinnacle of style and luxury—that she accepted the fact that Cristiano had hurt her feelings.

"You're being ridiculous," she muttered to herself, glaring down at her hands as she wound them together over the very crest of her bump. "He cannot take your word for it. How many women must turn up with paternity claims? He would be a fool if he did not verify this personally."

And if she knew anything about Cristiano Cassara, it was that he was never a fool.

That didn't make her feelings hurt any less, but it felt better to think about things practically. No matter how impractical she might feel on the inside.

Her mobile buzzed in her pocket and she pulled it out, not surprised to see that she'd missed a host of messages from Fleurette.

Did you tell him?

Was it terrible?

Are you okay?

She texted back.

I told him. He is confirming paternity.

And she slid her phone back in her pocket and muted it, because she knew too well what her sister's response to that would be.

After what seemed to her like a very long time, sitting there in silence in a house that was no longer hers—and had never been hers, if she was honest, or ever felt like more than the gift it had always been that she'd tried so hard to earn—she heard a noise at the door.

Julienne knew all she needed to about herself when her heart leaped at the notion that it might be him.

It wasn't.

"Have you booked into a hotel, Ms. Boucher?" the

man who stood there asked with a certain level of calm deference, as if Julienne might not recall that this was Massimo, Cristiano's secretary.

And Massimo was perfectly polite, as always. There was no reason for Julienne to interpret his question as aggressive. Or snide in some way.

Don't go making intrigue when there is only inquiry, she cautioned herself.

She named the hotel she'd checked into this morning, feeling outside herself as Massimo nodded, then withdrew.

And she was staring at her hands again when she felt the air change.

Because he didn't make a sound. Not one single sound.

There was that sense of some sort of disturbance, that was all. The hair on the back of her neck prickled. And Cristiano was there when she looked up, filling the doorway that led to the rest of the house and staring at her with that same raw fury making his dark eyes burn.

There were so many things she ought to have said. Julienne struggled to find the right words, but her tongue felt stiff. Heavy.

She realized then that she could still taste him on her tongue. That he could likely taste her, too.

Somehow, that made it all worse.

Her throat was tight. She couldn't tell if it was a sob or a scream. Or merely his name again.

And she understood as she stared back at him mutely that she'd been wrong about him all this time. Because she remembered him across all those years before that night in his hotel room in Monte Carlo. She remembered how cold and remote she'd thought him then. Always.

But she realized that he had not been cold at all.

Because now it was as if he was a block of frozen granite encased in sheets of ice.

His dark, bittersweet eyes glittered, but that was the only suggestion of heat she could see in him.

Everything else was ice. And the tension between them.

Taut. Harsh.

Julienne almost wished that he would say something. *Do* something. Even if it was terrible. Anything had to be better than this horrible silence.

She made herself swallow, though she felt as if there were knives in her throat. Perhaps actual knives would have been an improvement.

She swallowed again. Then cleared her throat. "If this situation is as terrible for you as it appears to be, I have a solution. I am perfectly happy to raise—"

"I would strongly suggest that you not finish that thought," Cristiano belted out, and she wished, then, that she had not been so desperate for him to speak.

Because it was worse when he did. His voice was so frigid she felt…chapped. And more, as if she was shaking apart at the seams, though it all seemed to be entirely inside her. As if she was built on a flimsy foundation that could tip over at the slightest provocation.

As if she had already, the longer he trained that pitch-dark gaze of his on her.

"You are carrying my child," he said, and there was no crack in his voice. No chink in the forbidding sheet of armor where his face should have been. Granite and ice. Ice and granite. "A boy."

"I know I am, thank you." Julienne forced a smile. "That's why I'm here, Cristiano."

"How could this happen?" he bit out. "And I would advise you not to get cute with me, Julienne. I understand the mechanics. But we used protection."

"Did we?" She sucked in a breath when his expression got, if possible, more forbidding. "That is to say, I can't claim that I was paying the slightest bit of attention."

His gaze was like flint. "I always use protection."

"So did my mother, as she liked to tell the world after a few drinks," Julienne said, with perhaps more flippant dark humor than necessary. "And yet here Fleurette and I are."

"What did you use?" he demanded. "Surely between the two of us, this should have been impossible."

"Whether it should have been impossible or not, it happened. Six months ago. It isn't going anywhere. *He* isn't going anywhere." But the way he was glaring at her seemed tinged with a kind of outrage, as if she'd done this to him. Deliberately. She blew out a breath. "And I was not using anything."

"Do you have habit of propositioning men, hoping they take care of the practicalities, and then failing to pay attention either way?"

"I don't have habit of men," she retorted, not sure where this wellspring of dark humor had come from. But she laughed anyway. "There has only ever been the one."

She saw his head tilt to the side, barely.

Barely.

And still, it was as if the room around them burst into flame.

Good job, Julienne, she snapped at herself. *Remember how you weren't going to tell him that? Ever?*

Across from her, Cristiano had gone glacial. "I beg your pardon?"

Julienne winced. She'd never wanted to tell him this truth. She'd never *planned* to tell him anything. He hadn't seemed to notice that night, and she'd assumed she'd never see him again. No need to burden him with the knowledge that he'd taken her virginity.

That was something she could hoard for herself. Like treasure.

But she rested her hands on the great roundness of her belly as she stared at him, so harsh and so bitterly cold, and really, what was the point of keeping these foolish secrets? What could any of it matter now?

"You do not habitually proposition men, is that what you're telling me?" he asked when she did nothing but gaze at him, and it was more knives then, slicing deep.

"I do not. Habitually or otherwise."

The tension between them rose even higher. She could hear it pressing against her ears. Making her head ache.

"I don't really know how to answer that," she continued brightly. "Perhaps I'll begin a habit of propositioning men, now that I am involved in so many new things." She rubbed her belly, and somehow found herself smiling at him over the child they'd made. The *child.* She forgave him his response because she wasn't exactly at peace with it herself. How could she blame him? "You were the first. And yes, before you ask. The first proposition. The first man. The first father to my first baby."

A terrible storm moved over his face, though his only physical reaction was the way his jaw worked. He looked away then, and she watched him press his finger and thumb to either side of his nose.

Fighting back something. She told herself she was glad.

But she found she was breathing far too heavily anyway.

"Very well then," he said after a long while, like a man facing the gallows. "It is done."

Julienne could still feel that shaking thing, making her feel fluttery inside in all the wrong ways. But she made herself laugh anyway.

"It's a baby, Cristiano. Not a harbinger of the end of days."

It seemed to take him a lifetime for him to turn his head back to her. And she wished he hadn't when that dark gaze of his landed on her with the weight of a great stone. Pressing the air from her lungs. Pressing the laughter out of her as if it had never been.

"I'm thrilled you find this so entertaining," he said, every syllable an accusation. More than an accusation, a verdict. And if a man's gaze could be a prison, she was sure she could see the metal doors clang shut all around her. Trapping her there in all that condemnation and cold. "I had no intention of continuing the Cassara bloodline."

Her mouth was dry while curiously, her palms were damp. "Surely continuing the bloodline is the first and foremost responsibility of a man of your position."

"Not for me." Again, that muscle in his jaw told her long, involved stories about how furious he was without him having to say a word. "My grandfather had two sons. One of them was by all accounts a good man, a credit to my grandfather, and an excellent steward of both the Cassara name and fortune. The other was my father. Miserable. Vicious. And deeply committed only to the bottle, never his family. Never his responsibilities. My uncle died in his twenties in a boating accident, taking my grandfather's dearest dreams with him. That left my father as the heir. To say that he was unable to live up to the expectations placed upon him would be to greatly understate the case."

He shook his head, but it looked like fury to Julienne, not sadness or loss, or even disappointment. "He bullied my mother. He would have treated me worse, had my grandfather not taken me in hand. But I vowed to myself a long time ago that it would end with me. I would never, ever take the risk that I would produce more Cassaras like my father."

"Then we won't." Julienne lifted her chin as she stared back at him. "This baby has just as much a chance to be a saint like your uncle as it does to turn out like your father."

"If you knew my father, you would understand that the risk is unacceptable."

"No one is born bad, Cristiano. They're made that way. The good news is, that means we can do our best to make sure we go in the opposite direction."

"Let us be clear what is at stake in this," Cristiano said darkly. "It is not simply a fortune. A corporation. The world is filled with both. It is also all the lives that hang in the balance of those things. Do you know how many people I employ? If I had been a man like my father, they all would have been ruined years ago. And you should be aware, Julienne, that I am more like my father than you would ever wish to know."

"That's ridiculous—" she began.

"A good man would never have touched you," he gritted out. "Much less the way I touched you, no matter what invitations you offered me after so many years. There is a darkness in me. There always has been, but you… You bring it out. And I can tell you from my experience with my own parents that such a darkness is no place to raise a child."

Her throat hurt again, and she had the sudden, terrible fear that it was tears waiting there, threatening to come out.

"I've already told you this, but you don't have to be involved," she managed to say, trying not to let her voice sound so thick. So obvious. And ignoring that sharp, stabbing sort of pain in her heart. "No one need ever know you have a son but you and me. I will take this baby away and raise him in Seattle, where he will grow up wrapped in flannel and immersed in technology, and who knows? Perhaps he will never come to Italy at all. It will be like it never happened."

And she could see that life stretch out before her, bright in its way and good, too—because she and Fleurette would care for this baby. They would devote themselves to him. They would do what they could to make sure he wanted for nothing.

But that sharp thing in her chest made it clear that wasn't the life she wanted. For her or the baby.

How had she managed to hide that from herself before now?

"I'm afraid that is impossible." And for a moment, Julienne could almost have sworn that the expression on Cristiano's face was that sadness, that loss, she'd been searching for before. "I don't know what you were expecting when you came here. But I will tell you now how it will be."

A kind of foreboding struck at her then, turning over inside her like a hot spike of pain. Of heat. Of something in between the two she wasn't sure she could name. "You don't get to decide how it will be."

His lips moved into something wholly mirthless, and darker than before. "My grandfather has an estate in Tuscany. It is quite remote, and will be a more than suitable place for you during your confinement."

"My...what did you say? My *what*?"

"I still don't know what you meant about your sister and you taking turns, but if that means that she must remain in Seattle, so be it. I'm not convinced that I care for her influence over you anyway."

Julienne let out something like a laugh. "You must have lost your mind."

"We already know that you have a habit of disappearing, Julienne." Those dark eyes glittered. "You will go to Tuscany. You will have the baby. And the two of you will remain there."

She was panting, her heart punching hard in her chest, but when he only gazed back at her as if what he'd said was perfectly reasonable, she found herself laughing again. In amazement.

"And how long will we remain there? The rest of our lives?"

His eyes glittered, glacial and harsh. "I can't say."

"You can't say because it's absurd. You can't really think that I'm going to let you hide me away somewhere. I have no desire to raise my child in a prison, thank you. Even one in scenic Tuscany."

"I'm afraid you will find that is not up to you to *let me* do anything," he replied, too softly "It is done."

She shot to her feet, cursing her new, pregnant body and how unsteady it made her feel on her own feet. And now the trembling inside of her had spread to the rest of her limbs. Now she simply shook, and there was no way he didn't see it.

He saw it, all right. What was clear was that he didn't care.

"This is not the stone age, Cristiano. What you're talking about is illegal. Kidnap. False imprisonment. Do you want me to go on?"

"You're welcome to put your complaint in writing, of course." His gaze was impassive. His expression like stone. "You are no longer employed by the company and can therefore claim no access to the human resources department, but I'll be certain to read any complaint of yours as closely as it deserves."

He only watched her as she gaped at him, and she couldn't help another incredulous laugh. "I'm not going to go with you, Cristiano. I will never, ever sign up to be locked away in some tower in the middle of nowhere, with or without my baby."

"Do you have an alternative?" he asked her quietly, that glittering thing in his gaze a weapon. And he'd hit his mark, dead center. "Ask yourself this, please. Can you run from me? And if you do, do you truly believe I will not catch you?"

"Cristiano..." she whispered, though she had the terrible feeling it was already too late.

And that his name was less a song on her lips tonight than it had been once.

Especially when his mouth moved into that grim, hard line. "The question is not whether or not I can do what I wish. It is not even whether or not I should. The question is, Julienne, what can you possibly do to stop me?"

CHAPTER SIX

THE VILLA CASSARA was as beautiful as it was quietly renowned. It was a triumph of Italian country glory set down to make the most of the gentle Tuscan hills where, it was rumored, Cassaras had dreamed of sweet things for many generations.

Julienne had been a little too aware of the difference between reality and corporate marketing after all her years as a glorified candy seller, but that didn't make the Cassara family home any less impressive. If she'd been an invited guest, she would no doubt have called the place a paradise.

But the villa wasn't hers for a holiday. It was a prison. And it didn't matter how beautiful a prison was. What mattered was that she couldn't leave it as she chose.

Julienne had succumbed with embarrassingly little trouble. Cristiano had been implacable, as ever, but worse—he'd been correct. She could not outrun him. She certainly couldn't fight him off.

She was six months pregnant and more debilitating by far, she had lost her heart to him a long time ago.

And so she had clung to what shreds of dignity she

had remaining. She had let him march her out of the house where she and Fleurette had once lived—where she had made him into a myth in her head. A legend of all that was good and right, when maybe that had been nothing but a fairy tale a lost girl told herself as she figured out how to find her way out of her own dark woods.

She rather thought it said unfortunate things about her that she felt more grief over the loss of her made-up version of Cristiano than she did about the fact he handed her into another car, escorted her to the Cassara Corporation offices, then took her to the roof where the Duomo rose in the distance. There he'd strapped her into his waiting helicopter.

Her priorities had shifted around when he hadn't boarded the helicopter himself, but let her fly away with his staff instead. She'd had nothing to do but think about the appropriate things to grieve as they flew through the night, away from the lights of Milan, then south toward Florence and the Tuscan countryside.

In the dark, as the helicopter came in to land, it was entirely too easy to see that there was absolutely nothing rolling out in all directions. Nothing but a vast inky black stretch, with only the villa casting off light, a small bright beacon in all the dark.

Her first, panicked assessment had not been wrong.

The next morning, Julienne had woken up in the room that the smiling housekeeper had escorted her to the night before. The room could easily have starred in a magazine spread on the wonders of Italian villas. Outside her windows, it didn't look any more real. It was a glorious stretch of pretty fields toward the horizon, the view studded with cypress trees, red poppies and purples wisteria.

But Julienne wasn't here to marvel at the pretty land and gardens. She was here against her will.

"You need to remember that," she told herself sternly.

The villa sat at the crest of a hill and no matter how high she climbed or how far she looked or walked in any direction, there was nothing. No other villas. No adorable Italian villages, tucked charmingly away beyond this hill or that.

Even if there hadn't been evident security, there to patrol the boundaries of the Cassara estate, it wasn't as if she could simply walk off and expect to get away. The estate didn't appear on any maps. It was so resolutely unmappable, in fact, that her mobile kept suggesting she was in the center of Florence.

She might have set off anyway, because Italy had been populated for thousands of years and she was bound to find *someone* if she walked far enough, but it wasn't just her she had to think about these days. And she didn't feel she could risk herself when she had the baby to consider.

It turned out that she could spend a lot of time brooding about that, too.

But it wasn't until later that first day that she truly realized exactly what it was that Cristiano had planned for her.

There was staff, but they only nodded and excused themselves. It became clear very quickly that they'd been instructed not to speak to her. Hours later, she found herself standing on one of the many patios, staring out at fields as the fog rolled in.

It was beautiful. And it was also…empty. No cars, no traffic. No signs of life. No indication that there was anything here, or anywhere near, but her.

Isolation to go along with her imprisonment, she understood then. Not just prison, but solitary confinement.

"You cannot expect me to live like this," she told him over the phone when she called him, shortly after that unpleasant revelation. "How can you remain in Milan, leaving me to molder away out in these fields?"

"Stranded in the prettiest prison on earth." His voice was a dark rasp that should have horrified her. It didn't. "My heart bleeds."

"I've lived in cities almost all my life." Because the oppressive silence of the hill town she'd grown up in haunted her still. The only sound had been the wind. And the endless judgment of the citizens. But she didn't tell him that. She hardly liked admitting it to herself. "Do you really think I will take to the pastoral experience? I'll explode if I stay here."

"There is no *if*, Julienne." His voice was glacial. As immovable as he was. "You will stay right where you are. Your every need is attended to and who knows? Perhaps a spot of quiet contemplation will do you some good."

"And what of you?" she snapped back at him, gripping her mobile so tightly she was surprised it didn't snap in half. "Do you plan to live your life as if you don't have a woman and a baby hidden away out here like some syphilitic eighteenth century nobleman?"

"Enjoy the fresh air," he growled at her. "Indulge in

la dolce vita. You are at the Villa Cassara, after all. The sweet life is guaranteed."

And it was only when he'd rung off that it occurred to her that really, he hadn't had to take her furious call in the first place. It wasn't as if the grand head of the Cassara Corporation answered his own phone, unless he wished it.

If he wanted to truly isolate her, if he wanted to keep her caged up here, there wasn't a single thing she could do about it unless she wanted to call the police.

Assuming there were police to call, this far away from anywhere.

Julienne wasn't proud of herself for crying, but she couldn't stop. Not for days, off and on. She blamed her hormones. But then, as one week ticked over into the next, something else kicked in.

She was a survivor, after all. She'd survived her beginnings in France, which was more than some could claim, her own poor, lost mother among them. And she hadn't accidentally survived it. She'd been prepared to do the unthinkable to rescue herself from that life. It made her stomach hurt to think of it now, but if Cristiano hadn't been sitting at that bar in Monte Carlo, someone else would have been. Some other man.

And Julienne would have done what she needed to do.

That thought often brought her shame. But now, left to her own devices in her lovely Tuscan prison, she decided instead to think of it as a strength.

She would do what she needed to do, because she always did.

Because that was who she was.

In this case, stranded here as she was, she had to accept that there was no way out. Unless she wanted to pull off an elaborate scheme that would involve stealing one of the vehicles—and behaving as if she wasn't pregnant. Maybe it would come to that, but first, she thought she'd try something else.

She'd always been extraordinarily good at doing her research. This had been a Cassara residence for generations. What she needed to do was gather as much information as possible where she was, and see where it led her.

And the more information, the better.

Because she intended to use it as a weapon.

"What do you mean, 'there are reporters'?" Cristiano asked in icy disbelief.

His secretary stood on the other side of the large desk and…quailed. When Massimo was normally unflappable. It was his superpower, in fact. Cristiano couldn't say that he liked the evidence that even the dependably immovable Massimo could look anything but in total control of all things, all the time.

Julienne, a voice inside him said. Foreboding, perhaps. Or simply a warning.

Because it couldn't be anything else.

"From what I can gather, sir, there are some questions about your grandfather's relationship with a woman," Massimo said, his face studiously blank. "A woman not your grandmother."

Cristiano ground his teeth together, but could not bring himself to speak.

Maybe that was a good thing.

Massimo gazed back at him as if, given his preference, he would have chopped off his own head rather than said such a thing. "I'm only repeating what the great mess of them had been shouting down in the lobby."

"The *mess* of them," Cristiano repeated. He had to fight for every scrap of advertising space across all media, but a whisper of scandal brought the vultures out in spades. But then, this was something he knew all too well after a lifetime as his father's son.

Cristiano wanted to do some shouting of his own. But he refrained.

Barely.

"They want to ask you questions about your grandparents, I believe," Massimo said apologetically. "And also, I'm afraid, about Sofia Tomasi."

Sofia Tomasi. A name Cristiano had hoped never to hear again.

His grandfather had died five years ago. Piero Cassara had personally built on an ancient Italian fortune to create Cassara Chocolates, the finest luxury chocolate brand in the world. And he had been a man of honor. So claimed the papers, his employees, even his rivals. Anything Cristiano knew about being a man—and not a sad example of one—he'd learned from his grandfather.

But his private life had been somewhat less sweet than the family business, particularly when thrust under the lens of public perception.

Cristiano wanted nothing to do with his grandmother, a bitter, dour old woman who still lived in a corner of the Tuscany estate, cared only for her own company, and was happy to tell anyone who asked that she'd turned her back on her husband, her marriage and her family long ago. Before Cristiano's uncle had died, in fact.

That she had never cared for her husband was an accepted fact of the Cassara storyline. Her parents had pressured her into marrying him, she'd done her duty, and once her two sons were born she'd wanted nothing to do with any Cassaras ever again. Cristiano had long imagined her his own, personal fairy-tale witch—hunkered down in a cottage on the edge of the property, bristling with malevolence anytime he ventured near.

He'd thought nothing of it. Just as he'd thought nothing of Sofia Tomasi, the woman his grandfather had called any number of things over the years. Housekeeper. Friend. Companion.

Mistress, Cristiano thought now.

Though the tabloids would start using much worse words, now they knew.

He supposed he'd always known what she was to his grandfather. Like his grandmother, it wasn't a story that bore repeating. It was simply a fact. Accordingly, no one had commented on the relationship in years, at least not in Cristiano's hearing. Because everyone already knew about it, Cristiano had thought. And because whatever provisions his grandfather had made for Sofia, they had not been in his will, and thus had never been subject to public review or comment.

But there was one person who could not have known

about Sofia, or the Cassara family's tacit agreement that she was far, far better for Piero than the angry old woman in the cottage ever could be. And that one person was currently at loose in the villa, clearly digging around in things she shouldn't.

Worse, Cristiano had put her there.

Meaning he had no one to blame for swarming reporters and a breaking new scandal his grandfather would have detested but himself.

He dismissed Massimo, even managing to thank the man. Meanwhile his jaw actually ached as he clenched it, so tight it was a miracle his teeth didn't shatter.

"I have told them to disperse," Massimo said as he walked out of Cristiano's office. "If they do not, I will contact the police."

Cristiano nodded, but there was no getting around what he needed to do, no matter how little he wanted to do it. He had done his best to carry on as usual, pretending there was no woman off in Tuscany and certainly no pregnancy to contend with. Because he had no earthly idea how to handle either one.

And he was not a man who usually suffered from uncertainty.

But he certainly couldn't have Julienne stirring up trouble and breathing life into old scandals that should have stayed buried with his grandfather.

He would have to go to her.

"I will have to go her," he said aloud, as if thinking it wasn't enough. "Damn her."

By the time the helicopter landed near the villa, his temper hadn't cooled a bit. If anything, being back in these rolling fields spiked with cypress trees with the scent of rosemary in the air only made it worse.

Cristiano had been raised mostly in Milan. His father had preferred the city, with its infinite bad choices spread out for him to choose between at his leisure, and he had been deeply scornful of the countryside where he'd been raised. Cristiano had always preferred it here, though he'd known better than to state a preference for anything. He associated the rolling fields and undulating hills so strongly with his grandfather that even now he expected to see the old man waiting for him. His seasons here at the villa were the only times in his life he'd ever really felt *right*.

You should not have brought her here, you fool, he told himself sharply as he made his way toward the sprawling main house his grandfather had restored and rebuilt over the years, so it felt appropriately storied and historic even though every detail had been modernized.

He braced himself as he walked inside, not sure what he expected. The statuary to be upended and left in chunks, perhaps. As if she'd pillaged the place in the week or so since he'd sent her here.

But everything was as he'd left it. And as he liked to leave it in the state his grandfather would recognize if he walked in the door this very evening, Cristiano didn't know how to feel about the fact that Julienne had done the same. Somehow that didn't seem to match a woman who would ring up the tabloids in the next breath.

He wandered through the rooms that looked precisely as they always had, with the same priceless art on the walls and the same furniture that managed to be both sophisticated and comfortable at once. A hall-mark of the villa, and in many ways, how he recalled his grandfather, too.

Cristiano wandered across the grand atrium in the center of the building. It was open to the deep blue Tuscany sky above, bursting with flowers, trees and the small pool he knew was stocked with plump, lazy fish.

On the other side, he did not find Julienne in the bedroom suite that had been set aside for her. Or any of the other suites in that wing of the house. And he could admit that he was beginning to feel the faintest sense of unease as he retraced his steps, looking in the various salons and studies and reception rooms, many of which had stood empty since his grandfather's death.

And that was where he found her.

He stopped in the door of the library, watching the light stream in from the great domed skylight above, carefully directed into the center of the space and the table that stood there. And not toward the floor to ceiling shelves that lined the walls. Julienne sat at the table, looking perfectly at her ease. Papers, books, his grandfather's collection of personal letters and a pad she was using to jot down notes were spread across the surface of the center table as if she'd made it her office.

He wanted to charge in and sweep the whole mess of it to the floor, but he couldn't seem to move. Because she was more beautiful than he remembered.

And God help him, but it caught at him. She caught at him and he had no earthly idea how to stop her.

Cristiano could no longer remember, now, how he'd managed to keep himself from noticing her all these many years. When she'd been nothing to him but another employee, if more ambitious and dependable than most. How had he turned this greed in him off? And why couldn't he do it again?

Her hair was not up in its normal twist today. It swirled down around her shoulders, gleaming gold in the sunlight. She had a faint frown of concentration between her brows, which he wanted to smooth with his fingers. And she tugged her lower lip between her teeth as she scribbled something on the pad before her.

And everything inside him was fire and fury, regret, and that other thing he couldn't quite name. That ache that he couldn't define and was doing his level best to ignore.

He didn't know when she became aware of him. But he knew when she did, even though she didn't react at first. She finished writing whatever she was scribbling on her pad, set her pen down with what struck him as unnecessary precision and only then lifted her gaze to his.

"You've sicced the press on me?" he demanded, his voice not much more than a growl, because that was better than analyzing the *punch* of her gaze. The way it made him want to rock back on his heels. Though he did not. "Do I need to confiscate your mobile, Julienne?"

"You can do that." Her voice was as cool and mild as her expression. Cristiano believed neither, not when he could still feel that punch. "But then you would have a much bigger problem."

"I find that difficult to believe."

"You've chosen not to deal with me," she said, her

eyes dark. "And lucky for you, I am accustomed to taking your orders. But you will find my sister more difficult to control."

"Is that it?" He didn't quite laugh, but he felt…bigger, suddenly. More in control of this mess he'd made. "Your little sister is the threat? Your big gun?"

Julienne smiled. "A key difference between Fleurette and me, among many others, is that she never liked you all that much to begin with."

And Cristiano didn't understand the pull he felt to this woman. He hadn't understood it that night in Monaco. He certainly hadn't understood it in the six long months that had followed. Today, when by rights he should despise her for discussing his family's business with reporters, he found himself leaning against the doorjamb instead. Almost lazily, when he was never lazy.

Almost as if this was some game they played.

"Impossible," he heard himself say, icily sardonic. "My charm is legendary."

"You are a distinctly charmless man," she replied. And there was no reason why Cristiano—who had never given a moment's thought to whether or not he was considered charming by anyone—should feel a sense of outrage at her offhanded, matter-of-fact tone. "You are known chiefly for your intensity, as I think you are well aware. And now, it seems, your upsetting criminal behavior."

Cristiano considered her, feeling as distinctly charmless as she'd called him. "I wonder that you did not call the police rather than the press, if your upset is so great."

She smiled again, but it was a different sort of smile. Far more of a weapon than the politely cool one he'd seen in the office.

"I realize this is not sitting well with you, Cristiano, but you are the father of this baby." Julienne rose then, clearly pointing her belly in his direction. In case he might have forgotten. "And it is not exactly ideal to have the father of my baby locked up forever in prison, as you surely would be if I called the police and explained to them that you're keeping me here against my will."

"You could walk to Florence, *cara*. It is not so many kilometers from here."

"It is, in fact, many hundreds of kilometers to Florence. I checked, and when the maps on my mobile failed, I asked one of your guards."

Cristiano wanted to hurl something back at her, but he was struck by all that light cascading down from above, bathing her in it. She *glowed*. There was no other word to describe it. He tried to tell himself it was a trick of the light, but somehow, he knew perfectly well it was not. It was her.

Julienne was...blooming.

Like the flowers outside in the atrium, she reminded him of spring. Bright and sweet and glowing, like the Roman goddesses who had once been worshiped on this same plot of earth.

"You want my attention, is that it?" he asked, forcing himself to stop thinking about goddesses and *glowing*. "Is that why you sent me your message in the form of a pack of reporters?"

He could hear the danger in his own voice. He

thought she heard it too, because she did that thing with her chin. That defiant tilt, as if, left to her own devices, she might fight him.

"It's the baby that needs your attention, Cristiano."

And he had to grit his teeth against that word. *Baby.* Against all the things that happened in him when he thought of it.

Because he knew better. He knew what he was.

"Neither you nor the child will want for anything." His lips thinned. "What more can you require of me than that?"

"Explain to me how this is going to go," she said, in the brisk manner he recognized too well from her days as one of his vice presidents. His favorite vice president, he could admit, now she'd vacated her post. "I will have the baby here, presumably? And I do not doubt that you will see to it that the finest medical team in Europe is on hand. After he is born, I'm sure you will produce nannies. Tutors. Do you anticipate that he will simply live here forever? That he and I will shuffle around the Tuscan hills until we are interred beneath the soil ourselves?"

His teeth ached. Again. "There's no need to be dramatic."

"My mistake. Because there is no inherent drama whatsoever in imprisoning the mother of your child against her will."

"Neither you nor the child will want for anything," he gritted out again, repeating himself.

"The child will want a father," she threw back at him. "And I—"

But she stopped herself. And he found himself roaming closer, not sure what it was that compelled him. That glow of hers, maybe, now mixed with the heat of her temper.

Cristiano had never seen anything so bright.

And he could not tell if he wanted to lock her away or put his hands on her instead. He could not tell which one hurt, which tempted him or how on earth he could possibly handle this. Her.

The baby.

"Finish your sentence," he dared her. "What is it *you* want, Julienne?"

"I have known you for a long time, Cristiano. A very long time. I have seen the best of you firsthand. I have also seen you on one of your cold rampages, striking terror into whole divisions with a single stare."

"And yet you do not know me at all," he retorted.

"I know enough. You have your rules, don't you? You like to be alone. No friends, no family, only work. You like a woman, but only for a night."

"In this, I think you'll find, I am no different than any other man."

"But you're not a playboy, forever in search of flesh and sin," she said, and there was a different kind of light in her dark eyes. He could feel the echo of it inside him. "You're afraid."

CHAPTER SEVEN

IF SHE'D THROWN a lit match at him, she doubted Cristiano would look more thunderstruck.

But that was good, she assured herself as that thunderstruck expression tipped over into something significantly more forbidding. He might not want to know how she felt, but she was compelled to tell him anyway, for her sins.

There had to be something deeply wrong with her that this man—her *captor*, lest she forgot—could stride in here with a look on his face that suggested she was already trying his patience, and she should want nothing more than to go to him. To put her hands on him. To press her mouth to his and feel the kick of that race through her all over again.

"Call the police," Fleurette had snapped at her, the first day. And every day since. "Or I will."

"I can't call the police," Julienne replied every time. Today she'd added, "think of the baby, please, Fleurette. Does he need to come into the world to find his father in jail?"

But her sister knew her too well, and had responded to that pious tone with a snort.

"Maybe you should think of the baby," she'd shot right back. "With your head, Julienne. Instead of whatever it is you're thinking with these days."

Julienne did not wish to examine what part of her person she might have been using lately, thank you. What mattered was that there would be no police. Paparazzi, perhaps, thanks to the wealth of personal letters Cristiano's grandfather had kept in this library. Passionate letters, both the ones he'd received and copies of those he'd sent, which meant Julienne had the full picture of his extramarital affair—a relationship filled with longing and complaint, years of yearning and plans for more. Always more.

And privately, she might have felt somewhat ashamed about sharing those sentiments with the world by calling some of the contacts she'd made in her time at Cassara Chocolates, then letting them run with what she'd dug up. Then again, who wasn't fascinated with stories of marital infidelity, long-term mistresses paraded around in plain view, and the truth about great men who had been very nearly canonized after their deaths?

Besides, she told herself now as Cristiano scowled at her, what else was she supposed to do? She was a kidnap victim. A kidnap victim held in glorious luxury, it was true, but all the lovely trappings in the world couldn't change the fact she couldn't leave.

Oh, said a voice inside her that sounded far too much like her sister, *do you* want *to leave? Because that certainly isn't clear.*

That landed like a punch. Because Julienne knew, now, that anything she might have told herself about her motivations was a lie. She'd known that the moment she'd looked up and seen him there, smoldering and furious and still with that darkness all over his face.

As if she had not simply surprised him with this baby. As if she'd broken him instead. A notion that made her want to reach out and make it better, somehow, with her hands.

Fleurette would be appalled, she knew. But then, Fleurette was often and easily appalled. It was part of her charm.

"I must have misheard you, Julienne," Cristiano said after what felt like a long, long while, in a conversational tone she in no way believed. Not when she could see that simmering fury in his dark gaze. "It sounded as if you called me a coward."

"It's a choice you have to make," she threw back at him, head high, as if he didn't get to her at all. Because he shouldn't have gotten to her. "You can be a father or you can be afraid. So far, it appears you've chosen the latter."

Because surely they could both figure out how to be better parents than the ones they'd had. She had to believe that was possible.

Cristiano's glower took on a new weight, but she refused to be cowed. And as he prowled toward her, she reminded herself that he hadn't exactly become less dangerous in the week he'd left her here.

What was wrong with her that something in her thrilled to that?

And worse, there was that melting between her legs.

As if her body had already made its choices and would happily, exultantly, make them all over again.

"You are not the only person I met in that bar ten years ago," he told her when he reached the table.

She felt a jolt at that, an awful kick. Was he trying to say…? But she couldn't even complete that question in her own head.

"I was there in the first place because I knew my father was there that night," he continued, sounding even darker than before. "He loved Monte Carlo. The excess soothed him. And when I found him, he was blind drunk, as ever. But in his blindness he retained a certain, vicious clarity. Particularly when it came to me."

"*In vino veritas* is a lie," Julienne said quietly, something she knew all too well. And she refused to acknowledge the sense of deep relief she felt that he was not telling her a story of how he'd had some other woman in that place she now thought of as theirs—the good and bad of it alike. "You must have learned the truth of this years ago."

Cristiano's mouth did something stark and bitter. "My father was not pleased to see me, which was the typical state of affairs between us."

That bitter curve to his mouth only deepened, leaving brackets in his hard face. And Julienne wished, suddenly, that he had not started to tell her this tale. She had a terrible feeling about where he was going with it.

But she couldn't seem to speak when she needed to most.

Cristiano kept going, one hand on the table between them. "We had a fundamental disagreement, my father and I. He believed that it was his right to behave as he wished, without a single thought for any other living human being. In particular, my mother, who he took great pleasure in bullying. And I believed that if he wanted to career about from one bottle to the next, then communicate with his fists, he should remove himself entirely from the rest of polite society. These were incompatible positions, obviously."

And there was something about the way he was looking at her, that bittersweet gaze of his direct. Intense. Daring her to…argue? Deny him the opportunity to tell this story? She couldn't tell. But whatever he was daring her to do, it made her pulse pick up. Her heart began to kick through her, slow and hard and insistent.

"I had long ago outgrown any need to rail at my father in the hope that he would become a different man before my eyes. Those are trials of adolescence and I had long ago become inured to his opinions of me. They mattered less and less in the course of my actual life and work. Left to my own devices, I rarely saw him."

"Except that night," Julienne managed to croak out, though her throat felt almost too tight to bear.

"That night it was necessary for me to seek him out," Cristiano agreed, the banked fury in that dark gaze of his making her neck prickle. "It was not a task I relished, though if I am honest, there was a part of me that wanted it, too. My grandfather was concerned about the future of the company he had spent his life building. He was as disgusted with my father as I was was—more, probably. And after many years spent waiting and hoping that my father might straighten himself out and rejoin the family and the company as a contributing member, my grandfather had made a final decision. He'd gone ahead and cut my father off entirely. And had written him out of his will to boot."

Julienne wanted to reach for him, but knew that Cristiano would never allow it. He stood too stiffly. His eyes were too dark. She braced her hands on the swell of her belly, and tried to focus on the story he was telling. And not how she longed to soothe a man who didn't want to feel better. Who would actively avoid it if possible, in fact.

"Why were you the messenger?" she asked quietly instead, a sense of injustice welling up in her on his behalf. "Shouldn't this have been something your grandfather told your father himself? It was his will."

"My father and I did not see each other much, but my father and my grandfather had not spoken in years," Cristiano said with a certain briskness that told Julienne a great many things about his family without him having to elaborate. And it occurred to her to wonder why she had always assumed that someone with his money must necessarily have no problems. Why she'd imagined that the money itself would protect him, when, of course, complicated people kept right on complicating things no matter their tax bracket. "It fell to me to deliver the news to him, if I chose."

"If you chose?"

"I didn't have to tell him that night. I could have waited for the inevitable explosion when he discovered his funding had disappeared, and for good. I might have, were it not for my mother."

Julienne blinked. "She wasn't still with him. Was she?"

"My mother believed deeply in the sanctity of marriage," Cristiano replied, his voice as hard as it was cold. As if he was turning to ice before her eyes. "Or perhaps it was more that she felt she had made her bed and was required to lie in it ever after. I can't say. I understood her very little, if I'm honest."

Julienne shook her head. "But surely she wasn't required to stay if your father was cruel to her."

"There is no 'get out of jail' card for a bad marriage," Cristiano said, a hard amusement in his voice that in no way made it to his eyes. "Not for my mother. She was raised to endure. This story you have dug up about my grandfather and Sofia Tomasi—I used to tell my mother that she should use it as her example. That it was possible to have something better. Different, anyway, even if she did choose to remain married. But she was horrified at the very idea."

"So she stayed."

"She endured." Cristiano blew out a breath. "I admired my grandfather deeply. In many ways, he is the only hero I have ever known. But when he cut off my father, I knew that he was condemning my mother to more abuse. It was the only time we fought."

Julienne searched his face, but there was only granite. "Did you think that if you spoke to your father he'd be nicer to your mother? I would have been afraid that it would make him go in the opposite direction."

"I did not beg a man like Giacomo Cassara to treat his wife better." Cristiano's eyes gleamed with that cold near amusement that made Julienne shiver. "I wanted him to know first that despite his best efforts, his inheritance was mine. And second, that I didn't care what he did with himself, but I would be watching over my mother. And prepared to take matters into my own hands if any harm befell her."

Julienne's mind spun. She tried to remember the bits and pieces of Cassara family history that had trickled down to her over the years. This rumor, that rumor. She knew his mother was no longer alive, of course. But did that mean…?

"My father proceeded to tell me that he thought about drowning me when I was a child. Repeatedly. Among other, less savory parental notions." Cristiano paused, his mouth in a flat, hard line. "And then he staggered out of the bar. He collected my mother where, unbeknownst to me, she was waiting for him in a rented flat, and told the valet that he was driving them back to Milan. Meanwhile, I looked up from a dark contemplation of the only example of fatherhood I knew personally…to find you there. Determined to sell yourself."

"Whatever your father said to you is a reflection of him, not you. You must know that."

"Spare me the pop psychology, please." His dark eyes glittered, remote and icily furious at once. "You and I can sit here and discuss at length the ways in which my father was a pathetic example of a man. But that does not change the fact there is something wrong with me. With this blood in my veins."

She opened her mouth to argue, but a frigid glare stopped her.

"I always think of my grandfather as a good man, but as you have uncovered, there are reasons to think otherwise. If you traipsed across the length of this property and found my grandmother, she would tell you that the Cassaras are nothing but monsters. Devils sent to this earth to plague the decent."

"In fairness, it seems your grandfather was fairly unrepentant about the fact he was cheating on her." Julienne gestured at the table and the collection of letters. "He even brags about it."

"There was only one good Cassara, and he died a long time ago," Cristiano said. Firmly. "I never had any plans for there to be another."

"Cristiano…"

"But there is more to the story." And she was too well trained to obey that commanding voice of his. She'd been doing it for years. She fell silent without even meaning to do so while he kept telling her this same story that bookended hers. "While I was busy making arrangements for you and your sister and having you transported out of the country, my father was driving to Milan. But he never made it."

The memory, foggy before, snapped back into place. There had been a car accident. She remembered the whispers she'd heard in the office about his past. And even more vaguely, the research she'd done on his family when he'd first installed them in the house in Milan.

But she didn't want him to say it. Not here. She wanted to leap across the sun-drenched library table and throw her hands over his mouth to keep his words in.

As if that could make it any better for him.

The baby kicked then. Hard. Sharing her distress, maybe, And for a moment she didn't have to wonder why she couldn't breathe.

"They say he lost control of the car in the Montferrat hills. But I know better. He was already drunk, and I had agitated him. And I'm not going to stand here and pretend to you that the loss of a man like my father keeps me up at night. It doesn't. It's my mother I can't let go." Cristiano's hard gaze bored into her. "He killed my mother, and it was my fault, and I have to live with that."

"Cristiano—"

"And then I have to ask myself, what kind of man does not care that he sent his own father to his death?"

"It wasn't your fault," Julienne said fiercely. She stepped out from behind the table and moved toward him, even though it was foolish. She couldn't seem to help herself. "You weren't the one who'd had too much to drink. You weren't driving the car."

"I knew what he was and I knew what might happen if he went off half-cocked. This is what I'm talking about, Julienne." And she could see something besides that glacial cold in his dark eyes as she came closer. The torture. The pain. Her stomach twisted—*for* him. "I killed my mother as surely as if I was behind the wheel. And I let my father kill the both of them, because some part of me cared that little about where he would go and what he would do once he left that bar. Because the truth is, there is nothing good in me. I play a good game, but scratch the surface, and I'm nothing but another Cassara monster. A breaker of vows. A bully. A son who took great pleasure in taunting his father into staggering off and getting behind the wheel. One way or another, that makes me a killer."

Julienne felt like crying. Or possibly already was. Her eyes were glassy and the library was becoming blurred at the edges.

But in the center of everything was Cristiano.

"None of that is true," she managed to say.

And then she closed the last bit of distance between them and slid her hands on his chest.

He jolted as if she'd shocked him. His hands moved to capture hers, and she thought he would push her away, but he didn't.

And for a very long moment, they stood there, frozen.

"You are nothing like your father," she told him with all the ferocity she could muster. "I knew your grandfather too, don't forget, and the difference between you and him is that you don't make vows unless you know you can keep them. Forever. There are a thousand things that can make an innocent child grow into a man like your father, but none of them are in your blood, Cristiano. Not one of them."

And before he could argue any further, she thrust herself up on her tiptoes, somehow balancing the weight of her belly, and pressed a kiss to his mouth.

She hadn't meant to do that.

Or maybe she had, because Lord knew, every night she tried to sleep in this villa—this gorgeous prison— and her head was full of nothing but him. Images of the things they'd done. Of the things they might yet do.

She woke up in the dark, her body one great throbbing pulse of need, and he was never there.

But Cristiano was here now. And he was hurting.

And somehow a kiss seemed to be the answer to everything. A give and a take. A soothing and a sharing, for both of them.

So she angled her head and took it deeper.

Just the way he'd taught her.

She felt him shake. It was as if he was melting, there while she touched him, and she knew that if he was in control of himself the way he normally was, he would never have allowed it. He would certainly never have let her *see* it.

She had the sense of glaciers melting, ice floes cracking.

Until slowly, almost reluctantly, he kissed her back.

And she forgot, for a moment, that he had spirited her off to this place. She forgot the baby. The great belly that was now pressed between them.

Cristiano kissed her and she forgot her own name.

She heard a faint noise, low and greedy, and only belatedly realized that it was her. That it was coming from her own throat.

And when he tore his mouth from hers, he looked hunted. *Haunted,* something in her supplied.

With perhaps more satisfaction than necessary.

"It is already too much," he said, dark and low. "It is already gone too far."

"I don't know what that means." But she understood well enough when he stepped away, backing away from her as if she'd *done something* to him. "Are you disgusted by my pregnancy?" Her voice was much too brittle, but she did nothing to stop it. She couldn't. "Is that what this is?"

"You *glow*," he bit out, as if the words erupted from within. "If it is possible, you're more beautiful now than you were before, damn you. And I think you know it."

That was meant to be an indictment, clearly. He threw it at her, then wheeled around, and stalked away.

And Julienne should no doubt have taken herself off for another good cry.

But instead, she found herself standing there where Cristiano had left her, her mouth still tingling from the taste of him, and a smile she couldn't quite control on her face.

CHAPTER EIGHT

THE WOMAN WAS a demon.

There was no other explanation for that kiss. The way he'd responded and worse, what he'd said to her as he walked away. This was precisely what he'd wanted to avoid. It was why he'd stashed her away in Tuscany in the first place.

Did you really think she wouldn't cause problems for you? a harsh voice inside him asked. *If you wanted to keep her out of trouble, you should have made sure she couldn't contact the outside world. A prison isn't much of a prison when a person has full access to her media contacts, is it?*

Cristiano meant to return to Milan. He needed to keep away from this woman who had unaccountably haunted him long before she'd turned up pregnant. But halfway to the helicopter, he thought better of it. Leaving Julienne to her own devices helped no one, least of all him. Especially not when he was stalked by the reporters she'd sent after the family secrets.

Unapologetically.

That was what he told himself, in any case, as he

sent for his things and then set up his usual remote office in the villa.

His intention—had anyone asked, which no one would dare—was simply to monitor the situation here. To repress any further attempts to stir up trouble.

Even if he still didn't know why he'd shared the details of that night in Monaco with her, when he'd never talked about that night with anyone. Much less the guilt and shame he carried with him even now.

And once in the villa, he expected her to show that relentless streak he'd so admired when she'd worked for him. He expected interrogations over his morning cappuccino, demands for further discussions at the end of his work day, or appearances in the middle of conference calls that would cause him difficulties with his colleagues when so many of them knew her.

But Julienne did none of these things.

She appeared at dinner that first night looking fresh and easy, seeming to shine even brighter than before. The smile she aimed his way was sunny, which had the direct result of making him glower.

"The staff tell me that you have insisted on a solitary dinner service every night," he said, sitting in his usual spot at the head of the grand table, the centerpiece of the formal dining room. "Right here at this table."

She beamed at him, sitting directly to his right. "There have to be some perks to finding oneself marooned in Tuscany. I decided I might as well make use of your fine staff and your truly excellent cook."

And when Cristiano could seem to do nothing at all

but stare darkly at her, she smiled again, even more sunnily. Then she turned her attention to her antipasti.

He resolved to use this experience—sharing the villa with her, against his will—as an opportunity for some immersion therapy. He did not wish to be haunted, thank you. He wanted her out of his head, his unfortunate dreams, his life. Cristiano felt certain that familiarity must breed its usual contempt, and that in short order this *thing* that ate away at him would disappear completely.

Once it did, he could approach the rest of this rationally. Carefully.

But everywhere he went, she seemed to be there. Even if she was not physically in the room, there was some reminder of her. Her scent on the breeze, or the sound of her laughter from across the atrium.

More than that, the woman he associated so strongly with a particular corporate sleekness and style of dress preferred to go about…naked.

Well. Not precisely *naked*.

But as the weather got warmer, Julienne could often be found out at the swimming pool, set slightly down the hill from the house, sunning herself.

Wearing absolutely nothing but a bikini.

And he had not lied to her that day in the library. He found her new, impossibly lush body astonishingly beautiful. Almost too beautiful to bear.

He might not want to think of his impending fatherhood. He actively avoided it, in fact. But it was impossible not to look at Julienne and think of fertility. Of spring and sunshine, colorful new flowers and the fresh green of new growth.

She was bright and round and ripe, and every moment he did not have his hands on her was a torment.

Cristiano found himself in his own hell. Here at the villa, where he had always come for sanity. For an escape from the tumultuous life his parents led. One week led into the next, a riot of longing and fury, Julienne's knowing smiles, and those dinners that required more self-control than they should have.

Familiarity with Julienne bred nothing like contempt. On the contrary, it ignited nothing short of an obsession.

But he knew addicts too well. And he knew that succumbing to the itch was always worse, in the long run. Always. Far better to white knuckle his way through this without sampling her again.

Sooner or later, this vice grip she had on him would fade. He was sure of it.

One night at dinner, she looked up from the gazpacho that had been served as their first course and announced that the doctor would be coming the following morning.

"It was so thoughtful of you to set up an obstetrician's office of sorts in one of the studies," she said, in that tone of hers he spent far too much time analyzing. Was she mocking him? Was that a hint of a sardonic slap? Or had he gone utterly mad and was now *parsing* her tone? "If you come to the appointment tomorrow, you'll be able to see—"

"'Come'?" Cristiano stared at her from across the table, the icy distance he preferred to keep between them crumbling into so much ash. "Why would I attend your doctor's appointment?"

And for the first time since he'd come here, that sunny, breezy demeanor of hers cracked.

First, that smile tumbled from her face. Her gaze darkened. She put her fork down and took a breath, as if he was trying her patience. And more—messing with her head the way she was doing with his.

Funny how that seemed a hollow victory.

"What game are you playing, Cristiano?" she demanded, an undercurrent in her voice that made his chest tight. "Why would you be here, however reluctantly, if you didn't want some part in your son's life?"

Cristiano stared back at her as if he was made entirely from stone. It would be easier if he was, he knew. "I'm here to encourage you not to continue to seed the voracious Italian press with scandalous stories about my grandfather," he told her, crisply, as if he couldn't see the dark thing between them. Not even now it was all over her lovely face. "And if I cannot encourage you to stop, to prevent you from doing it all the same."

Julienne sat back in her seat, her belly taking up most of the room between them. Or so it seemed to him, because that gloriously round belly was all he could see.

She studied him for far too long. With a considering sort of look in her clever eyes that made him feel far too exposed. "Let me guess. This is your fear talking. Again."

He didn't like that. "I am who I am. Who I have always been in all the years you have known me. It is hardly my fault if you cannot accept this now that you are with child." He shrugged. "Perhaps this is an example of the pregnancy hormones I have heard so much about."

There was hot color on her cheeks, then, and something perilously close to disappointment in her eyes. When, if he was honest with himself, it had been his intention to prick her temper.

Not disappoint her.

He had already disappointed the first woman who had ever meant something to him. He couldn't bear the idea that he was doing it again.

"People choose who they are," Julienne told him, her voice much too quiet. Not shrill, not furious. Just that quiet directness that scraped at him, leaving deep grooves inside her. "Every day, you choose. It's not destiny that makes a man, or his bloodline. It's how he behaves."

"You have no idea what you're talking about."

"You forget how you met me," she shot back.

Cristiano had not forgotten. And now, because of what had happened ten years later, all his memories of her were infused with an eroticism the reality had not possessed. Like all those years in offices around the world when he somehow hadn't fully looked at her. He remembered them like torture now. And when he thought of Monte Carlo now, she was this version of Julienne both times—not the terrified sixteen-year-old she'd been then.

You are sick, he accused himself. *Do you need any further proof?*

But then, he had despaired of himself for the whole of the last decade.

"You never asked either one of us too much about where we came from," Julienne said now, still sitting back in her chair and frowning at him. "Which was a mercy, as neither Fleurette nor I ever wanted to speak of it. You told me that first night that you assumed that if selling my body was my only option, my other options must be wretched indeed."

"You have mentioned your mother before," he said darkly. He didn't wish to have this conversation. Or any conversation. He wanted to remain in merry ignorance forever, if that would keep this woman at arm's length. If that was what he wanted. Which, he assured himself forcefully then, he did. Of course he did. "I understand that your childhood was unpleasant."

If she heard his repressive tones, she ignored it.

"In my village, they called my mother a 'party girl,'" Julienne told him. "A lovely euphemism, is it not? When what she was, always, was an addict. She had me when she was seventeen. Sometimes she liked to claim that I ruined her life, but even as a child, I knew that wasn't true. She was the one who ruined her life, over and over again."

"I don't see what the story has to do with our situation," Cristiano said gruffly.

Because the last thing he needed was to have more reasons to *feel things* where this woman was concerned.

"It's hard for me to look back and figure out what I knew then and what I know now, thanks to the passing of so many years." Julienne sighed. "But my mother would do anything for a good time. At a certain point they began to tease me about it in school. Everyone knew who the easiest woman in the village was, and how they could get their hands on her. So you see, when I decided to sell myself, I knew what to do. I thought I would try to differentiate myself from my poor mother by charging more than a pack of cigarettes or a ride home."

His jaw was so tight he worried it might shatter. "I do not see the purpose of wandering off down memory lane, Julienne."

But she didn't relent. "Men began to look at me early. Too early. There were leers, suggestive comments. One of my mother's friends told me that the Boucher women had a certain look. That anyone could tell they were made to be whores. And yes, he said *women*. He wanted to be sure to include Fleurette, who could not have been more than eight at the time. It was as if we had price tags around our necks, and a clock counting down. All the men in that village were waiting for was the opportunity."

That chin of hers rose, defiant and something more.

And there was a howl in him that Cristiano doubted would ever fade.

Julienne's smile was brittle. "On the day I decided to leave that town forever, I had been propositioned no less than three times. It was just an ordinary day. And I knew, you see, that it was only a matter of time before I surrendered to my fate. There was nowhere to go on that cursed hill. No one would hire one of the Boucher women to do an honest job. Who would have a whore like that behind the counter? Or even sweeping a floor where decent people might go?"

"Why are you telling me this?" Cristiano demanded, convinced there was ground glass in his mouth as he spoke. "Is it your intention that I find this village and burn it to the ground?"

He would do it personally. And with pleasure.

"You are a Cassara," she threw at him, her voice fierce, then. "The blood you are so ashamed to have in your veins makes you a billionaire twice over. You can buy anything you wish. You were never trapped in a forgotten hill town, doomed to be a whore. And yes, I was lucky enough to stumble upon a benefactor at the least likely moment. But I didn't lounge about, bemoaning my good luck. I claimed it. Don't you see? I worked night and day to be worthy of my rescue."

Cristiano didn't know when he had stopped pretending to pick at his dinner. Or when they'd faced off, there at the corner of the great table in the dining room, staring each other down as if at any moment one of them might throw a punch.

What was wrong with him that he almost thought it would be a relief?

"I know you cannot be suggesting that I am...lazy, is it?"

"Not lazy, perhaps. But you certainly do work at your self-pity the way others work for a paycheck."

He growled. "Be very, very careful, *cara*."

"Or what?" Julienne asked wildly, and laughed in a way he could not say he enjoyed at all. "Let me guess. You will imprison me on a remote property and leave me to live out my days in forced solitude. That will show me."

"Here is one thing you apparently did not learn in your vicious little hill town." He leaned closer to her, which was a mistake. "Things can always get worse. They often do."

Julienne sighed, a great heaving sound, as if plagued. By him, presumably.

"When our son is old enough, will you sit right here this table and tell him these things?" she demanded. When he was used to making the demands in all situations. "Will you make certain to let him know that he's cursed already? As doomed as I was? How will you make sure that he's aware of the Cassara corrosion that already pollutes him?"

Cristiano found he couldn't answer that. He only stared back at her, something dark and edgy gripping him. Crushing him.

"When he seeks his father for comfort, will you push him down to the ground? Slap him until he cries— or stops crying? That's what your father did to you, didn't he?"

"Stop it," he ordered her, with a stranger's voice.

But her eyes were too bright with an emotion he couldn't identify.

"I know. You'll wait until he really needs you. When he's a man grown but still needs a father figure. You'll get drunk. You'll say appalling things, calculated to slice him into pieces. Then you'll totter out of the bar, hurt yourself, and blame him for it."

She might as well have thrown a bomb at him. Cristiano wished she had.

"That is more than enough," he growled at her. "I believe you've made your point."

But he could see that wild thing was still on her, in her. She stared straight at him, challenge stamped on every inch of her, opened her mouth—

And Cristiano did not want to hear whatever came next.

He pushed back from his chair, hardly aware that he was moving, and then he was looming over her. But that was good, because she sucked in a breath. And did not say whatever shattering thing was next on her list.

A win, as far as he was concerned.

He pulled out her chair so he could lean down over her and brace himself on the arms, holding her there.

And he remembered, with an electric flash of need and longing, that night in Monte Carlo. That alcove he'd found off the lobby.

He could tell from the way her breath changed and her color heightened that she remembered it too.

"You poke and poke and poke," he said, his voice so low he wasn't certain it was anything more than a dark rumble. "You must know that this cannot end well, Julienne."

"That's the point," she threw back at him, defiant to the end, which made him feel…something almost like helpless, in the face of all her beauty and resolve. "It never will end, Cristiano. If all goes according to plan, a father dies before his son. And you have to ask yourself a question, right now. Do you want your son to talk about you the way you talk about your own father? Or do you want something better for both of you?"

"I told you, no more. No more, Julienne."

He didn't raise his voice so much as he leaned into the way he said the words, staining them both with all that intensity inside of him.

Julienne didn't flinch. She didn't so much as bat an eye. He watched her breathe, watched those extra full breasts move, and her belly with it. And it occurred to him that he was most furious with her not because she was wrong.

But because he had the terrible suspicion that she was right.

Cristiano couldn't face it. So he bent down instead, took her defiant chin in his hand, and kissed her.

And he could not have said the things that battled inside him, then. He wouldn't have known where to begin.

The losses he had suffered, one after the next. His enduring shame and guilt, first because there was something about him that had made his own father hate him as a child. And then later, that he had hated his father enough in return to let him stumble out of that bar and toward the certain death he should have anticipated would steal away his mother, too.

He had let it happen. Or he hadn't cared enough to stop it.

His hands were stained with the blood of two deaths that he could have prevented.

If only he had been a different man.

He wanted to forget. He wanted her shine, her light, *that glow* instead.

Cristiano kissed her and he kissed her.

He kissed her for the baby she carried, the son he'd

never wanted. He kissed her for the challenges she'd thrown at him, her refusal to quietly disappear the way he'd wanted, and because she still haunted him. Here, now, while he touched her, she haunted him.

Something in him rang, deep and hard, and he had the uncomfortable notion she always would.

And then, somehow, he was sinking down to his knees before her, to worship her properly.

Again.

"Cristiano…" she breathed, but he didn't want her words.

He wanted her passion. He wanted her taste in his mouth and the molten hot clench of her body on his. He *wanted*—and he was done restraining himself.

Julienne liked to dress for dinner, in what he was certain was—like that bikini of hers—a calculated campaign to make him lose his mind. It obviously worked all too well. Tonight's selection was a formfitting, stretchy sort of dress that covered her modestly enough and yet was deeply, spectacularly immodest at the same time because it welded itself to her curves. It emphasized those full, heavy breasts, all but making love to her enormous bump.

Cristiano did the same.

He found her breasts with his hands and teased her nipples in his palms. Slowly, carefully, not sure what kind of sensation she would like now, he moved his hands in circles.

And watched her come apart.

Her head fell back. She let out a moan he was fairly certain he'd last heard when he was deep inside of her, and he felt the spike of it like her mouth along the length of him.

He kept going, playing with one nipple, then the other. He watched in fascination as her cheeks went red, goose bumps rose along her skin, and then, unmistakably, she convulsed.

She bucked in the chair and he moved closer, wedging his body between her legs. Then he hissed out a breath when he felt the molten center of her against his thigh.

"You have said a great deal tonight, *cara*," he told her, murmuring the words into the side of her neck. "But as always, I'm only interested in one word. My name. I think we both know how easily it falls off your tongue."

And then he moved down her body, helping himself to every last voluptuous inch of this new body of hers. Her glorious breasts, that swollen belly. And when he got to her thighs, he pushed the stretchy material of her dress out of his way, then up further, until he bared her to his view. He made short work of the panties she wore, tossing them aside, and then settling down to get a taste of her. Rich, sweet.

Ripe and entirely his.

He hadn't allowed himself to think too closely about all the various things she'd said to him since she'd reappeared in his life, but suddenly, all he could think about was the fact of her innocence that night in Monte Carlo.

Only mine, a dark voice in him intoned. *Only and ever mine.*

He took a deep, lush taste, and kept going until she

was squirming against him, panting out his name the way he liked. Only then did he pull away.

He lifted her up, enjoying the extra heft her round-ness gave her. He moved her onto the gleaming, pol-ished table, then spread her out beneath the sparkling chandelier that dated back to the time of kings and royal guests at Villa Cassara.

Then, finally, he pulled that dress from her body, and made short work of her bra. And then she was there before him in all her glory. His very own goddess, her eyes glazed with heat and need.

He pulled himself out from his trousers, already huge and ready. And he watched her face change, going hungry.

It was the sexiest thing he'd ever seen.

Cristiano braced himself on the tabletop, moved his hips to hers, and slowly, deliberately, sheathed himself in the molten grasp of her core with a single, relent-less thrust.

Julienne shattered at once. Her back arched, offer-ing all her deliciously full curves to him.

But he waited. He gritted his teeth as her pleasure washed over him, through him, and nearly sent him spiraling off into his own.

Once her initial storm passed, he began to move.

He went carefully at first, but when her response was nothing but enthusiastic, he thrust a little harder. A little deeper.

Until the two of them were moving as one, fighting together to get to that same great height that had stalked him since Monaco. That sweet rush that haunted him, night and day.

And she said his name the way he'd told her to. She sang it, over and over, until he could not tell the difference between the melody and the name itself.

Between his name and her and this magic they made between the two of them.

And when it all broke apart, sending them both shattering, he was the one who cried out. He was the one who called her name like a summoning, a reckoning.

Like a new song.

And he didn't know how long they stayed like that, there on that antique table where his grandfather had entertained Europe's finest, in his time.

He didn't care, either. Minutes, hours, years. As long as she was with him, curled around him, a part of him—

But he didn't allow himself to finish that thought.

He pulled himself away from her with more reluctance than was healthy or wise. He tucked himself into his trousers, and then, without thinking it through, lifted her up into his arms.

She dropped her head to his shoulder, and he felt a surge of feeling he couldn't begin to identify wash over him. Something he might have called tender, if he was that kind of man. If there was anything soft inside him.

If there was, it was only hers.

A thought that should have disturbed him, but he shoved it aside.

And he carried her from the grand dining room, through the villa, until he found the master bedroom. Once there, he settled her in his bed.

He did not question himself. He did not analyze what he was doing. He simply did it.

Cristiano busied himself removing his own clothes. He was crawling back into the bed beside her when she opened her eyes again, fixed them on him and smiled.

Light. Heat.

Joy, even.

And he didn't know what to do with the things in him that rose to meet that smile. Something like wonder, God help him. And a strange tenderness that would likely appall him, come morning.

But it was still night. And more than anything else, there was still that driving greed that made him reach for her all over again.

"Am I allowed to talk yet?" she asked softly, her smile firming into a solemn line, though her eyes still laughed at him, toffee-colored and sweet.

"Of course," he said, rolling her into him. "You have one word, as always. Use it well."

Cristiano did not need words. He didn't know the right ones—or worse, he did, but could not bring himself to say them. Because he had always known who he was. He had always known that he did not have the same capacities in him that others did, or his own father would not have despised him. And he, in turn, would not have let him leave that bar in Monaco while so impaired.

Love was for other people. Tenderness was a dream.

He had always prided himself on his directness instead.

So he used his mouth on her in other ways, his hands

and the hardest part of him too, while she sang that song of hers.

That beautiful song that was in him now. The song he knew he would never escape, as long as he lived.

He used what he had and he told her all those things he could never say out loud, never in words. He told her over and over again, until dawn.

When the sun rose over the Tuscan hills and Cristiano was still himself.

Always and ever himself, and destined therefore to remain alone.

CHAPTER NINE

CRISTIANO WAS NOT in the bed when she woke.

"That's quite all right," Julienne muttered to herself, running her hand over her belly to say her usual hello to the baby. "It would be far more surprising if he was here, really."

And the baby was still sleeping, or unwilling to give her even a little kick, so she heaved herself up and over to the side of the bed. After hesitating a moment, she stole a silk robe from his vast dressing room, then padded her way down the hall to her own suite.

Where, if she wanted to have an emotion or two in her shower or while fixing her hair, that was no one's business but hers.

She expected to see him at breakfast out on one of the patios these warm, bright mornings, while Tuscany outdid itself with its spring splendor in all directions. But when she made it to the patio in question, Cristiano was nowhere to be found.

That's just as well, too, she told herself stoutly.

Maybe if she kept telling herself that she'd believe it.

The gardeners had outdone themselves with the rose

bushes, and it was strange how little she fancied cut roses, as ubiquitous as they were. And yet here, where they grew exultantly around the villa, seemingly on the verge of going wild at any moment, she couldn't seem to get enough of them.

And there was a lesson there, likely having to do with the thorns.

But then, all things involving the Cassara family were bad for her in one way or another. And here she still was. With the next Cassara currently inside her, pressing hard on her solar plexus when he was in a mood.

And she knew she was a goner when the image of a tiny little Cassara deliberately kicking at her made her laugh.

"I'll be mounting a rescue operation," Fleurette announced later that morning, her voice tense over the phone. "I don't think I've ever gone this long without seeing you. It's not okay. You know that, I hope. *None of this is okay.* If I have to storm Tuscany to make it clear to that man, I will."

Julienne laughed. She had spent some more time with Piero Cassara's letters after breakfast, but somehow hadn't been able to bring herself to make any further calls to her contacts. Fleurette's number flashing on her phone had been a relief—because anything was better than facing her own weaknesses, surely. Even sharp conversations with her sister.

"One does not storm Tuscany, Fleurette," she said, still laughing. "One flies into Florence, becomes operatic at the sight of the Arno, and loses oneself for days between the Ponte Vecchio and Neptune's marble penis."

"I've waited in line for the Uffizi, thank you, and it wasn't worth it. This isn't a joke that you can tell about penises on Florentine statues, Julienne. We're talking about Cristiano Cassara locking you away forever. I'm not going to let him do that. And while we're on the topic, he's certainly not barring me from my nephew's birth, either. I don't care what he did for us ten years ago."

"Fleurette." Julienne kept her voice as mild as possible, because she knew her sister well. And she knew where Fleurette's vehemence came from. "You know I love you. And I know that there are very good reasons that you want to rescue me this time. But I don't need rescuing. I'm not Maman."

"Are you sure about that?" Her sister asked, her voice thick with those memories she usually pretended not to have. "Because an addict is an addict as far as I can see."

And then rang off before Julienne could counter, which might have been childish, but was also effective.

Maybe too effective, because she left Julienne stewing.

So much, in fact, that Julienne was late to her own doctor's appointment, even if it was conveniently located right there in the villa. She'd been too busy thinking about addictions. About all the different ways a person could give herself over to something more powerful than she was, particularly when it was bad for her.

She'd seen what it had done to Annette. But she'd never given any thought to the fact that before her mother's many crushes, there was first the exultation.

And she wasn't sure how she felt about the fact that she understood that now.

"I'm so sorry," she said as she walked into the study that had been made into a remarkably well-furnished doctor's office, just for her. "I didn't mean to keep you waiting."

The doctor gave her a slight bow, which struck her as strange. *He thinks you're the new lady of the manor,* a voice inside piped up, *and now that Cristiano is here, he thinks he needs to treat you with more respect.*

Julienne really should have made it clear that she and Cristiano weren't…anything. Not really, or she wouldn't be here alone, would she? But she was late this morning. And slightly off balance for any number of reasons, from last night to her sister to her own inability to be as ruthless as she knew she should have been, so she… said nothing. The doctor could think what he liked.

She answered the usual questions, then got up on the exam table and waited while he and his nurse hooked her up to all the state-of-the-art machines Cristiano's people had installed in here.

Because Cristiano might claim he wanted nothing to do with his baby, but he still made sure that both Julienne and that baby were well cared for. No matter what.

At the very least, that made him better than methamphetamines. Or heroin. Or any of the other things she either knew or suspected her mother had tried in her day. But even as she thought that, she could hear her sister's voice as if Fleurette was standing there beside her.

Are you really sure that "better than meth" is a decent recommendation?

Shut up, Fleurette, Julienne thought ferociously.

And then startled, there on the table, when the door to the room opened again. And Cristiano walked in.

His gaze met hers, and she hardly recognized what she saw there.

Beneath the glacial arrogance that was all Cristiano, there was something else. Something that made her hold her breath as he ventured near, nodding coldly at the doctor to continue.

Together they stared at the screen before them, and the unearthly picture that didn't seem to make sense— until it did.

Cristiano stood next to where she lay, and she stared up at him as his throat convulsed. Once, then again.

The doctor pointed out the baby's features, and Julienne looked from the screen to Cristiano's stricken expression. And at the hand that flexed slightly at his side. Then, following an urge that came straight from the swell of emotion in her heart that made it beat too hard and too loud, she dared to reach over and slide her hand into his.

She made a great show of looking at the screen, not at him while she did it.

Cristiano stiffened. Julienne expected him to shake her hand off.

But then, a breath later, his hand wrapped around hers. And held her fast.

That evening, Julienne dressed for dinner the way she always did. She smoothed her way into another stretchy dress, this one with a longer skirt that brushed the floor as she moved. It made her feel prettier somehow. Especially since the baby had been particularly active all day, kicking and punching like he had a score to settle.

"Or," she murmured, rubbing her belly as she walked out of her room and into the atrium, "like a little baby boy whose papa saw his face at last."

She could hardly put into words how that made her feel. It hadn't mattered to her that Cristiano had walked out with the doctor, and had not returned. Or it hadn't mattered *much*. Not when she could still feel the sensation of his hand on hers. The way he clenched so tight, and kept holding on to her even after they finished with the picture part of the examination.

Her fingers flexed of their own accord. And she could still feel the heat of his grip. The strength.

It was a beautiful spring evening and against her will, Julienne took a deep, almost happy sort of breath. She loved this villa more every day, though she tried so hard not to let it charm her. The graceful colonnade that formed the border of the atrium, wound with flowering vines. The atrium itself, a beautiful central garden that made every room in the house feel a part of the wild, surrounded by so much Tuscan beauty on both sides. She made her way down the path that cut from the guest suite to the formal part of the villa, with its many reception rooms. The stones beneath her feet were still warm from the day. The trees that stretched above her head provided a canopy of shade and birdsong. The small pond had a little fountain on one end, so the sound of water spilling and falling filled the whole of the villa like a happy song.

She couldn't help but smile as she made it to the dining room. But to her surprise, the table was not set. The housekeeper stood there instead, and nodded diffidently when she entered.

"Mr. Cassara requests the pleasure of your company on the west terrace," the housekeeper said.

Julienne wanted to argue. She wanted to demand that Cristiano come to her, and that they continue this tradition that she'd put into place when he'd left her here. Because maybe she wanted to play at being the lady of the manor—the lady of *this* manor, anyway.

His lady, something in her whispered.

She made herself smile at the waiting housekeeper, which was better than crying at her own foolishness. "We wouldn't want to keep Mr. Cassara waiting."

And she followed the housekeeper around to the west side of the villa, through one pretty, airy salon after the next. Eventually they walked out onto a stone terrace surrounded by wrought iron, also festooned with flowers and greenery. The terrace sat up above a slope of vineyard that rolled down into the valley below. It was not quite dark, and the light was magical, making the red rooftops of the villa's outbuildings and guest cottages gleam, while the marching pairs of cypress trees along the estate's winding lanes seemed to head straight for the setting sun.

She told herself the light was the reason Cristiano looked the way he did then, standing at the rail with all that soft gold licking over his strong, gloriously perfect body.

The body she knew better now, having refreshed her recollection of him last night.

And it amazed her that she could still blush after the things they'd done, but she did. Hard and hot. She hoped he would mistake it for another trick of the light.

He turned at her approach. And though his face was cast in shadow, then, she could still feel the impact of his intense gaze.

And everything felt fraught, suddenly. As if that intensity that emanated from him was part of the silky Tuscan golden light between them. And it was all around her, too, pressing in tight. Until she wasn't sure which one of them might burst.

She didn't know what to do. And the baby was kicking, her face was aflame and she could *feel* the way he looked at her, all that hunger and hope. Not that she imagined he'd admit that last part. She flexed her hand again, then she walked to him because she couldn't think of a single other thing to do.

And her heart stuttered as she drew close, because he reached out his hand and took hers.

Of his own volition this time.

And then, stunning her, he pulled her close.

"I thought we would eat here," Cristiano said, sounding formal and stuffy and delicious. And the way he gazed down at her, she was not entirely certain what sort of meal he meant. "To take advantage of the view."

Her head was tipped back so she could look him full in the face, though she had no memory of doing that of her own volition. "I like the view," she said softly.

His gaze dropped to her mouth, and she felt everything inside her shudder to life. Then bloom, in a riot of sensation and need.

But he did not kiss her.

"Thank you," Cristiano said instead, his voice like gravel. "I cannot describe to you what it was like to see the baby." That look in his gaze, as stricken as it had been earlier, sharpened. "My son."

And Julienne could blame her hormones all she liked, because it hardly mattered when the end result was the same. Her eyes welled up, then spilled over.

"Our baby," she whispered. "Our son."

And for a moment, there was nothing but the deep red and thick gold of the setting sun, his hands on hers, and the new life they'd made between them as they stood, not quite kissing.

Finally, she thought, a dangerous hope careening around inside of her.

Because she'd imagined this moment, but she'd never thought it would happen. Never.

And as if he knew they were discussing him, the baby kicked. Hard.

Julienne took Cristiano's hands in hers, then slid them down onto her belly. She pressed them in, smiling up at him as she waited. Then smiled even wider when the baby kicked.

"He's saying hello," she whispered. "To his father."

Cristiano jolted. Julienne could feel the electric charge go through him. And then his face changed. She saw a flash of wonder. His dark eyes lit up, and in that instant, he was…unguarded. Disarmed.

The baby kept kicking, and Cristiano's hands molded to her belly. She could feel all their heat and strength. She could feel the baby kicking. And she had the indescribable joy of watching a smile creep its way across Cristiano Cassara's austere face.

She could feel how wet her cheeks were, and it didn't occur to her to wipe them dry. Julienne could have stood where they were forever, and she wanted to—lost in this moment that felt as old as the hills and fields around them. A man and a woman and their coming child. She felt ancient. Connected to the earth, the seasons, every woman who'd come before her and all the women who would follow.

Julienne had understood that she'd gotten pregnant, of course. And she'd understood how. She had been overwhelmed by what that meant, for both of them. And apprehensive about his reaction.

But it was not until now, with only the soft, golden sunset in Tuscany as their witness, that she truly understood what it meant that she and Cristiano had *made a new life* together.

She felt her heart break open inside her chest, but it wasn't a heartbreak in the classic sense. It was more love, not less. It made more of her heart to go around, suddenly. All the shattered pieces fused back together, better than before.

More, not less.

"We did this," she whispered now. "You and me."

"This feels like a miracle, Julienne," he replied, his voice a mere thread of sound.

And then he broke her heart into pieces all over again, then stitched them back together in the same breath, as he sank down to his knees before her.

Julienne couldn't believe that any of this was happening. That she was here, with him, and that look on his face. That Cristiano was looking at her—or her belly, anyway—with so much tenderness. So much obvious, astonished delight. He spread his hands out to cover as much of her bump as he could, and then he leaned forward and placed a kiss there where his thumbs nearly met.

She couldn't stop crying, and she had never been quite so far from sad in all her life.

He looked up at her, this beautiful man, his eyes so bright they blocked out all that Tuscan gold. Like another miracle, right here on this terrace.

"We will marry," he said, a gruff command. "We must marry."

"I will marry you," she replied. "Of course, I'll marry you."

But it wasn't until she'd said it that she realized he hadn't exactly asked.

"He will be one of the good ones," Cristiano said fiercely. "I will see to it personally."

"He will be absolutely perfect," she agreed, because this was their son. And there were no curses, no poisoned blood. And the life inside her would turn into a boy who would never know the vile things others might predict about him. She would be his mother, and unlike her own, Julienne would make sure of it.

Cristiano stood then, this man she had loved for as long as she'd known him. First as a teenage girl with a crush, then as a hopeless employee he never once saw as a woman. And now, she knew all too well what it was like to have his mouth between her legs, his hands on her breasts, and best of all, the hardest part of him deep inside her, again and again.

And she loved him more.

Julienne wished that she could go back in time and tell that terrified sixteen-year-old how it would all turn out. That Cristiano would save her from the Boucher women's fate. That she would love him. That they would make a son together.

And then he would become her husband, and a father, and if there was a happier version of ever after, Julienne knew that neither she nor the teenage version of herself could possibly imagine it.

He led her over to the table she hadn't even seen, so lost was she in him. In this. He sat her down so she could look out at the vineyard, and the hills that rolled into forever, as the sun finally inched its way below the horizon.

This is everything you ever wanted, she kept telling herself, waiting for it to feel believable. Or real.

Beside her, Cristiano kept touching her belly, and even began speaking sternly to her bump, man to man.

She was so full to bursting, that it wasn't until later, when they'd eaten their dinner, and were sitting, enjoying the mild evening, that she realized one crucial thing was missing.

Cristiano had talked of parenting, and of marrying. He'd told her his plans of how it would be between them, and Julienne had agreed, but he had never once mentioned the most important thing of all.

Love.

CHAPTER TEN

"WE WILL MARRY at once," Cristiano announced the following morning, watching Julienne as she settled herself across from him, wearing nothing but the sheet they'd kicked off the bed early. His wife, he thought, with a stamp of possessive fire. The mother of the son he nearly hadn't gone to see—and had, in the end, because of that tenderness that only she brought out in him. It only made him more determined to move quickly now—before the realities of life as a Cassara set in, as he knew they would. They always did. And before that tender thing he could not put into words curdled and died like everything else he touched. "I will have a special license and priest here by nightfall."

"How romantic," she said dryly, and there was a flicker of something he couldn't say he liked in her toffee-colored eyes.

He studied her a moment, telling himself he was imagining things. This was the woman who had cried, she was so happy. And then cried for entirely different reasons in his bed all night.

"These are practicalities, Julienne," he said, aware

that there were landmines here, though he couldn't understand why. "The sooner they are dealt with, the less we need speak of them."

"And, naturally, our only purpose here is to be practical." She shifted the sheet she'd wrapped around her, hiking it higher over her breasts. Cristiano wondered if she knew how very much she looked like a Roman goddess, toga and all. "While also having sex."

"Is that a complaint?"

She was looking out at the scenery, the rolling hills and the thicket of rosebushes. "I wouldn't dream of lodging a complaint. Besides, you don't care for my methods. Too scandalous."

"I thought we were in agreement," he said, mildly enough.

She looked different this morning, though he couldn't have said why. It wasn't the sheet or the fact she was sitting here on his private terrace, though that was certainly new and different. She had her hair up again, but in haphazard sort of pile instead of the sleek chignon that he recalled from the office. Maybe that was it. Maybe she no longer bothered with sleekness, which made him wonder why any woman did. When the other side of it was this—all soft woman, rosy cheeks and clear toffee eyes.

"I said I would marry you, yes," she said, and he realized after a beat that she was mimicking his own excessively mild tone. Exactly. "But there's no rush, surely. The world will not be ending at nightfall."

"I see no reason to wait."

"I cannot marry without my sister present." She

shook her head at him, but at least that meant she was looking at him instead of out into the distance. "And don't you have a grandmother? Right here in Tuscany?"

Cristiano did not frown. Because he ordered himself not to frown. "Technically. But my grandmother would have no interest in attending my wedding. I'm not sure she would bother to attend my funeral, and of the two, it would likely bring her far greater joy."

Julienne laughed, but when he didn't join in—and, in fact, only stared at her implacably—she sobered. "You can't be serious."

"I know you have decided she is a sympathetic figure, Julienne, but my grandmother is an unpleasant woman. She takes pride in it. When I was a child, I was convinced that every fairy tale involving a witch and the forest was about her."

Julienne's gaze cooled, and too late, he remembered what she'd told him about the way the women in her family had been treated in France. And the way she had already come to his grandmother's defense. "You will forgive me, but can you really trust any stories you heard about her? Your grandfather was hardly an objective source."

Cristiano felt he should have received commendations for remaining calm in the face of such provocation. Medals, at the very least. But none appeared forthcoming, so he pinched his nose and wished for strength. "You are basing this on the letters you read, is that it?"

"The letters, yes, and the long-term marital affair that was celebrated in each and every one of those letters." Julienne's brows rose. "As the person you decided should marry you *tonight*, you should perhaps take note. I don't like cheaters or liars. And if my husband treated me the way your grandfather treated your grandmother, I would not waft off into the nearest forest and make myself into a fairy tale. I would burn him down."

He felt his gaze narrow. "Noted. But has it occurred to you that my grandfather was not the villain of this tale?"

"I understand why you want to believe that." Her throat worked, but it took her a moment to speak. "Then again, this is how men tell stories about women they can't control, isn't it? Whores. Witches."

"Wives?" he supplied, sardonically. Then regretted it when she turned that dark glare on him. He sighed. "Life is not black-and-white, especially when it comes to marriages. People are not all one thing or another."

"But in the case of your grandparents, one of them carried on an affair that went on for decades. The other lives by herself in a cottage, cut off from the world. One was considered a great man and celebrated internationally when he died. The other is loathed even by her own grandson." She shrugged. "It feels black-and-white, doesn't it?"

Cristiano studied the flush on her cheeks, realizing belatedly that it was temper. "Do you have grandparents too?" he asked. "Is that what this is about? Or is this something more prosaic than a sudden, deep concern for a woman you've never met…like second thoughts about a wedding, for example?"

Not that he would entertain her second thoughts.

"They say my grandmother died of shame," Julienne

said, with a certain starkness that tore at him. "Not long after I was born. My grandfather had died when my mother was still young, which everyone agreed was a great blessing. Because he never had to know what became of her."

"And what of your father? Your father's family?"

"The man I think was my father also died, but no one is quite certain where he came from. Or if he left any family behind him. I've heard theories that his accent was Parisian by way of Marseille. But then again, some argued that he was very clearly not French at all. Who can say? All I know is, he overdosed when I was twelve, and I have never known how to feel about it, because I hardly knew him."

"I know my grandmother very little," Cristiano said, because every story she told him about her past was worse than the one before. And wasn't that the point of this? They would make something new. They would make it all better. "But it is enough."

"Is she a heroin addict?" Julienne asked, dryly. "I had heard many parts of the Cassara family legend, but not that."

Cristiano wanted to snap back at her, the way he would at an underling, but she no longer worked for him. Failing that, he wanted to get his hands on her and use the language they were both far more fluent in.

"I do not understand this intriguing take on a woman you've never met," he said, fighting to keep his voice calm. And not sure that he succeeded when her eyes flashed. "Surely you can allow for the possibility that

I might be the expert on her motivations here? Since of the two of us, I'm the only one who knows her."

"Maybe your grandmother loved your grandfather to a distraction," Julienne said softly, and her pretty face was unreadable. "So much so that it drove her crazy when he met someone else. Have you ever stopped to think about that?"

"There will be a special license and a priest here by nightfall," Cristiano told her evenly. "Unless you have some further objection? Preferably not one that is based on your imaginary version of my grandmother?"

And when Julienne looked away, she did not look back for a very long time.

"I cannot marry without my sister here," she said again. "I won't."

"Then, *cara*, I would suggest you stop arguing about my grandparents' marriage and get her on a plane," Cristiano said silkily. "Because the wedding will happen. Tonight."

Fleurette arrived that evening, grumpier than usual, but with the same giant chip on her tattooed shoulder.

Julienne was so glad to see her, it hurt.

"You know you don't actually have to marry him, right?" Fleurette asked as she sat in Julienne's bedchamber in the guest suite with her, watching balefully as Julienne smoothed out the bodice of the dress that had appeared on her bed, as if by magic.

Not magic, she knew. Cristiano.

Cristiano, who could go to the trouble to pick out a beautiful dress for her to wear to what would no doubt be a beautiful wedding, but couldn't love her. Didn't love her.

Does he love anything? the voice inside her asked, sounding entirely too much like her sister. *Can he?*

"Why wouldn't I marry him?" Julienne asked, catching Fleurette's gaze in the mirror's reflection. And choosing to keep her thoughts on love to herself. "He's the father of my child. And as you've pointed out to me repeatedly over the past ten years, I have been hopeless about him from the start."

"I realize it gets confusing here in Europe," Fleurette said dryly. "But it is not necessary to marry a man simply because he got you pregnant. I know Italy *looks* medieval, but it's still the modern world here too, no matter the age of the buildings. No one cares anymore if a child is born out of wedlock."

"You don't care," Julienne corrected her quietly. "But that is not to say that others share your views."

Fleurette rolled her eyes. "Do I need to remind you that neither one of us was born on the right side of the blanket? We don't even have the same father."

"You don't know that. It's as likely that we have the same father as that we don't."

"This is the difference between us, Julienne," Fleurette said softly. Sadly. "You want so badly to believe there might be goodness in the world that you'll sacrifice yourself on the off chance you might find it. I know better. A sacrifice is a sacrifice. All it means is that you lose something."

And if Julienne could have, she would have bundled up her sister in cotton wool and made the world so good she would have no choice but to accept it—but that didn't work. She'd tried. And yes, it had worked out much better than planned, but Fleurette never forgot what could have happened that night in Monte Carlo. What would have happened if Julienne had approached a different man.

Sometimes Julienne thought it haunted her sister more than it haunted her.

"I want better for my son," Julienne said now. "I want to give him absolutely everything, and I don't need you to try to make me feel badly about that."

"I'm not trying to make you feel badly," Fleurette said, her voice tight. "I came, didn't I? I'm wearing a pastel dress that makes me feel dead inside. I'm perfectly appropriate and ready to applaud. But I'm also your sister."

"Fleurette. Please."

"And you once sacrificed yourself *for me*, so I think you can do me the courtesy of listening to me. I'm not asking you to hide in an alley and save yourself."

Julienne met her sister's gaze in the mirror. And it was there between them, the way it always was. That same dark night. What she'd been prepared to do. What Fleurette would have had to live with. The ghost of what could have been.

She found she couldn't speak, so she nodded. Jerkily.

"I don't think you're doing any of this for the right reasons," Fleurette said. Julienne said nothing, but rubbed her belly ostentatiously. Her sister rolled her eyes. "Yes, I'm aware that you're pregnant. But I think you want to wrap all of this up in a pretty little bow.

You saved yourself for this man. You ranted on and on about bookends, and then you went out of your way to make it happen. I don't want to speculate how you ended up pregnant."

"The usual way, I assure you."

Another eye roll. "My point is, we got a raw deal. We never had a chance. If you'd walked up to any other man in that bar, neither one of us would be standing here right now. We both know where we'd be, if not the precise street address."

"Do you think I don't think about that every day?"

"I know you do." Fleurette's voice and gaze were intense. "And I understand why you want this to be neat. Tidy. If you marry the man who saved us all those years ago, does it wipe the slate clean? If you have his baby, and live with him, do you wash all the sin away?"

"Because it can't possibly be true that I love him."

But Julienne's voice sounded tinny and hollow, and there was a great weight deep in her belly that felt too much like a stone.

"Maybe you love him and maybe you don't," Fleurette said, her undertone something like urgent. "Maybe you've confused love with a sense of obligation. But none of that matters."

"It matters to me quite a lot, actually."

"Julienne, you deserve someone who loves *you*," Fleurette said, scowling at her. "You deserve to be loved, full stop. You deserve someone who loves every single thing about you, always. Someone who does not require acts of sacrifice in return for simply not being disgusting in a bar ten years ago. You've spent a life surviving and sacrificing—for me, for us, for your baby. But what about you? What would happen if you lived *for you* instead?"

"I've never felt more alive in my life," Julienne threw at her. "Ever."

And she expected her sister to fight back, but she didn't. She only held Julienne's gaze for a long, long time, then nodded.

"Then I'm thrilled to be here to celebrate you," she said quietly.

But Julienne couldn't get those words out of her head. *What about you?*

Fleurette did not disrupt the wedding, as promised. And Julienne couldn't have said why there was a part of her that found that disappointing. Did she want the excuse?

You want an enemy, came that voice inside, again sounding too much like the too-wise Fleurette. *You want to fight your way into this marriage, and better still, have something to fight against.*

And she found her hands were damp as she walked along the colonnade, and out to meet her fate. Her husband. With no enemies and no fights.

It was a quiet, simple affair, out on the terrace where Cristiano had gone down to his knees and kissed her baby. His baby.

Our baby, she thought fiercely.

It was quiet, simple, and fast. The priest intoned their vows, they both responded appropriately, and then Julienne watched as if from a great distance as Cristiano slid a pair of rings onto her hand. He provided her with one to put on his hand in return.

And then it was done.

She was married to Cristiano Cassara. Just as she'd always dreamed.

There was a small, pleasant dinner. Then Fleurette took her leave, and the sisters stared at each other. Neither one mentioning how strange it was that Fleurette had flown across the planet to witness a decidedly unromantic wedding ceremony and wasn't even staying the night.

"I love you," Fleurette said fiercely, and hugged her, hard. "Always."

"I love you too," Julienne replied.

She waited until she heard the helicopter blades begin to whir. She watched it rise into the air to whisk Fleurette back to an airfield outside of Florence, where one of the Cassara jets waited for her.

Then she went back into the villa, a married woman, to find her husband waiting for her.

She should have been dancing for joy. Or at least simmering with it, somewhere inside. She wore a lovely white dress. She had his rings on her finger. And when she came into the salon where he waited, staring down at one of those tumblers of whiskey he never drank, he gazed at her with a look on his face that she could only describe as possessive.

This was what she'd wanted.

Wasn't it?

"I've taken the liberty of moving your things into the master bedroom," he told her in his calm, certain way. "And now, wife, I think it is time we consummate this marriage. Unless you would like to take this opportunity to further debate my grandparents' marriage."

She wanted to smile, but her mouth felt funny. "I would not."

Cristiano's smile was not funny at all. It was savage. Erotic.

He swept her into his arms, lifting her as if she weighed nothing at all though she was seven months pregnant. He carried her through the villa, then bore her into the master bedroom, where he lay her down on the bed as if she was fragile.

And wasn't that a funny thing, because she certainly felt fragile.

His mouth was demanding on hers, and it didn't matter what oddities she felt in her heart tonight, because her body was his.

Always, only, and ever his.

His hands moved over her, as if he was learning her anew. As if the fact she was now *his wife* made her a stranger he needed to reacquaint himself with. Inch by inch.

She wanted to burst into tears, or let out a terrible sob she wasn't sure would ever end. Instead, she poured it into her own kisses. She took it out on his body, peeling off the gorgeously tailored suit he wore to find the glory of his flesh beneath.

And this time, he lifted her to straddle him and then watched her as she rode them both toward that bliss, his eyes a fierce claiming all their own.

She sobbed all right, passion and that odd stone inside her together making her too raw to do anything but let it out. Again and again and again.

And she loved him. And she was married to him now. And somehow, she had to come to terms with what all of that meant.

Because it wasn't what she thought it would mean, back when she'd fantasized about things like this. About him.

He poured himself into her, and then they lay there together. They both fought to catch their breath as the breeze came in through the windows smelling of jasmine, the deep green of growing things and the dark brown earth, and the faintest touch of rosemary.

She thought about bookends. She thought about that dark, grim life she and Fleurette had escaped in the hills of France. She thought about that awful bus ride down into Monte Carlo with the last of their euros, the stolen dress and the longest walk of her life into that hotel bar.

"You deserve to be loved," Fleurette had said.

And maybe, just maybe, Julienne also deserved to ask for more. Instead of simply accepting what came her way and thinking that was the height of what life had to offer. She understood his grandmother, that was the thing. She understood the decision to live as she liked, to be *alive*, even if it meant living all alone in exile and scaring children while she did it. Just because most women didn't make that choice didn't mean she couldn't feel the temptation of it, like another bit of jasmine in the air, blooming just for her.

"Cristiano," she said, as much to the dark ceiling above her as to the man who lay beside her. The man who had married her in haste, despite the fact everyone knew how that went, traditionally. But would he be the one doing the repenting? Or would she? "Husband."

"Wife," he said, as if in agreement.

She shifted to look at him, propping herself up on her elbow and wishing her belly didn't make her feel quite so ungainly.

"Why do you look so serious?" he asked. "Everything is settled now. You and me. Our son. If you truly wish it, I will introduce you to my grandmother, though I will have to insist you maintain a reasonable distance. You never know if she'll throw things."

"I love you," she said, and she could hear the foreboding in her own voice. The worry. But she said it, and that startled, thunderstruck look on his face didn't make her take it back. "I love you, Cristiano. I always have. I loved you when I was a teenager you happened to save, and I loved you as a businesswoman who sought your good opinion in the office. I loved you when I came to you in that hotel six months ago, and I loved you even before you recognized our son. I have loved you a thousand ways already, and I imagine I will love you in a thousand more before we're done."

And she wasn't surprised when all he did was stare at her, his expression arrested. Frozen, almost.

Hurt, yes. But not surprised.

"You deserve someone who loves you," Fleurette had said so fiercely.

"There's no need to talk of love," he said, sounding as if he was being strangled.

"Of course there's a need," she said, and it was hard

to keep her voice soft. To keep her gaze on his, when he looked very nearly horrified and her heart ached the way it did. "Love is the entire point, Cristiano."

"No," Cristiano said in a low voice. And this time, when he broke her heart, it was a devastation. "*Cara. Julienne.* Don't do this. Surely you, of all people, must know that love is a lie."

CHAPTER ELEVEN

FINALLY EVERYTHING WAS going according to plan.

Cristiano might not have originally planned to marry and have children, but now that one was done and the other imminent, he found he rather liked the surprising peace of domesticity. It was far better than being haunted. And the new plan made sense.

He gave up his sleek, modern penthouse and moved back into the house he'd once given to Julienne and her sister. It was a home, not a bachelor's residence, and he liked the idea of his son playing in the garden, or tearing up and down the stairs. Especially once he bought the attached house next door and began making plans to create one, far better home for his family.

His family.

He liked that word, even if he only admitted that to himself privately.

But then, he liked having Julienne there, in his house. With him. He particularly liked her in his bed.

Even if she did have a terrible habit of speaking about love. Of all things.

He could not have picked words to describe the things

he felt and if he did, he would have chosen other ones. That terrible, wrecking tenderness that swamped him when he touched her, or when he thought of the baby she carried. The weakness he felt in him at the sight of her.

"Of course your father loves you," his mother had told him when he was still small, but old enough to know better. *"He loves both of us. He struggles to show it, that's all."*

What was *love* but a tiny word that served as a gateway to despair?

Their wedding night, she'd stared at him with those eyes of hers he liked to think of as the precise shade of Cassara's finest toffee. Though that night, there had been a shine to them that had trickled into his gut, kicked around in there and made him…edgy.

"Imagine if your father had loved your mother," she'd said. "And if your grandfather had loved your grandmother. Who would you be now, do you think?"

"I respect you," he had growled in return, shifting closer to her so he could put his hands on her body. And once again, speak to her in terms they both understood completely. "I want you. I will raise our son the way my grandfather raised me."

"To be happy?" she had asked in her quiet way. "No matter who it hurts?"

"To be good," he had retorted, feeling unaccountably challenged.

But he had handled it the way he dealt with all things involving Julienne.

With his mouth, his hands. With the near inexpressible pleasure of burying himself deep inside of her.

And as far as he was concerned, the conversation was over.

He moved them back to Milan, installing her in his house. His bed. Right where he wanted her—with the added bonus of it being *her*. Julienne Boucher, the most formidable of all his vice presidents. Cristiano rather liked that he could come home from work and actually discuss it with her, because her opinion was always learned, careful and most of the time, right.

The research that Massimo had provided him, on pregnancy, parenthood and everything else he knew he would have to contend with, and soon, suggested that a woman's preferences might change once she became a mother. Then again, they might not. He was happy enough to let Julienne do as she pleased, but he couldn't help hoping that what would please her most would be—after an appropriate amount of leave—to join him at the Cassara Corporation again.

"Because it is not nepotism if we're already married?" she asked one night, as she sat in the bedroom that was now theirs. She was rubbing lotion into her enormous belly in an attempt to control her stretch marks, a job that Cristiano sometimes took upon himself, because there was no part of her he didn't find beautiful. Marks and all.

Tonight, he only watched. His wife and the son he would meet soon enough. Sometimes the sight of her so close to giving birth made his heart careen about dangerously in his chest.

Appropriate anxiety, he assured himself. It was what anyone would feel.

"Nothing inappropriate happened between us while you were my subordinate," he said, with a shrug. "And I would be a fool indeed not to take advantage of the fact that one of the greatest minds that has ever worked for the company has returned to me."

"To you, Cristiano," she said, in that mild way she always used these days. That cool, calm voice while something too dark for comfort gleamed in her gaze. "I came back to Italy to tell you that you are to be a father. Not to concern myself with bolstering your corporate profile."

He didn't like her tone. But he only gazed back at her. "I fail to see why it cannot be both."

She stopped rubbing the lotion into her skin, and put the top back on the jar of the thick salve she was using. He couldn't help but think that her movements were jerky.

"Surely the benefits of marrying a man of your wealth and consequence is that I need not concern myself with work." And though there was no hint of temper on her face, he felt it in the air between them, anyway. "If I, for example, wish to do nothing at all but welcome our son into the world by loving him fiercely, wholeheartedly and with singular focus, that should be fine, shouldn't it?"

"I wasn't aware that you had to choose between the two," he replied. "That is the true benefit of marrying me. You don't have to choose a thing. You can have it all, whatever you like."

"Not quite *whatever* I like." And her eyes were on him in a way that made him…distinctly uncomfortable.

"You don't believe in love. Why pretend you can offer me things you can't, Cristiano?"

She launched herself from the bed, one hand going to support the small of her back as she moved, and then she swept out of the bedroom. Leaving him there.

To think about her obsession with *love*.

And that was not the first inkling he'd had that all was not quite as rosy for his new wife as he'd imagined. But it was most direct.

Julienne never denied him. At night, their passion only seemed to grow, wilder and hotter, even as they moved into her final stage of pregnancy. And she always cried out his name in that same perfect song.

She indulged him when he wanted to get his hands on her bump, or put his mouth there so he could speak to his son.

But they were not far off from her due date when he realized that it wasn't that there was a different light in her eyes when she looked at him these days. It was that there was an absence of light.

He didn't know how he could have missed it.

And what made it worse was that he didn't figure out what it was that was getting so deeply beneath his skin until Fleurette appeared, in her usual defiant state, a few days before Julienne was due.

"I can't miss the birth of my nephew," Fleurette announced when she saw him, and *her* gaze, Cristiano could not help but notice, was bright and hot and not particularly friendly. "I won't."

"Of course not," he murmured.

And then he'd been called upon to handle a near disaster at one of their processing facilities. He'd spent all day handling the various politics between his plant manager and the local government in that country, and a full contingent of his attorneys.

When he arrived home, it was late. He was surprised to find lights still on, when Julienne had taken to a far earlier bedtime these days.

He nodded at his housekeeper as he entered, accepting the mail and messages she'd prepared for him.

And then he drifted further into the house, following a sound he'd very rarely heard here.

Had never heard here, or any place he'd ever lived in Milan, if he was honest.

Laughter.

He loosened his tie as he followed the surprising burst of it, past the study and the rooms he normally used to the small salon Julienne had claimed as her own in the back of the house. In the month that she had lived with him here, she had slowly substituted some of the furnishings, making it less a random collection of items a designer had chosen, and more hers.

Tonight, as he stood at the threshold, out in the dark hall beyond, the first thing he noticed was the light.

Endless, glorious light, and not only from the lamps she'd lit.

It was all over her face. Julienne sat in a comfortable armchair that she'd told him would be perfect for nursing his son. Before her, Fleurette was telling a story, sitting cross-legged on the floor gesticulating widely while also doing something with Julienne's feet.

Painting her nails, he realized in the next moment.

Or supposedly painting them, when she wasn't waving her arms about.

And Julienne looked...*alive.*

Her eyes shone, sweet and bright, all toffee and no darkness. Her face was filled with laughter, and hope and that astonishing quicksilver song he only heard when he was deep inside her and she was calling out his name.

Cristiano felt his heart flip in his chest, as if heralding a cardiac event.

He felt frozen where he stood, staring at this woman. His wife. As if he'd never seen her before.

Perhaps you haven't, a dark voice inside him suggested. *Why would you deserve her?*

He didn't think he made a sound, so caught was he in all her brightness. The glorious shine of it.

Cristiano could have stared at her forever. He felt thirsty. Ravenous. And only that light and joy she generated could make it better. Could make *him* better.

But that was when she turned, saw him standing there and blinked.

"Cristiano," she said, her voice changing. And her face changing with it. "I didn't hear you come in."

And he watched, feeling as if there was a hatchet buried deep in his chest, as all that light dimmed.

As if looking at him switched it off, that quickly.

Something in him thudded then, unpleasantly.

"I only just arrived," he heard himself say.

He glanced at her sister, but Fleurette's face was studiously blank. A condemnation in itself.

Cristiano felt his pulse kick in when he looked back

at Julienne, because she was looking at him the exact same way she had since the night of their wedding. Calmly, yes. Coolly, even.

But with no trace whatsoever of all that glorious light.

"I will not disturb you," he said shortly, and left them there.

He went to his office in the house, but he couldn't focus on the work he needed to do, no matter how long he sat at his desk. And when he stopped pretending to work and stared at a shot of whiskey instead, daring himself to truly become his father once and for all, there was something in him that longed for the oblivion.

More than usual.

It would be so much easier *not* to feel anything. He could imagine it so clearly.

But he didn't take the drink. He didn't take the easy way out.

And when he climbed the stairs to the master bedroom and found Julienne there, he felt his heart stutter inside him when she looked at him in that same mild, empty way.

"Your sister being here makes you very happy," he said, studying Julienne's face for signs of…something. Something to stave off this panicked thing inside him.

"She's not really my sister. Or not only my sister. She's also my best friend." Her gaze rested on him. "And she loves me with every last cell in her body."

"Because you rescued her," Cristiano said.

And he saw a flash of *something* across her face

then, but it wasn't that same light he'd seen earlier. It was temper.

But it was better than nothing.

And even as he thought that, it occurred to him that he felt most connected to Julienne—the person, if he was honest, he felt most connected to on the planet— through passion. Whether that passion was based in anger or desire, it was the only language he knew.

It was the only vocabulary he possessed.

And so perhaps it was not surprising that he felt something far too close to bereft as he watched her fight it back.

"You don't love someone because they do things for you," Julienne said, and though her gaze was hard on his, her voice was resolute. "You love them. That's all. And if a situation arises where you can do something for them, then you do it. But it's not a transaction."

And Cristiano understood, in a sickening flash, that transactions were all he knew.

That the people who had raised him had taught him passion, and he had equated it with their brand of drama. Theatrics. Operatic displays, cruelty and fiery conclusions.

He stared at this woman, ripe and round with his child, and for the first time in his life, Cristiano didn't have the slightest idea what to do. How to reach her, or find a way back to that beautiful light of hers that he was very much afraid he had already extinguished.

And this time he didn't think he could ignore the uncertainty and make it go away.

"I see how you're looking at me," Julienne said, and

didn't quite roll her eyes. Because she was not her sister. Not yet. "Don't worry. I'm not going to ask anything of you that you can't give, Cristiano. I married you knowing exactly who you are."

And a week ago, a month ago, he might have accepted that. He might have nodded, thought that sounded like a perfectly reasonable bargain and carried on.

Tonight, those words sounded like an indictment.

But everything was different now.

Because *she* was different, and he had made her that way, and he wasn't sure that he could stand it.

He moved toward her, getting his hands on her body. Filling his fingers with the thick fall of her pretty hair, and then taking her mouth with his.

Because these were the only words he knew. This was the only passion that made sense to him.

This was the only way that he could make her sing with joy, for him.

And he proved it, to himself and to her, over and over again that night.

But in the morning, he left her with her sister, entirely too aware of the way she only seemed to relax once Fleurette was near. And he knew that as soon as the door closed behind him, she would once again light up the way she hadn't for him—not since their wedding.

And it was with a sense of fatalism, or possibly surrender—not that he'd ever had such a sensation before—that instead of going into his office, he went to Tuscany.

When the helicopter delivered him to his usual spot

near the villa, he did not go inside. He took one of the property's hardy SUVs instead, and drove out into the hills.

An hour or so later, he wound around on a bumpy dirt lane, having left the cultivated part of the Cassara fields behind some time ago. And there the cottage sat, right where he remembered it, solid and defiant in the middle of nowhere.

Summer was coming, and the clearing where the cottage stood was carpeted with wildflowers. He walked toward the front of the small home, lecturing himself on the strange prickling he felt all over his body. It was not a wicked enchantment. She was not a witch.

Those had been the fancies of the boy he'd been, who'd been taught to hate her.

And it was only when he drew close that he realized that she was there. Right there. Folded into a chair on the front porch, watching his approach.

She looked wrinkled and wise, but her dark eyes still burned. She was dressed all in black, though he doubted very much that was any kind of nod to her widowhood. Her hands were like claws, her knuckles large as they clutched the head of her cane.

"You have the look of a salesman about you," she said, and her voice was precisely as he recalled it. More robust than a woman should sound on the cusp of ninety, to his way of thinking, and threaded through with a deep and abiding dislike. "A Cassara salesman, no less. The very worst kind."

"Hello, Grandmother," he replied.

The old woman sniffed. "Whatever it is you've come

to say, I'm not interested. I do not require assistance. I do not wish to be placed in a home with other old people. I will die as I have lived here, happily alone and usually left to my own devices—as God intended."

"I didn't come here to put you in a home. Or argue with you, for that matter."

But it seemed she was making a list. "My health is none of your business, but it is excellent, since you've come looking. If you wish to develop this land, you will have to do so over my dead body. But never fear. I may be thriving at the moment but an old woman can only live so long. You may have to learn to wait for what you want—a trait no man in your family has ever possessed."

"I don't need your land. For God's sake."

"The last time you were here, boy, I thought I might make you cry. Is that why you returned? To test yourself against childhood nightmares? I'm delighted to try again."

She laughed and that part he remembered too well. Because it wasn't the demure, carefully cultivated laughter of the women he'd always known. He'd considered it unhinged when he'd been younger. But now, he understood.

It was joy. Pure joy, the kind Julienne shared with her sister and never him. It was uncontrolled. Untamed.

This is how men tell stories about women they can't control, Julienne had told him. *Whores. Witches.*

His grandfather had made his wife into a witch. How had Cristiano never seen that? And Piero was the one who had been heralded as a hero upon his death. When what he'd been was a selfish man who did as he liked. Who selected the people he would care for—Sofia Tomasi, Cristiano—and discarded those he disdained, like the woman he'd married and his only remaining son.

Nor had he ever seemed unduly concerned about the consequences.

It was like a mountain crumbling on top of him, sucking him under and crushing him there.

And Cristiano understood, with a pang of a deep, harsh grief, that this take on his beloved grandfather was not something he could unknow. It was not something he could pretend he hadn't seen.

"I do not think I will cry," he said to the grandmother he should have known all these years, his voice low. "If I am honest, I would sooner dig out my eyes and feed them to the crows."

She hooted derisively. "What do crows want with a rich man's eyes?"

He should not have been here, no matter what revelations might have come to him overnight. Making this her problem was proving that he was like all the rest of his family. That he was just like them, selfish to the core.

Cristiano had no idea what he hoped to gain.

But he stayed where he was, there on the porch of this cottage he'd avoided for most of his life.

"Grandmother," he said, with a stiff formality that in no way matched the moment but he thought she deserved nonetheless. "I've come to talk to you about love."

"Love?" The old woman cackled. "Your father was

a drunk and his father a liar. They raised you in their spitting image. Too rich, too pampered and cruel with it. What can you possibly know of love?"

He didn't flinch away from the glare she settled on him.

"Nothing at all," he said quietly.

His grandmother studied him for what felt to Cristiano like a very long time. A lifetime, perhaps. The lifetime he might have known this woman, if things had been different. If his grandfather had been the hero Cristiano had always seen in him, instead of the man he was.

"If there is no love, there is no life," she said at last, and again he had the sense of some enchantment after all. Some spell she was casting as she spoke, and not because she was a witch. But because she might well be magic. "You can live on, mind. But it's nothing but going through the motions. I would not have imagined a Cassara would care about this distinction. You don't have to be fully alive to count all the money, after all."

"I have a wife," Cristiano heard himself say, as if the words were torn from somewhere deep inside him. Torn from the mouth of a version of himself he had never been—a version of himself who did things like ask for advice. "She says she loves me."

This old woman looked at him with canny, clever eyes, as if she'd known him all his life. And knew him better than he knew himself.

"But you, naturally, cannot be asked to concern yourself with the petty concerns of the heart. Not when you have sweet things to shove down throats. Sugar in place of character will never end well, boy. What do you want me to do? Build your poor wife a cottage next door? Or direct her to a coffin like your mother's?" And there wasn't the faintest trace of age in the look she leveled on him, then. "Those are the only two options for Cassara wives, as I understand it."

Cristiano did not argue, though he wanted to. Desperately.

"There has to be a third option," he said, his voice gruff. "There has to be."

"There is." His grandmother lifted her cane and pointed it at him. "You. Change yourself, boy. Not her. She's changed enough already if she's with you."

CHAPTER TWELVE

WHEN THE DOOR to her bedroom swung open, Julienne told herself that she was prepared.

Because what had this last month or so since their wedding been if not an exercise in preparation?

She arranged her face in a polite smile. She'd become good at it, she thought. She would remain calm and cool no matter what. She would not give up, the way his grandmother had, no matter the provocation. She was not sacrificing herself, no matter what Fleurette thought, she was *choosing*—

But the usual litany she chanted at herself blew away like smoke.

Because the man who came to the door was not her husband.

It was Cristiano, but a version of him she had not seen in a long time.

Not since that night in Monte Carlo, in fact. The second time around, when he had proven to her that, in truth, she hardly knew him at all.

He'd proven it again and again, deliciously.

And that's the reason you're in this state now, she reminded herself tartly. *About to have a baby in a marriage that feels like you're choking and drowning, daily.*

She might have resolved to live with it. But the man who slammed the bedroom door behind him made her jump a bit, there in their bed where she was propped up against the pillows, supposedly reading a book on breastfeeding.

"What has happened?" she asked, staring at him.

And Julienne was unable, in the face of all the ferocity she saw in him, to keep her tone even at all. The way she'd been doing since their brusque wedding, because it was that or start screaming. And she was afraid that once she started screaming she wouldn't stop. She'd felt it claw in her, those screams she wouldn't let loose, when she'd told him she loved him and he'd told her love was a lie.

A lie.

And had very clearly meant it.

"I've been to Tuscany," Cristiano said, and his voice wasn't his. Not really. It was gruff, dark. But there was a different undercurrent. It was one she didn't know.

"Did something happen to the villa?"

"Villa Cassara has stood for hundreds of years. It will stand forever. And in any case, I didn't go to the villa."

"Cristiano." She used the repressive tone she sometimes employed on her sister, and it had about the same effect. One of his arrogant brows rose, with no hint of repentance. "I can't tell if something is wrong or not. Is it?"

"Something is terribly wrong," he told her, dark and urgent. "You are wrong."

He might as well have hauled off and punched her in the belly. Julienne felt her jaw drop open, even as in the next moment she told herself that she *absolutely refused* to give him the satisfaction of seeing her react like that. Or at all.

"Perhaps you missed the news," she managed to say crisply. "I have married a Cassara. I think you know full well that's a fast track to wrongness." She inclined her head in a fair mockery of the aristocratic way he did it. "I will accept your condolences."

"You have changed, Julienne."

He moved closer to the bed, where she'd been agitatedly turning pages in her book but failing to read a single word. Because the office had called, looking for him, and that told her only that he was off doing something he didn't want anyone to know about.

Had it started already? Was he off looking for his own long-term mistress to install in the house and push her out? Or had he lost himself in the whiskey she'd seen he'd left out on his desk, in an imitation of the father he hated and feared becoming?

And what did it say about her that she wasn't entirely sure which route was worse?

Then his words penetrated and she frowned. "I don't think I've changed. Perhaps you have. Or, more likely, you're paying more attention than you did before because we're living in the same house."

"No," he replied sternly, in that tone she recalled from the office. The one that brooked absolutely no argument. "There's a sadness in your eyes all the time now. Do you think I don't see it?"

"I'm sure you're mistaken. And I'm equally sure that you don't really care. Because if you did, you might have mentioned your thoughts on love before getting married."

Julienne had not meant to say that.

She was horrified that she'd said that.

She flushed, and hated the fact that she was so big now that she couldn't simply leap to her feet and walk away from her own embarrassment. Not without a struggle. Instead, she had to stay where she was, anchored to the bed by her giant belly.

By the child she was bringing into this mess. Into the arms of a man who didn't believe in love. It was bad enough for her. What would it do to their son?

Then again, she already knew. Cristiano was a walking advertisement for exactly what would happen.

"It doesn't matter now," she said, nervously, because she couldn't read that intense expression on his face. He seemed even more austere than usual. Almost as if he was in pain. And she could not bear that. "We are married. Our son will be here soon enough. We can love him, instead."

Or I will, she promised the baby. *I will love you enough for both of us.*

"I went to see my grandmother," he said as he came to a stop at the foot of the bed.

And had he said that he had personally flown himself to the moon and back, Julienne could not possibly have been more surprised.

"Your grandmother?" She gaped at him. "The fairy-tale witch?"

"Her name is Paola DeMarco." His voice was gruff again, his face grim. "She does not use her married name, which will perhaps not surprise you."

"Why did you go to see her?" Julienne asked. The baby kicked, hard enough to make her wince. And she told herself that was why her heart began to pound. "Did she cast a spell on you after all?"

"Because you spoke to me of whores and witches." And that grimness on his face began to look…ravaged, instead. "You made me question who it was who told me that particular fairy tale, and why. And because you married me and began at once to fade. And I want you to understand this, if nothing else, Julienne. I have no intention of repeating any of this history."

"I told you I would burn it to the ground," Julienne told him fiercely, thinking of that cold, sick feeling in her belly when his office had called. And the gloating letters from his grandfather's mistress. "I meant it."

His gaze on hers was savage. And beautiful. "There is nothing to burn save the empty, hollow carcass of the man I was before I met you."

And there was no pretending, then, that her heart wasn't beating hard and mad for him.

For hope.

But she couldn't seem to make herself speak.

"I told myself all was well," Cristiano said in that same tone. "And I wanted to believe it. But all the while, you looked at me through a stranger's eyes. No light. No joy. And in all the time I have known you, Julienne, you have never looked at me like that."

"You don't have to do this," she managed to get out. "Really."

And there was a kind of panic in her then. She fought against it, trying to roll herself out of the nest she'd made of too many pillows, but then he was there.

Cristiano was at the side of the bed, and then he was sitting there beside her. And this time, he didn't put his hands on her belly, or address himself to her bump.

He took her hands. And he looked into her eyes.

"Last night I came upon you laughing with your sister," he said, and she'd never heard him sound like this. Gravel and ice, certainly, but something hot and alive beneath. "And I couldn't help but think to myself that I had extinguished all that light. All that joy. Because when you look at me now, there's nothing but heartbreak on your face. And *tesoro mio*, you must know that I cannot bear for you to be broken. *I cannot bear it.*"

Julienne wanted to reach out to him. She wanted to fix this, whatever it was. It was as if the ice in him had cracked at last, she realized. And what she was seeing was the man beneath it.

Uncontrolled. Untamed.

Real, a voice in her whispered.

Cristiano kept going, his hands on hers. "My whole life I have equated emotion with pain. Terror. Grief and loss. The deeper the emotion, the more passion in its display, and the worse it has always been. I have watched a man I respected act as if what he'd done to his wife was something she deserved. That she'd brought upon herself. He was *proud* of it."

He shook his head, a cynicism she'd never seen

before in his gaze, not when he spoke of his beloved grandfather. And Julienne didn't entirely understand how she could feel all that same cynicism when it came to Piero Cassara, but want to soothe it away from Cristiano. With her hands, her mouth, whatever worked.

But he was still speaking, intent and low. "And I watched another man I never respected abuse my mother, who, it must be said, put more energy into martyring herself to her marriage than she ever did into raising her own child. These were the emotions I knew growing up. This was the passion that marked the Cassara family. Of course I told you that love was a lie. Do you know the only person who ever used that word in my hearing?" His mouth, firm and hard, thinned into grimness again. "Sofia Tomasi, the housekeeper who welcomed my grandmother into the Villa when Paola was a shy eighteen-year-old bride. Sofia loved my father, or so she liked to tell me, and she showed that love by undermining my grandmother at every turn. Pretending to befriend her and then using her confidences against her."

He shook his head, but the gaze he kept trained on her was fierce. "Every example of love I have ever seen has been a lie, Julienne. Save yours."

And his hands were on hers, so she gripped him, hard. She didn't care about the wetness on her cheeks, not as long as she could keep looking at him. At his face, torn apart by something deep and strong. *Ravaged,* she thought again.

She would take from him in an instant if she could. If only she could.

"You have loved me unwaveringly," Cristiano said and there was a kind of wonder in his voice. "You loved me when I was a bitter, angry man who had just sent his own parents to their deaths."

She did her best not to shout, *That is not your fault.*

He shifted, his fingers laced with hers now. "That you are so fierce about that is only further testament to the kind of person you are. You loved me then, Julienne. You loved me when I threw you and your sister into this house, then threw money at you to assuage my guilt, and did absolutely nothing to help you make your way in the world."

"Aside from paying for it."

"Money does not keep anyone warm, try as they might," he growled.

And it was her turn to smile, through the tears that blurred her vision. "Cristiano. I do love you. I have always loved you. But please, take it from me, the money to pay a heating bill in a cold winter keeps anyone warm enough. Everything else is icing on the cake."

He reached over and traced that smile on her mouth with his fingers, as if it was a priceless work of art. As if she was.

"That smile."

And his voice was so intense, then, it nearly hurt to hear him. Nearly. Instead, she melted.

"I have missed that smile."

"Cristiano—"

"That you love me at all humbles me," he told her, as if he was making vows. And not with the briskness he'd displayed at their wedding. "You, who have been through so much. I thought that the purpose of my life was to distinguish myself from my father. I wanted so desperately to be nothing like him. But somehow, I never saw that I was as drunk on my own perceived virtue as he ever was on whiskey. Until you."

"None of this is necessary. Really."

"It is more than necessary." And his voice was like thunder, then. "It is past due. This whole time, I have thought that I could avoid saying these words that I barely know how to form if I expressed myself another way. I thought that while I heard that beautiful song of yours, so passionate and all mine, you would hear the truth in my heart as well."

Julienne found she was holding her breath.

"The things you make me feel terrify me," he said, and she understood that she was seeing the real Cristiano now. No ice. All flesh and man. And all hers. "They make me feel mortal, weak and wrong. And all my life, I have considered it my duty to exorcise anything I felt. Better to be like ice. Better by far to be half-dead—but you make me feel alive, Julienne. You forced me, against my will and inclination, to face up to the things I wanted so badly I'd locked them away inside myself. And then you systematically broke down each and every one of my compartments."

She didn't know if she should melt or apologize. But Cristiano took one of her hands and brought it to his chest. Then placed her palm over his heart. "I'm going to tell you a fairy tale."

"Does it involve witches?" she managed to ask, not sure if she was laughing or crying.

With his free hand, he reached over and wiped away the water beneath her eyes.

"Once upon a time there was a fool," he told her, his voice a low rumble that she could feel, now, as well as hear. "He was raised by an ogre and a troll. The ogre taught him airs and graces. The troll taught him pain. The fool knew no better, and imagined that one was a king and the other a jailer."

"This is already a very sad story."

Cristiano's dark eyes gleamed, but he kept on. "Time went on, and the fool allowed his king to color his world. He thought that made him a man. A hero, even. Until one day, at the end of a very low hour when he had indulged his innate selfishness and would soon learn that there would be consequences for his folly, he had the opportunity instead to play the hero he'd always imagined he was. For in walked a girl, and he saved her."

"Oh, okay," she said. "I like *this* story."

"But you see, like any fool, he thought saving her was enough. He turned his back on her, told himself it was a virtue and made a career out of turning himself to stone."

Beneath her hand, his heart beat, hard and strong. Beautiful. And inside her, she felt their son's feet poke at her, and if this wasn't love—physical and real and true—she was sure she didn't know the meaning of the word.

"And then one day, years later, the girl found him again," Cristiano said, still telling his story. Or maybe this was really their story. "She flattered him, flirted with him. For she had grown up to become a beautiful princess, and the fool thought—*of course*. He considered himself a hero, so why shouldn't he have a princess? So he kissed her, but when he woke the next morning, it was to find that the princess had disappeared. And worse, that she had prized off the stone he wore instead of a heart and had taken it with her."

"Not a princess," Julienne whispered. "And you've never been a fool."

"Six months passed," he said, a faintly reproving note in his voice. "And the fool knew that he was not the same. His stone was gone, and that meant that he could feel that beating, untamable organ beneath. Suddenly, there was blood in his veins. Suddenly, he wanted things he knew he couldn't have. But he ignored it all, and assumed that if he locked himself away in eternal winter, he could find another stone. The world has no shortage of stones, after all."

Julienne's hand was still there on his chest, splayed wide over his flat pectoral muscle, and all she felt was his heart. The kick of it, insistent and strong.

No stones to be found.

"One day, the princess returned. She gazed at our fool, and to his astonishment, he could see in her eyes that what she saw was a hero. 'Look,' she said, and showed him her big, round belly, swollen with child. 'I have taken the stone that lay upon your heart, and see what I've made with it.'"

"A son," Julienne whispered.

"A son," he agreed. "But the fool knew that he was no hero, you see. And more, he was afraid of the princess, and the things she made him feel, and that hollow where his stone once lay. He knew that the princess was filled with light, and it was only a matter of time before she looked deep enough to see that there was nothing in him but darkness. He had an idea. He would marry the princess, and pile stones on top of her, muting her light. Saving himself in the process."

"Some princesses like stones," Julienne argued, astonished to hear the thickness in her voice. "Or they wouldn't take them from unsuspecting hearts in the first place, would they?"

"A princess might like to collect stones," Cristiano said, shaking his head at her. "But no one likes to have them stacked on top of their chest. Crushing out the will to live. The fool kept going, for he knew no other way. Every day he lay another stone upon the princess, and every day, he watched the light in her fade. Until one day, he realized that when she looked at him, all she saw was stone. That he was no longer a hero at all. And the fool knew then that if he continued along this path, it would only end one way. First he would kill the princess, as surely as if he choked her with his own hand. And then, inevitably, he would do the same to his son."

"Cristiano," she said.

And it was only his name. But it held whole worlds in it.

"More than that, he understood at last that the ogre and the troll were neither kings nor jailers, but had once been fools themselves. And once he understood that, everywhere he looked, he saw the stones his ancestors had piled up like walls."

She tried again, but she couldn't seem to speak. And

she knew she didn't have stones on her chest, but love. So much love it hurt.

"That was when the fool remembered there had been another princess, long ago. A princess so feared that every ogre and troll in the kingdom called her a witch instead. And the fool ran, then, over the hills and into the forest. And he found an old woman who had once been a princess living alone in a cottage on the edge of a deep, dark wood."

"Your grandmother."

"A fool is a fool until the very end," Cristiano said. "'How can I help the princess?' he asked the old woman. 'How can I dislodge the stones enough to keep her breathing?' The old woman laughed, and she told him that the stone was a stone. It could never be changed. It was weight and heft, and when piled upon a princess would crush her, sure enough. ''But the princess took a stone and made a son of it,' the fool argued."

Julienne's heart beat so hard, she wondered if she was made of stone herself.

"The old woman looked him straight in the eye. And she said, 'She didn't take a stone from you, child. She took your heart. And all you've done since is pretend you can function without it.'"

Cristiano smiled then, and Julienne held her breath.

"'You can, but you must kill her first in order to do it. And when you're done killing her, you must destroy your son, so he too becomes a fool. A fool becomes an ogre or troll, and if you squint, you can see which one he'll be. Which one you are.'"

"She sounds like a wise woman," Julienne managed to say, feeling wrecked. And a bit dizzy, too. "And scary, if I'm honest." She shifted where she sat, searching his face. "And I love a fairy tale, Cristiano, but I really would love to jump to the end of this one. The 'they lived happily ever after' part. Is that where we're headed?"

Though she wasn't sure what she'd do if he said no.

He held her gaze. Then he reached into the pocket of his trousers and pulled something out. And she didn't know why she was holding her breath again, because she already wore his rings. Beautiful, priceless works of stone and metal that declared her not only his, but forever a Cassara bride. His wife, no matter what.

Still, she watched as he opened his palm.

And then she blinked.

Because sitting there in his hand was a stone. At first she thought it was misshapen—but then she realized.

It looked like a heart.

"I'm not sure I have ever loved anything in my life," Cristiano told her, his voice deep and strong. "I have long hated the word. I have considered it nothing but the harbinger of doom, if I am honest. But I can think of no other word that explains how I feel about you, Julienne. You are the sun, the stars, the moon. You are all the light in the world, and I do not deserve you, and I don't know that I ever will. You think I saved you, when all the while, you must know that you are the one who has saved me. You took the stone away from my heart and taught me how to make it beat again. You have loved me completely, always. You are carrying my son. Everything is dark and cold without you. Me most of all."

She whispered his name again, but this time, perhaps it was a kind of incantation.

Hope, love and joy.

Cristiano.

"You already have my heart," he said. "I want you to have this, too. Because if I keep it, I think we both know that I will use whatever stones I have to build as many walls as possible. But not you, my beautiful Julienne. You make life. You make love. And I want nothing else than to dedicate myself to making you happy."

"Cristiano," she said, and this time, he did not cut her off. And she did not falter. "I love you. And I don't want to be a princess. You are not a fool, and I am your wife, and we will love each other as best we can, for as long as we can, so that our son grows up and doesn't spend his time worried about stones and ogres and trolls. But rather, happiness. Family. Love. All the things that make life worth living."

"I can think of no better happy-ever-after than that," he said, there against her mouth.

This time, when he kissed her, it tasted like forever.

And kiss by kiss, and stone by stone, they made it so.

CHAPTER THIRTEEN

JULIENNE WENT INTO labor the following morning, and by nightfall, their son was born.

And in Cristiano's wholly unbiased opinion, he was perfect.

They named him Pietro, which meant rock, because he was the greatest magic either one of them could imagine. And something far bigger and better than a mere stone.

And the more Cristiano allowed himself to love, the more magic there was to be found.

It took him the better part of a year, but he convinced Paola to start attending family functions, such as they were. To meet her great-grandson, and better still, the woman who had convinced a Cassara man to change.

"Perhaps it is not me who is the witch, then," the old woman cackled with glee, the first time she and Julienne met.

"I will take that as the highest compliment imaginable," Julienne replied.

It took him another year to convince Paola to move into the villa, where she could be mistress of the house at last. And his grandmother might have been in her nineties, but she ran the villa with an iron fist. And ordered Cristiano, Pietro and the three other sons Julienne bore him around at her leisure.

"It is not difficult to make a good man," the old woman told him on her hundredth birthday, grinning at him over her cane. "All it takes is a woman's firm hand."

Cristiano could not disagree.

But the hands he preferred on him belonged to his wife.

Julienne was his north star, his lodestone. She carried his babies, she raised his sons and when she was not busy creating tiny humans, she served on the Cassara Corporation board as well.

And, finally, together, they made it the family company it never had been in his grandfather's hands.

"That's because you are the man your grandfather never was," Julienne told him, year after year. "You love your wife. You would die for your family. You have honored your grandmother, and yes, Cristiano, you have rescued each and every one of us. Over and over again."

But Cristiano always knew the truth.

Julienne might have been the one to walk into that bar, determined to sell herself. But she had been the one to do the rescuing.

"I love you," he told her, every day of their lives.

And better still, showed her.

In any way he could, in every way that mattered, he showed her.

How he loved her. How crucial she was not only to his happiness, but to the mechanics that kept the world turning. How perfect she was and always had been, just as she was.

And in tougher times, or when things seemed the darkest, they would take out that stone that was shaped like a heart, and it would make them laugh.

Cristiano would tell her stories about ogres and trolls and terrible fools. Julienne would tell him stories about princesses who were born on hilltops, who came down to the sea to find their Prince Charmings.

Again and again, they wove their stories around themselves until they were right again.

Until they were whole.

"Happy-ever-after isn't made," Julienne liked to say as they lay in their bed, still wrapped around each other tightly twenty years on. "It's mended. The days are the thread, the years are the colors, and all we have to do is sew."

"I love you," Cristiano told her. *"Ti amo, mi amore. Tu mi completi."*

His heart, his love, his wife.

His whole life, gleaming there before him. Light and joy.

And then he rolled her over, and showed her how he loved her in the language he was most fluent in, once again.

Until she sang their love back to him, the way he loved best.

The way she always did, and always would, all the rest of their days.

* * * * *

COMING SOON!

We really hope you enjoyed reading this book. If you're looking for more romance, be sure to head to the shops when new books are available on

Thursday 16th April

To see which titles are coming soon, please visit
millsandboon.co.uk/nextmonth

MILLS & BOON

Coming next month

THE SECRET KEPT FROM THE KING
Clare Connelly

'No.' He held onto her wrist as though he could tell she was about to run from the room. 'Stop.'

Her eyes lifted to his and she jerked on her wrist so she could lift her fingers to her eyes and brush away her tears. Panic was filling her, panic and disbelief at the mess she found herself in.

'How is this upsetting to you?' he asked more gently, pressing his hands to her shoulders, stroking his thumbs over her collarbone. 'We agreed at the hotel that we could only have two nights together, and you were fine with that. I'm offering you three months, on exactly those same terms, and you're acting as though I've asked you to parade naked through the streets of Shajarah.'

'You're ashamed of me,' she said simply. 'In New York we were two people who wanted to be together. What you're proposing turns me into your possession.'

He stared at her, his eyes narrowed. 'The money I will give you is beside the point.'

More tears sparkled on her lashes. 'Not to me it's not.'

'Then don't take the money,' he said, urgently. 'Come to the RKH and be my lover because you want to be with me.'

'I can't.' Tears fell freely down her face now. 'I need that money. I need it.'

A muscle jerked in his jaw. 'So have both.'

'No, you don't understand.'

She was a live wire of panic but she had to tell him, so that he understood why his offer was so revolting to her.

She pulled away from him, pacing towards the windows, looking out on this city she loved. The trees at Bryant Park whistled in the fall breeze and she watched them for a moment, remembering the first time she'd seen them. She'd been a little girl, five, maybe six, and her dad had been performing at the restaurant on the fringes of the park. She'd worn her Very Best dress, and, despite the heat, she'd worn tights that were so uncomfortable she could vividly remember that feeling now. But the park had been beautiful and her dad's music had, as always, filled her heart with pleasure and joy.

Sariq was behind her now, she felt him, but didn't turn to look at him.

'I'm glad you were so honest with me today.' Her voice was hollow. 'It makes it easier for me, in a way, because I know exactly how you feel, how you see me, and what you want from me.' Her voice was hollow, completely devoid of emotion when she had a thousand throbbing inside her.

He said nothing. He didn't try to deny it. Good. Just as she'd said, it was easier when things were black and white.

'I don't want money so I can attend the Juilliard, Your Highness.' It pleased her to use his title, to use that as a point of difference, to put a line between them that neither of them could cross.

Silence. Heavy, loaded with questions. And finally, 'Then what do you need such a sum for?'

She bit down on her lip, her tummy squeezing tight. 'I'm pregnant. And you're the father.'

Continue reading
THE SECRET KEPT FROM THE KING
Clare Connelly

Available next month
www.millsandboon.co.uk

LET'S TALK
Romance

For exclusive extracts, competitions
and special offers, find us online:

- facebook.com/millsandboon
- @MillsandBoon
- @MillsandBoonUK

Get in touch on 01413 063232

For all the latest titles coming soon, visit
millsandboon.co.uk/nextmonth

JOIN US ON SOCIAL MEDIA!

Stay up to date with our latest releases, author news and gossip, special offers and discounts, and all the behind-the-scenes action from Mills & Boon...

 millsandboon

 millsandboonuk

 millsandboon

It might just be true love...